THE WONDERS OF THE LITTLE WORLD

A novel by Bill Meissner

STEPHEN F. AUSTIN STATE UNIVERSITY PRESS

Copyright ©2024 Stephen F. Austin State University
All rights reserved. Printed in the United States of America. No part of this book may be used or reproduced in any manner whatsoever without the writer's permission except in the case of brief quotations in critical articles or reviews.

For more information:
Stephen F. Austin State University Press
P.O. Box 13007 SFA Station
Nacogdoches, Texas 75962
sfapress@sfasu.edu
www.sfasu.edu/sfapress

Managing Editor: Kimberly Verhines
Assistant Editor: Mallory LeCroy
Cover Design: Mallory LeCroy
Distributed by Texas A&M Consortium
www.tamupress.com

ISBN: 978-1-62288-252-6

Acknowledgments

I'd like to express my appreciation to friends, colleagues, former students, and family members who have supported my writing over the years. I'd also like to send a shout-out to the EZ Writers group for their valuable advice and friendship. Thanks to my editor, Kimberly Verhines, for her belief in my writing. I'm grateful to Felicia Eth of the Felicia Eth Literary Agency, who commented on the very early versions of this novel.

This book is in memory of my mother, who was born in Prague and often said she had psychic powers (and I believed her), and my father, who marveled at circus acts and who drove the rural roads of Iowa and Wisconsin as a traveling salesperson to give his family a better life. When I was nine, my parents took me to an Iowa fair where I wandered among the rides and sideshows and was amazed by a contortionist, and a woman—born with no arms—who sewed with a needle and thread using her toes.

My heartfelt appreciation to my son Nate for his support of my writing over the years, his design wizardry, and for joining me on annual treks to the crazy Benton County Fair.

Most of all, I am grateful to my wife Christine for her always-intelligent suggestions and critiques, and for her love. Decades ago, when I asked her to dance in a loud, crowded, smoky bar, I'm glad she finally said Yes.

*   *   *

Brief sections of this novel first appeared in "Mesmerizing Minnie: Another Life" and "Skip Remembers: The Tug of War" in the short story collection *The Road to Cosmos* (University of Notre Dame Press). Other brief passages first appeared in *The Mapmaker's Dream* (Finishing Line Press) and *Learning to Breathe Underwater* (Ohio University Press). All three books are by Bill Meissner and are used with permission of the publishers.

This is a work of fiction, and all the characters and events in the story are invented. Any similarities to actual people, living or dead, are purely coincidental.

For Christine and Nathan—always the greatest companions, on and off the midway.

PART ONE

CHAPTER ONE
August 1968

Ariel

The Bird Child. Ariel couldn't stop thinking about it. And tonight, in the darkness, she did something she never expected to do, but it was something she needed to do. She knew her mother, Estelle, would be upset with her if she found out. But Ariel pushed that hesitation aside. Nimbly twisting a bobby pin left, then right, then left, she began to pick the lock of the exhibition shed at the end of the midway until she heard a faint click. She'd learned this trick a couple of years ago, when she was nine, from Fast Eddie, her favorite carny mentor and a pal of her dad's. Like a lot of carnies, the guy could break into just about anything.

Stepping over the red velvet rope that kept the steady line of customers at bay, she unlatched the lid of the wood and glass display case. She lifted the five-gallon jar, filled with formaldehyde that surrounded The Bird Child. It felt slippery in her hands, heavier than she had expected, so she clutched it close to her frail, bony chest to keep from dropping it.

Ariel had come here, alone, after hours, every night this week to stare at The Bird Child. She wasn't sure why. Sometimes she flipped on the overhead spotlight for a few minutes to see it illuminated. Other times she just pondered its form in the dark. No matter what, she always wondered: Who created a creature like this, anyway? What kind of God made this cruel joke, this thing that ended up half in one world, half in another? And was it really part bird? Could it ever fly?

Unlike the other exhibits featured in their carnival, like the Six-legged Calf, the Horse-headed Lamb, or even the Devil Pig with its frighteningly pinched face, this display haunted her. The gaudy black and orange painted sign claimed:

THE AMAZING BIRD CHILD
An Oddity of Nature!
An Eighth Wonder of the World!

The creature had two flesh-colored wings on its back, about the size of a dove's. The boy or girl—no one knew for sure—was curled in a fetal position, opaque eyes bulbous, head bent to its chest as if praying. Its pale, whiteish skin was almost transparent beneath the bright light. Ariel always felt sorry for The Bird Child, on display, suspended there for eternity, people paying fifty cents to shuffle past and gawk and smirk and ridicule it.

This evening as she hugged the jar against her stomach and carried it down the midway, she could see, up close, The Bird Child's eggshell-like eyes, which seemed to be studying her in surprise. The creature looked ridiculous now, outside the display booth, with no spotlights to illuminate it. Like a cheap doll, almost, as though it was made of plastic in someone's basement.

She passed the closed Bust-Em Balloon Toss and Knock-A-Milk-Bottle game tents with their tarps tied down.

The Bird Child seemed to gain weight as she carried it, the liquid sloshing side to side in the jar like a small murky ocean. As she walked, her right leg felt whole and strong, but her left leg—which was shorter than her right leg—felt weak. She'd had that short leg all of her eleven years. A birth defect, the doctors called it. She called it an embarrassment since it caused her to walk with a limp, which she was doing right now. She felt like some awkward sleepwalker who wasn't sure which way to go.

Beyond the skeleton arms of the Tarantula ride, she veered behind her mother's fortune-telling tent. It was the place where people lined up, waiting for Estelle the Teller to peer into a crystal ball and dish out advice about their lives.

"It's mostly true," her mom had assured her once when Ariel quizzed her about fortune telling.

"So what's the true part?" Ariel asked.

"You never know," Estelle replied. "That's the fun of it." She paused, then added, "And maybe the curse of it, too. Anyway," she continued, laughing a little, "Guess it makes me part psychologist, part fortune teller, and part something else."

"What's the something else?" Ariel quizzed. She was waiting for a big secret of some kind. Estelle's only answer was a smile that floated across her face.

Balancing precariously on her right foot, Ariel lifted her knee to unlatch the gate of the cyclone fence and stepped outside the carnival grounds. She felt suddenly victorious out there like she'd just won some kind of marathon.

Above her was a nearly full moon, visible but glazed by a cloud, and beyond it, a few stars that looked dull and blurry. She thought about Virgil Sand. He was the self-important boss of Sand's Magical Shows and Amusements, based in the outskirts of less-than-magical town of Wanley, Minnesota. She knew he would be more than a little angry when he'd discover that the display was tampered with, that his prize, money-making Bird Child was gone. He would stomp—from the Kamikaze to the Merry-Go-Round—ranting and raving and swearing, like when, after a tractor-pull contest, someone accidentally backed a John Deere over the Ferris wheel's generator.

But she didn't care. She needed to do this.

She came to a stop on the asphalt and raised the jar. As she held it in front of her face for a few seconds, she was certain that she saw The Bird Child trembling with expectation. "No more holding your breath, kiddo," she said quietly like she was talking to herself. Then, without hesitating, she let it go and it fell, in slow motion, to the hard surface.

When it hit, the glass shattered with a sharp sigh, and the pungent-smelling liquid drained, forming a dark, spreading, star-shaped puddle. It was a sound she would hear in her dreams for a long time.

The Bird Child lay there motionless, its body coated by a layer of moonlight.

Ariel stepped to the edge of the asphalt and dug a shallow hole in the soft soil with the garden trowel she had brought along. Then she lifted the tiny body, surrounded by the cloudy shards of glass.

Its touch scared her.

Not plastic, she thought, and it didn't feel like rubber. Its skin was heavier and silkier than she had expected, something that might actually have been alive once. It seemed softened and preserved so well that it could have lasted a hundred years, millions of people pointing and laughing as they filed past.

But no more, she thought. It'll be protected from all that now. The Bird Child will finally be safe.

She pulled some bubble wrap from her back pocket, wrapped it around The Bird Child up as if to cushion it, then covered the frail body with a layer of earth. In her head, said a little prayer for it—not a church prayer, since, though she wanted to, she never went to church on Sundays due to the carnival's town-to-town schedule. So she just said a few of her own words to wish it well, to pray for its soul, in case it really had one.

"Goodbye," she whispered. She straightened and limped back toward her trailer.

If her mother—who might be up late, reading a tattered romance novel—looked up at her and asked where she'd been, she'd tell her she was just taking a long and innocent walk, just trying to count the sugary stars above the cotton-candy booth on the far end of the grounds.

Her father, though, would understand. Wouldn't he? This was the kind of crazy, impulsive stunt that Tony, AKA The Dashing Desdiolo, might come up with. Her mother once described Tony as the wildest and most wonderful guy on the planet.

But now he was nowhere to be found. He had left them. Not just for days, but weeks, with no word. Lately, Ariel felt like her heart was a red balloon someone had popped with a dart. "He's somewhere...," Estelle said, letting her slim hands, circling vaguely in the air, attempt to do the explaining. Though Ariel asked, her mother could never say exactly where that place was. She was supposed to be clairvoyant, to see the future, and all that, but when it came to Tony, her mind was a blank.

Since he'd been gone, Ariel felt like she'd been holding her breath. She missed him terribly. And so did her mom. After all, they both loved him.

Tomorrow morning, Ariel figured, someone will discover that the almost world-famous Bird Child is missing. The word would spread quickly among the carnies, but Ariel wouldn't let on what she knows. If anyone asks her where she'd been that night, or what she was doing, she'll simply tell them she was dreaming.

CHAPTER TWO

Estelle and Ariel

Towing the weight of the pink and cream trailer behind her, Estelle Esmeralda eased her car toward the carnival exit gate. The car wobbled and dipped across the rutted dirt path toward the entryway, with its huge red, white, and blue banner announcing SAND'S MAGICAL SHOWS AND AMUSEMENTS. Reaching the banner, Estelle braked, shifted the car into neutral, and idled beneath it.

What am I doing? she asked herself as she glanced at the pair of fuzzy dice swinging back and forth from the rearview mirror.

She understood that once she drove beyond the carnival entryway and that gaudy flapping canvas banner, she'd be leaving her old life behind. But what world would she enter?

After all, the carnival was a place that had been her home for the past years, and the weird familiarity of Splat the Clown, Fast Eddie, Old Whiskers, Jumpin' Johnny, and the metallic click-clacking sound of the Octopus ride next to her fortune-telling tent had always given her an odd sense of comfort. After more than a decade of being here, the place seemed to have a pull on her, as if it controlled her with invisible but powerful strings.

But now one person was pulling her in a different direction.

It was her husband Tony, of course. Tony Desdiolo. Tony—a tightrope walker who seemed able to balance his way across any length of wire without falling. He was a tightrope walker who, suddenly, had left with no explanation, no message. It was as if, on the far end of that wire, he tiptoed into a swirling layer of fog and disappeared. And now, with her home-on-wheels in a trailer behind her and her eleven-year-old daughter Ariel next to her, she had decided to search for him.

She glanced out the window at the Toss-Em Ping Pong booth, and her mind rushed back to the first time she met Tony.

* * *

It was 1957, eleven years ago, when she first joined the carnival, and she was walking past Tony's booth after hours.

"Want to play a game?" he had called as he motioned her over.

"I thought you were closed," she had said, stepping to the booth.

"Nope. For you, I'm staying open," he replied. Tony reached out and placed several white ping pong balls into her hand. The whole cluster of them seemed to weigh nothing in her palm. "Consider it a private game," Tony added, "On the house." His high cheekbones were buoyed up by a grin. There was something captivating about him at the time, though Estelle couldn't exactly identify it. An aura. An inexplicable magnetism.

"Well, okay," Estelle replied.

Tony lifted one eyebrow flirtatiously. "But if I let you play, what do I get in return?" he quizzed.

"A free reading, maybe," she replied, referring to her fortune-telling tent with a sign above the entryway proclaiming ESTELLE THE TELLER. HAVE YOUR FORTUNE READ!

"Hey, cool." Tony gave her a look filled with his usual opposites: confident but somehow shy, experienced yet still boyishly innocent and open.

"So go ahead," he said, nodding at her hand and then toward the plywood platform clustered with shot glasses, "Toss away."

She flipped the ping pong balls underhanded, and watched ball after ball bounce crazily over the lips of the glasses, hopping forward and backward like Mexican jumping beans. She laughed lightly at their erratic jittering motions.

"Careful," Tony cautioned. "Sometimes they have minds of their own."

"Does anyone ever land one in the first prize glasses?" she asked, referring to the six glasses clustered in the center of the board. The rims of the glasses were painted lipstick red. The next two circles of glasses were yellow-rimmed, indicating a small prize, like a rabbit's foot or a cheap key chain. The largest section of glasses, around the perimeter, were rimmed with white, the *no prize* category.

"Rarely," he answered. "Very rarely."

"So the odds are that much against me?"

"Yes and no." He ran his hand through his dark wavy hair that curled at the collar of his tight denim shirt with the sleeves rolled halfway up. "It's a little like gambling in Vegas. But hey, keep trying. You never know what might happen."

She threw another ten ping pong balls, each of them skittering around the lips of the glasses, none of them coming to rest in a winning glass. "This game's not fair."

"Just chance, is all," Tony said, tapping a wooden pointer in his palm. "Nothing more, nothing less."

With her next toss, the ball hopped left, then right. In mid-bounce, Tony angled the wooden pointer toward the ball and nudged it with the tip. The ball jumped sideways and finally settled right in the center of a red-rimmed glass.

Estelle cheered and clapped her hands. Then she turned to him. "You cheated, though."

"So? For you, maybe, I'd cheat." He gave her an in-between smile, the charismatic smile he became famous for.

"What do I win?" she asked anxiously.

He reached to the wood rafters of the booth and plucked one of the big prizes—an oversized pair of foam fuzzy dice—from a hook. "These," he said, holding the black dice with white spots. As she reached out for them, he pulled them back teasingly. "And me."

"What if I only want the dice?" she asked coyly.

"Can't have just the dice. It's a two-for-one deal." His brown eyes locked with hers. "Either both, or nothing."

She felt a chill rise through her as he handed the dice to her, then leaned forward and surprised her by kissing her lightly on the lips.

"Wow," she sighed, "Some prize."

"Yeah." He stared into her eyes with a steady gaze that seemed so intense it could melt candle wax. "Some prize."

* * *

"Mom, what are you waiting for?" Ariel called from the passenger's side, startling Estelle back to the present.

"I'm not waiting," she replied, feeling, beneath the soles of her feet, the vibrating floorboards as the engine idled.

"Then why are we just sitting here?" Ariel questioned. "You forget something?"

"No. We're going. You ready?"

"Sure," Ariel chirped.

She pressed her purple silk slipper on the gas pedal, and the car lurched forward and through the gates of the carnival grounds, leaving a small blue globe of exhaust behind it. The fuzzy dice circled each other, waltzing briefly, their black cords winding and unwinding.

In the rearview mirror, Estelle saw the shrinking banner which now read:

SAND'S MAGICAL SHOWS AND AMUSEMENTS

She felt, for a moment, that maybe her life was in reverse, too, and that she'd made the wrong decision. The clear map she had envisioned in her mind suddenly branched out like cracks from a nicked windshield. But she had to start thinking forward, she told herself. To whatever was ahead and waiting out there. To the wide, gleaming future—the kind of future that she always tried to predict for her customers.

This trip was a gamble, she knew. A game of chance. A crazy roll of the dice. At a stop sign at the edge of town, she accelerated onto the narrow county road that seemed to stretch all the way to the hazy horizon—a place where, she knew, she would either be lost, or found, or something in between.

CHAPTER THREE
One Week Earlier

Estelle and Ariel

Estelle opened a black wooden box, lifted her crystal ball from a purple velvet bag, and lowered it gently to the kitchen counter. She dusted it off with a soft cloth. It would be ready, she thought, when she opened her fortune teller's tent in a half hour, ready for whatever images might appear within it.

"Orange stars, yellow moons, pink hearts," Ariel said as she sat at the breakfast table.

Estelle turned and gave her a puzzled look.

"That's what Lucky Charms are made up of." Ariel pointed to the cereal floating in her bowl. "So, Mom," she said, changing the subject, "when do you think we'll hear from Dad?" She spooned the last few pieces, rescuing the shapes from drowning in the milk.

Not having an answer at the moment, Estelle stepped back to the breakfast table and cupped her hands around her mug of chamomile tea, the steam rising from it in thin whisps.

She could hear the squawking sounds of crows piercing through the walls of their 1950s Rollohome Dream Home trailer, which she and Tony had bought years ago on a year-end closeout sale. It featured two doors, a stand-up shower, and slightly-rounded windows with Venetian blinds. Its pastel pink and blue exterior was dimpled with small dents, and it always seemed to rest at a slant so that a tennis ball could roll across the living room floor.

"When, Mom?" Ariel insisted.

Estelle took a bite of her toast—a little too dry—and washed it down with a sip of tea. "Soon, I think," she finally answered, seeing that anxious expression fill her daughter's face. It was a lie, of course, but she didn't want to say what she was really thinking.

"Soon?" Ariel asked insistently. "Soon is a stupid word. Soon isn't soon enough."

Estelle felt a pang in her stomach as Ariel's words sunk in. For the past two weeks, Tony—her husband of ten years—was just plain gone, and his unexplained absence was a gap in their lives. With each passing day, that gap grew painfully wider. Big enough to fill their whole trailer. Their whole hearts. Their whole lives. She kept expecting him to step through the door at any moment, but he didn't.

She poured two glasses of orange juice, set one in front of Ariel, then sat down again at the table beneath the overhead fluorescent kitchen fixture that always flickered and fluttered, like a wing of light, about to take off.

Estelle checked her watch. "Aren't you almost late for tutoring?" she asked. "The smartest kid on earth better get going."

"Okay." Ariel gulped her glass of juice. "But promise me you won't touch my secret laboratory while I'm gone. Or my observatory telescope."

"Don't worry," Estelle said with a laugh, "I'll save them just for you."

With that, Ariel rinsed her cereal bowl in the sink and headed to her bedroom to get dressed.

* * *

Thoughts of Tony filtered through Estelle's mind. She pictured him, performing his tightrope walking act. It was a talent, the way Tony made his audiences believe. He was always confident and freewheeling, and people were drawn to him and liked him. He was part carny, part tightrope artist, part dreamer. And she loved him like crazy for those qualities, for all those things she could never be.

On the wire, his performance in front of the caramel corn-munching small-town crowds in Wisconsin and Minnesota and Ohio included an agile toe-stand while he juggled three realistic-looking rubber knives. At the end of the show, he'd do his patented swan-song bow, bending over suavely, his dark, shiny hair waving in an unseen wind, an ear-of-corn grin widening on his face. All the while, his size thirteen and a half foot gripped the wire as the crowd gasped. "Like they'd just seen Jesus or somebody," Tony once joked. They'd never witnessed a man bending so low, so gracefully, and still managing to stay on a thin wire thirty feet off the ground. Estelle figured that some people's lives in the audience had not gone the way they expected, or had tipped and fallen off-kilter, and somehow this agile man straightened it for them, at least for a few minutes. His smile seemed to briefly brighten the darkness inside their skulls, his impossibly turquoise eyes hypnotizing them into believing that the whole planet was right, and level, and balanced.

Tony made Estelle believe that, too, even if it wasn't true. Twelve years ago, Tony had swept Estelle off her feet as easily as the clowns, with their oversized push-brooms, whisked away balloons after a show.

And now, sitting in the kitchen, she closed her eyes and pictured Tony, stepping agilely on that tightrope and walking right back to her.

Then a disturbing memory pushed that image away. It was a rainy evening, three weeks ago. After a couple of beers, Tony had said, almost casually, "Don't be surprised if I have to leave for a while. You know—for a few days, maybe. Or longer, even."

Surprised by his comment, she turned toward him as they sat on the couch. "What do you mean?"

"Just that," he answered, and he drew a vague shape in the air with one hand. "Something's come up. And, I mean, if it happens, then, well…" he faltered and went silent. She leaned toward him with a blank look, anticipating what he'd say next. Then he turned toward the black and white TV where the audience on "What's My Line?" burst into laughter. His eyes glazed over as if there was something else on his mind besides that show on the snowy screen. He stood abruptly, strolled to the darkened kitchen, and opened the refrigerator door. She followed him there and saw him peering in a little too long as if searching for something, though his bottles of Bud were on the shelf right in front.

"Really, Tony," she insisted. "What's this all about?"

His face was half lit by the milky glow from the refrigerator light, half in shadow. He just lifted both hands in the air, like an innocent man being arrested, and curtly ended the conversation with "Aw, damn. Just forget I said that. Okay?"

How could she forget about it? she asked herself now. Why did she go silent? When he dodged her question, she should have insisted that he tell her what he meant. Why didn't she just pin him down and demand: "What the hell are you talking about, Tony?"

The first few days he was gone, she had expected him to return—hopefully, with an explanation. She had asked around about Tony's mysterious absence. But it was futile. No one—not his buddy Fast Eddie, not Old Whiskers, or Splat the Clown—knew why he would have left, or where he went. "Sorry, Estelle," Fast Eddie had said with a wince. "Wish I could help you out. But I've got nothing." Virgil Sand, the self-important owner of the carnival, was fuming about it, of course. He confronted Estelle near the Fireball ride. "Tony back yet?" he asked. It was more of a demand than a question.

Not wanting to talk about it, she just shook her head.

"Well shoot," Sand continued anyway, "I've had to cancel his goddamn tightrope show every night. All because of your famous husband. And his damn disappearing act. It's costing me big bucks, you know." When she kept walking, he called to her: "When you see him, tell him to get his ass into my office. Right away."

"Sure. That's my first priority," she said sarcastically, but, as usual, he missed her tone.

With each passing day, Estelle worried more and more about her daughter. A couple months ago, Ariel had pasted a few glow-in-the-dark planets and stars to the ceiling of her small bedroom. She always focused on them in the darkness before she fell asleep. But since Tony left, Ariel kept a tiny lamp on all night. Mornings, she'd claim that she left it on because she'd fallen asleep while reading, but Estelle knew that wasn't the real reason.

Ariel had started asking lots of questions that had no answers. Questions like: "Where do think he is?" Or "Did something happen between you guys, or what?" Or: "Think he'll walk in on us at breakfast tomorrow?" Estelle could tell, by the cracked-glass expression on Ariel's face, that those questions tormented her. After all, Ariel loved him. And so did she. And Tony still loved the both of them, too, she thought. She had to believe that.

Dressed and carrying a notebook for her tutoring session, Ariel emerged from her bedroom. "Guess what I found in my Lucky Charms this morning?" she said.

"What?"

She lifted a paper napkin toward Estelle. In its center was a single greenish piece of cereal. "A clover. A clover!"

"Oh?"

"Yes. A clover is the rarest of the cereal pieces, I heard. All the kids say so. There's only one in every ten or twelve boxes."

"Hmmm," Estelle tipped her head toward the napkin and nodded.

"It's a little soggy, but still." Ariel squinted one eye at it. "So," she asked, "does that mean I'm lucky? Or just that I'm dumb because I believe what the back of the cereal box tells me?"

"Both, maybe," Estelle replied with a light laugh.

After Ariel kissed Estelle on the cheek and said goodbye, Estelle lifted a pencil, and crossed another day off the wall calendar with a thick X. She turned and looked out the small window above the sink, a window which allowed a narrow, squashed view of the outside world. That world consisted of the stained canvas backs of the game booths that marched both directions and into the distance. And in the center of the view was the corroded steel underside of the Round Up, a ride with a fifty-foot rotating platform. On the ride, the spinning wheel was steadily raised by a huge hydraulic arm until it was spinning vertically. Estelle, with her fear of heights, had never been on it. When you rode it, everybody said that the centrifugal force pressed your body to the mesh of the back wall. You could let go of the metal safety chain at your waist, extend your arms straight up, and you wouldn't fall. Even inside her trailer, she could always hear the riders screaming as if they were being tortured and needed to be rescued.

She should do something to find Tony, she told herself. She should swing into action and not be so indecisive, so passive, so damn helpless. But then her doubts whirled around inside her head, bumping together and blurring like some Tilt-a-Whirl gone mad, and she felt numb, immobile. How would she begin? Where would she go?

She looked over at the crystal ball in the corner. She knew she had a kind of power with it, or, more like it—the ball gave her a kind of power. Though she wasn't totally convinced about it, she was told she had the gift; her Andalucian grandmother Rosalinda assured her of that when she was a little girl.

Estelle could never really explain her visions to anyone, much less herself. When she began a telling session, she would let herself soften, as if in sleep, her eyelids closing halfway. Soon she could feel herself become almost transparent, like a spring-fed mountain lake that was growing deeper by the second. She became ten times as deep as her normal self. She felt clear. Distilled. Pure. But still waiting. Waiting for an unexplained glimmer of light, or a cloud of darkness, or whatever was in between.

Sometimes she felt like she was seeing events that might soon happen, or pain that was longing to be healed. She might envision tears on someone's cheek, or hear laughter, or the song of a bird, or the voice of silence. The world: ugly or beautiful, was there, and it spoke to her, through her. Most times, she was convinced that she didn't see the world; maybe it was the world that saw her.

At times like that, she knew it was not just some carnival gimmick. She performed her act out of love, out of caring.

The more she tapped into her psychic self, the more she became convinced that our lives weren't just flesh and bone, life and death, heaven and hell like her childhood catechism taught her while the black and white nuns hovered over her shoulder. Lately, she began to think that there were other spheres, other realms—infinitely bigger and more complicated—that no humans could comprehend.

This morning, though she was already late for setting up her fortune-telling tent, she stepped close to the crystal ball and circled her delicate hands like clouds around the ball's surface. She closed her eyes, let herself go into her relaxed trance, then opened her eyes and gazed into it.

She kept staring into it, waiting for that soft electrical pulse she sometimes felt. Waiting for some doors to softly open within her. Waiting for feathery blue lights to form themselves into shapes. Images. Answers. A direction.

Instead, she saw nothing. No orange stars, yellow moons, pink hearts, or lucky clovers. And definitely no Tony. All she could see were the slightly magnified scratches on the linoleum counter beneath the ball.

CHAPTER FOUR

Tony

    Tony followed the asphalt carpet that kept unrolling in front of him. If a highway was some kind of hypnotist, he thought, then this early morning it definitely seemed like it. No traffic, and a mesmerizing white line that sometimes blinked at him, sometimes just pulled him toward the hazy blue distance. Suddenly he had the sensation that he wasn't moving forward in his truck; instead, he was standing still, and the landscape was steadily sliding past him. It would be easy to doze off out here, he thought, a hundred miles between towns. It would be easy to get lulled by the endless flatness and to wake up dead, the truck wrapped around some utility pole. So he focused on staying awake. He took a gulp of coffee from his silver thermos. He clicked on the radio, spun the dial, and found some faraway country station that was laced with static. He fought off the numbness, imagining himself slugging it in his brain like a boxer.

    This trip needed to be the opposite of numbness. He had a mission, a destination he needed to reach. He had to focus, to find out. No falling asleep on the damn drive, he told himself, even though, as he rode over an uneven surface in the road, the steering wheel rocked back and forth like a cradle.

*   *   *

    That night he had left the carnival, he glanced once in the rearview mirror and saw the glow of the security lights quickly evaporating. He took another slug from his bottle of Jack Daniels, turned the radio up loud, and fixed his eyes straight ahead. He drove hard and fast, the truck's headlights poking two holes in the darkness. His '62 blue Chevy Fleetside pickup was a half-ton metal compass needle gone crazy, heading haphazardly on the back roads as if it couldn't decide which direction to go. He felt the engine's metallic heat rising through the dash. He imagined that the highway was on fire.

Meanwhile, he sipped more whiskey. He knew Estelle claimed that Jack made him crazy and reckless. Sometimes too much of it made him wild, but not wild in a good way, and maybe she was right. It permeated his brain with impulsiveness, moodiness, and sometimes anger at himself. It was his weakness behind his usually strong façade, his liquid Achilles heel.

With his left elbow resting on the open window, his right wrist draped over the steering wheel, he accelerated, the sound of his tire treads on the road rising in pitch like a song. He veered down the yellow-lined asphalt county roads that reminded him of flattened garter snakes. Or black, dotted tongues, calling him. Then, as if finally finding its way, the truck aimed itself south on County 21. Then west, toward Highway 66. Yes, he thought. West. Steadily west.

Sometime past midnight, he had stopped at a small-town bar—called Jerry's Hideaway—just beyond the Iowa border. A couple of locals—heavy-set middle-aged farmers wearing overalls and feed caps—gawked at him, making him feel like he was some kind of alien. One of the men rotated his head and asked, "So where abouts you from, fella?" Tony knew how out-of-place he looked with his tight jeans, dark blue tank top, a tattoo on one bicep, and hair flowing toward his shoulders. Tony downed a shot of tequila, then answered, "Outer space. Where else?" which quickly shut the man up.

Those were some of the last things he remembered of the night. From then on, he *was* in outer space. He bumped from bar to bar like some silver ball in a pinball machine. Only a few fragments of the night remained: dropping quarters in a jukebox and playing Janis Joplin over and over, neon Schlitz signs glaring at him and stinging his eyes, tipping a barstool over, a blurred barkeep leaning toward him and saying "You've had enough. You're cut off, buster," to which Tony replied with a slur "You're telling me." He knew it was damn foolish to drive around in that condition, but maybe that was him: damn foolish.

The next day, when he woke on a wayside outside that small town, a hangover tightened a vice on his temples, and doubts jabbed their fists at him. Debating about whether he was on a pointless journey and should turn back, he pulled into the next small town and checked into a cheap motel. No neon sign, just the word *Motel* painted on a wooden rectangle beside the road.

When Tony stepped into the musty lobby, a gaunt older man, reading a newspaper on a red vinyl reclining chair, gave him a blank look from behind the counter. "This place have a name?" Tony had asked as the man slid a registration card toward him.

"Nope," the man had replied. He laughed a deep-down raspy laugh that sounded like you were opening a paper bag. "Don't need one. We're the only one in town." Behind him on the wall, a calendar that sported a girl in a bikini lying on a red Chevvy, and a sign that said TV and Shower in All Rooms. Air Condition. No Refunds.

"Huh," Tony replied, shaking his head. He wrote his first name on the registration card, then before he filled in his last name in the second box, he hesitated. He let the pen linger in the air, then drew a straight line in the box. He wasn't sure why. He just did. There were a lot of things he did in his life without knowing why, without questioning. Impulsive, Estelle called him once. And she was right. Maybe too right. Last week, after hours, he walked across a wire in the dark and tried out a new stunt: bending backward while on the wire and touching it with his fingertips. No way could he do it. He ended up falling on his goddamn ass. It seemed like he was falling from the wire—even during shows—more and more often lately, and that bothered him a lot. Virgil Sand even questioned him, saying, "Shit, Tony. Looks like you're losin' it. You gotta shape up your goddamn act, or the crowd's not gonna like it."

Tony slid the registration card toward the man.

"You forgot your last name," the man commented.

"Don't need one," Tony countered wryly, and the man chuckled, getting his drift.

The man squinted at Tony. "You on the run from something, or what?"

"Running *to* something is more like it," Tony replied, taking the room key, attached to a plastic keyholder the shape of a pine tree.

For the next three days in that darkly paneled room, he was anonymous. He was Tony with a line after his name. Just Tony———, a nameless guy in a nameless run-down town staying at a nameless motel. A guy who was grappling with what he should do, and what his next step would be. He wrestled with his conscience, his doubts wringing his brain until it felt dry. He knew he could return to the carnival, which was only a day's drive away. He could do his familiar tiptoe walk across a wire each evening. He could return to the loving safety net of Estelle and Ariel. They were always there to catch him. He missed them, of course, and felt bad about leaving the two of them.

For the next three days, he bought junk food at the local hamburger stand or at the quick mart, took it back to the motel, and ate next to the hot plate and the coffee maker with a stack of Styrofoam cups and powdered Coffee De-lite. He opened a map of the U.S. and studied the spidery blue and black roads. He ran his thumb over them as if he could feel the texture of the pavement.

Three days he sat in that room while, in the background, Captain Kangaroo and Have Gun Will Travel or Mission Impossible played on the screen of a small TV that kept filling with snow, then coming into focus, then filling with snow again.

Those three days, he felt suspended, almost, and strangely unable to move forward or backward. Like a damn bubble caught halfway to the surface of something. He was beginning to think that maybe this whole idea was stupid. An aimless plan. But he knew he had to ease his mind, answer some questions that had been haunting him ever since he got that letter. It had arrived straight out of his past from thirteen years ago. From her. There was no return address, but there was a ghostly postmark from California. She was being coy and sort of elusive, he thought, just like she was back then when what they had between them fell away and shattered to pieces.

The letter stirred up memories of a time he never told Estelle about. It was their agreement not to talk about past relationships. "Life started the day we met each other, right?" he told her, and she nodded. The trouble was, that letter dredged up not just all the memories, but all the guilt. All the unfinished business. It made him decide to step out the door and aim his truck, head-on, into the night.

After the third nearly sleepless night, Tony woke up early, unwrapped himself from sweat-stained sheets, and slid out of the saggy motel bed. It was still before dawn. No light sliding through the blinds of the picture window.

He clicked on the gooseneck desk lamp. He noticed, beneath the pale triangle of light, the road map of creases on his palms. Too many, for a guy who was only thirty-three. Which ones should he follow?

He slid the envelope from the back pocket of his rumpled jeans and studied the handwriting, the letters coiling, intertwining with each other. He put the letter away, packed his things in a duffle bag, gathered his belongings, and shouldered through the warped aluminum screen door. Standing there for a few minutes in the parking lot, Tony looked out at the barbed wire fence in the field adjacent to the motel where the weathered wooden fenceposts marched off into the distance. The bleak pre-dawn landscape was just beginning to brighten.

He felt resurrected, almost. He'd finally made his decision. He would go on. He'd make things right if he could. He'd plunge headfirst into it, this little odyssey of his. Succeed or fail, this was something he just had to do.

He veered his truck onto the gravel access road. Through the windshield, he spotted the pale but still luminous full moon, which was setting on the horizon on the road ahead of him. And, in the rear-view mirror, the blood-red lip of the sun began to lift itself directly behind him. Moonset, sunrise: both of them perfectly aligned on opposite sides of the highway.

A sign, he had thought. Some kind of amazing equinox. And I'm here, right in the middle of it, driving on a nameless road toward whatever's out there.

He passed a dented Drive With Caution sign and floored the truck through an intersection, a cloud of gravel dust swirling behind him.

* * *

Now, today, as he drove, the faraway radio station faded in and out. It was a song he didn't recognize, but he turned the volume up anyway. He took another gulp of bitter coffee, steadied the wheel with his right hand. One step at a time, he told himself. One foot in front of the other. Don't fall this time, damn you. Don't fall.

CHAPTER FIVE

Ariel

Sideshow #1

    Hello. My name is Ariel, I'm eleven years old, and I steal Bird Children.

Sideshow #2

    Hello. My name is Ariel, and you don't know me yet, but you will. If you keep reading, that is. I write in a secret journal. My Mom and Dad don't know about it. It has a nice blue cover, so I call it my Blue Sky Notebook. (It's like a little square of the sky.) I call my entries sideshows because I guess my life is kind of a sideshow. I have hundreds of entries, in case you're wondering. Thousands, eventually. I keep the journal inside another notebook I've labeled *Tutoring Notes, and Stuff,* like it's from my meetings with Mrs. Chadouir. She's a teacher who stops to tutor us carnival kids. We learn about math, science, English, the importance of posture, and all that. She once said to me "Ariel, I swear you'll be a poet someday. Or some kind of writer, at least." (That made me smile.)

    My Blue Sky Notebook is filled with all kinds of happy (and sometimes sad) thoughts. Those kinds of thoughts always swirl inside my brain. About Mom. About Dad. About me. About my life. Depending on the type of thought, I dress it up. I use a rainbow of green or red or pink ink from my set of colored pens. Pretty fancy, I know!

    Oh, by the way—if you happen to find this after I'm dead, don't publish it or anything. And don't show it to my handsome (but very smart) boyfriend of the future, either. I mean, I'd be pretty embarrassed in my grave.

    I write mostly late at night. Then I slide my journal under my pillow when I sleep. That's a good place for it, I've decided. Because that way, all my dreams can seep into it.

Sideshow #6

My left leg is shorter than the other. Anisomelia, the doctors call it. Or short-leg syndrome. Sometimes, when I walk, it feels like the earth is tilted to one side. So I limp a little. Which really bothers me. "I don't advise that you enter any marathons," one doctor told me. He gave me a klutzy cork insert in my left shoe. "Can I run a marathon now?" I asked. "If I fall into a swimming pool, will the cork keep me afloat?" He didn't answer either question.

Anisomelia. The word has a sort of pretty sound to it. It reminds me of the name of a royal Egyptian woman who rides camels across the Sahara. Princess Anisomelia. Her attendants fan her with big palm leaves.

Yeah, the name reminds me of that. Or maybe it just reminds me that one leg is shorter than the other. (Very funny, Ariel. Academy award for that one.)

Sideshow #9

I live inside a carnival. It's kind of my miniature world, I guess. It has pretty much everything I need. My friends are here—a few carney kids are about my age, and we meet up every day. My school is here. I have a lot of fun here. I mean, if you count the free rides on the Tilt-a-Whirl. And an occasional spin on the Ferris wheel. After hours, Lily's daughter Maria Luz and I get to stroll the arcade and play games. All for free. Plus, the carnival is filled with sweet treats. Cotton candy, sno-cones, candy apples, mini-donuts, funnel cakes. (Health foods, Mom calls them. Yuk yuk.) Lily brings me a cup from the lemonade stand. I ask you—if you have all that, what else do you need? (Okay, I'm being a little funny here.) It's a corny place, I know. But I love it.

And did I mention that I have a Mom and Dad who love me? If not, I'm mentioning it now.

I'm not sure why, but everybody who works here has a nickname. I'm known as A-Plus Ariel. I hope it's because I'm kinda smart? Then there's Puerto Rico Lily, Splat the Clown (just don't try to joke with him), Fast Eddie, Jumpin' Johnny (in charge of the World's Smallest Horse), Kandy Korn Kim, Proto Pup Pete, Three Finger Louie (ticket taker—what else?), Boom Boom Bruno (former human cannonball, now deaf), Cotton Candy Mandy (how sweet can you get?), The Flying Santiago (a very down-to-earth guy from Mexico), Sizzler Ernie, Rowdy Rodrigo, Higgie (carnival busybody and mail deliver-er) Texas Slim, Ol' Whiskers (carnival historian. No one knows how old he really is, but some say one-hundred and two!), Reptile Ray (only when we do Iowa shows), The Psycho Cycler, Mexico Manuel, Jambalaya Jamaica (from the Caribbean, & the chief mess tent cook). Last but not least there's The Dashing Desdiolo (my dad), and Estelle the Tella (my mom).

As you can see, the carnies who work here come from all kinds of different places. I guess nobody here is a regular ordinary person, with a regular plain old name. And that's a good thing.

Something else…No one comes to a carnival to be sad. I've lived in one for all of my eleven years, and I've noticed that. No one comes here to cry. Everybody's pretty much happy. Sure, you win or lose at games. Either you get a goldfish in a plastic bag, or you don't. But that's life, everyone tells me. Who knows?—maybe someday, I'll get out there into the big world. And I'll find out.

CHAPTER SIX

Tony

Karl Wallenda. Now there was a real high wire artist, Tony thought as he followed the straightaway that unrolled in front of the windshield. He listened to the humming pavement sing to him and he pictured the angled sunlight gleaming off the license plate.

He had a lot of time to think on this drive, and this morning he focused on his hero, Karl Wallenda. The guy could walk any length of wire. Between buildings. Between canyons, even. Some people called him a daredevil, but that didn't describe him. He was a performer. Even though he was already 63 years old—thirty years older than Tony—Wallenda was still touring the country with his act.

Tony had read articles about Wallenda, and always remembered what he once said: "Being on the tightrope is living; everything else is waiting." And he was right, Tony thought. So goddamn right.

What's life, Tony thought, if you don't take chances? Where's the adrenaline rush if you sit on a La-Z-Boy somewhere and watch some damn soap operas all afternoon? Where is the joy of climbing those rungs to a thin wire that you can almost hear singing with a high-pitched sound? Where's the thrill of taking your first step on it?

Tony recalled those first times when he attempted to walk the tightrope. It was all because of Estelle. He wanted her to admire him. Not just admire him, but more than that. Way more. He wanted her to see that he wasn't just some game jock, idling away the day as customers handed him fifty cents or a buck to throw some ping pong balls. Those pale white spheres had hardly any weight and were mostly air.

So he asked The Flying Santiago to teach him, and the guy agreed to coach Tony after hours.

When he first tried walking on the wire, suspended just a couple feet off the ground and attached to two trees, Tony realized how hard it was. The wire—like some nervous, living thing that was cold—kept shivering beneath his feet. It jiggled rapidly left and right and left, and he'd drop off. "Damn!" he'd exclaim, shaking his head. A dozen times he tried it, and the shimmying wire, like some silver bronco in a rodeo, kept shaking him off. The ground was unforgiving.

"Get those arms out to your sides, amigo," Santiago barked. He sat on a stump, sipping some gin, as he often did after the carnival closed its gates. Santiago was an immigrant from Mexico City, and he used to do a high wire act with the Ringlings back in the day when he was a twenty-year-old. His family troupe was called The Flying Santiagos. Now, thirty-some years later, with bad legs and a back brace, he was relegated to jockeying the ring toss game and other odd jobs. "Vamos!" he called to Tony, using his usual mix of English and Spanish. "Don't clamp your hands to your sides. You look muy asustado. Like you're scared shitless!"

"Maybe I am scared shitless," Tony called back to him with a laugh. "And the damn wire's too loose."

"Wire's not loose. No esta suelto." Santiago countered. "You're just not good enough at it."

"Take a hike," Tony snapped back with a laugh. But he did follow Santiago's advice, extending his arms, and it helped to steady himself. He soon realized that—to be great at this, not just good—he needed to reach toward both horizons and grab onto them for support. He needed to grab the whole world and hold on tight to it.

Eventually, he learned the skill, and, by raising the height of the wire each time, he got better and better at it. "Keep your shoulders back," Santiago advised. "And look straight ahead. "No abajo. Not down. The ground, she'll jump up at you if you look down at it. Comprendo?"

"Comprendo, I think," Tony called back.

"And trust in your feet," the old man added. "Soon they'll know where to go." Odd and unique advice, Tony had thought at the time, but it seemed to work.

The middle was always the worst part. That was where the wire sagged slightly, and it always wavered, as if there was a slight wind blowing it. So he had to get past it, and walk the second half gracefully but quickly.

He learned to fight gravity and to ignore the dizziness up there where the atmosphere always seemed to be thin and almost ethereal. He slipped and fell from six feet up to the soft sawdust many times, of course. But he just got back up there with bruises on his knees and elbows. Bruises will heal, he always thought. You had to be positive about it. You need to forget the falls like they never happened. Don't question yourself. You had to imagine yourself always making it to the other side, to your destination. That was the only way to get there.

Soon the wire was thirty feet up, and Virgil Sand plastered a banner over the small performance tent that proclaimed: Thrilling Tightrope Walk by The Dashing Desdiolo! Shows Daily at 3:00, 5:00, and 7 p.m. Sand always wanted to make his carnival bigger and better, with a few circus-like performances, so he was happy to have Tony's act as part of the show. "More thrill," Sand beamed, "more money in the till."

Tony didn't prefer chaotic psychedelic rock music all that much, or cheesy calliope music, which Sand often piped into the midway through some tinny speakers. Instead, he chose a classy John Phillip Sousa march—Semper Fidelis—which would begin to play as soon as his gray slipper touched the wire. Always timing it perfectly, his walk was completed at the end of the song, when he took a deep bow and felt the flutter of applause rising toward him.

In the silence before his performance, as Tony climbed the twelve wooden rungs, he believed he could hear the wire humming. He could almost hear it calling his name. Other times, he imagined that the wire was on fire. He felt like he could be one of those firewalkers, those religious zealots in Greece who walked, unscathed, across hot coals for purification and healing.

Whenever he took that first step, Tony felt like he was taking a first step on the moon, as if he was one of the Apollo astronauts. Tony always felt an adrenalin rush filling his head as he walked. He began to believe there was magic in the soles of his feet.

He was no longer a stuntman, as Virgil Sand once referred to him. He was no corny novelty act. He was an artist. He wouldn't settle for just being good at this; he wanted to be great. In fact, he wanted to be famous. A star, known throughout the entertainment business, his picture splashed on the covers of magazines. A man who had, finally, achieved perfection.

Yesterday, as he drove, he added up the length he had walked on the wire—100 feet—and multiplied it times the number of times he stepped across it during the last ten years. He realized he could have walked a tightrope that stretched across the state and all the way to Minneapolis. Eventually, maybe even all the way across America.

He recalled Estelle questioning him about his act one evening when they sat in the empty wooden bleachers. "How can you do that,

Tony?" she asked, looking up at the glistening thread of the wire. "I'd be terrified."

"It's easy," he had lied, trying to be suave. To be honest, he always felt a flash of fear when he began his trek. "You have to caress the wire," he continued. "Tame it." When she gave him a questioning look, he added, "You know—make it part of your world."

"Hmmm, Tony," she replied. "That sounds almost poetic."

"And speaking of worlds" he added, turning to her, "You're mine." He slid his arms around her and gave her a kiss. He knew all along that when he was on the wire, it wasn't about the audience's applause that encouraged him. It was Estelle's loving gaze that buoyed him up. It gave him confidence as she watched him, her nervous expression smoothing over with an encouraging smile. It made him feel almost weightless.

Each day as he performed, the sold-out crowd gasped and rose to their feet, spilling their caramel corn to the sawdust floor. Tony knew the tightrope was in love with him at the same time that he was in love with the tightrope. And as he walked across it for those few moments, he almost believed that the earth's not round, or flat, like some people say, but thin and narrow, like a wire.

*   *   *

A large snake—a rattler or sidewinder, he wasn't sure—slithered across the road and Tony swerved the truck to avoid it. He glanced at the speedometer; he was pushing 90 and not realizing it. He couldn't afford a ticket, so he took his foot off the gas a little.

For the next few hours, he drove across the flat, unremarkable landscape. No trees. Just dried brush and a few rotted fenceposts scraping the haze. The mottled sky seemed to taper to a point.

He stopped at an empty wayside to stretch and noticed the moon, which hadn't set yet. It was pale and ghostly, but still visible in the sky. He pictured the astronauts, orbiting around it. They'd put a man on the moon soon, he figured. It would be an awesome journey, to get there, and back. As a kid, Tony always fantasized about being an astronaut, or a scientist, an astronomer who studied novas and galaxies. In grade school, he used to tote stacks of books home from the library with subjects like rocketry and famous inventions and constellations. A young kid's dreams.

Then, when he was eight years old, there was a day that erased his dreams, a day that has haunted him ever since. It was a couple of years after his mother passed away from cancer. In his mind, Tony sees his father, Roy, in the living room of their small apartment. His father's narrow, deep-set eyes turn steely as he flicks the ash of a cigarette into an ashtray, then rises slowly from the sofa, a glass of bourbon in his hand, the ice cubes clinking. "Well…" his dad says. Just that one word. That one goddamn word. Young Tony didn't really understand what that word meant, the weight of it, or why it trailed off so quickly without more words to follow it. Then, later, there were other voices, voices of his aunt and uncle, trying to be assuring, voices Tony heard so often that year: "He'll come back, right?" they said. "Any day now, he'll come back."

They were wrong. He never saw his father again.

Tony remembers Estelle asking him numerous times, "Want to talk about it?"

"Um, no," he always answered. "Not really." It was his private side, the side he wouldn't let anyone in on. His personal dark side of the moon.

The distant honking sound of geese, flying along the small stream beyond the rest area, brought Tony back. Silhouetted above the line of sharp, jagged trees, the geese looked like crosses gliding across the dark blue sky. They kept flying until they merged with the thin gray line of the horizon.

The sight made him feel lost, and the lost feeling seemed to grow larger, and larger, and he could feel it press on him from the inside like an overinflated tire. But before the feeling overwhelmed him and made him cry out in anguish, he jogged back to the truck, clicked the ignition, then floored it onto the highway. His tires spun in the gravel behind the truck, leaving two ruts as the Chevy lurched forward.

But he couldn't outrace his thoughts. What happened to those dreams he had as a kid? he asked himself. Instead of walking on the moon, he ended up working at a carnival at age 18 and inflating the gaudy Moon Walk for kids so they could bounce up and down on its plastic surface.

Later, when he began to develop his tightrope act, he longed to be the center of the universe on the greatest show on Earth. But these past months, all he heard was the floppy applause from a few overweight fairgoers holding nachos and tubs of popcorn in the sweaty crooks of their arms. He was going on thirty-four already, for cripes sake, and now he was beginning to realize what he was—a past-his-prime carny performing in a run-down show in towns where people could care less. He was no astronaut. He walked on the plain earth, and when he jumped into the air, he didn't rise and float upward, higher than anyone, as if he was blessed with a different kind of gravity.

*   *   *

For the next hours, he kept driving across this big middle—this long, empty, stretch of highway that told him he had no choice but to keep going. No hesitating. No more stopping for a break even though his legs ached with cramps.

Then, like a few times before, his thoughts backtracked a little. By taking this chance, was he risking a fall? he wondered. And if he was, how bruised would he be when he finally landed on the hardpacked ground?

CHAPTER SEVEN

Estelle and Ariel

A rapping on the trailer's tin door startled Estelle. She opened the door to see Dickie Higgins, the red-faced, Leprechaun of a man who ran the Go-Kart-a-Rama, a ride for little kids. Some of the 12-year-olds were taller than he was. He was also in charge of dropping off mail he picked up at the carnival's post office box in downtown Wanley, population 4,821.

"Top 'o the mornin', you two," Higgie crooned with his Irish accent, which everyone said was fake. He also claimed he attended the U. of Notre Dame for a year and made the football team practice squad as a field goal kicker, which people knew was a lie. "So have ya heard th' latest news?"

"What's that?" Estelle inquired.

"Guess the Bird Child's missin.'"

"Really? What happened?" Estelle asked.

"Yeah, what happened?" Ariel echoed in her best innocent voice.

"Nobody knows fer sure. But shucks," he said, laughing a high-pitched laugh that sounded like a giggle, "I always thought the thing was made of plastic or somethin' anyways. Just a pickled punk. Still, Sand's all in a tizzy about it." He held up an envelope. "But lookie here. Got somethin' for bonny lil' Ariel."

Higgie handed her the letter addressed to Miss Ariel Esmeralda-Desdiolo.

Estelle's eyelids blinked hard as if a sudden gust of wind just blew dust into her face.

It was Tony's handwriting.

Estelle leaned forward as Ariel anxiously tore open the white envelope and slid out a flimsy greeting card. On the cover was a cartoon of a smiling penguin, surrounded by multicolored flowers that looked like snowflakes. A feather slipped from the envelope and floated to the floor. With her high, wispy voice, Ariel read the note inside the blank card:

Hi Ariel,
Happy birthday!
Sorry about not being in touch.
  Miss ya, kid. —Your Dad.

Ariel picked up the dark gray, striped feather by its sharp quill, and twirled it around and around. It looked like it might have come from an eagle, maybe, or a hawk. "It's soft," she said, running her finger along its edge. "And really pretty. Think he wants me to wear it in my hair or something?"

"Um, sure," Estelle said as she squinted at the cramped, slanting letters of the handwriting on the envelope. No return address. And the postmark was unreadable, a smudged circle covered by wavy lines like inky ripples on top of water. But it looked like it might be Iowa or Illinois. She appreciated it that Tony remembered Ariel's birthday, but at the same time, it was maddening that he revealed nothing about where he was or why he was gone. Still, Estelle couldn't help but think this was some kind of clue, a gesture from Tony to tell them that he was out there and wanted to connect with them.

Ariel studied the card, then climbed on a stool and propped it on the windowsill, where the sun angled off its sharp but slightly bent edges.

A few minutes later, Ariel skipped through the room and left to meet her friends.

*   *   *

Estelle stood next to the kitchen table. I should get ready for my tent, she told herself. I should put on my makeup and get my fortune-telling garb on. I should transform myself with bracelets and shiny necklaces like I do each morning. I should be what everyone expects me to be. I should be able to know my own future, to know what's ahead for me. Instead, I'm just standing here in a cramped kitchen, unable to move forward or backward, weighed down by the weight of a thousand questions. Questions like Should I go on a search for him, and if I do, then where would I go? Or should I just wait? I keep thinking that he'll return in a couple of hours, stepping through the door, kissing me on the cheek, and saying "Sorry, Es. I'm such an idiot."

She turned and focused on the thin card on the windowsill as if it had the answers. But in the shaft of morning light, the translucent card just sat there: mute, flat, unmoving, like a single wing torn from something that once knew how to fly.

CHAPTER EIGHT

Estelle

    The girl, who looked about sixteen, slipped tentatively through the front flap of Estelle's tent. It was later that evening, the day Tony's birthday card arrived. The girl's mouse-brown hair was scraggly, unwashed, and she was dressed in baggy bell bottoms and a sweatshirt with a high school logo. Tugging nervously at the strap of her backpack, the girl asked, in a monotone voice, "Can I, um, get a reading or something?"

    "That's why I'm here," Estelle said with her warm voice, motioning to a chair in front of her table. Her reading tent was inviting, but with simple décor. No gaudy red velvet curtains or shelves with statues of mystical wizards and glass unicorns. No candles, incense, or hanging strings of crystals. Just two plain wood-slat chairs, and a small round pedestal table with a large crème colored doily, or tapete, as her Spanish grandmother called it, in its center. The doily, crocheted by her grandmother, was a delicate, circular pattern called a 'Wish on a Star.' The crystal ball rested on a red wooden stand. Next to it was a rose-colored glass flute vase that held three impatiens Estelle picked from her flower box. Estelle was always ready to meet her customers with her mauve eye makeup around her eyes, her gauze blouse embroidered with red stitching, her purple lips. A scarlet scarf in her long, blonde-streaked auburn hair added flair. "Please sit down," Estelle said, nodding to the chairs.

    But the girl didn't sit, just stood there, fidgeting. Estelle couldn't help but notice a desperate look on her pale face. "So," the girl said tentatively, "Are you for real? I mean, like, can you really predict things?"

    "I'll try," Estelle said. Sensing the girl's distress, Estelle asked "What's the matter, honey? You in trouble of some kind?"

    "Ha. You could say that." She pressed her fingertips to the front of her sweatshirt. "Or you could just say I'm pregnant," she blurted. With that, she burst into tears.

    Estelle stepped around the table and circled her with her arms. "I keep thinking about running away," the girl said as she sobbed. Mascara sliding down her cheeks in little gray funnels, she pulled back. "What should I do?" she pleaded. "Tell me."

Estelle opened her mouth, hoping to give her a few words of wisdom, but nothing came out. She had no pat replies. She wanted to be strong for this girl, but at the moment, the right words were eluding her, like butterflies scattering across a field. So instead she just said, empathetically, "Talk to me. About what you're feeling."

The girl proceeded to pour out her story about her ex-boyfriend, who was already dating another girl. About her father, who she claimed would disown her and throw her out of the house. Or send her to, as she called it, "Some preggie home with a bunch of mean nuns." She talked rapidly, winding her worries together like a tangled line on a fishing reel.

A few minutes later, the girl calmed down and turned to leave. "Thanks," she said. "I mean, for listening, at least."

"We can talk again, if you want," Estelle assured her. "Just stop any time." She picked up the five crumpled bills the girl had placed on the table, and handed them back to her. "Here," Estelle said. "I don't need these."

*   *   *

As soon as the girl left, Estelle closed her tent an hour early and hurried toward home.

On her way back, as she cut between the Guess-Your-Weight stand and the Sling-a-Ring Toss, she couldn't stop thinking about the desperate expression on the teen's face.

She couldn't help but remember that afternoon, twelve years ago, when she searched frantically for Tony. The two of them had been going out for several months. When she finally found him, Tony was setting up the Fun House on the far end of the lot with Fast Eddie and a couple of other guys.

He and his best buddy Fast Eddie—a thin Native American guy with long brown hair tied back so it hung down his back straight as a broomstick—were lifting a plywood panel with an amateur-looking painting of a laughing Mardi Gras jester in a five-cornered hat. Tony wore a denim shirt, cut off at the sleeves, a faded black Nascar ball cap, and reflector sunglasses. A Lucky cigarette bobbed in his mouth. As she approached, Tony and the guys were laughing about something.

"Tony," she had said. He didn't turn, as if he didn't hear her, or didn't want to hear her at the moment. "Tony," she repeated, more urgently.

He finally faced her. "What's up?"

"I have to talk to you." She couldn't see his eyes, only her own image, convex and panicky, in the silver lens of his sunglasses.

"Just give me a minute, okay? We've got to finish this." He nodded toward the panel, the jester's huge, toothy grin near his knuckles. "Can't exactly drop it."

"As soon as you're done, then," she acquiesced.

He tipped the panel to one side, adjusted it on the hinges, and hurriedly tapped some cotter pins in. The big colorful panels—added to both sides and the roof of the small Fun House trailer—lured in customers by making the attraction look twice the size than it really was. Sand liked the idea and bought it from a show in South Dakota.

"Hang on," Tony said to the rest of the crew. "I guess I'm on call. You boys can keep building your muscles while I'm gone."

Fast Eddie slid his t-shirt sleeve up to his shoulder and flexed the bicep of his thin arm. Then he smirked in his hatchet-faced, pointed-nose way.

Estelle led Tony between the corrugated metal walls of two parked semi-trucks, then spun around and faced him. "Tony," she said, in a shaking voice, "I think I'm pregnant."

At first, he didn't respond. He just tipped his hat back slightly on his forehead, exposing sweat-damp waves of his dark hair.

"Tony, did you hear what I said?"

"You think you're pregnant," he said, flattening out the words.

"No," she said, feeling her tingling face flush red, "I don't think I'm pregnant. I *know* I am."

"Oh," Tony exhaled. It was the sound a person might make when someone unexpectedly punched them in the gut. Then again: "Oh. Oh." Estelle felt his gasps in her midsection, too. She was hoping there wouldn't be that much of a hesitation from him, and wanted him, instead, to give her an encouraging look.

Instead, he slid off his sunglasses and looked down at the packed dirt. A tin bucket there, half full of rusty bolts. He nudged it with the toe of his leather work boot and the bolts clinked. Finally, he lifted his gaze back toward her. He grabbed her hand and slipped his arm around her waist. They swayed back and forth gently, and then he spun her around. "Okay," he said. "We're waltzing."

She couldn't help but laugh a little. "There's no music, Tony."

"Yeah," he replied, looking into her eyes. "There's music." His face gathered into a smile. "We make music." Then he leaned in and gave her a smoky kiss.

Just then, Fast Eddie, making his way between the semis, called "C'mon, Tony! We only got an hour to get this frickin' thing set up." Seeing Tony's arms around Estelle, Eddie squinted one eye. "The hell you two lovebirds doin' back here? Makin' out?"

"You got it," Tony replied, "We're makin' out. "And..." he paused. "We're getting married."

With those few words, Tony had proposed to her.

It wasn't how Estelle ever imagined it would happen. If it did happen, she wanted it to be dreamy and extravagant, like a scene out of some romance novel: Tony, galloping up to her on a white and grey dappled horse as she stood in a meadow exploding with lavender. Tony, lifting her onto the horse. Tony, proposing to her, and the two of them riding down a trail to a beach cove, where aqua waves crashed into black lava rocks. Or at the very least, she wanted it to happen in a lovely setting: in a garland-twined veranda in a park, maybe, two glasses of merlot glistening between them as they clinked them together in a toast. Fantasies, she knew.

Instead, it happened here, in a carnival, between the trailers of two semi-trucks. It happened there, with the two of them dancing without music, and in its own way, it was real and romantic, and amazing.

Pow! The sudden sound—as a Bust-Em Balloon Toss customer struck a balloon with a sharp dart—jolted her back to the present, and she paused there, halfway down the midway.

At that moment, she felt like the carnival was closing in on her. In front of her, she noticed the red stains from spilled sno-cones and the orange confetti of torn ticket stubs. Cotton candy cones, like flattened beige paper trumpets, embedded themselves in the mud. The metallic clunking and clacking of the nearby rides assaulted her ears. The air was filled with the wafting scent of toasted caramel corn mixed with the burnt-rubber scent of overheated generators. She winced as she heard old Herman, a maintenance worker—loaded again on booze, she assumed—puking behind one of the booths. Sour calliope music spilled from buzzing, frayed speakers near the corn dog stand. Young kids holding slushies squealed as they won a trinket at the Ring Toss game.

The whole place seemed like a confusing mix of happy and sad, sweet and bitter.

Just like everything she felt, these past days, about Tony.

She tipped her head back. The swirl of blinking carnival lights ignited the dark sky, making the constellations seem insignificant.

At that moment, Estelle felt insignificant, too. Standing there in the center, the heart of Sand's Magical Shows and Amusements, she felt anything but magical. It was like her life was tied up in thick ropes and the slowly passing days were knots, tightening around her.

But she'd finally made a decision, and she knew she had to act on it.

When she opened the trailer door, her mood was lifted when she was bathed in the familiar bluish glow filtering from the living room. There, Ariel, reclining on the worn, lime green couch in her pink pajamas, was watching TV. With her left leg propped on the scratched maple coffee table, Ariel read a book in her lap while the grainy screen played a rerun of The Newlywed Game.

Estelle greeted her with a kiss on the cheek, then went straight to the bedroom, where she flung open the hollow core bifold closet door. The sudden vacuum made Tony's three white T-shirts, hanging on the far side of the wooden pole, sway slightly, like laundry left hanging on a line with an approaching thunderstorm. In the back corner, hiding in the shadow, were the three pairs of shoes. Work boots. Tennies. Gray slippers. The three sides of Tony, she thought. His work, his leisurely moments, his tightrope act. Was there another side she didn't know about? She picked up the pair of slippers Tony had used for his act. She pictured Tony, beginning his walk, those suede-soled slippers stepping nimbly off the plywood platform and curling softly around the wire. She wondered—if he abandoned these three pairs here, then what shoes was he wearing that night he left? Was he walking on solid ground, or was he walking on glass, on ice, on fire, like she was with each passing day that he was gone? And how many more days will there be? She hated it that when Virgil Sand passed her today, he referred to Tony as "your damn escape artist husband." Is that what he was?

The t-shirts hovered in front of her like three ghosts made of sagging cotton. She didn't want to see them there anymore, so she pulled them free, leaving their black metal hangers clinking together and swaying like pendulums, then slid the shirts into a plastic Glad kitchen bag. Then she grabbed the shoes and boots, stuffed them into the bag, pulled the drawstring, and cinched the top shut.

She could hear The Newlywed Game on the TV, Bob Eubanks saying "Okay, ladies. Let's see just how well you know your spouse. Here's our first question: It bugs you when your husband does this at night."

She carried the bag through the living room and plopped it beside the back door.

Ariel, a Melmac bowl of Sugar Pops on her chest and an empty bottle of Nehi strawberry soda perched next to her on the table, craned her neck and called, "What's in the bag, Mom?"

"Just some old clothes."

"You donating them, or what?"

"Don't know for sure." Estelle shrugged one shoulder, bare above her sequined scarlet dress. She hadn't really asked herself what she planned to do with Tony's things. Maybe, once they found him, she'd throw the shoes at him and say Why did you just walk away from us like that? "But I do know that we're leaving," she said to Ariel. "Tomorrow morning."

Ariel stood and brushed off the pieces of cereal that were stuck to the front of her pilled pajamas. "Tomorrow? Is the show moving out?"

On the TV, one embarrassed wife stammered a little, then answered "Snores." The woman's face formed a cutesy pout when her husband sheepishly held up his card and said the word "Sleepwalks." The audience burst into laughter.

"No, not the carnival," Estelle explained, stepping back into the room. "Just us. We're going on a little adventure."

"Oh," Ariel responded. "One of those." Ariel had gotten used to Estelle's impractical schemes that didn't seem to work out, even though they were supposed to be mother-daughter bonding time. Like last spring when the show was in South Dakota and Estelle drove them to Reptile Gardens in the Black Hills. By the time they arrived, the place was closed. Or when they camped in a park in Iowa where mosquitoes attacked them all night. "So where are we going this time?" Ariel quizzed, sounding skeptical, though in reality, she liked the idea.

Estelle turned the TV volume off, silencing Bob Eubanks and the bantering contestants. "Close your eyes, my little one," Estelle said, exaggerating a slight Spanish accent.

"Oh, Mom..." Ariel whined, but she happily complied.

Estelle gestured, her hands rising and falling like waves in the air. "Okay. Imagine a road. A road made of asphalt. Can you see it?"

"I guess."

"Good. Now picture a car driving on it. It's clunky, but still sort of streamlined."

"Okay…"

"That's us. And that's the road we're taking."

Ariel's eyes snapped open. "So we're looking for Dad. Right?"

Estelle lowered her hands, surprised that Ariel seemed to be reading her mind. "Finish your snack," she said, returning to her normal tone of voice. "No late night TV. You're going to need a good night's sleep."

Ariel didn't beg, like she sometimes did, to stay up a couple extra hours and read, or watch the Steve Allen show or a rerun of Mr. Lucky, with that eerie theme song. She just lifted her plastic bowl, and slurped out the rest of the milk, leaving the last pieces of Sugar Pops to beach themselves at the base of the Melmac.

After Estelle tucked Ariel in bed, she walked to the back door and placed her car keys on the counter next to it. On the floor, the pale plastic bag had slumped sideways, its top falling open like a mouth. From it, the toe of one dark slipper stuck out like a tongue that was either mocking her or else trying to tell her something.

CHAPTER NINE

Estelle and Virgil Sand

"What the heck?" Virgil Sand barked when Estelle stopped at his makeshift office early the next morning. "You can't just up and leave like that." His office in his double-wide trailer was scented with a mixture of the half-empty glass of scotch on his desk and the stale cologne he always wore. He tipped back in his wooden chair, his herringbone sport coat wrinkling, his chubby body centered on the seat like a ball of clay. For some reason no one understood, he wore two watches on his left wrist—one with the current time, the other set to daylight savings time. Above him, a corny red and white sign, a somewhat puzzling motto he'd made up: Have You Hugged Your Carnival Today?

"Um, it's just, just for a while…," Estelle offered. She nervously shifted her eyes to the framed carnival celebrity photos on the wall behind him. One with "Best Wishes to Virgil" was signed by Percilla, the hairy, bearded Monkey Girl. Another featured Joanie, a woman born with no legs who was known as the famous Half Girl. Dottie, the Fat Lady, filled out most of a third frame, though she managed, with a Sharpie pen, to fit a squat pink heart and signature in one corner. In a fourth photo, a younger, thinner Virgil Sand stood proudly in front of a tent with a banner strung above him, clutching a cheap plaque presented to him by a local businessman's association.

"Well, tell you what. It's a damn bad idea." Above his beady, deep-set eyes, Virgil's eyebrows moved like caterpillars wiggling to find something. "You got a contract here. You can't just take off on some goddamn vacation."

"It's not a vacation, really," she said hesitantly, and then added, "And there's no contract, anyway, is there?"

"Oh, but you're wrong there, missy. Everybody's on it. It's an unspoken contract." Sand emphasized each syllable when he spoke, making everything seem important as if all his words were underlined or italicized.

She played nervously with the fringes on her blouse. Her eyes skipped up to the tweed Sherlock Holmes-style hat on a hook—a hat Sand wore around the grounds once in a while. Nobody knew why. "Call it whatever you want," Estelle said. "But…"

"I most certainly, positively can," he interrupted with a snort. "After all, I am the captain of this outfit. I keep this ship on course."

Sand was famous for instituting hundreds of rules for the crew. They ranged from who gets to line up first for food, to curfews for the carnie kids, to a Keep Off Grass sign in front of his main office trailer, even though there were only a few sprigs of grass. He taped his poorly-written notes with instructions on everything from the utility poles (Do Not Back Into) to the portable toilets (Please Close Door, After Usage) to the dashboards of the hauling trucks (If You Speed, You Will Pay Fine, Not Me) to mess tent conduct (No Drinking Aloud) and (Please, Clean Up, After Yourself) to the tiny pen for the World's Smallest Horse (Do Not Tease Nor Play With). Fast Eddie called Sand's domain "The land of ten thousand reminders."

Sand stood and stepped to the side of his desk, closer to Estelle. He clasped his small hands in front of his bronze South Dakota-shaped belt buckle he acquired when they passed through Mitchell. "You know, I started this whole show, right from the ground up. I had a vision. Yep, almost ten years ago, it was…"

Here comes the mini-donut speech, she thought. Sand was also famous for steering off course, for pouring the opaque liquid of his words into a clear glass and clouding any conversation. "I know about that…" Estelle said, trying to get back to the point.

Virgil took a breath, puffed up like a balloon inflating itself, and tipped his head toward the asbestos ceiling tiles, faintly speckled with gold paint. "It was back in 1958," he continued. "I used my hard-earned cash to buy a mini donut stand and a couple of rusty kiddie rides. Set 'em up in the parking lots of dinky strip malls," he continued, "and hoped for a couple stragglers coming out of The Salvation Army Store."

Estelle, and everyone else in the carnival, had heard Virgil's windy ramblings about his success story. He'd tell and retell the story to anyone he could corner, embellishing it a little more each time. Before his carnival days, Virgil started a taxidermy business in his basement; he'd stuffed his share of pheasants and fish and deer. When a customer came in with a two-headed pig to be stuffed, the idea for a carnival struck him. Or so the legend went.

"It was just a little, two-bit operation," Sand continued, "but, hey—look at us now." He spread his stubby arms. "I'm president of this whole organization. Best amusements in the whole damn Midwest. Sideshow acts, even. Everybody loves it. We're not just a carnival anymore. I've added acts so that now we're half carnival, half circus. A sort of *circuval*." He beamed at his invented word. "You know, when I first started, people called me a carny. But all that's changed. I'm a showman now. A showman. Just think of it..."

"I'm just here to get my check for last month," Estelle interrupted.

Sand ambled to the front of his rectangular oak desk—too big for the cramped room—and plopped down on one corner. On the opposite corner of the desk, a stack of jumbo-sized boxes of Dots teetered. The boxes were flanked, on both sides, with Sand's decorative taxidermy: two mangy stuffed squirrels holding miniature guns, wearing cowboy hats and tiny suede vests. "Now, about your fortune-telling biz...," he began, rolling his eyes upward in a mock thoughtful pose. "I mean, the income it brings in is pretty damn good. Without Estelle the Tella, we're going to be one star attraction short. And, now, with the Bird Child missing and all...I mean, that bugs the hell out of me. Where'd that goddamn thing go?"

She shrugged.

"So who'll be taking over for you, then?" he continued. "Certainly not...Cotton Candy Mandy or some part-time gal from the sno-cone wagon." He fell into a reflective pause. "You see, Estelle, it leaves me in a kind of bind. A quandary, as they say." He glanced down at an owl on a shelf in the corner, half-stuffed, a few of its beige feathers like fallen leaves on its plywood base. "I mean, if you leave, then some of the magic is gone from this place. So, my question is, who can I possibly replace you with?"

"How about Lily?" Estelle suggested.

"Nope," he replied. He paced back and forth in his shiny brown wing-tip shoes, waddling clumsily. "Lily doesn't have the finesse. Plus, being Puerto Rican and all, I mean, she's—shall we say—a little too ethnic looking."

"Lily is an attractive woman," Estelle interjected, but Sand ignored her.

"And…" He stopped pacing, pondered, then continued walking. "And, to be honest, none of the other gals would look half as believable, or as good as you in those fortune-telling duds. You're easy on the eyes, you know." He rubbed his double chin thoughtfully. "Also, people say you have the knack." He leaned close to her, his bloodshot capillaries expanding in the whites of his eyes. "Knack. That's what counts around here, doesn't it? We all have it for something." He nodded with himself. "I mean, shoot," he said. "Some of us have a knack for hawking." His voice rose and fell grandly like he was an MC at the Academy Awards. "And some, they have a talent for getting laughs, and others…" He swung one arm and gestured to the pictures of the three women on the wall. "Others," he chuckled, "others just have a knack for being gazed at—I mean, if you're a little bit deformed, that is. Of course, I have a knack for—shall we say—financial virtuosity. For making the big bucks." He gave her a fleshy wink. "Yep, back when I started this show from the ground up, almost twenty years ago…."

"I don't have that much time," Estelle said, cutting him off again. "I'm leaving first thing tomorrow morning. Could I please please please just get my check?"

"Hold your horses," Virgil exclaimed. "You'll get it. You'll get it. In due time." He pursed his lips. "You know," he said, lowering his voice and sidling up to her, "it can get real lonely out on the road. Especially with no man around or anything…." He inched closer. "Without your carnival family. And big daddy Sand." He put his hand on Estelle's wrist, then slid it up her arm to her shoulder.

As he did, she recalled Lily, telling her that Sand always managed to casually fondle her rear whenever he slipped past her in the mess tent. Everyone heard the rumors that he made sexual advances in his office, groping several of the young part-time women workers. One woman he mauled even quit the show because of it.

"Come on, Estelle," Sand said, his voice almost crooning. "Let's face it. I could take real good care of you. If you let me. I could make things better for you around here. A lot better." He snorted softly. "I'm The Sandman, remember? Mister Sandman. I bring people dreams. We're like Disney around here, you know? And I can make your dreams come true." He slid his other arm around her waist. Her nostrils filled with the pungent mix of scotch and sweat and Brut cologne.

Caught off guard, she didn't know how to react at first. "Stop," she said weakly, backing away.

Virgil straightened his spine and his face turned a mottled red. "Okay," he said, his voice suddenly harsh. He sauntered back to his chair. "If that's the way you're going to be." He sat down hard, and the stuffed squirrels wobbled on their pedestals. "Have it your way, then." He tugged at the lapels of his rumpled jacket. "So, dammit, I guess I have no choice but to dock you." When Estelle gave him a questioning look, he added, "That's right. You're costing the show money. So you'll only get half pay for the last month."

"But I worked the whole month. That's not fair."

"Hey," he said, laughing lightly and throwing his hands into the air in mock innocence, "Fair is fair, and I'm always fair. No favors for me, no favors for you, I always say. I'll lose money if you're gone, you know. It's just business, is all. Nothing personal." He winked at her. "No hard feelings, I hope." His face puckered with a patronizing expression. "Oh, and by the way—if you ever say anything about this meeting, I'll just deny it."

Estelle shook her head at him in disgust, then took a step toward the door.

"Hey, young lady," Virgil called, his jowls lifting an artificial smile, "Don't forget this." He lifted a checkbook from a drawer, scribbled with a pen, and held a check toward her.

When she reached for the check, he pulled it away from her teasingly. "I gave you more than half. Full pay, almost. Just as a courtesy."

Estelle snatched the check from his stubby fingers.

"Still friends?" he said. "Still friends with Papa Sand, right?"

She spun around and hurried toward the door.

"That's my girl," he called to her back, "That's my pretty little girl."

CHAPTER TEN

Ariel

Sideshow #9

I'm waiting for the future. It's really important. (Mom always says that.) It's what's ahead of us, she says, and we have to be ready for it. Sometimes I think that it's waiting for me, just outside the trailer door. But when I open the door, everything looks just the same. The Rock-O-Plane ride has its usual line of customers (because it's ten-cents-a-ride day). The teenage girls and their boyfriends sit in those metal cages with their arms around each other. When the car flips upside down, they scream like crazy. Like they're just being born or else they're dying. I don't tell anyone, but that's just how I feel some days.

Sideshow #19

My mom is Estelle the Teller. You might have heard of her. I have, and I love her dearly.

I sort of know how her fortune-telling thing works. I've peered in through an opening in the back of her tent. The customers drop a five into the fishbowl on the table and wait. Mom talks to them a little, then begins the session. She lets her hands swirl over the crystal ball. ("Like delicate clouds," she said). She closes and opens her eyes and flutters her eyelids. She always looks so pretty when she does this. (I've tried it, in the mirror, but it doesn't work for me. I just look like a kid who's blinking.) Then she holds her breath a few seconds as if she's going into a trance.

"I sense them out," Mom once explained to me. "I figure out what they want. What they need."

"Oh?" I replied.

Then she said "It's sort of like a phone's been ringing a long time deep inside their skulls, and they finally pick it up and say 'Hello?' They think it's me, but it's really their own voice on the other end of the line. That way, I let them talk to themselves."

To me, it seemed like decent advice, in any profession. That's Mom for you—always practical in a mystical sort of way.

"So, how do I look?" Mom asked me yesterday before she headed to her tent. She just got all dressed up for her gig: long dress, beads, some makeup but not too much, jingling silver bracelets.

"You look like my mom," I replied. "And also like the greatest fortune teller ever."

"I wish," she said with a laugh.

I'm always kind of amazed that Mom can sort of transform herself. In just a couple minutes, even. Early mornings, she's just my ordinary mom, wearing a pale blouse that's spotted with bleach. She clacks dishes in the sink. But a few minutes later, she becomes a colorful gossamer butterfly of a gypsy (Cool description, eh? Tony called her that once, and I never forgot it). She seems ready to break out of a cocoon. Ready to mesmerize the world with her beauty. And all her clairvoyant powers (some days I call her Claire Voyant).

The best thing is, Mom always makes me believe there's magic inside all of us. She says we just have to find it, pull it out.

She kisses me goodbye. Then she leaves the trailer for her fortune teller tent. I sometimes think that she doesn't have to trudge across the muddy carnival grounds like everybody else. Instead, I imagine she can fly.

Sideshow # 20

My dad is The Dashing Desdiolo. You might have heard of him. I have, and I love him dearly. He walks tightropes as easily as you or I could walk across a solid field. I'm pretty sure the soles of his feet have mystical powers. Trouble is, he's stepped away from us. And we don't know where he is. Sometimes, late at night, I feel like I should try to follow that tightrope and catch up to him. But I'm kinda clumsy. There's no way I could do that. Not with my legs. So I only walk the wire in my dreams. But even in those dreams, the wire always disappears into some kind of dark cloud. And all I can do is just wobble there, and call out his name.

Sideshow #22

I'm going through some changes soon. My mom and her friends keep telling me that. The birthdays keep happening, and the next thing you know, I'll be thirteen or fourteen. Changes, soon. But who will I be then?

You'll grow wings, My Mom says. You'll fly.

But where? I wonder.

Sideshow #24

My mom's a fortune teller, but she can't predict her own future. My dad's a tightrope walker, but it looks like he walked away. And me—I'm not a grown-up, but I'm not a kid, either. I'm somewhere in between. I guess that makes me kind of a lost girl.

CHAPTER 11

Tony

The first time he saw her, he stubbed his toe.

As he drove, Tony had a lot of time to let his mind wander, and this memory of Estelle was a pleasant one.

It was eleven years ago. That morning, Tony didn't know what he tripped on—maybe it was one of those electrical cords that wasn't flattened to the ground with duct tape. Whatever—when he noticed Estelle near the front gate, sliding languidly out of a powder-blue two-door Nash, he stumbled forward, his knee bumping the plywood platform of his Toss-Em Ping Pong game, the rims of the shot glasses clinking together. He couldn't believe how gorgeously she parted the air around her as she swayed lithely past him in her tight black pedal pusher pants and a slinky violet top. Her long auburn ponytail swayed like it was dreaming of wind. But she didn't seem to notice him, ogling her as she headed straight to Virgil Sand's trailer and knocked on the door.

Tony wanted to meet her, of course, and introduce himself. He knew, instinctively, somehow, that she was more than just looks. Something about her seemed deep. So right then and there, Tony decided that he had to change his name. Everybody at the carnival had started calling him Ping Pong Tony, but it was just too ordinary and unflattering, he figured. That nickname would never impress a woman of her style.

A couple days later, he spotted her at the mess tent. He timed it so he could slide his tray into the line right in front of her. He was always good at timing.

"Hey, mind if I cut in?" he asked, sporting his best grin.

She looked surprised at first, eyelashes fluttering like dark brown butterflies. "Go right ahead. You're Ping Pong Tony, right?"

He was flattered that she knew him and hoped she'd been asking around about him. "That's not my name," he answered glibly but still trying to sound friendly.

"Sorry. Guess I don't know everybody around here yet. Do I have the wrong person?"

"Nope. You've got exactly the right person. But I'm not Ping Pong Tony."

As she gave him a questioning look, her brown eyes were lovely and intense, and her skin seemed to glow from the inside, brightening the dusty air inside the gloomy beige canvas tent.

"I've officially changed my name," he explained. "And my gig." He was about to tell her about his plan to learn tightrope walking. "I'm now The Dashing Desdiolo." He waited, counting the seconds, hoping for some reaction. He took it as a good sign when she—at least—tilted her head slightly to the side and raised one eyebrow.

"Yeah," he added. "And I'm the purveyor of a new act."

"Oh? What act?"

"Balancing."

"Balancing what?"

"Myself. That's what." He straightened his broad, muscular shoulders.

"Seems like an admirable goal," she agreed.

"It is," he nodded, the brim of his dark blue ball cap bobbing. "It really is."

Then she glanced down and laughed lightly. "Especially since your gravy is sliding right off your tray."

"Oops," he said, wincing in embarrassment as he looked down at his tipped tray. He quickly wiped the brown river of overflowing gravy with a napkin, shrugged, and mustered a chuckle. "Guess I got a little work to do."

"Guess so." She smiled and seemed to study him a moment, and an odd sensation came over him. He suddenly felt like his skin was a layer of cellophane, and she could see right through it to his deepest layers, to who he really was. And he liked that sensation as he stood close to her, with just some stringy roast beef, pale green beans, and mashed potatoes on the trays between them.

* * *

But that pleasant memory was years ago. Today, some other memories were pulling and pulling at him. Guilt was pulling at him. All triggered by that single, one-page letter.

As he drove in his pickup, he thought about the journey ahead. He pictured a map, unfolding in his brain, a map that widened into uncharted territory, the highways and county roads spidering out in all directions. Blue roads and black roads: arteries branching into capillaries, capillaries thinning out and disappearing. He hoped he was following the clearest route—not blurry, not detouring or reaching some damn dead end.

As he thought of his plan, and how poorly thought out and random it might seem, he pulled his foot off the gas pedal, and the truck slowed. He knew he should ask himself a lot of questions about what he intended to do on this trip. Thirty-three hours, hugging the road, not counting stops. But he didn't ask himself anything because he knew he had no answers. And even if he did, those answers would just throw him off kilter. All he knew was that he just had to keep following the road that kept beckoning him with its long asphalt tongue. So he pressed lightly on the accelerator, balancing himself between where he was now and where he wanted—no, not just wanted, but needed to go.

CHAPTER 12

Estelle and Ariel

As three scruffy crows fluttered up in front of her windshield, Estelle kept a steady speed on a rural county highway. The road was flanked by tall stalks of corn; their shiny green leaves seemed to be waving at her in the angled morning sun. The corn looked ripe and ready to be picked.

As she drove, Estelle's mind filtered back to a childhood memory.

When she was eight years old, her mother, Lucia, ushered her to the couch and lifted the ball from a black, paint-chipped wooden box with rusty nails loosened on one side.

"This," Lucia had announced with a lilting voice, "This was your grandmother's."

"Was she a fortune teller?" young Estelle had asked.

"She never called herself that. She just referred to herself as a seer. A knower," Lucia confided. Estelle's grandmother—who had ancestors in the village of Lebrija, in Andalucia, Spain—had immigrated to Ellis Island and settled in the Midwest. One day, Grandma Rosalinda passed the ball to Estelle's mother, telling her that it was something special. "She told me this ball was a family keepsake," Lucia continued. "And that someone should nurture their gift."

"What kind of gift?" young Estelle asked.

Her mother brushed the light coating of dust from the surface of the ball with a soft cloth. "The crystal ball could help her sing," she said. Help her fill with duende."

"Duende?" Estelle questioned.

"It's a Spanish word. It can't be translated, really. But it has to do with the inner spirit, the soul, the power. She told me duende didn't just come from the throat when you sing, or from the words you speak." She nodded at Estelle. "It climbs up from inside you, from the soles of the feet." Lucia set the ball on a wooden end table covered with hand-crocheted creme doilies. "One night, your grandmother," Lucia hesitated, trying not to choke up, "It was the night before she…" her voice cracked, "before she died. That night, she passed the crystal ball on to me." A tear traveled down her mother's cheek. Estelle looked into her face and noticed how worn and pale it seemed lately. The creases on her forehead were pronounced as the clotheslines strung between the brick tenements of what people referred to as Gypsy Town, a run-down neighborhood in New York City where her parents had settled.

"Is something wrong, Mother?" Estelle asked, suddenly worried.

Her mother, proud and stoic as always, just stood, parted the lace curtains, and looked toward their small patch of a garden that she always tended. "The tomatoes will be ripe by August," she announced. "You have to promise to pick them before they fall off the vine."

"Why am *I* supposed to pick them?" Estelle questioned. "You always pick them with Papa."

Her mother just peered out at the garden in silence.

"You aren't sick, are you?" Estelle asked, feeling a sudden sense of dread.

Instead of answering, her mother stepped back to Estelle and lowered the crystal ball into her small hands. "This is for you."

"What if I don't want it?" Estelle protested. "What if I don't have the gift?"

"Just accept it. Keep it. Treasure it. Who knows?" Lucia added with a husky laugh, "You might find a whole universe inside. You might even find duende."

Estelle learned later that her mother had been diagnosed with lymphoma cancer, and had only weeks to live. And by the end of that summer, she was gone.

"Alabama, Alaska, Arizona," a voice interrupted Estelle's memory. It was Ariel, naming the states as she rode in the passenger's seat. "Delaware, District of Columbia, Florida…."

Estelle focused again on the highway that was unreeling itself like a gray ribbon. Her plan, for day one, was to drive to Waterloo, Iowa, where she heard a carnival was setting up this weekend. She'd gotten the scoop—a list of Midwest carnivals, and their usual circuits—from old Whiskers, a guy in his eighties who had worked carnivals all his life. She'd start there, on their first day on the road; she'd ask around, showing Tony's black and white photo that she kept in the glove compartment. Every of couple days, from a phone booth, she'd call Lily, her best friend back at the carnival, just in case there was any news about Tony. And Ariel could also chat a little with her friend Maria Luz, Lily's daughter.

During this trip, Estelle planned to let Ariel traverse the midways and play a few games in the arcade. They might go to parks in the towns, where Ariel would hop on the swings or show off on the jungle gym, imitating a trapeze artist. At night, they might take in a movie at a local theatre. They'd take some detours, and have a little fun. After all, she reasoned, she really needed a break from the confinements of Sand and his all-important carnival.

She didn't want to think about it as a desperate search for Tony, but rather a casual vacation, a trip where, maybe, on the way, she'd find out a little more about herself, too. When she couldn't quite come up with a prediction for a customer who stepped into her fortune-teller tent, she would advise: "Exhale the past and let it go. Then inhale what's ahead." Now she was saying those words to herself. She knew her future was out there, somewhere in the shimmering distance, almost unreachable. But still, she had to keep moving toward it.

"Illinois, Indiana, Iowa…" Ariel recited, her eleven-year-old voice squeaky, like a hinge that needed oil. She paused in her litany. "Mom, how many towns and states do you think we'll visit?"

"Don't know," Estelle said softly. But she thought Not that many, I hope. Maybe we'll find Tony in Waterloo when we stop at a café for dinner. Maybe he'll be strolling the sidewalk in his jeans and blue denim shirt and leather vest. The past weeks, she had pictured him a thousand times: Tony, pausing mid-step, then turning slowly toward her as she pulled her car to the curb next to him. But what would happen next? she wondered. Would he turn to her with an apologetic half-smile? Or would he just stare at her indifferently, as if a gray cloud was crossing his face? Or, worse, would he be walking with some woman, who would ask "Um, Tony, who's that?" Whenever she speculated about it, her questions always faded without answers, like a frantically scribbling pen suddenly running out of ink.

In reality, Estelle doubted that their next destination would bring them to Tony. Their next stop would most likely be a dingy café with a dusty picture window on which teens would write *Wash me*, a water tower teetering on wobbly stilts, a narrow main street in the middle of a small town in the middle of a bigger middle.

"Think we might visit that island with the wild ponies?" Ariel asked. "It's off the coast of Virginia."

"Hmmm," Estelle replied, "maybe."

Ariel often talked about that place after she read about it in National Geographic. Chincoteague Island was a small island inhabited mainly by wild ponies and horses, and she always fantasized about going there and seeing them galloping across the dunes. She often made pencil drawings of what the horses would look like.

"Good," Ariel said. "Because I dream about those ponies all the time."

"I can't promise that we'll get there, though," Estelle cautioned.

"Why not?"

"Just can't. Because promises sometimes get, well, you know, broken."

"You mean trampled? You mean stampeded on?"

Catching her drift, Estelle pursed her lips and didn't reply. So Ariel went back to her list of the states, talking over the announcer's voice buzzing through the single dashboard speaker of the AM radio. News stories about the upcoming Apollo 8 launch, scheduled to orbit the moon and then return to earth, and a Black rights protest against police brutality in Detroit.

Estelle didn't know much about either topic. She hadn't followed recent affairs or politics. Over the years, life at the carnival—like some thick, glittering insulated quilt—had shielded her from all that. Her days were predictable: each morning, it was an 11 a.m. walk from their trailer to her fortune-telling tent, and then back to the trailer again at 7:00 p.m.—always too late for the national news. Then she'd make dinner for Tony and Ariel and they'd watch The Wild Wild West or Lost in Space on their small TV that only picked up three channels. Now, as she listened to the radio, those news reports seemed to come from a country that was so far away. What mattered right now were the most immediate things: the soothing sound of her daughter's voice, and how far they were from the next state line. She checked the odometer. Another fifty miles or so.

"Kansas...," continued Ariel. "Isn't that where Dorothy got spun up by a tornado?"

"That's the place," Estelle replied, knowing Ariel was referring to The Wizard of Oz, one of her favorite books.

"I wonder what that feels like," Ariel mused. "It would be quite a crazy ride."

"I'm sure it would be," Estelle replied with a light laugh. "I prefer to keep my feet on the ground."

As the wind rippled through the cornfields, Estelle felt their small trailer behind them shift in the wind, making their red 1962 Ford Falcon Futura station wagon lurch slightly left, then right. Whenever the carnival moved from town to town, their Rollohome trailer tagged along behind them. Tony usually towed it with his truck. It was their two-bedroom home on wheels—always right behind them on the hitch, wearing out the engine. Always pushing them forward toward something as they drove down a hill, or slowing them on the inclines, dragging behind them like the past itself.

Whoosh. In the oncoming lane, a semi-truck, loaded with cattle, roared past in the opposite lane, and the rush of air through the open window caused the dice to spin. Estelle's thoughts slipped back to that evening, years ago, when she won them at Tony's Ping Pong Toss game, and he had walked her back to her trailer. They stood there beneath a flickering floodlight on a wooden post. Though Estelle felt strongly attracted to him, she said "I'm not kissing you goodnight or inviting you in, you know."

"I don't expect you to," he replied. Then he added flirtatiously, "But I do expect you to stay with me the rest of my life."

She laughed. "That's not too much to ask, I guess."

"No, it's not," he said, gazing at her intensely. At that moment she felt a warm sensation rush through her, and she couldn't move. She couldn't turn and step back into her trailer, nor could she—though she felt compelled to—slide her arm around his neck and give him a kiss. She just stood there, surrounded by swirling emotions and suspended in the present.

"Washington," Ariel said. "I've almost got them all, Mom." She lifted a tube of strawberry lip balm and applied it to her lips.

"You hear the latest about the Bird Child mystery?" Estelle asked.

"No," Ariel replied, feigning innocence. "What's up?"

"Virgil Sand went on an all-out search in everybody's trailers. He accused Splat the Clown of stealing it and selling it to another carnival. But Splat denied it. Nobody knows where it is. It's just gone. Missing."

"Hmmm," Ariel replied. "Maybe the bird just flew away." Then she went back to her list of states. "Wisconsin, Wyoming." Then she added one more. "Wherever."

"Wherever?" Estelle questioned.

"Yeah. I'm adding that one to the list." She looked over at Estelle. "You know, it's dumb to memorize the states in alphabetical order."

"Why?"

"Because. You never travel to them that way," she explained. "I mean, you never cross the border from Alaska to Alabama, or Colorado to Connecticut."

"Maybe it's just a memory trick," Estelle offered. "To keep them organized in your mind."

"I think teachers make you learn them that way to confuse you. So you never know where you're going next."

An hour later, Ariel took a nap, her forehead softly bobbing on the pink pillow that she propped against the window.

The black and white sponge dice, hanging from the rearview mirror, kept distracting Estelle. Their black dots seemed to stare at her. Sixes and deuces and snake eyes. If she was really a psychic, she said to herself, then couldn't she hold one of them in her hand and visualize where Tony had gone? Or would it just sit there stupidly in her palm, all those airy holes making it feel too light to be real? Why couldn't she predict things for herself? Thinking she should toss them to the back seat and out of sight, she reached up to pull them from the base of the mirror. But then she hesitated and drew her hand back.

She shook her head and concentrated on what was ahead of her: The white lines, leapfrogging in the center of the dark asphalt lane. Road signs: Do Not Pass. Pass With Caution. Waterloo 77. As the uneven road rose and fell, Estelle had an odd sensation. It felt like the earth was swaying a little, as though their car and trailer were floating on water rather than solid ground. As if, beneath the tires, the prairie of southern Minnesota was rippling—a liquid green ocean rather than solid fields. And once they were out there, far from shore, would they have to swim and swim to keep from drowning?

She knew she couldn't express any of those worries to Ariel. She glanced over at her sweet daughter, dreaming on her pillow. Did those fifty states—all out of order—grow cartoon legs and start dancing in her head? she wondered. Were the wild ponies galloping out a steady beat in there?

A half-hour later, the setting sun sent out a red splash, and the sky overhead was fading from bright blue to dull gray. She passed a road sign: Speed Limit 55 Day, 45 Night. So, Estelle asked herself, did that mean she had to quickly take her foot off the gas and slow to 45? After all, she always diligently obeyed the speed limit.

Level farm fields surrounded the steadily darkening road, and suddenly she felt like the four directions were pulling at her from all sides. North, south, east, west: all four of them, stretching her until she felt like she'd be pulled limb from limb. Her doubts were pulling at her, too. Were the odds against her, and would this trip be aimless, like a feather spiraling in the gusting wind? She hoped not. Still, she wasn't used to taking chances like this.

As she approached a slow-moving vehicle, she hit the brake. It was a trundling farmer's truck, hauling a couple of Holstein cows in a dented steel trailer. She followed it for about a mile as it crawled along at thirty miles an hour. Then, surprising herself, she pressed the accelerator hard and, with the muffler rattling, swerved the car into the left lane to pass.

The farmer's doughy face turned toward her with a startled look as she roared past the truck. The speedometer needle edged toward eighty. As she angled back into the right lane and steadied the vibrating wheel, she noticed the dice swaying nervously back and forth, their thin chords twisting together, then untwisting, then twisting again.

CHAPTER 13

Tony

As he drove, his mind drifted back to a few weeks ago, and what happened made him wince. That day, at practice, he slipped from the tightrope wire and fell into the net. Angry at himself, he climbed back onto the wire, then slipped again.

That evening before the show, Tony had taken a couple shots of Jack Daniels before his act to bolster his confidence. Jack would help him find that balance, he assured himself.

But halfway into his act, in front of a crowd that had paid extra, he wavered, rotating his arms in quick, small circles, then slipped from the wire again. "Damn," he exclaimed as he caught the cable awkwardly with his hands, swung from it a couple of times, then dropped to the net. He bounded onto the sawdust floor. His palms stung where the wire burned them, but what stung more was the humiliation. His act was only half over, and the scratchy instrumental music kept playing from the speakers. So, as if it was all part of the act, he did a spontaneous little tap dance, then took a bow in front of the onlookers in the makeshift bleachers. He noticed that one boy in the front row, his face melting into a frown. The kid's mother grabbed his hand and pulled him through the tent flap, muttering that Tony's act was a waste of time. Through the open flap of the small tent, he noticed Virgil Sand, shaking his head admonishingly.

"Knock it off." Tony chided himself aloud as he drove, trying to expel the negative thoughts that burned in his mind like cigarettes on a countertop. He clicked on the radio, spun the dial, and finally picked up a faraway station. "Don't Think Twice" was playing. It was followed by "Mr. Tambourine Man." Tony sang along with The Byrds in his baritone voice while tapping his fingers on the wheel. The song was about wandering through the morning to find a better place. He let his thoughts drift to that place. It was there, right ahead of him. He had to believe that.

When his tires hit the shoulder, the truck swayed. He quickly jostled the steering wheel and centered the truck back in the lane. He had to stay focused, to veer his thoughts to the positive. This journey. A journey to find that missing piece. He thought about it almost daily, his deep-down guilt keeping him off balance.

He had to face the darkness of his past. To make it right, before it was too late. Before it was out of reach, like that shimmering water mirage he kept seeing on the asphalt ahead of him. A silvery mirage that, the more he kept driving toward it, the further away it seemed to be.

CHAPTER 14

Ariel

There was no Tony in Waterloo. Neither Estelle nor Ariel expected that.

"So we're moving on," Estelle announced as they woke up the next morning.

"Where to?" Ariel asked.

"How does Central and Southern Iowa sound to you?"

"Hmmm. It sounds a lot like Central and Southern Iowa," Ariel replied wryly.

*   *   *

Today, as they drove between the seemingly endless farm fields, Ariel recalled the days, earlier this summer, when she helped out at the Bust-Em Balloon Toss game. Lily—her mom's best friend, and the woman everyone called Puerto Rico Lily—ran the game. Ariel always admired Lily's smooth brown complexion and her black, shiny hair, not to mention her enthusiasm as she called out to the customers with her unique Spanish accent. Lily was always quick to laugh, and Ariel liked being around her.

Lily put Ariel in charge of blowing up the balloons, then tacking them to the cork panel on the back wall. "Sergeant at Arms in charge of breath," Lily called her. Meanwhile, Lily beckoned the passersby: "Pop one balloon and you get a small prize! Pop two for a medium! Pop a grand prize balloon and you get the largest prize!" There was just one Large Prize card hidden behind a balloon on the entire wall, though. The card was behind a balloon that only Ariel and Lily knew about. Just one balloon, up there in the top left corner, among the fifty balloons on the wall. That was the beauty, and the secret, of the game. It was the only way you'd get a long-necked giraffe or an oversized teddy bear or a wide-eyed white unicorn.

After helping at the game several times, Ariel became proficient at tossing the darts. Once, when a little kid didn't hit any balloons and his face sunk into a frown, Ariel, without even looking, threw a dart over her shoulder, popped a balloon, and then called out "Winner!" so that the kid could choose a trinket.

The balloons always inflated so easily, Ariel often thought, like bright red or blue or pink plastic lungs. "You've got good wind, kid," Lily complimented Ariel. "I'm hiring you as my permanent inflater."

"Swell," Ariel replied with her usual wit. "Breathing is a full-time job. Guess I have a great career ahead of me."

"We all do," Lily chuckled.

"So," Ariel inquired, "do they have carnivals like this down in Puerto Rico?"

"Not like this," Lily replied.

"What was it like there?"

"When I was growing up in La Perla, in San Juan," Lily replied, "we were very poor. To help out, my mother and I made bread and sold it on a stand on the street. We did whatever we needed to do to get by."

"Did it get you by?"

"Of course. We didn't have much, but we were happy with what we had," Lily added. "Happiness. That's what counts the most, doesn't it?"

On this road trip, Ariel had a lot of time to think about The Bird Child. She wondered if The Bird Child, too, had lungs. She wondered if some fragile, thin sacs inside its frail chest once inhaled fresh air, its heart pumping that oxygen through its network of arteries and capillaries and all the way to its deformed legs and the tiny pale wings sprouting from its back. But would that have mattered, anyway? she asked herself. Or, when it was still alive—if it ever was—did it just lie there in a crib or in a blanket, never destined to walk, or to fly?

How long did The Bird Child survive until it was condemned to the inside of that glass jar? A minute, an hour, a day, a week? Such a short, unhappy life, Ariel decided. But merciful, maybe, since it never had to grow up and see, in a mirror, how strange it looked, and how deformed it was.

It never had to suffer, she hoped.

Today, as she rode in silence with her Mom, Ariel tried to picture The Bird Child's last moments. When it finally passed from this life, was it a slow death? Did it exhale one last, agonizing breath, trying in vain to explain itself, so people wouldn't have to ponder it?

Or was it all over in an instant, the air bursting from its lungs as if the silver point of a cruel dart suddenly punctured them?

Such questions. Such big and small questions.

She closed her eyes and pictured herself in the Pop-Em booth. She pictured herself grabbing another thin-skinned balloon from the cellophane package, then blowing it up just right, and watching its skin inflate, stretching, stretching almost to popping, but not quite. Not quite.

CHAPTER 15

Tony

Tony woke in his truck and shivered. It was still pre-dawn, and the landscape looked grainy. He was parked in a gravel wayside where, last night, he'd decided to stop his truck and get some shuteye. Thoughts rushed through his head, as they did each day when he woke. He slid the letter out of the glove box and clicked on the ignition. In the orange glow of the dash lights, he read the letter again, as he had a dozen times:

> *Hi Tony,*
>
> *Hey, it's me, Charlotte. Bet you're pretty surprised to get this letter. I'm writing at about three a.m., so never mind my lousy penmanship.*
>
> *It's been a long, time! Don't I know. I hear from the grapevine (I still have a couple friends in Minn.) that you're still in the carny business, that your tightrope shows are getting kinda famous. Good for you. That doesn't surprise me one bit.*
>
> *A lot has happened since we last saw each other. A whole lot. I'm still working the tourist crowd and the rubes, of course. You know me. It gets me by. (It also gets me buy. Ha ha.)*
>
> *I guess I never told you what happened back when we split and I left town. I really was pregnant. So, guess what? You actually have a kid, walking around on the planet. And because of that, I think you owe me. I mean, those years of child support, and all that.*
>
> *Okay. So I'm wondering if your carnival ever travels anywhere near the pacific coast circuit.*
>
> *If so, we'd like to see you.*
>
>   *Over and out,*
>   *--Charlotte*
>
> *p.s. By the way, in case I forgot to say it, which I did, I'm in Santa Monica.*

A kid, walking around on the planet. The words repeated in Tony's head, surprising him just as they had the first time he read them. Then there were her other words: Child support, and all that.

His mind jumped back thirteen years, to that day when Charlotte told him the news. They both were working in a carnival in central Wisconsin. Charlotte, who lived in town, took a summer job at the funnel cake stand, and Tony was an assistant game jockey at the Bust a Record game with Sarge. Sarge was famous for cake-cutting, or short-changing customers. Sarge liked Tony because he could demonstrate the game for potential customers, throwing a fast pitch with a baseball and cracking one of the old '78 records propped up at the back of the booth.

Tony and Charlotte had been going out for half a year. Tony was 19, and she was 18 and had just graduated from high school in June. They claimed to each other that they were in love. It was a careless and turbulent romance, the two of them naïve, and looking for some kind of stability in their lives. Tony, no longer at foster homes, had taken over an abandoned trailer on the carnival lot where he had a hot plate, a mattress, and free reign.

"So, um, you said you're pregnant?" he had asked.

"I'm not even sure about it. But I think I might be. I mean, I missed my time. So what am I going to do?" she asked. Instead of her usual sassy self, she sounded soft, her lips smeared, her voice scared. She just finished her shift at the funnel cake stand, and she still had powdered sugar on her wrists. "If my mom found out, she'd want me to put rocks in my dress and walk into the ocean. And my dad. Jeez. He'd have me burned at the stake. They're staunch Catholics, you know. They have the priests over for dinner, and all that."

Tony glanced down at her stomach, which still looked flat. "Well, um..." he mumbled, waiting to hear where she was going with this.

"So," she continued, "if I'm pregnant, we're not getting married or anything. We don't have real jobs. I mean," she said, gesturing to the dingy row of food stands, "look where we work."

"Right," he agreed. "We're young, and all that." He was nervous of course, his eyes skittering back and forth, looking anywhere but in her face. He toed the soil with his tennis shoe. "So, um...then what?" he asked.

"I don't know what." She burst into tears. "I have a whole life ahead of me," she sobbed.

"Well, yeah." Tony shifted his feet awkwardly. "My life. I mean, I have a life, too." He reached out, and she let him embrace her momentarily. Her body was limp, almost too pliable. Then she pushed him away. "But we'll figure it out," he offered. "It's not the end of the world, is it?"

"Then why do I feel like I'm falling off it?" she asked. Of course, he couldn't answer her.

That night, Tony couldn't sleep. He wrestled with his conscience, wondering what they should do. He pictured the two of them, in the living room of her parents' house, telling them about it. He'd be staring at the floor, and Charlotte would sit there, her knees clamped together. He tried not to picture Charlotte's dad's stony face when he heard the news. He'd glare at Tony and growl something like "Damn you. Get out of my house."

The next day, during his morning break, Tony stopped at the funnel cake stand. He planned to talk to Charlotte, figure out some solutions. Bettyjo, the overweight middle-aged woman who ran the stand, slid open a cloudy glass window.

"Charlotte here?" Tony asked.

"Nope."

"Where, then?"

Bettyjo's oval face, framed in greasy brown hair, puckered. "She up and left."

"Left? Where?"

"Dunno. Settled up her pay this morning. Said she's quitting." Tony just stood there in disbelief. A couple of customers behind him looked impatiently over his shoulder. "So," Bettyjo finally asked, "you plannin' to buy something, or not?"

Tony later learned from a friend of Charlotte's that she had taken a Greyhound bus to somewhere on the West Coast. After that, rumors about Charlotte spread among her friends and the younger carnival workers. Someone said Charlotte wasn't even sure she was pregnant in the first place, but just wanted to get away from her suffocating parents. Another person said she confessed to her mom and dad, and they kicked her out of the house. A third rumor—one which really bothered Tony—claimed that she was planning to abort the baby. No matter what, Tony never heard from Charlotte again. No phone call, no message, no letter. At least not until now.

* * *

Tony slid the letter back into the glove box, then stepped out of the truck to try to clear his head. As he stood in the parking lot, the first blinding shafts of morning sunlight flooded over him, making his shadow long and dark. He pinched his eyes shut from the glare.

He formulated his plan for the day. Like the previous mornings, he'd rely on his pickup to point him in the right direction. He'd pull onto Route 66 and hug that road with his tires until the asphalt learned to recognize him.

He knew it wouldn't be easy, and that he'd have to cross lines—city limits, county lines, state lines. There'd be other lines, too—lines from the past that he'd almost erased, that he'd have to try to find again and follow. It would ease his conscience, and make his life feel whole and level again. Maybe even rescue his soul.

It was an impulsive move, he knew, to just leave Estelle and Ariel the way he did. But he was in the middle of it now, and once he started something, he couldn't turn back. After all, you don't try to walk backwards on a tightrope, because you're damn sure to fall.

He climbed into his truck again, and though the steering wheel felt cool in his hands, he believed he could already feel it turning. He clicked the key, the engine waking from its deep metallic slumber.

It was a kind of love, Tony thought, that made him press his foot gently but firmly on the accelerator. That was it, he decided: A kind of love that made him keep driving toward the answers that waited for him out there.

CHAPTER 16

Ariel

As she rode with Estelle, Ariel had quite a few questions about The Bird Child. Not just a few—A zillion, actually, she wrote in her journal.

Did The Bird Child ever dream? She wondered. Did it have visions while it slept? Or was its head just filled with foam or plastic or cotton, like some ordinary doll made in a toy factory?

Its eyes looked sort of like two eggshells. Or ping pong balls. Could it see through them? Did they ever open and see the morning sky? Then there was its thin mouth, with no lips. Did it ever make any sound?

How old or young was it? Was it one of those mutants that lived a few lonely years in someone's barn? Did the family hide it there, keeping it in a hayloft because they feared what the neighbors would think? Was the family scared of it? Did they call a priest to bless it, maybe? Or maybe even give it an exorcism? Ariel had read all about that once in an article, though Estelle told her not to.

Was it the devil's child, or an angel's child? Both of them had wings, didn't they? Or was it no one's child? Just an odd orphan, something no mother or father would claim?

Did it know it was part child, part bird? Did it realize it was half of one creature, half of another? But not really part of either one?

Questions like those fluttered around inside Ariel's head, haunting her.

It seemed like her whole life was filled with questions lately. Some nights they swirled around her, and she felt like she was in the center of a tornado. Where is my dad? Why did he leave? Will we ever find him? Doesn't he love me anymore?

No matter how many questions she asked, or how often she asked them, there were never any answers. Just a lot of silence. Just that loud, maddening Bird Child silence.

CHAPTER 17

Tony

I'm here, he thought, finally. Tony approached a gold and black roadside sign—Welcome to Santa Monica—and gunned his truck past it.

He knew he'd made it. To the coast. Highway 66—what people called The Mother Road—had led him here, across the country's heart and all the way to this golden shore.

At the beginning of his journey, the left rear tire of his truck had a slow leak and was beginning to bulge. He must have stopped at ten different gas stations to put more air in it, and as he did, he wondered how long it would last before it went totally flat. Some mornings he felt like he was that damn tire, slowly losing air.

But today all those hesitations were behind him. Though there was a lot of uncertainty left, he'd conquered the first leg of his journey. Rolling down the window, he took a deep breath as the two lanes widened to four lanes. The traffic began to surround him and he entered the suburbs, then continued into the city itself. Commuters in Mercedes and sleek Oldsmobiles paralleled his truck. He glided through a couple of stoplights just as they turned from yellow to red. The Beach Boys' "Surfin USA" played on the radio, a local California station coming in clearly. Tony cranked it up louder and tapped his palm to the beat on the steering wheel.

He needed to keep going until he finally reached it: the expanse of blue he'd heard so much about all his life. He knew that Highway 66 ended at Santa Monica Pier, but, noting a sign for a beach, he detoured. He'd never been to the ocean before, and he longed to see it. It seemed like the perfect place to take a break on this clear, sunny morning. He followed the city streets that led to a gravel parking lot, then stepped out at a small beach park where the waves rolled in steadily, chasing each other with white foam.

If one of his carny buddies asked him where he had gone on this road trip, he'd simply reply with something glib and casual, like Yep, I just let ol' Highway 66 pull me west, 'til it ran out of pavement. Like so many people before him, he'd explain, he drove all the way to the edge of America, just to see it, just to be there. It would be a lie, of course. This trip had much more meaning than that.

Leaving the door open, and jogged toward the small beach. Except for a woman and her small child at a picnic table on the far side of the park, he was the only other person at this time of the morning.

On the beach, he reveled as the warm wind, blowing off the water, touched him like a lover. He let the wind cup his face and felt his T-shirt ripple like a white flag, though he wasn't surrendering. He was just beginning this journey, this search. This quest to fill the hole he fell through each night in his nightmares. In his dreams, he always seemed to be standing at the edge of it, and it was steadily collapsing beneath his feet, pulling him toward it with its dark mouth.

Then there was that other hole inside him. He had thought about it a lot during his drive out here. It was the hole within the hole—one that opened when he was eight years old. It was always there, a hollow spot, like a bubble of air moving through his arteries, back to his heart, and then away again. He saw, again, a fleeting image of his father, lifting a glass of bourbon to his lips, gulping it, then setting it down, the ice cubes clinking in it. "Well…" Roy said. A tentative, word. So distant. A hundred miles away. "Well…" The word meant nothing to young Tony, and he wasn't sure if he replied or not. His dad didn't say anything else; he just turned, slowly, as if he was on a rotating wheel. He turned. Turned. Turned and walked out the door.

As he reached the beach, Tony shook his head, expelling the painful memories. He focused instead on there here, the now. The ocean: the blue breakers crashing to pale white, while little commas of seagulls banked and hovered above them. Spontaneously, he slid his T-shirt over his head, tossed it in the air, and it fluttered to the ground.

Beyond the breakers, the azure stretch of water seemed to go on forever. It was mesmerizing. The ebb and flow of life, he thought, and this beach was definitely on the flow, the tide coming in. He kicked off his shoes and socks and faced the line of rushing waves that lifted their foaming heads and pushed each other toward him. He stepped into the water in his jeans, and then, without hesitating, kept wading deeper. The waves hit his thighs and waist and bare arms, stinging his skin with their sudden powerful slap.

When the water reached his shoulders, he dove forward and lunged into a crawl stroke. Left arm, right arm, breathe, he told himself. Left arm, right arm, breathe. He wanted to be one with it.

The swimming made him feel better. Cleansed.

He reached the calmer water, beyond the breaking waves, and it felt good to be out there. Good to stay buoyant in the blue palm of mother ocean, good to do the backstroke, facing the flocks of clouds, feeling the steady blue swells rise and fall beneath him. He felt exhilarated, as though he could swim there a long time, as though he could swim there for the rest of his life, away from dry land, away from everything.

Still, he knew he had to return to shore eventually. He had no choice. He had to face the unknown. He needed answers, closure.

He needed to find Charlotte.

For thirteen years, these doubts, and this guilt, like dark stones, were far beneath his surface, but still always faintly visible. He realized his plan might sound poorly thought out, or even crazy. But he was almost reaching his destination, pushing against the tide, and there was no turning back. Left arm, right arm, breathe. One, two, breathe.

Finally, tiring a little and beginning to pant, he angled back toward the beach. As soon as his feet could reach the sandy bottom again, he stood. Suddenly a large, rolling ten-foot-high wave struck him from behind, knocking him to his hands and knees. The wall of rabid foam rushed over him, the salt stinging his eyes and nose. He tried to get up, but the soft sand shifted beneath his feet and he wobbled. He felt suddenly weak, knocked down by that wave, and he hated that feeling. He was stronger than that, right? he told himself. When he stood again, a second rogue wave curled over his head and slammed into him. As it churned him under, he inhaled a mouthful of brine, then struggled to his feet again.

Back on the beach, exhausted, he fell to his knees, his shoulders shuddering as he coughed out the seawater and gasped for air. The woman and kid looked over at him. He realized that, from where they were sitting, he might look like some castaway, a man lost at sea for weeks who—sobbing with joy and relief—had finally made it back to shore.

PART TWO

CHAPTER 18

Estelle and Ariel

"Where are we?" Ariel asked, her voice coated with sleep after a nap in the front seat of the car.

"We're approaching Oz," Estelle replied as they passed a gray farmhouse and a vintage barn, its boards warped. A couple of appaloosa horses stood motionless in front of a white fence. Then she added ironically, "We're not in Kansas anymore."

"Oh Mom," Ariel chirped, sitting up, "You're always quoting the Wizard of Oz." They both loved that movie and had watched it several times. "I'm always Dorothy," Ariel continued, "and you're always the cowardly lion, Fast Eddie is the tin man, Lily is the scarecrow, and Tony, well, Tony….." her voice trailed away.

Is the Wizard, Estelle thought, finishing her sentence. Ariel sometimes referred to Tony as The Wizard. They were a trio for all those years of Ariel's life, a family unit, relying on each other when any one of them needed a heart or a brain or courage. And courage, Estelle realized, was something she lacked; she always counted on Tony for that.

Ariel glanced out the side window at the skeleton frame of a windmill in a farm field with one of the wooden blades missing. "Tony's sort of a wizard, though," Ariel said tentatively. "Isn't he?"

"He's whatever you think he is, honey." She steadied the car as a sudden gust of wind blew across the fields and buffed against the side of their trailer.

Last night they had stopped at a carnival called Tip Top Rides and Attractions. It was an outfit Tony worked for just before joining Virgil Sand's crew.

"Nope," said Sal Roebling, the proprietor said to Estelle. "Haven't really heard from 'im since he quit my show. I mean, that was a long time ago. More than a decade, even." The man tipped the brim of his straw hat. "He's pretty much ancient history around here, Maam."

"Oh," Estelle had replied. "Ancient history."

"Why you lookin' for him?" the man quizzed. "You his girlfriend, then? Wife?"

She just nodded, as if that answered the man's questions.

*   *   *

Ariel gave her pillow a soft punch, plumping it up, and peered out the passenger side window. "So where we stopping today?"

"At Ottumwa. A carnival's supposed to be there this week."

"Oh-dumb-what?" Ariel quipped. "Who names these towns, anyway?"

"It's Ottumwa. A Native American word."

"Oh, I get it. In that case, it's cool."

"In Native American, I guess the name means perseverance. Or Land of the rippling waters."

"So which is it, then? The land of the persevering waters, then. Or land of the rippling perseverance."

"I'm not sure. Either way, it's home of the Corn Belt Calf and Cow Conference. I read it in a brochure from the Iowa Welcome Center."

"Gee whiz. That sounds fascinating. A Calf and Cow Conference. So, you're the cow, and I guess that makes me the calf."

"Plus," Estelle laughed, "you'll be happy to know that Ottumwa is not too far from Oskaloosa."

"Fabulous. Oscar's loose. That town sounds even better. If they have a Red Goose shoe store, can we stop in and get my feet X-rayed? That would be quite exciting."

"I think you need your head X-rayed instead," Estelle joked.

"So," Ariel asked, her voice turning suddenly brittle, "you're asking around about Dad at that carnival?"

"Sure," Estelle said, trying to sound casual about this whole search-for-Tony quest they were on. "I suppose I could." A tumbleweed, dry and brown and asymmetrical, spun across the center line like it knew where it was going.

"Yep," Ariel responded, playing along with the casualness. "Wouldn't hurt, right? Maybe he'll be behind a velvet curtain, running a control panel, talking to us from a big video screen." She blew a bubble with her bubble gum, popped it. "So, what will happen if we do find him?"

"Haven't thought much about that."

"Oh, jeez," Ariel sighed, crossing her arms. "Can't you just predict it?" she asked, frustrated. "Can't you tell what will happen in the stupid future? I mean, so we don't have to waste a lot of time?"

Estelle had no answer and focused on the crows, like black commas, that carved the air above the highway. She appreciated Ariel for wanting answers. Ariel was a girl who—though she was trying at times—wanted nothing more than to click her heels together and find her home again. Estelle understood exactly what she felt.

These past weeks, Estelle sometimes felt like she was walking on some high window ledge without a safety net. But day by day, Ariel was becoming that net. All Ariel had to do was say the word *Mom*, and the word spread out below her like ripples in a soft pond, ready to soften her falls, to buoy her up.

"So," Ariel asked, "can I go on a couple rides when we get there?"

"Of course. But not those scary ones, like the Rock-O-Plane. They make you sick, don't they?"

"Not anymore. And I've outgrown the kiddy rides. Like those dumb dancing teacups. Or those rinky-dink cars that just go in a circle at one mile an hour. I'm way too old for that."

"Oh," Estelle said condescendingly, "I forgot. You're so grown up. You're so *old*."

An hour later, they waited at a stoplight at a city limits sign where a banner over Main Street announced Welcome to Ottumwa, Iowa. You Can Get There from Here.

"Catchy slogan," Ariel mused. "So where's the there that you're getting to?"

"Very good question," Estelle said as she adjusted the steering wheel on a curve. They bumped over a set of railroad tracks at the edge of town. She wondered what answers, if any, this town might have in store for her. It had been a long day behind the wheel. She glanced at the needle on the gas gauge, leaning toward empty. She needed fuel. She needed a break. She needed more courage. She needed....what? she wondered. What else did she need?

"I had a dream when I napped this morning," Ariel said, interrupting Estelle's worries.

"What about?"

"About The Bird Child. It keeps popping up in my dreams a lot lately."

"Is that a good thing, or a bad thing?"

"I don't know. Both, maybe."

Estelle turned a corner toward the local fairgrounds. "That day Virgil Sand found out it was gone," she said, "he lined up all the workers and questioned them. I guess he ranted and raved and threatened them. Like a cop trying to get a confession. He even offered a cash reward to anyone who could find it. But he never got any answers."

"Wanted," Ariel announced, imitating of Sand's guttural, authoritative voice. "The Bird Child. One million dollars reward!"

Estelle chuckled. "I guess that he eventually decided that some local teens raided the display. On a dare or something."

"Those darn teen delinquents," Ariel scoffed. "Them and their dares."

"I wonder what did happened to it…"

For a split second, Ariel thought about confessing that she had done it, that she was the wild, soon-to-be-teenager who stole the little creature and gave it a decent burial. But instead, she kept quiet about it. "Yeah," she finally added wistfully, "I wonder."

CHAPTER 19

Tony

At Pacific Ocean Park, he thought he spotted her at the far end of the Santa Monica pier.

He made his way down the pier, past the Playland arcade, a cheesy souvenir stand, the wooden scaffolds of the roller coaster, and Neptune's Garden, where tourists plunged into the ocean inside a metal sphere.

As he approached, he realized it was Charlotte. Wearing red clog heels, a shiny scarlet vinyl mini-skirt, and a bright green halter top, she leaned against a metal railing with what looked like a thick, pale-yellow collar around her neck.

Hoping to find her out here, Tony had asked around about her when he encountered a couple of street performers in Santa Monica. One man told him she sometimes frequented the pier with buskers and musicians who passed the hat for donations.

A few yards from her, Tony realized what the yellow collar was, and he paused. Two snakes wrapped themselves around her neck and oozed along her bare shoulders. Small boa constrictors. Albinos, he figured. Wearing dark aviator sunglasses and his blue ball cap with the brim pulled low, Tony watched her. Charlotte hawked passing tourists to convince them—for a buck—to take a picture of themselves with a snake.

When the tourists left, she turned toward Tony. "Hey, guy!" her raspy voice called. "Wanna try on a snake?" She grabbed a section of her long, purple-streaked blonde hair and tossed it over her tattooed shoulder. "Sure would look good on you!"

When he pulled off his ball cap, she narrowed her thick-lashed eyes at him.

"Tony?" she exclaimed. "Tony? What the hell? Is that you?"

He pried off his sunglasses. "Yeah. Yours truly."

"Ohmahgod!" she cried as she threw her arms around his neck in a quick hug. As the snakes grazed his chest, he didn't hug her back, just stood awkwardly, hands at his sides.

Charlotte looked somewhat the same as when he knew her over a decade ago, but the years had drawn faint creases in her face beneath her thick makeup, and a new series of intricate blue tattoos crawled along her arms and shoulders. The word LOVE was scrolled in bold on her left wrist. On her right wrist was scrolled EVOL.

Without another word, Charlotte lifted the six-foot snakes from around her neck, folded them like thick sticks of yellow licorice, and stuffed them into a gray canvas backpack. "Here," she said abruptly, holding the bag toward Tony. "Hold these. I've gotta pee." Surprised, Tony had no choice but to take it. "Don't go anywhere, promise?"

"But what if they get out?" Tony protested.

She clomped in her clogs toward the outdoor toilet a few yards away. "Don't worry," she called back with a wheezy laugh. "They're very well-behaved."

Tony felt uneasy, holding the bag by the straps, the two snakes inside it. They felt heavy, considering they were rather thin snakes. And he could feel them move, could see their coiled shapes pressing against the sides of the canvas as they oozed in slow motion.

When Charlotte returned, she slid the snakes out of the backpack and onto her shoulders again, where they uncoiled gradually, like something melting in the hot sun. "So Tony," she exclaimed. "Tony Desdiolo. I can't frickin' believe it's you." The words slid out from her too-bright red lipstick. "I thought you were in Minnesota. Or on the moon or somewhere."

"I was. I am. In Minnesota, I mean."

"So what are you doing here, then?"

"To see you, I guess. I mean, you sent me that letter." Tony was sweating a little, not knowing how this conversation might go. He wiped a drop from his sideburn. He noticed her studying his face, which, he figured, had gathered a few creases of its own over the years.

"Oh, yeah," she said. "That letter. I send all my ex-boyfriends letters." When Tony gave her a questioning look, she cackled and added, "Just kidding." She studied him, not smiling, but not frowning either. "It's been a lot of years, Tony. I mean...you know what I mean?"

"Yeah. A lot of years," he agreed. "But listen. We need to talk. I wanted to ask you some things."

"Don't ask me anything," she replied quickly with a change of tone as she tossed her hair back. "I don't give answers. It's against my religion."

"And what religion would that be?"

She spread her arms to her sides. Long fingers, with nail polish alternating on every other finger: fire red, blue, fire red. "The religion of now. The religion of here. The church of Santa Monica pier. That's what. I'm living my life free out here, and that's what I want to do. Questions just weigh you down, man."

Her motions were quick and almost frenetic as she looked left, then right as if she was expecting to recognize someone she knew. Tony thought about asking her if she was high. He didn't though, because the tips of a couple of reefers sticking from the zipper pocket of her backpack confirmed it. Half the buskers he met in Santa Monica so far seemed to be stoned, or talking about the next time they could be stoned. She still seemed a little like the teenage Charlotte he had known back in the day, but she'd evolved into someone wilder, more dramatic, and definitely more abrasive.

She peered over Tony's shoulder, then called to an overweight tourist wearing a gaudy Hawaiian shirt and carrying a Nikon camera. "Hey handsome! When's the last time you had a picture with an albino boa?"

The man shuffled over, and she lowered one of the snakes to his shoulder. "Pics are a dollar." She pointed to the upside-down straw beach hat next to her backpack. "Best bargain on the whole damn pier."

She grabbed his camera and snapped his picture. The man fished a dollar out of his wallet and dropped it in the hat.

"Hey," she said as she slid the boa from him, "Watch this." She opened her mouth wide, then held the snake's head inside her mouth for a couple of seconds.

"Wow," The man exclaimed, and he snapped another picture of her, then dropped another dollar into the hat.

She draped the snake back on her shoulder and said, "Yeah. I'm all about wow."

"Jesus," Tony exclaimed after the man left, "this is how you make a living?"

"Any which way you can," she replied flippantly. "Beats searching for coins under seat cushions."

"I suppose...."

"Hey, sometimes you're on your own, and you do what you have to. You—of all people—should know that, Tony. You're still a carny, right?"

He nodded, then pointed to the snake. "Aren't you afraid that thing would bite you?"

"Bite me? No." She let her eyelids go half-closed. "These snakes are my lovers."

"Oh?"

"Yeah. They're far out." She held one of the albino snakes up to the sun. Its tail curled, spiraling around her wrist. "I've worked with lots of different kinds. Snakes are basic. No legs or arms. One long spine. They never pretend to be anything than what they are. Mysterious, kind of."

He noticed the small, hand-lettered sign tacked to the railing behind her. CHARLOTTE THE SNAKE CHARMER. PHOTOS: ONE MEASLY BUCK. "You're wackier now than when I first met you. You know that?" Tony said.

"I am. I'm frickin' wacky," she whined, twisting her lips. Then her face took on an intense expression. "No wackier than you are," she added, lowering her voice, "walking out on this pier after all these years." Her steady gaze made him nervous.

Tony was silent, not sure what to say next. He heard the slosh of an ocean wave below, rushing against the dark green algae-coated pillars of the pier. Gray and white gulls swooped above him, then dove, squawking, as a small boy tossed them a few pieces of bread. A feather twirled down from one of the gulls, and Tony picked it up by the quill and spun it around between his thumb and index finger. "I've got a few questions Charlotte. I mean, about us. And thirteen years ago."

"Ask me no questions and I'll tell you no frickin' lies." With that, she touched his lips flirtatiously with her fingertips, then draped one of the boas around his neck and pulled an Instamatic camera out of her backpack. "This pic's a freebie. No strings." And before Tony could squirm out of the way, she leaned her head next to his, held the camera at arm's length, and snapped the shutter. "That one'll look great. Our engagement picture," she laughed. "Right?"

He didn't answer.

She lifted the snake from his shoulders and studied him. "Damn, Tony. You look great." Her bright lips seemed larger and more exaggerated as if they were inflated. "And, here we are again. Like old times, eh?"

"No," he uttered, "Not like old times."

"Why not?" Her face melted into an exaggerated pout.

"We never had a snake between us."

"That's what you think," she snapped. "So, I bet you're married by now, right?"

"I am. You?"

"Nope. Boyfriends, though. And a girlfriend, sort of, once." She laughed. "So, there's a wife, back home, then?"

"Right. And an offspring, even." He slid the gull's feather into his shirt pocket.

Charlotte reached down, pulled the bills from her straw hat, and began counting them. "Lucky you," she finally said. "So why aren't you with them?"

"I told you. I'm here to talk." Then he added, hearing his voice shaking a little, "I mean, about the kid."

"The kid," she repeated the word like it was a dry piece of cardboard on her tongue.

"Yeah. The kid. You know what I mean."

She shifted her eyes to the bills in her hand.

Tony's cheek twitched slightly, anticipating her reply. He could smell her perfume that seemed to move toward him in waves: a thick, musky scent, like incense. In the background, he heard the clack-clack-clack of the roller coaster on the far end of the pier as the riders in the metal cars rose slowly to the top of a pinnacle. Then they pierced the air with squeals as the coaster dove down the tracks.

"Thirteen years is a long time, Tony," she finally said, her voice softer, but tinged with bitterness. "A way long time. I mean, we really connected back then. But let's face it—we both went separate ways. There's so much water over the—you know—the goddamn dam." She turned, and stared at a wave, breaking alongside the pier, its white foam folding under. "Love goes down the drain, I guess."

"Tell me about it."

"But still, you owe me, you know."

"Yeah. I understand that. So," he persisted, "When can we talk? In private somewhere, maybe?"

She didn't reply, just rolled the bills into a spiral and stuffed them into her cleavage. "Hey, I got twenty-three bucks already," she exclaimed. "Not bad for a frickin' Tuesday."

CHAPTER 20

Ariel

Sideshow #32

I live in a room made of words. My room is stacked with books. On my desk, on shelves, in the closet, on the windowsill, under my bed. Pretty much everywhere. My mom bought a lot of them for me, and Splat the Clown delivers some, too. "Here, kiddo. Some brain food," he always says as he hands me a book. "So you don't end up clowning your life away." (Hearty har!). He finds them at garage sales and rummage sales. I know that some some are from libraries, because they still have a stamp on them. But Splat tells me they were phasing them out. Once, when my mom tried to pay Splat for a stack of books, he just said "Words are free."

Mom claims that if I collect any more books, the trailer will start to lean to one side. But I do give some of them away to the other carnival kids so that doesn't happen. Like my best friend Maria Luz. I gave her Alice in Wonderland since I'd read it about a hundred times.

Travel books are my favorites. Every day I'm visiting exotic places, sort of. Though I never leave the carnival, I'm at the Eiffel Tower in France. I climb Machu Picchu. I'm inside an Egyptian pyramid looking at hieroglyphs on the wall. (Very cool!) I'm migrating with monarch butterflies. I'm swimming at an ocean reef. I'm riding a horse at a Navajo sheep farm. I enjoy a fiesta in San Miguel de Allende, Mexico. I'm climbing the cliffs of Patagonia. I'm diving into The Great Blue Hole in Belize. (Wow, let me tell you it is really blue. And really great.) I'm spotting the Madagascar Pochard, the rarest duck on the planet. Yes, let me just say being in my cramped bedroom at the back of the trailer is quite an adventure.

Sideshow #75

Sometimes I imagine that I'm writing words in the sky. It's sort of like those skywriting planes that advertise our carnival when we visit a town. Virgil Sand hired the guy from the local airport. Anyway, the words are white and puffy like clouds. And they form slowly, up there in the blue. And in a few minutes, they fade.

But who knows? Maybe my words in this Blue Sky Notebook will last a little longer than that. I hope so, anyway.

CHAPTER 21

Estelle and Ariel

Farmhouses with leaning porches and rickety barns rose into view and then were absorbed by the landscape as Estelle and Ariel passed them.

Estelle was crossing carnival stops off her list. First, South Dakota, then Iowa, then Ohio, and eventually, if it was necessary, she'd head east and then south. She kept an extensive list—compiled by Old Whiskers—in the glove compartment.

She looked over at Ariel, who was focusing on counting the fence posts between towns. Estelle felt relieved, seeing that Ariel was, for the moment, entertained. Still, she couldn't help but worry that Ariel would get bored or restless on this road trip. And she worried a little about their car, which was making a faint pinging noise under the hood. Pinging noises were never good, she knew. Their used Ford Falcon—which she bought two years ago in '66—had already logged in 221 thousand miles. After being parked in the sun and rain from town to town on the carnival circuit, the car's fenders were a little rust-bitten, and its two-tone red paint's sheen had faded. Still, it sported wide beige Venetian blinds on the back window to show off its style, and a batch of bumper stickers from around the country to attest to its fortitude and adventurousness.

"Why'd they name it after a bird?" Ariel asked once, noting that the Falcon was anything but sleek and streamlined. "It's more like a turtle with a red shell." She giggled and said, "I'm calling it The Turtle from now on."

Estelle agreed, and the name stuck. She knew Ariel was right: The car was no swooping Falcon, no majestic bird of prey. Some days, rather than starting when Estelle cranked the key, the car did a little laryngitis imitation. Other times, when Estelle pushed the gas pedal to get through an intersection, the car hesitated, as if it was deciding something. The steering wheel was mounted off-center, so the Ford emblem always tipped slightly sideways. In busy parking lots, Estelle maneuvered the car carefully, the way you'd steer a three-wheeled shopping cart around a precarious display of light bulbs. Then there was the muffler that made an odd noise. Ariel said it sounded like a thundercloud was riding under their car. And when they turned a corner, something loose in the undercarriage made a sound like pebbles rolling inside a metal bin.

The Turtle's scratchy a.m. radio was intermittent, sometimes shorting out when they tried to use the tuner, sometimes bringing in a distant station where the announcer read the latest news. Ariel spun the dial and picked up Bob Dylan's "Subterranean Homesick Blues." Dylan's high, nasal voice slid through the small holes of the tinny speaker on top of the padded dash. Then an oldie played. It was Doris Day crooning "Que Sera Sera." Estelle sang softly along.

"Help!" by The Beatles played next, and Ariel sang along with the song she had memorized when she was eight. Minutes later, a serious expression washed over Ariel's face. "Mom," she asked, "is our family sort of broken?"

"Why do you ask that?" Estelle was surprised at the question.

"One of the kids said that to me. Back at the carnival."

"Well, they shouldn't have. That's not very nice." Estelle pondered Ariel's words, then added, "But maybe sometimes people just need something."

"What do you mean?" Ariel twisted on the seat and faced her.

"Everyone has something they want, but don't have. Some piece missing, maybe. But no, our family's not broken." She glanced out the window at a windmill, then back at Ariel. "It just needs a little repairing, maybe."

As they reached the city limits of a small town, a green and white sign at the edge of town boasted: GRAVITY, IOWA. WE'RE DOWN TO EARTH and IF GRAVITY GOES, WE ALL GO. The sign made both of them laugh. "Quite the amusing place," Estelle commented.

"Very," Ariel said. "Hearty har. I think I suddenly weigh a few more pounds." She spun the radio dial again and found a station. Aretha Franklin belted out "R-E-S-P-E-C-T" amid the crackle. As they drove down the almost empty main street, Estelle sang softly along with the song.

"Louder!" Ariel demanded.

"What?"

"Sing it louder," Ariel goaded. "Come on Mom. Everybody says you're always kind of soft-spoken. I dare you. Sing it way louder!" She turned up the volume.

With that, Estelle laughed, rolled down the window, and they both sang the lyric so loud that it echoed off the two-story brick storefronts.

An older man and woman, sauntering on the sidewalk in canes, turned their heads in surprise and tossed scowls at them.

The song ended, and they both laughed. Passing a grain elevator and a ten-foot concrete statue of a kernel of corn, they exited the town limits, and the two-lane county highway pulled them forward again.

Ariel fiddled with the dial, trying to get the radio station to come in clearer. "Where do you think that station is?" Ariel asked.

"Far away," Estelle mused. "As far away as we are from home."

"Yeah, the carnival. It's our home."

"But who knows…." Estelle mused, "Maybe we're not meant to be carnies forever."

"Aren't we?" It was the only existence Ariel knew, so she never questioned it.

"No, we're not, honey. You know that old saying, 'Once a carny, always a carny?'"

Ariel nodded.

"Well, that's not necessarily us. I mean, there might be another career for us someday."

"So we're part-time carnies, then? Half carnies, half something else?"

"I guess you could say that," Estelle replied.

Do Not Pass, a road sign commanded as Estelle continued on the county road. There were no vehicles to pass out there, though—just the road reinventing itself mile after mile. She approached a road sign—Ames: 21. She pictured the downtown that she'd driven through with the carnival many times. The whole place seemed frozen in the 1950s. A Fastco Drug with its cramped aisles. The Tip Top Sandwich Shop, where she might stop for a Cherry Coke for herself and a Sparkle Bar for Ariel. Further down Main, Adams Funeral Home, run by a creepy Addams Family, no doubt, she often mused. Then there was the Whattoff Motor Company, where they'd stopped for gas. Smirking, Ariel always asked the gruff owner, "What's on today, Mr. Whattoff?" He never answered.

Estelle glanced over at her daughter, blowing a translucent pink bubble from her Double Bubble as she went back to counting the wooden fence posts on the roadside.

"How many now?" Estelle inquired.

"One thousand, five hundred twenty-one," Ariel replied, glancing at Estelle and then back to the roadside. "No, make that one thousand five hundred twenty-two."

"So how many posts do you think there are between Wanley and Ames?" Estelle asked.

"A million, at least. They'll go on into infinity, I bet."

"That's quite the big word."

"Sure is." Ariel popped a small bubble with a snap. "Learned it in the dictionary. With all the other little words."

"You know," Estelle said, changing the subject, "you don't talk much about Tony. About what you feel."

Ariel frowned. "I know."

"You count fence posts, comment on the miles between towns, and all that. But you haven't said much about your dad."

"But, um, sometimes I write about it."

"Write?" Estelle gave her a surprised look.

"Yeah."

"Where do you write?"

"It's secret. They're like words in the sky, kind of," she said illusively. She was thinking, of course, of her Blue Sky Notebook.

"Well, I'd like to read those words."

"Maybe someday, you'll look up, and you'll see them."

"Hmmm," Estelle said with a chuckle, "this all sounds sort of mystical."

"It is mystical. I'm your daughter, after all."

"Right. You're my daughter." Estelle thought for a moment. "And you're also my future. I count on you to do great things when you grow up."

"No, Mom," Ariel countered. "You're *my* future."

"Okay. Maybe we're both right."

A few miles later, Ariel focused again on counting fenceposts. "Mom, how many fence posts do you think there will be in the next hour?"

"Don't know. Hundreds. Thousands, maybe."

"And then what's next for us? Another town?"

"Sure. Another town." Estelle could tell that Ariel was beginning to question this rather random journey, and where it would—or wouldn't—take them next. Words from the Doris Day song played through her head. Whatever will be, will be. Did she believe that, or was the future hers to see, like in the song?

It occurred to Estelle how much she had in common with her daughter. Estelle, too, found herself wondering what was next. How many fenceposts, how many mile markers, how many dead-end carnivals, how many missing pieces? And how long, she wondered, could she keep driving toward them? Sometimes she pictured her future as being like some big, curved mirror that she kept trying to peer into. And her reflection—which she hoped would be clear and bright—was, instead, blurry, and a little distorted around the edges.

CHAPTER 22

Tony

"So," Tony was saying, "Are we going to talk, or what?"

It was early evening, and Tony stood in the living room of Charlotte's apartment off Hollywood Boulevard. It was a cheap brick apartment, built in the '40s. She had decorated the place with posters on the walls: Buffed-up surfers riding waves at the Big Sur, Marlon Brando in a biker film, and another one—La Dolce Vita—from a Fellini film fest. A wood oak pedestal table anchored the dining area; on top of it, a mosaic vase with a few bright pink paper-mâché flowers sprouting from it.

"What about?" Charlotte looked up from the couch as she applied bright nail polish to her fingernails. She wore a leopard-skin patterned leotard top and toreador pants. Multi-colored ribbons decorated her hair and miniature dream catcher hoop earrings dangled from her ear lobes.

"What you wrote about. In that letter," Tony said. He felt uneasy about being at Charlotte's apartment, and the conversation he planned to have. But she had told him to stop over after she was back from her stint with her snakes on the pier, so he figured this was the time and place.

"Right. Um, yeah." She brushed her hair back from her face but didn't look up from her fingernails.

"Okay, then. Let's talk about it. I mean, you had the baby, and …" Tony began tentatively.

"Oh. So you wanna talk about the old days," she said, her voice expressionless. She twisted the cap on the bottle of nail polish. The polish sent out a strong scent, like insect repellant, which mixed with the incense in the room. "The old days are old and gone. That's why we call them that. These are the frickin' new days. These are the now days." She stepped over to a bookshelf, pulled an incense stick from a glass jar, and lit it. "And the now days call for a celebration. Celebrate now, talk later, I always say. Right?" She spun around and faced Tony. "So how 'bout a joint?" She nodded at the reefers and a couple of glass pipes on the scratched coffee table. Not waiting for his answer, she stepped over, lit up one of them, and inhaled.

"I don't smoke that shit," Tony admitted. He had seen some weed back at the carnival, and Jumpin' Johnny once offered him a baggie of it, but Tony, figuring he might spin out of control on it, never tried any.

"Aw, hell, Tony. You're such a prude," Charlotte scoffed. "It's the best stuff. Panama Red, actually. My friend Buzzy goes down there from Malibu and picks it up himself. Hashish. And Maui Wowie, too. He takes his yacht over." When Tony didn't react, she asked "So what do you want? You can't just stand there with your hands in your pockets."

"Maybe just a beer," Tony relented.

"Beer it is." Charlotte swayed toward the kitchen and leaned into the well-stocked refrigerator. Pulling out two cans of Schlitz, she popped the tops, sauntered over, and handed one to Tony. "Here you go. It's just plain old boring beer for boring old Tony." She lifted her can to toast Tony. He didn't reciprocate.

"Come on, Tony. It's just a friendly toast, for God's sake."

"What are we toasting?"

"How 'bout To us? How 'bout "How 'bout we're glad to finally see you?" Charlotte gazed fondly at him, making him nervous.

"Who's we?" he asked, remembering her using that word in her letter. At the time, he thought it meant her and the child.

"We is me, and my two snakes. They're like family, you know," she laughed. She held the can again toward Tony, who still hadn't sat down. "So come on, let's toast."

"How 'bout we just skip all that?"

"Okay, then. I'll drink to that." She raised the can in the air. "To skipping all that!" she exclaimed, then took a long drink. She plopped on the couch with the wild-looking red and orange cushions. "C'mon, Tony. Quit standing there with a poker up your butt." She patted the stuffed pillow next to her. "Make yourself at home."

He finally sat down. "So," he said, "Tell me about, um…the kid."

"You can at least finish your beer first, right?"

Tony shook his head. "I'm not here to drink."

"Jeese, Tony. You seem so uptight. So guarded, kinda. It's like you're wearing a bulletproof vest or something."

"Protecting my heart, maybe," he replied.

"Very funny. Aren't we all?" She lifted her beer, fingers curling around it with orange and violet fingernails. "Okay. I have an idea. I'll race you," she said, holding the can to her lips. When he declined, she tipped her can up, and rapidly chugged the rest of the beer. "Yummie," she exhaled. "Did you know I once won a chugging contest at The Beachball Bar and Grille?"

"No. Guess I missed it on the nightly news."

"Well, I won. I even beat some surfer dudes at the bar." Charlotte swung her arms to her sides dramatically, the empty can in one hand, the joint in the other.

"Sounds like quite an accomplishment," Tony uttered, hoping she'd pick up on his sarcasm.

Instead, she just held her wrist up to his face. "So, tell me, how do you like my new bracelet?" she asked. "Got it down in Venice Beach. Bought it from a funky lady on the boardwalk, even." To Tony, it looked gaudy, cheap. Tangled circles of brass and macramé, with a couple of tiny fake gold unicorns dangling from it. "And how about my new ring?" she said, holding her hand too close to his face. "It's a mood ring. Way cool, eh?"

"Um, yeah," Tony mustered.

"See? It's purple. It tells me I'm always in the mood," she said with a hoarse laugh.

*   *   *

A half-hour later, after they finished a couple more beers, Charlotte brought out a bong—with water and tubes—and set it on the table. "Ta-daaa!" she announced triumphantly. "Got this at the head shop. Let the par-tay begin!" She took a long toke on it, then followed it with a shot of bourbon. "Makes the smoke go down so much easier," she explained.

"You mix all that shit together?" Tony said incredulously. I mean, bourbon, dope…"

"The more the merrier, I always say," she said, cutting him off.

"Listen, Charlotte," Tony said, trying to steer her back into the subject he needed to discuss. "About the kid…"

"The kid. The kid. The kid. Is that all you want to talk about?" she whined.

"Well, yeah. It is."

She stood and walked toward the large glass terrarium below a macramé plant holder. The two albino boa constrictors moved slowly across the artificial rocks at the bottom. She lifted the cloudy glass cover and peered in. "Look at these two. Just look at them. All tangled up like that. Aren't they far out?"

She ambled back to the couch and lowered herself close to Tony. "Wow, you're really handsome," she said, her voice sliding down to a low, sensuous pitch. "When was the last time I told you that?"

"A million years ago," he said, brushing her off.

"Come on. Take a hit." She pointed to the bong. "You seem so damn stressed, kinda. You need to relax. Then maybe we'll talk. Just do it," she coaxed when he hesitated. "Or has crazy fun Tony suddenly turned into dull and dreary Tony?"

Oh what the hell, he thought, giving in, and he reluctantly inhaled the smoke from the mouthpiece. Bubbles rose through the water. The filtered smoke tasted like silage, but he soon felt a quick rush massaging his brain.

She took another long drag, held it, and then released a plume of bluish-white smoke. Inside the cloud were the words "Foster homes."

"Huh?"

"Yeah, foster homes. That's where the kid went." Before Tony could respond, she jumped up. "Oh, oh. Need a bathroom break." She shuttled to a door in the back hall, and pulled the door shut behind her.

Foster homes, Tony thought. Tony closed his eyes and a disturbing memory entered his brain again, blistering it. He's eight years old, standing in the living room of his apartment. The summer his dad just took off and left him. The sad, watery eyes of his aunt and uncle and his grandma as they gathered around him. Can't take him in. You have to understand, Tony. Can't possibly. Sorry. Then, a helpless shaking of heads, and other words. Damn that Roy. Where'd he go? Just walked out like that. He'll be back, right?

"I gave the kid up." Charlotte's voice brought Tony back. She was sitting next to him again. "I mean, first I took care of the kid for a couple years. Then it was way too much. I had to give him up."

"To a foster home?"

"Yeah. That's where he went."

"He?" Tony leaned toward her anxiously. "So it was a boy?"

"What's a boy?"

"The baby you had. You said he. It's a boy, then?"

"Yeah." She stared straight ahead absently, seemingly mesmerized by the glowing lava lamp in the corner. Pink globes slowly rose and fell in it.

She blinked, eyelashes twitching. "Tony, those were bad times. Times I'd rather forget. I was frickin' messed up." Suddenly hyper, she stood and paced the living room floor as the words poured out quickly. "When I got out here, I wandered the beach at night, wondering what to do." Reaching the wall, she pivoted and walked back the other way. "My older sister was out here, in San Fran, so that helped. But then the delivery—it was hell. Shit—I didn't know if I was up or down in the hospital." She ran her finger around one hoop earring. "Drinking half a bottle of Wild Turkey didn't exactly help things."

"Sheesh, Charlotte."

"Don't sheesh me, Tony," she rasped. "You've never been frickin' eighteen and pregnant."

"It must have been…I mean, really tough," Tony agreed. As he said the words, he had the sensation that as he pushed them out, they were pushing him backward. As if his whole body was moving backward at a high rate of speed.

"Tough?" Charlotte said with a sad laugh, rolling her eyes toward the low plaster ceiling where a couple of Led Zeppelin posters were taped. "That's one way to put it."

She sniffed, pushed a tear out of the corner of her eye, pulled a Kleenex from a box, dabbed it on her face, balled it up in her fist, then threw it hard to the carpet. "And you, the loyal father. You owe me some child support. You know that, don't you? I mean three years. You owe me something for those years, Tony."

"I understand," Tony said, lowering his head.

"I talked to a girlfriend who had a kid. Out of wedlock, too. Said the father sent her a check for a hundred bucks a month. But you. You were half a country away."

"I was," Tony acknowledged. "But so were you. And I'm sorry. I mean, about the way it worked out," he said. "But I came out here to make things right. To do the right thing."

"Do the right thing?" she snapped. "Shit, you should have thought of that. Like about thirteen frickin' years ago."

Feeling trapped by the conversation, he nervously took a hit of the bong. He was already spaced out, but another hit made it worse. "First…" Tony exhaled. "I want to find him. "Then I'll…I'll settle up. Child support, I mean."

"Why don't you just settle up now?" she asked. "Finding him's gonna take time. A way long time."

Tony just looked down.

"Hey," she blurted, "I need reinforcements." She spun around and strolled to the kitchen. Scooping up a glass of ice from the refrigerator, she poured bourbon over it. Walking back, the bottle in her hand, she stood in front of him, swirling the glass, the ice cubes clinking, clinking. She was saying something about the flavor of the bourbon, but Tony couldn't concentrate on her words.

All he could hear was that clinking sound.

He closed his eyes again and couldn't help but picture his father, holding a glass of bourbon as he stood, rotated slowly, and stepped toward the door. Roy Desdiolo, his father. The man who couldn't stick to any job, the man who drifted from a factory job to the VFW Bar to another factory job. Roy Desdiolo: master of nothing, king of nothing, owner of nothing. Roy Desdiolo, a father to no one, except for his amber bottle that he held each night, the bottle he lifted gently from the cupboard some mornings like someone would lift a fragile baby, about to cry, from its crib. Roy Desdiolo, deadbeat dad. Disappearing dad. Tony couldn't stop picturing himself, at eight years old, pushing through the heavy oak front door of a run-down foster home. He wondered what love was, and how it disappeared between a father and a son.

"Want some?" Charlotte asked, jolting him back. She was holding the bottle toward Tony.

"Um, no," Tony heard himself say. He began to feel like he was underwater, or floating on top of the water, or both. He felt like he was about to sob. He began to wonder if the weed in Charlotte's bong was laced with something. "I just need to…I mean, to find the kid," he blurted. "That's all. You know—connect, I mean."

"Connect?" Charlotte's voice pronounced the word from far away. "Shit. He might be in San Diego. Or San Francisco. Timbuktu. Who knows?" Turning, she fanned the smoke from an incense stick toward her. "Ummm," she crooned. "Look at the way that smoke curls. And don't you just love the scent?"

Tony was silent. In his brain, a thick oak door was opening in front of him, then closing.

"Jasmine." She tipped her head to one side. "Makes me think of endless summer."

She turned to Tony, and gave him a longing look. Her black pupils were dilated, huge. "God, I love endless summer. Don't you?" She wobbled to the corner, put an album on the stereo with the big floor speakers, and cranked up the volume. "Come on!" she called, beginning to dance. She gyrated toward him, the glass of bourbon in one hand. "Let's boogaloo!"

Tony wanted to shout at her. "No! This isn't about dancing!" He wanted to ask her more questions. Anything to push his search forward. Anything to find out where the boy was. But for some reason, everything was getting too chaotic, and when he grasped for words and tried to place them in the right order into a sentence, they didn't quite form. His thoughts were like water, pouring through a sieve.

He wished Charlotte would stop whirling around the room, her blurry arms flailing above her head, the tiny unicorns on her bracelet jangling. The clinking ice cubes in Charlotte's glass seemed to get louder and louder.

At that moment, a panicky sensation rushed through him, and he knew he had to leave. There was no use continuing the conversation.

He jumped from the couch and stepped toward the door.

Oblivious, Charlotte just kept grooving to the music. He hated the ice cubes in Charlotte's glass that kept making that awful clinking sound. He wanted to stop picturing his father, downing his glass of bourbon, turning, turning, turning, then walking out the door for the last time. He wanted to stop picturing himself, riding in the musty back seat of a sputtering car toward his first foster home. Despite the blaring song that filled Charlotte's room, the memory of Tony's relative's voices ricocheted back and forth in his head like tennis balls bouncing off a wall: *Damn that Roy. Just took off. He'll come back, right? He'll be in touch, eventually, right?*

When he shut her apartment door behind him, the voices and the music and the clinking finally stopped.

CHAPTER 23

Estelle and Ariel

Estelle knocked on the door of the silver Airstream. No answer. She rapped on the door again. The boss of Sal's Amusements finally appeared in the doorway, and Estelle held up a picture of Tony. The man wagged his head. "Never seen him before," he said, a cigar jammed into the corner of his mouth. Then she strolled from booth to booth, showing the carnies—most of them men in their 20s, dressed in undershirts and jeans—the photo.

"Nope," one man gaunt and sporting a suede cowboy hat and drinking a Slurpee replied, "Don't recognize 'im." He handed the photo back to Estelle and then admired her, his eyes sliding up and down her body. "What?" he inquired, "He get you in trouble or something?"

Estelle didn't dignify his comment with a reply.

That evening, disappointed and tired, Estelle parked the trailer in a local Ottumwa campground for the night.

With Ariel sleeping, Estelle sat at the kitchen table, below the small window, and focused on the crystal ball for a few minutes. It was her form of meditation, her way of relaxing before bed. As usual, she held the ball at least ten or twelve inches away from her face; if she held it too close, she never saw anything in it. She closed her eyes, then opened them again and, though it wasn't really there, she imagined Tony's face appearing inside it, staring at her from its center.

He gave her his warm yet mysterious smile, a kind of mesmerizing expression. He always was illusive like that, wasn't he? she thought. You could never quite tell what was going on inside that head of his. In an instant, she was back in Wanley again, two years ago, when Tony was working on his truck, sliding beneath it on a wooden creeper in his tight white undershirt and worn jeans. He was repairing the clutch.

He slid out from under the car and sat up. "Done," he announced, rubbing the grease from his hands with a pink rag. "The cosmos is fixed."

That was pure Tony, Estelle thought: One minute attaching the cold metal clamps on an exhaust pipe, the next minute he'd be passionately tracing the contour of her body as they lay in bed. Later he might sit on a card table chair, paging through a book he bought at a used bookstore, something he often did when they were on the road. The books encompassed his two main interests: great circus performers and tightrope walkers, and planets and the solar system. Estelle knew you could never pin Tony down or anchor him to an expectation or nickname. You might find him under a metal chassis, or balancing on a wire, or spinning with satellites around the sun, or propping himself close to her in bed, his eyelids soft and moonlike. Dashing Desdiolo didn't describe the whole Tony. It didn't encompass him at all.

Sometimes she'd see him in the evening before sunset, sitting alone on the wood flatbed of a semi-truck, smoking a Lucky and staring into the distance. The tip of the cigarette glowed orange, like a firefly hovering a few inches from his lips.

"What are you thinking?" Estelle asked, sliding alongside him in blue jean cut-offs, her legs, below her shorts, tanned from the long days of summer. She hoped he'd notice, but he didn't seem to.

"Nothing, really," Tony said illusively.

Estelle knew he sometimes got moody when what she called that lost boy feeling came over him, like when he brooded about the way his father abandoned him when he was young. He was taken in by impersonal foster homes in Wisconsin and Iowa who took in foster kids just to get a stipend from the state. When he was about to turn 18, he ran away from one home and ended up in a carnival.

"Come on," she insisted. "Let me in on it. You're thinking about something." She always had to pry at Tony to find out what was going on inside him.

"About that horizon out there, I guess." He motioned with his cigarette toward the flat land beyond the eastern South Dakota town. Out there, only a few telephone poles, like eyelashes, stood between them and the horizon.

"What about it?"

His eyes narrowed at the distant flat line, a few thin clouds with scarlet underbellies just above it. "Just thinking that no matter how long you drove toward it, you'd never really reach it. It would just keep pulling away."

Estelle narrowed her eyes, trying to see what he was seeing. "So, are you thinking of driving toward it?"

"Don't know," he shrugged. "Maybe." He lifted a can of Hamm's, took a long drink, emptying it. Then he tipped his head back and let out a spontaneous laugh.

As he did, Estelle had wondered: Did he revolve around the universe, or did the universe revolve around him, like he sometimes jokingly claimed?

When he was doing his tightrope walk, she sometimes noticed a certain look in his eye, a look that came over him when he was halfway across the wire, which was the most dangerous part. The small crowd always gasped as he centered himself there, his jittery feet almost dancing. It was a look in his eyes that said I'm all confidence. I'm not going to fall. And if I do, you'll never know it. I'll land on tiptoes like some cat as though I planned it. Then I'll take my bow.

So why did he just take off from her? Estelle wondered now. He loved her; she knew that, and she felt it every day. He loved Ariel, though he didn't always spend as much time with her as Estelle would have liked. So what was it that made him suddenly, one day, turn and disappear, like a cloud of dust swirled away by the wind?

She blamed herself. It was something she did or didn't do. Maybe she bored him with her passiveness. Or maybe he was bored with himself. She thought of the possibility that—although he never talked about it—he felt trapped, feeling obliged to marry her when she was pregnant with Ariel. She wondered if he'd suddenly fallen in love with another woman. Estella was aware that there was always a slight distance between her and Tony—a hollow space shaped like a question mark. It was something unspoken that she couldn't quite identify. She speculated endlessly—enough to drive herself mad, Lily cautioned. Her doubts kept clicking and clicking against each other like the silver spheres that swung back and forth in a perpetual motion machine. All she knew was that she wished she could answer some of those questions to solve the mystery of Tony.

But there were no answers. Sometimes Estelle felt like she was walking alone through an endless empty fairground where a carnival had pulled up stakes days before. The only clues left behind were a couple of flattened red and white boxes and, next to them, pieces of spilled popcorn pressed into the mud like dull, yellowed stars.

And now, tonight, Tony's face still stared out at her from the crystal ball. Seconds later, white pellets appeared on a black background around his face. His mouth opened as if he was about to say something. Or was he pleading? She wasn't sure. Seconds later, all the images faded. She leaned close to the ball, anxious to see more, but nothing was there. What did it mean? She asked herself. She'd seen the same fleeting images just a few days ago, and she'd lost sleep over them.

"You're looking for Tony in there." Ariel's voice startled Estelle. It was past eleven o'clock already, and she had assumed Ariel was sound asleep. Ariel nodded at the ball. "Aren't you."

It made Estelle uneasy that Ariel seemed to be inside her head, to know what she was thinking. She wondered what knowledge, what untapped power might be lurking behind her daughter's innocent face.

"Go back to bed," Estelle finally said, pushing the ball aside. "I'm just looking out the window. That's all."

CHAPTER 24

Tony

Tony propped himself on one elbow on the cool sand and watched the strobe lights flashing on the gyrating crowd—some of them moving slowly and languidly, others whirling frantically in a drug-fueled frenzy. The big rectangular speakers, perched on the concrete sea wall in front of Buzzy's house, stuck up like wooden teeth. The woofers and tweeters kicked out psychedelic Jimi Hendrix songs from the *Are You Experienced* album, and Tony could practically feel the beach vibrate beneath him. The hot tub on Buzzy's deck was packed with people laughing and toasting drinks. To his left, a circle of partiers sat around a campfire, passing a pipe and smoking reefers. On the fringe, in the grainy darkness, couples—not necessarily of the opposite sex—made out, some of them naked and moaning as they writhed in the sand. The woman next to Tony had eyes that seemed to roll independently in their sockets. She passed the reefer to him with fingers that were circled by silver rings dotted with rubies. Without thinking, he took one toke of the doobie, a thickly rolled joint that looked more like a cigar. The strong dope, added to the beers he'd finished—kicked in quickly, and he tipped his head back to the sand. He couldn't help but wonder what the hell he was doing here, on this unfamiliar beach with a group of strange people he didn't relate to. He let out a long sigh. The sound of his breath reminded him of something. The air being let out of a tire, maybe.

Tonight Tony ended up at Malibu, courtesy of Charlotte, and Buzzy's lavish beach house. The never-ending par-tay, she had called it.

Charlotte had convinced Tony to take her here.

"Malibu?" Tony had questioned a few hours ago.

"Yeah. Out at Buzzy's place. His parties are Fridays and Saturdays. And Wednesdays." She giggled. "And sometimes Tuesdays, too." The first time she went, she had tagged along with a friend. Though Buzzy and the partygoers were clearly out of Charlotte's league, Buzzy liked her, approving of her wildness and, of course, her looks, so he kept inviting her back.

"Go ahead, if you want to," Tony had said. "I didn't plan on any parties."

"Well, I kinda...I mean, I lost my license." She cupped her hand on one side of her mouth as if revealing a confidential secret. "Don't ever have a stash of reefers in your ashtray when a frickin' cop stops you," she whispered. "Not a good idea." She broke into a high-pitched laugh that sounded like someone chipping wood with a small axe. "So," she said, "I nominate you to be my friendly chauffeur."

"I didn't come out here to drive you around. Or to party. I just came out...."

"Come on, Tony," she said, cutting him off. "Don't be such a damn stick in the mud. It's only twenty-five minutes on the One. You don't even have to jump on a freeway."

Charlotte had told Tony that some nights, the beach party featured a mini-concert, courtesy of The Electric Now, Buzzy's personal party band. While a light show with blobs of liquid color was projected onto a screen, the group played psychedelic music by Big Brother and the Holding Company and Jefferson Airplane and The Grateful Dead.

"I feel like it's another day wasted," Tony said. "The agency, the..."

"It'll take time, they say," Charlotte said cutting him off. She pulled a few strands of her hair in front of her face and studied them. "All that frickin' red tape with the adoption agency," she continued, "I mean—it's going to take a while. They keep putting me off. I've made appointments. Their records from back then are all screwed up. But hey—you've got nothing better to do than sit in that crappy motel, right?" She winked. "So let's hang out." Her words sounded inviting, flirtatious. "Not such a terrible idea, is it?"

Tony had no answer for her. He wanted more information from Charlotte, but it was getting more complicated than he expected. Since she was the legal mother, he couldn't make any inquiries about the child. He hadn't planned to stay out here any longer than he had to, but delays in the adoption office, and Charlotte's illusiveness were all adding up. He knew he had no choice but to wait it out. Sure, Charlotte was frustrating to be around. Her flightiness, her escapism. She was obnoxious, and grating on him, but he had to stick with his plan. Still, these last couple of days, he couldn't help but feel like he was constantly compromising. He felt trapped, caught in limbo. Sort of like that wasp he noticed back at his motel—the one caught between two hazy windowpanes.

"Besides, you'll like Buzzy," Charlotte had crooned in her final pitch to convince Tony to chauffeur her. "He's far out. He's got a yacht, even.

It's New Year's Eve every night, and he really really really knows how to throw a party."

* * *

"Wow," one girl called to Buzzy tonight as she strolled past Tony. "Who's the new hunk?" Her Audrey Hepburn-ish head pivoted on a long, thin neck. She was darkly-tanned, and clad in a skimpy white bikini that was almost see-through.

"Friend of Char's, I guess," Buzzy replied. He was perched on a stack of multi-colored surfboards. "Dude came all the way out here from Minnesota to see Snake Charmer Girl."

"Oh?" the girl questioned.

"By the looks of it, she seems to have the hots for him."

"Like really?" she said, a little irritated, "I thought I was Snake Girl's girl, sort of."

"Well shit, Lotus," Buzzy mused, "Maybe you were, for one night. Snake Girl goes with pretty much everybody. Depends on which night, right?" He shook his head and laughed. "The chick is a siren, headed for a fire or something."

"Yeah, whatever…" She angled away, reached both arms above her head, and started to twirl on the sand with no one in particular.

Buzzy lifted himself from the surfboards, strolled over to Tony, and said, "Dude, ever been on a yacht?"

"Nope. I'm a landlubber, I guess."

Buzzy took a long hit from his reefer, flipped the rest of it to the sand, then set his bottle of imported St. Pauli Girl on a lounge chair. "That means it's cruise time."

"Huh?"

"Yeah. New kids always get a free ride." He nodded to his yacht—a white boat with a high cabin—parked a hundred yards offshore. The tall mast bobbed as the waves rolled under it. "Up for an adventure, dude? Or," he challenged, "is the Midwest boy afraid he'll get seasick?"

"Yep, and nope," Tony replied, noticing Buzzy's sarcastic tone. "Always up."

Buzzy's real name was Stuart Lewis Anthony, one admiring female partygoer had told Tony, but everyone called him Buzzy, or The

Buzzmaster, or sometimes Crazy Buzz. He got a big inheritance from his father, who was a CEO of a Fortune 500 company. Good Time Buzzy—tall and blonde and surfer-dude handsome—was not only the host of the parties, but the wildest of the bunch, making out with the women, drinking, smoking, and handing out some reds and LSD-laced sugar cubes once in a while. His medicine cabinet was like a candy store of fun, the girl claimed with a giggle.

"Then let's go, man." Buzzy broke into a languid jog toward the far end of the beach, his shoulder-length blonde-streaked hair fluttering in the wind.

Tony followed Buzzy into the shallows where an inflated Zodiac skiff was anchored. "Don't know much about boats," Tony admitted, not sure what Buzzy was planning.

"Just get in," Buzzy commanded.

Tony climbed over the inflated side of the skiff.

Buzzy started the outboard motor, then pulled a thick reefer from the pocket of his white cargo shorts, lit it, and passed it to Tony.

Tony waved it away. "I think I've had enough."

"What are you?" Buzzy scoffed, raising his voice above the whirr of the motor, "A short-hitter or something?"

Tony acquiesced, took the reefer, and inhaled.

"It's good shit, isn't it?" Buzzy laughed.

"You could say that."

"I just did," Buzzy said, his voice abrasive.

As they motored through the waves, the round nose of the skiff rising and falling, Tony heard Hendrix's "Third Stone from the Sun," with its dissonant guitar screams, skipping across the water. The lights of the beach house began to blur as he turned his head toward them, then back to the darkness of the ocean. Charlotte was back there in her string bikini, dancing wildly around the campfire with a couple of other girls.

"So, Char's your old girl, then?" Buzzy inquired.

Tony laughed. "Nope. I'm married, actually."

"Really?" he replied. Tony could hear the disdain in Buzzy's voice. "What the hell's *that* like?"

"It's good. Real good." Tony already heard the rumors that Buzzy had sex with several of the party-going women—sometimes two of them at once. A regular Hugh Hefner, Tony figured, his Malibu house like an ocean-side Playboy Mansion.

"What the hell you doing here with Char, then?" Buzzy's interrogation sounded suspicious, and Tony could pick up a hint of jealousy. On the beach a few minutes ago, one of the girls, after snorting some cocaine powder, whispered to Tony that Buzzy and Charlotte sometimes shacked up after the parties.

"Dunno." Tony tried to keep it elusive.

"Don't bullshit me, man." Buzzy snarled, tossing his hair back. "I mean, Jesus, she talks about you like you're her long-lost lover or something. So what are you?"

"Her long-lost lover, I guess. Way long-lost, though."

"So what the hell are you—long, or lost?" Buzzy asked with a smirk.

"I'm both," Tony said, tossing a smirk back at him.

Buzzy tipped his head back toward the sky and stared upward with a stoned look. His eyes seemed to lose their focus for a moment. "Jesus Christ," he exclaimed. "Nights like this, I feel like the sky is falling."

"Oh?"

"Yep, the frickin' sky's falling. But hey, you gotta do something to stop it. Right?" With that, Buzzy held up the stub of the reefer as if toasting it to the stars, took one more hit from it, and flicked it into the dark water.

"See the Sea Princess?" Buzzy asked.

"I don't see any princess."

"That's not what I meant, man," Buzzy barked. "My frickin' boat is named Sea Princess." Tony couldn't help noticing that Crazy Buzz, with each passing minute, seemed a little less crazy and a little more hostile. "Shit, are you dudes from the Midwest a little slow, or what?"

"Or what," Tony replied, letting the insult slide.

They reached the yacht and Buzzy pulled up behind it. "She's loaded with power," he said. "Five-hundred HP under the lid. This baby flies."

"Oh." Tony looked up at the white hull, rimmed with gleaming chrome and gold trim.

"She cost me a hundred grand. Peanuts, man. It's a Coronado, forty-footer. I could buy ten of these babies," he bragged, "and I've already bought two. The first one was just a thirty-seven-footer. But I smashed that one up." He snickered. "Doing eighty into the waves at night. And she sort of flipped."

"Impressive," Tony replied flatly.

"I'll show you impressive," Buzzy said as he grabbed the braided nylon line attached to the front of the skiff. He dove from the skiff, swam to the side of the yacht, climbed the ladder to the deck, then tied the rope to an iron bar near the stern.

Tony rose to his feet, ready to swim to the yacht, too.

"No," Buzzy ordered. "Stay where you are." Before Tony knew it, Buzzy had started the boat. The water from the propeller pushed a rush of bubbles beneath the skiff, and the yacht lunged forward, its bow nosing up.

"Okay, hot shot!" Buzzy shouted, looking back at him, his muscles bulging beneath his polo shirt. "It's time for a joy ride!"

As the skiff jolted and then scooted forward, Tony fell backward, then grabbed the side ropes and held on. The skiff swayed left and right as it fought through the waves.

Buzzy accelerated and the skiff slapped the water as it bounced hard.

"Yahoo!" Buzzy yelled, letting the boat slow a little. "You like the ride, dude?"

"Why not?" Tony called back.

"Not fast enough for you? Let's see what she can do." Buzzy slowed the boat a moment, then pushed the throttle, and Tony could taste the exhaust from the whirring dual engines as the slack rope went taut and then pulled the skiff with a jerk.

The boat reached nearly forty miles an hour, and Buzzy cranked the steering wheel, turning the yacht sharply. The skiff leaped, airborne, over the wake as it swung to the far side. Tony stayed low, gripping the rope hard.

Then the motors rose in pitch as Buzzy cranked up the speed. "How's the ride now?" Buzzy shouted.

"Smooth," Tony lied, realizing that this little boat ride was turning into a threatening challenge. In reality, he was frightened of falling from the boat in this deep water at night. He knew something could be out here in the dark waters. Sharks, maybe.

"I'll show you smooth!" Buzzy yelled, and he accelerated even faster, cranking the steering wheel, veering the boat far to the left, then far to the right so the skiff swung wildly on its tether.

As the skiff slammed into a large wave from the wake, it bounced in the air and flipped, sending Tony flying into the air. As he hit the cold water hard and went under, it stung like needles. He found the surface, coughing the water from his lungs. The yacht sped away into the darkness, dragging the bouncing, upside-down skiff behind it. Tony looked anxiously toward the shore where the beach houses were just tiny shimmering lights. A long way to swim, he knew.

Trying not to panic, Tony dog paddled, tipping his face back to keep it above the waves. The next thing he knew, he heard the engine of the Sea Princess idling with a gurgle, then rising to an ear-splitting whine. Then he saw the red and white lights on the bow.

The boat was heading straight at him.

The boat accelerated, roaring closer and closer. Thinking that Buzzy didn't see him bobbing there, Tony panicked. He lifted one hand in the air and waved, yelling "Hey! Hey!" He knew, at the speed it was approaching, the boat's hull would knock him unconscious or that its huge whirling propellers could just about cut him in half. He tried desperately to swim out of the boat's path, pulling frantically at the water with both arms. But he couldn't swim fast enough.

Just as the speeding boat got within a few feet of him, it veered away, cutting the water, sending out a wave that slapped him hard in the face. Buzzy laughed hysterically as he passed, his long blonde hair blowing back.

Buzzy made a wide turn, then pulled beside Tony, slowly this time, the engines making a low-pitched growling sound. Buzzy killed the engines and the boat rocked there.

"Had enough?" Buzzy called, guffawing. His eyes looked manic. Good Time Buzzy definitely wasn't as amiable and freewheeling as the partygoers said he was. "Or do you want a few more drive-bys?"

"Enough," Tony admitted, wanting this whole episode to end.

After Buzzy threw him a rope, Tony climbed aboard in his soaking wet jeans and t-shirt. Buzzy, stood there smugly, his shoulders arched. The first thing Tony felt like doing was grabbing Buzzy by the shirt and yelling "What the hell was that?" Instead, Tony restrained himself. "Guess I passed the audition, right?" he uttered.

"Maybe. Now you're officially allowed to drink my beer and smoke my goddamn dope," Buzzy said as he took a hit from a joint and exhaled the smoke toward Tony.

"I already have," Tony replied, still angry.

Buzzy started the inboard motors again, flipped his hair, and nodded toward the lights of the beach. "My party's waiting!"

"Hey," Tony said, feeling light-headed but with a rush of confidence after passing Buzzy's initiation challenge. "Mind if I drive this thing back to the pier?"

"If you think you can, dude." He could tell Buzzy didn't like the idea, but he stepped aside anyway, and Tony grabbed the wheel.

"Just one little thing, man," Buzzy blurted. "You put a scratch on my boat and I'll kill you."

"Yeah," Tony said with a laugh, "Sure."

Buzzy grabbed Tony by the neck of his T-shirt. His ice-gray stare was chilling. "I kid you not, dude," he hissed through gritted teeth. "You put one little scratch on my baby, and I'll fuckin' kill you."

CHAPTER 25

Ariel

While Estelle left for the grocery store to pick up some supplies, Ariel stayed in the trailer parked at a campground.

She tiptoed into Estelle's and Tony's bedroom and spotted the wooden box in a corner of the closet. Estelle always kept the crystal ball there. She said the plain black wooden box was simple and unassuming, and not ornate, and that's where something prized and valuable should always be kept. Not under lock and key—but instead nearby, and accessible.

Ariel pulled the box out, set it on the bedspread, then opened the lid.

She lifted the ball from the red velvet bag. It was a little heavier than she expected. The ball was seven inches in diameter, but it was solid crystal. She wondered, again, about the stories her mother told about the ball. Sometimes her mom joked that she bought the ball from a warehouse in New Jersey. Other times she said she found it at a pawn shop, or that it was presented to her by someone who said she was a female wizard. Another time, she claimed the ball was quarried from a crystal cave deep down in the earth. She claimed that the cave was full of huge crystals that gave off so much energy that you could actually hear the low-pitched sound of their humming. "I'll tell you the real story sometime," Estelle once said to Ariel, "when you're ready."

Ariel set it on the dresser on its wooden swivel stand, then leaned close to the ball, almost touching her nose to it. The ball was as clear as a mountain stream. Like a large, perfect bubble, holding its breath.

She remembered her mother telling her a bedtime story with a happy ending. It was about Harry Houdini, the great escape artist. Estella told it this way: One winter day, Houdini leaped from a bridge on the Detroit River through a hole in the ice. Shackled in handcuffs and leg irons, he struggled free, but the current had swept him downstream beneath the thick layer of ice. He panicked as he swam beneath it, not sure how long he could hold his breath. Suddenly he heard his mother's voice, calling him. He followed that voice, and it led him toward a small opening in the ice, and he made it out alive.

I always listen to my mother's voice, Ariel thought now. It's what daughters do to survive. Maybe someday, she thought, I will even become my mother. I could be a fortune teller, too. I'll look a lot like her, but I'll try not to make some of the same mistakes. No hesitating. No self-doubting, or double thinking myself. No staring at glass that's sometimes cloudy.

Ariel closed her eyes, as she'd seen Estelle do, and let her mind relax. She waited to feel like her brain was floating on soft waves. Then she opened her eyes and peered into the ball for visions, the way her mom always seemed to do so easily.

Ariel kept looking, hoping for some images to appear. Herself, maybe, a blossoming sixteen-year-old, gazing back at the gawky, skinny 11-year-old kid. Herself as a grown woman—a 21-year-old—beaming at the man who was about to be her husband. She hoped to see her Dad, pulling his truck next to the trailer again and jumping out to hug her and Estelle. She wished for a healing rainbow to arch over their trailer, like after the tornado in The Wizard of Oz.

Let me see something, she thought, squinting. Hurry up. Show me something. Anything.

Minutes passed. All she saw was the flicker of her eyelashes. All she saw was the concave face of a young girl, looking for answers about who she was or who she would be. A girl who was just too young for anything. A girl with a curved face, her lips small and pale, her brownish blonde hair flat and stringy. A girl whose father was gone. A girl with glistening tears rolling down her convex cheeks.

Forget it, she thought. Just forget it. She was only a kid, trying to be her glamorous and wise mother, and there's no way she could suddenly transform into that. My hands are too small, she thought. And I have no powers. Guess I'm not ready for the real story.

She glanced at the clock. She knew she had better put the ball away before her mom returned. When she lifted it, it felt even heavier than before. Maybe it was the weight of all those dreams inside it, she thought. But they were suspended somewhere in the crystal, so there was no way that—for now, at least—they could come true.

CHAPTER 26

Estelle and Ariel

Halfway to somewhere, it happened. Things always seemed to happen to Estelle halfway to somewhere.

At first, a faint orange light on the dashboard of the Falcon winked at her.

Estelle ignored it, for a while at least. She glanced into the side view mirror and saw the small swirls of tan dust devils, circling on the roadside behind them.

"Does that light mean something?" Ariel inquired, twirling a few strands of her hair alongside her face.

Estelle didn't reply. The light, sunken into the padded dash, kept opening and closing its eye.

"Maybe it means The Turtle wants a drink. A rest. A nap." Ariel mused. "Or it wants to pull back into its shell."

"Whatever," Estelle chimed in, "we better stop at the next town."

"And where's that?"

"I saw a sign for a town in 30 miles. Check the map, would you?"

Estelle had appointed Ariel as the designated navigator, so she could calculate, by the inch, how far to the next destination, and how long it would take. She'd lean over the road map in the front seat and run her finger along the highways, estimating the miles with her thumb or pinkie. Then she'd call it out, like a co-pilot reporting to a crew commander. "Donovan, fifteen miles. Walsburg, thirty-two miles. Akron, one twenty-four. Moon, two-hundred thirty-eight thousand, nine hundred. Give or take a few."

They followed the county highway, the gusting wind blowing dry dust across the road in front of them in rippling waves. Estelle kept the accelerator steady as the car cut through them. A couple of miles later, the car began to lurch a little. Then it lurched again, and when it did, Estelle slowed down from 60 to 45.

She pressed on the accelerator again, but the car didn't speed up. She pressed it all the way to the floor, but the engine had already killed and the car was steadily slowing.

"Mom," Ariel cried in alarm, stretching out the word so it had three syllables, the first one high pitched, the second lower, and the third high pitched again. Then, as the car coasted to a stop, she said the word again, this time as a quick, one syllable question. "Mom?"

"Yeah, I know. Something seems to be wrong here." She felt panic swirling inside her as she eased the car onto the shoulder of the road, the pebbles popping under the tires like acorns. The car came to a complete stop. "Great," she exclaimed. "Wonderful." She inwardly cursed herself for deciding to take this small county highway somewhere in Ohio, just to see the countryside.

"Now what do we do?" Ariel asked.

"We're going to….well, we'll…well, I don't really know. I suppose we could hitchhike to the nearest town."

"Great idea, mom. We'll take a ride with whoever doesn't look like a mass murderer, right?"

"Exactly," Estelle said, playing along. "We'll refuse to ride with any criminals. We'll check their credentials." Estelle looked up at a herd of grazing cows on the roadside. They were black and white Holsteins. Whenever she saw them, Estelle always wondered if they were black with white spots or white with black spots. One cow, its big ears flapping to ward off flies, turned its large, clumsy head toward her and stared dully at them. Estelle glared back at it. "What are you looking at?" she shouted in exasperation, causing Ariel to burst into laughter.

"Mooooooo," the cow bellowed. Estelle couldn't tell if the reply was sarcastic or not.

After they locked the car and the trailer behind it, they stood on the shoulder and Estelle reluctantly stuck her thumb into the air. A few minutes later, an older lady in her late sixties pulled over in an old Buick and picked them up.

After Estelle thanked her profusely, the woman, dressed in a pastel green pantsuit, scolded her.

"You ain't hippies nor nothing, are you?" she asked suspiciously, her eyes sliding up and down Estelle's outfit, which consisted of worn bell-bottom jeans, an earth-tone gauze top, dangling dark emerald earrings passed down from her grandmother, and sandaled feet.

"Um, no," Estelle responded.

"Well, good," the woman said.

"We're just carnies," Ariel piped in from the back seat.

"How amusing," remarked the woman, who had bluish hair and who had doused herself with strong-smelling perfume. Estelle noticed the amber bottle of Max Factor Primitif perched in the ash tray. "Whatever, you shouldn't be hitchhiking out here. Not with the youngster, anyways."

"I know," Estelle replied. "It's not the greatest idea. But we didn't have a choice, really. Our car broke down and…"

"Well, I'm heading to the Beauty Barn on Main," the woman said, cutting her off. "I can let you off by the gas station. They happen to have a tow truck. So you're darn lucky you broke down near our town."

"I guess."

"And you're lucky you didn't try to rob me," the woman added.

Estelle assumed the woman was joking. "We weren't planning that," she said pleasantly.

"Good. 'Cause I have a gun in my hand bag." The woman nodded at the green and pink embroidered purse on the seat between them. "I'm part of the Right to Carry Club in my town. We're anti-Commie, you know, and pro-Nixon. We want him to get elected in November. We want him to bomb the hell out of Hanoi."

"Oh?" Estelle said.

"You know. Show them who's boss."

Estelle was surprised since the woman seemed more like the type who'd be interested in bridge club and quilting than guns and bombs.

"Yes indeed. And you can bet I can really blast with that pistol. Got first place in the annual target practice contest," she exclaimed with a tittering laugh, "in my age bracket, that is."

"Good for you," Estelle said politely.

"And just so you know, I'm the only person in my age bracket in the gun club. But," she added, a pleased expression crinkling her face, "I can still blast with that thing."

When they reached the town, Estelle and Ariel hopped out quickly, happy to be free from the cloying scent of the woman's perfume. Estelle never wore perfume, preferring to be natural, and the scent of some brands almost gagged her.

Estelle thanked the woman and held out two dollars for her.

"Don't need that," the woman said, waving the bills away. "I go to church Sundays."

During the twenty-minute trip in a tow truck back to their stalled car, Estelle chatted with the driver, who introduced himself as Cody.

The man—in his early thirties—wore a green plaid shirt with the sleeves rolled up. His sandy hair was swept back and longish. He talked in a lively voice about his aunts and uncles who lived in town, the Elks Club he belonged to, the softball team he played on. "Our town's just a speck on the planet," he told her, pride sounding in his voice, "But still a decent place to live." Estelle couldn't help but notice that he was sort of handsome in a rural I-grew-up-on-a-healthy-farm sort of way.

* * *

The tow truck tugged the Falcon, and the trailer behind it, as the dust, blowing in sheets, almost erased the road ahead of them.

"Is it always this dusty?" Estelle inquired.

"Had a pretty dry spring," the man replied. He fiddled with the radio dial, picking up a station with less static. "But hey, just a little dust. The crops still seemed to come in okay. And the highway crew keeps re-painting the lines on the highways, so people can tell which lane they're in." He gave her a nod. "If nothing else, we're known for our straight lines around here."

Country songs slid through the dash speaker. Hank Williams crooning "I'm so Lonesome I Could Cry," followed by Loretta Lynn and Johnny Cash. "So," Cody inquired, "you have AAA or anything?"

"I wish."

"You really are stranded, then, aren't you?"

"You could say that," Estelle sighed.

"Where'd you say you were from?"

"We're not from any one place," Ariel, sitting next to the window, spouted.

"You don't say?"

"My dad once said that the road is our home," Ariel explained. "So we're from all kinds of places."

Like which ones?" Cody inquired.

"Like Wanley, Minnesota. OnAlaska, Wisconsin. Sleepy Eye, Minnesota. Or Mount Zion, Illinois," Ariel said, naming some of the stops on their annual carnival circuit. "Those kinds of metropolises."

He beamed at Ariel's list, then shifted his eyes to Estelle. "So what it is you do, ma'am?"

"I work for, um, a carnival." As usual, she tried to keep her occupation as generic as possible. She knew the reaction she sometimes got from small town people, who, when she related that, automatically assumed she was a con artist and a thief.

"Interesting." He turned the oldies country station volume down slightly, Patsy Cline's smooth voice crooning "Walking After Midnight." "So why aren't you with your carnival, then, if you don't mind my asking?"

"I am, but I'm not, really," Estelle stammered, not sure how to explain it. "I mean, I'm taking a kind of vacation from it."

"She's a crystal ball reader," Ariel interjected confidently, doing her best to clarify the vagueness of the conversation. "And she's very good at it."

"Crystal ball?" Cody repeated. "So you actually tell the future?" Unlike most non-carnies, he sounded genuinely intrigued by the idea.

"Not exactly. I…."

"Hmmm. So how does it happen?" Cody asked. Seeing their stalled station wagon and trailer, he slowed the truck.

"It's complicated. If you had an hour, I could try to explain it. I'm a little more like an adviser. I like to help people through their lives."

"So it's intuitive, then," Cody said turning his tawny face to her. His eyes were deep set, inquisitive.

"That's a good word for it," Estelle agreed, surprised by his vocabulary.

With Estelle and Ariel standing behind him, Cody studied the car's engine. He lifted his head and wiped his fingers on a rag. "Battery looks good. Let me try to start it." He slid into the driver's seat and clicked the ignition. The car let out an odd, raspy sound, but it didn't start.

He looked at the dash, tried the key again, with the same result. He stepped out, leaving the door part-way open. "Ever check your oil?"

"Oil?"

"Yeah. When's the last time you checked it?"

"Um, I'm not sure," she admitted. That was always Tony's domain—doing maintenance on the car and keeping it running, and she realized that she hadn't checked it lately.

"Well, your oil light's on. There's probably nothing left in the crank case."

Estelle winced.

He leaned under the hood again, pulled out the oil stick, and checked the level. "That's what I thought. Bone dry." He turned to Estelle. "The whole engine might be shot." He gave the trailer a woeful glance. "Plus, you're dragging all that weight behind you."

You don't know how right you are, Estelle thought.

When he closed the hood with a metallic clunk, she asked "Will it survive?"

"Depends on how long you've been running without oil. It can burn the heart out of a car. They're like people, you know. You've gotta feed them once in a while."

"Oh." Estelle felt ignorant. She thought back to yesterday when she smelled a faint, burnt-wire scent that should have been a warning to her. But what did she know? She was out here, on some untraveled county road, near a God-forsaken town, and without Tony, she was helpless. Stupid to feel that way, she knew. It was a mistake to rely on Tony to know everything about everything—from the wiring and the plumbing in the trailer to the car—and to always take care of it for her. Stupid to not be at least a little independent. Stupid to just stand there, on the side of a county road, staring helplessly at the small dent in the fender, the place where—one night after an argument—Tony kicked his boot hard against it, and then, his anger vented, took her in his arms and apologized. Stupid not to know where he was now, or to know exactly how he felt about her.

* * *

Back at the garage in town, Cody lowered the front end of the car, bent to one knee, unhitched the bumper from the tow truck's harness, then straightened on his tall, slim frame. "So," he said, spreading his arms, "Welcome to Elmwood Place, Ohio, population one thousand six hundred and twenty-one. It even made the list of Top 100 U.S. small towns," he said, a little humor sounding in his voice. "We were ranked number 98 on that, you know."

"Right up there with Darwin, Minnesota," Ariel commented from behind.

"How long will it take to check out the car?" Estelle asked, focusing back on the lame vehicle.

"Shop closes at five," he said, glancing at his watch, "and it's past five already. So I won't get around to it until tomorrow morning."

"Oh," she sighed, disappointed. She knew that meant an overnight stay at one of the two run-down local motels. She had seen one dreary-looking place called the Royale Motel on the way in.

"So we're staying here tonight?" Ariel's tone revealed, quite clearly, that she didn't exactly appreciate this little town with the sheets of dust rising and falling on the narrow main street.

"Don't worry, sweetie."

Ariel's face pinched into a skeptical look. "I know what it means when you say don't worry. I'm twice as worried now." She wandered from the dank, oil-scented concrete block garage—where the walls were decorated with fan belts and bent fenders and stacks of batteries—and into the cramped 1940s-style front office with dark woodwork and an anchored oak desk. She parked herself in front of a penny gumball machine, a glass globe filled with a kaleidoscope of red, green, yellow, blue and pink gumballs.

"So what do I owe you for the tow?" Estelle asked Cody, who stood near the hoist, jotting something in a ledger book.

"Didn't you say you were a crystal ball reader?"

Estelle didn't reply.

"So, can't you just predict the bill?" he said with a laugh and a wink that made her think he might be flirting with her.

She just shook her head.

"Well, I can." He tipped his head toward the wooden braces near the ceiling, gray exhaust pipes angled across them. "Let's see. I predict you don't owe me a thing."

"What do you mean?"

"Well," he said, his face flushing a little, "You two were good company. So the tow's on the house. And my guess is that once we run a few tests on the engine, and get some oil into it, check the plugs and get a new fuel pump fuse, your car will be up and running again." He set the ledger on a cluttered wooden counter. "So you'll probably be on your way by tomorrow morning. Where were you headed, if you don't mind my asking?"

"We're not sure yet. Just...well, I don't really know. I know that sounds sort of irrational, but..."

"I've been there," he filled in quickly. He strolled to the corner sink, picked up a bar of Lava soap, washed his hands, then dried them on a towel. "So, you have plans for tonight?"

"Plans?"

"Well, it is a Friday night."

A blank expression crossed her face. She'd lost track of time; it hadn't even dawned on her what day of the week it was. "I guess my plans include waiting for a broken-down car. And a night in scenic downtown Elmwood Place, Ohio."

"Sounds like loads of fun," he laughed, picking up on her tone. "And the town is pretty darn nice. In its own way. When you don't have much, you celebrate the small things you do have." He pressed a switch and one of the paneled garage doors slid down on greased rollers. "Anyway, I'm headed to the Flat Iron later. He gestured toward the tavern sign further down Elmwood Avenue. "Why don't you stop over? For an hour, anyway. I mean, if you're not too busy."

She felt flustered and didn't know how to respond, so she just replied, "I don't think I can. Ariel....I mean, my daughter. I need to stay with my daughter."

He pondered this while sweeping some metal flakes from the floor with a push broom. "Well, I have a niece who could hang out in the motel with her, if you want. She's fifteen already. Does a lot of babysitting. Reliable kid. And the bar's only a block from the motel. You could still check on your girl from time to time." Seeing her hesitant expression, he backtracked a little. "Then again, maybe I'm getting ahead of myself. I don't mean to be forward or anything. Maybe there's someone..."

She lowered her eyes quickly to the gray oil stains, darkening the floor of the garage, a vague rainbow meandering on its surface. She thought about it briefly, but she couldn't get herself to answer. *Yes, someone*, a voice in her head announced. *It's someone, all right. My husband, wherever he is*. Finally, she just mustered a polite smile.

"So you'll stop over, then?" he said. "I'll introduce you to some of the locals."

"Maybe," Estelle replied. With that, she stepped into the front office to get Ariel, who stood there, her frowning face close to the glass globe of the gumball machine. She put one penny into the slot, then another, and then pushed and pushed at the handle that seemed to be stuck.

CHAPTER 27

Tony

After a night at Buzzy's rollicking party, Tony dropped Charlotte off at three a.m.

Days had passed. There was still no word from the adoption agency. Charlotte promised a report from them any day. So Tony found himself just waiting around, and, in the evening, for lack of anything else to do, driving Charlotte to Buzzy's never-ending party.

"Fun," Charlotte blurted as he pulled up in her apartment parking lot. "Thanks for the ride again, Tone. It was, like, great being with you."

"Yeah," he managed.

"You coming in?" she questioned.

"No," he replied curtly.

"Awww," she scolded. "Mister prude strikes again."

"Good night, Charlotte," he replied, and she reluctantly stepped out of the car and climbed the stairs to her apartment.

Tony was high, higher than he thought from the mix he had consumed at the party. He didn't intend to get this way. He was sitting alone at the edge of the beach, guitar riffs from Buzzy's psychedelic house band screeching in his ears. A couple drinks lowered his inhibition, and he thought *Oh what the hell* and made the bad choice to take some kind of pill that a partygoer offered him. He wasn't sure what it was.

Tony slid out of his truck and meandered into the yard behind the apartment. He needed to clear his head. But it wasn't easy. As he walked, he felt as if his feet weren't attached to his legs. His skull seemed to lift slowly from his head, then drop back down. His mind was like a bird's nest, woven together with a random mix of twigs, leaves, and stray threads. At the party, Charlotte, surrounded by haze, laughed as she held a sugar cube between her fingertips. Was it acid? he wondered now. Is that what she was into? And what the hell am I getting myself into? One thing he did know for sure—he had to try to sober up before he drove back to his motel off Sunset.

Beneath a moon that seemed like a piece of paper pasted in the sky, he noticed the paint-chipped clothesline posts. Three wires stretched from one cross-shaped post to the other.

"Okay," he barked to the six-foot clothesline post as if it could hear him. "If you insist." Without even thinking, he kicked off his tennies and socks, grabbed the upper T of the post, and lifted himself to his waist. On the far side, two worn, striped kiddie T-shirts—left by their owner—still hung from the wire by wooden clothespins.

With a grunt, he raised one leg and positioned his bare foot on the cold steel pipe. He lifted the other leg and rose from his crouch, then spread his arms to the sides. The motion was quick, smooth, effortless, like on his best nights back at the carnival—a place that felt so far away from him lately. But now, as he centered himself on this post, everything felt right.

He was a gymnast, an athlete, an artist, a lover, all at once. All at once. Tony Desdiolo had command over himself again, and his audience, which, at the moment, consisted of a line of scraggly poplars, two blue plastic trash barrels, and, above, an opaque skin of night sky.

He thought he could hear the hum of the distant Milky Way as it watched him in appreciation. Or was it just another galaxy—remote and distant, like always? The hum grew to a pulsing roar. Maybe it was just the blood rushing through his temples, he wasn't sure.

He didn't care. It didn't matter. What did matter was that he was lowering his bare foot to the taut, braided steel wire. What mattered was he'd try to make it to the other side. The other side.

He felt the skin of his sole caress the wire, tame it from wobbling. For an instant, he hesitated. Would this one hostile coiled strand of steel hold him up, or reject him? The thirty feet between the clothesline posts suddenly seemed to stretch farther away, as if he was trying to cross above Niagara Falls, and he thought maybe he shouldn't even try it at all. He thought of Virgil Sand a few weeks ago, who told him that he was losing it because he was falling more often. "Damn it, Desdiolo," Sand had muttered, "you gotta shape up your act. Or the crowd ain't gonna like it." And Tony knew it was true. He'd been doing this for over a decade, and now, at thirty-goddamn three, he knew he was not as sharp as he was when he was in his twenties.

Tony always told himself that confidence is nine-tenths of the law. He told himself it was the only way to be Tony Desdiolo, King of the Wild Wire. Titan of the Tightrope. Prince of Balance. But at this moment, he wasn't used to this uncertainty, these hammering doubts, this crumbling confidence, this aimless feeling of being in-between.

"C'mon," he coaxed himself aloud, "C'mon, damn you." And he took a second step, his right foot coming down precisely, just enough weight, but not too much. The key to a tightrope walker, he always told himself, was to make yourself almost weightless, to float on the wire. And when you walked, it was all or nothing: the crowd either roared in appreciation, or you heard a disappointed sigh of disgust.

For an instant, as he stood there, he wasn't just plain Tony Desdiolo anymore. His ego inflated again, and he was back to who he used to be—the famous Dashing Desdiolo, the guy who could defy the odds, the guy who could accomplish anything, who could cross any chasm and amaze the masses. The two small T-shirts bobbed in delight with each step. For those few moments, he loved the world again, and the world loved him.

Still, something was missing. Something he couldn't tiptoe toward and reach, as much as he tried. It was like the damn wire was strung between the past and the future.

He took another step. The Milky Way studied him with its thousands of tiny blinking eyes. The dark apartment windows watched with half-closed lids. The headlights of the beat-up muscle cars, in their assigned slots in the parking lot, stared steadily, suddenly taking notice of his skills. Their grills gleamed faintly like chrome smiles in the moonlight.

He imagined his son somewhere out there, too, watching him across the wide gap of thirteen years. A son he would rescue, save from being bounced around—like some scuffed-up basketball—from foster home to foster home. Finding that boy had turned into an obsession, a quest. He vowed that he'd never abandon a child, the way his father did, and he had to carry out that vow. He'd stay in Cal as long as it took, despite the delays, despite the roadblocks at the adoption agency in San Francisco. He had to find him; he had to look into the kid's eyes, hoping that he would simply say, "Dad." Or would the boy just turn away bitterly with a snarl, saying "Who the hell are you? And what are you doing here?" He hoped not. In the best-case scenario, if the boy was still in foster care, Tony would begin the process of adopting him.

At that moment it began. Just a slight tremor in his toes at first. A tiny earthquake. But it magnified as it rose to the bones of his feet and into his ankles. It slid up through his calves and then to his thighs, making them quiver, much as he tried to steady them. The two T-shirts snapped loose from their clothespins and fluttered to the ground, deflated ghosts. The next thing he knew, the quake was shaking the earth, turning it on its end. The San Andreas fault, opening its mouth wide.

As he fell, he seemed to drop through the air in slow motion, and for an instant he pictured his elbows, shattering easily as the flickering florescent tubes decorating The Scrambler ride at the carnival.

He landed with a thud, the earth knocking the wind out of him with its hard shoulder. For a few seconds, he lay there, writhing in the grass, a guttural Uhhhh escaping from his lungs that couldn't seem to pull any air back into them.

Finally, he sat up. The crowd—the windows and headlights and the night sky—was disappointed. Failure, they seemed to say to him. What a failure. He could hear them hissing at him. Then that sound was replaced by the steady high-pitched scree of distant crickets in the small swamp beyond the apartment.

He touched his temple and felt something wet. Still, The Dashing Desdiolo pulled himself to his feet. He clipped the two T-shirts back on the line. He stood by the silhouetted cross of the clothesline post, then took a brief bow to assure his imaginary audience that the fall was intentional. It was just part of his act. His comeback, his little resurrection.

Limping a little, he walked to his waiting truck, feeling the pain in his ribs, like brass knuckles punching at him from the inside.

He clicked the key and wiped the blood from his temple. He wasn't hurt, he told himself; there was nothing he couldn't overcome. He had to believe that. He told himself he could always rise from the dead like some damned Jesus the savior. He let out a quick laugh, just thinking about it: Jesus the tightrope walker. Jesus with nine lives. Jesus with wings.

CHAPTER 28

Estelle

Estelle followed the sidewalk along Elmwood Avenue, passing a general store and a Laundromat where a few women in pin curlers watched their clothes circle around and around in the large white dryers. She'd only stay for a few minutes, she told herself. Just one drink, then back to the motel, where Cody's niece had agreed to stay with Ariel.

Halfway down the block, Estelle hesitated in front of the picture window of the closed Betty's Beauty Barn, wondering exactly what she was doing. She knew she could just turn back now and spend the evening playing a game of Sorry or watching TV with Ariel. It would be a much safer, more prudent choice, wouldn't it? She noticed a faded cardboard cutout of a 1950s-style woman in an apron holding a bottle of shampoo. Got to Look Good for My Man, the sign on her apron proclaimed. Behind her, a gray row of hair-drying hoods and, next to them on the glass counter, stacks of *Family Circle* and *Woman's Day* magazines. On the back wall, a large vintage clock advertising Breck Shampoo, its second hand stuck, unmoving. She focused on the reflection of her face. Was that a new line on her forehead, she wondered, or just an imperfection in the wavy picture window?

Her thoughts shifted to Tony. She couldn't help but wonder where he was, couldn't help but feel a little anger and resentment toward him.

It was then that the words *Okay, go,* spoke in her head, surprising her. Those two words made her turn and keep walking toward the bar.

When Estelle stepped through the front door of the squat brick rectangular Flat Iron, blaring jukebox music filled her ears. She wrinkled her nose as she smelled the grease from the blackened grill in the back of the bar. Bar signs—their bright neon tubes bent into shapes to spell Hamms, Blatz, and Schlitz—glowed within the layers of cigarette smoke. Tiers of half-empty liquor bottles stacked themselves against a beveled mirror behind a long wooden oak bar with two carved pillars on each end.

The bar was crowded with locals who jammed the place with clamorous laughter and raised voices. A few of them, nearest to her, rotated their heads toward Estelle, who wore a red and orange gauze blouse, worn jeans and leather sandals. Her auburn hair was twisted in a long braid that hung down her right shoulder. She could tell they wondered who she was, and what she was doing in the Flatiron Tavern in Elmwood Place, Ohio, population 1,621 on a Friday night. She wondered the same.

Before her doubts made her turn and walk back out the door, Estelle spotted Cody, squeezing through the crowd and toward her. "Saved a place for you," he said, his voice raised over the din. He led her to a red vinyl stool, close to the jukebox on the back end of the long wooden bar. "Hope it's okay. It's the best bar in town," he chuckled. "Well, the only bar in town, but still the best. What do you want?"

Just a Bud Light, she thought at first. *No, something else. Something besides what I always order.* "A whiskey sour," she blurted. She hadn't had one since she was a teen and snuck some liquor with her girlfriends out of her father's liquor cabinet.

The drink flowed down easily as the two of them talked, and the next thing she knew, she had another one in front of her on the ring-stained bar, and then another. Each time she took a long drink, the whiskey tasted smoother and smoother. Not used to drinking that much alcohol, the whiskey swirled in a whirlpool inside her head as Johnny Paycheck sang from the jukebox. "Take This Job and Shove It." Then she found herself singing softly along to the Monkees' "Last Train to Clarksville," then tapped her toe to a parade of early Beatles' songs. Meanwhile, Cody was charming, telling her about his life and asking her about hers. She was guarded, of course, and tiptoed around the whole story of Tony, not wanting to go into it. And she felt guilty, too, of course.

Cody talked about how he ended up working in a local gas station and towing company. "I went to junior college over in Akron," he told her. "Only lasted a year."

"Why'd you quit?"

"I could have finished, I guess. But accounting and me don't mix," he laughed, then took a long sip from a 16-ounce can of Pabst. "Then I moved back to Elmwood. Good people. Softball picnics in spring. I know just about everybody here, and I like it that way. A batch of family members still live here, too. Sometimes I feel like I couldn't leave, even if I wanted to. So," he questioned, "you ever go to college?"

"Me? Just a semester, when I was eighteen. Never finished."

"Why not? You seem like you'd do really well in school."

"I did. But I was from a family of carnies. My mother handed me a crystal ball when I was a kid. After I dropped out of college, I thought about going back again, but never did." She glanced at herself in the back mirror. Her eyes looked bloodshot, her braid a bit frayed. "Never thought about a lot of things."

"You do that often?"

"Do what?"

"Not think. Hold back on things." Cody surprised her with his inquiry.

She just gave a shrug, noticed that her scoop-necked blouse had slipped down on one shoulder, and slid it back up.

He rotated his stool toward her so the knees of his jeans brushed hers. "It seems like you're starving for something, sort of," he offered.

"Aren't we all," she replied, leaving it hazy, like the pungent, smoky air that was almost making her eyes water. "Aren't we all holding back on a lot of things?"

"I guess."

"What are you holding back on, then?"

"I guess this is just as far as I go in life. Nothing more out there for me. I resigned myself to that."

"Really?" She frowned. "Seems kind of limiting."

"Maybe it is. But okay, then, what is it with you?" he pried. "You're not just on some vacation like you claimed. I can tell."

Her answer was to take a long drink of the whiskey sour, finishing it.

"Darts?" a voice called from behind. It was a man in his 20s, wearing a feed cap and a Playboy University sweatshirt, and a woman in jeans and a too-tight T-shirt standing next to him.

Cody shifted his eyes to Estelle. "Darts?"

"What?" she replied, feeling the room begin to rotate around her as if there was a shift in the earth's crust.

"Want to play darts?" Cody clarified. "It's a Friday tradition here. And we've just been challenged."

"Well sure," she said, "Yeah," raising her voice above the sounds of the bar, the way a person would while driving at seventy with the windows down.

"Have you ever played? These two are champs of the dart league, you know."

The couple pulled six steel-pointed darts from a personalized vinyl case and smirked. They introduced themselves as Darrin and Sheila.

"I've played a little before," Estelle replied humbly. "I'm average, or just below." She didn't admit that she'd tossed a lot of darts at Lily's Bust-Em Balloon game after hours at the carnival, and she got to be pretty good at it.

The couple challenged them to play 301, a game where you count down from 301 with each score you make, and the first person to reach exact zero wins. "Okay," Cody said, clunking his can of Pabst down on the bar. "We'll get our asses kicked, but so what?"

"Yeah, so what," Estelle echoed. She could hear a slight giddiness in her voice.

After a few rounds, Darrin called "Pause for refreshment," as he returned with a sticky tray with four shot glasses on it.

"What's this?" Estelle inquired, looking at the amber liquid in the shot glasses.

"Tequila, of course," Darrin proclaimed. He nodded to Shelia. "Makes her a way better darts player. And," he said with a snort, "Tequila makes her wanna wear less clothes, too." The two of them burst into laughter as Sheila—adorned with too-red lips and a thick quilt of too much makeup—elbowed Darrin in the ribs, and he bent over in exaggerated agony.

"Idiot," Shelia crooned. "But I hafta love him."

Estelle tossed the shot back in one gulp, and felt what seemed like a stream of lit gasoline pouring down her throat.

After a few minutes of playing, Cody and Estelle, as a team, lowered their score to 50. The other couple had a score of 97. On her turn, Estelle poised her toes at the duct-taped line on the bar floor and aimed. The floor felt soft beneath her feet, and the target seemed to move a little from side to side. It was like stepping off a five-minute Octopus ride, her stomach being stirred like soup. No, she thought—don't think about the carnival. She was so far away from Tony and the carnival, far from everything, far from herself. A million miles away, and that made her feel, somehow, free. The floor shifted again, but she concentrated and made it stop. She could always make things stop, or start, just by concentrating on them, she told herself, the rush of alcohol giving her sudden confidence. She drew her arm back and held it there, the dart held loosely but steadily between her index finger and thumb. Behind her, the jukebox blared "Day Tripper" by the Beatles. "What are you waiting for?" Cody called from behind. "Fire it!"

She focused on the dark red circle at the very center of the target. A red heart. Tony's heart. She whipped her arm forward and flung the dart. To everyone's surprise, she hit the double bull's eye—a 50-point shot. Exactly where she was aiming. Flashing lights circled the electric dart board and giddy, upbeat music blared from it as the recorded voice called out "Winner!"

Stunned, Sheila pouted, and Darrin let out a moan and blurted "Shit! Gol-damn!"

"Hey!" Cody called. "Great shot, Estelle!"

Estelle clapped a few times, and the next thing she knew, Cody grabbed both of her hands and circled her clumsily, doing a little victory celebration. She laughed, strands of her hair straying from her braid falling over her face as she spun. Then Cody pulled her closer in a hug, and she could feel the strength of his arms, the tingle of his breath on her bare shoulder.

As he held her, she realized she was enjoying the embrace, not wanting it to end. Then she felt his lips brush against the base of her neck, and then suddenly slide up to her lips and he kissed her. Estelle let the kiss linger on her lips a moment.

Then a sudden guilt made her pull away. *What am I doing?* a voice—sobering as a splash of cold water—asked inside her head. Cody kept staring into her eyes. She felt her face blush; it felt warm enough to melt the makeup from her cheeks.

She turned, stumbling on Cody's tennis shoe. "I've got to get back," she said, her words slurring a little. "Ariel. You know, she's waiting." She started toward the door, then turned back to Cody. "But, thanks. For the night, I mean."

Cody looked confused and a little upset, but all he said was "Okay, sure." Then he called "Wait! Let me walk you back." But Estelle had already pushed her way through the shoulder-to-shoulder crowd that had grown in size as the hours passed. She glanced at a clock at the front of the bar. Time had somehow collapsed, and she realized it was already almost one a.m. She let the bowed screen door flap shut behind her and ran down the sidewalk toward the Royale Motel.

* * *

"Mom," Ariel scolded as she noticed Estelle walking unsteadily to the bathroom and washing off her face in the sink. "You just washed your makeup off five minutes ago."

"Oh. Um, did I?"

"Have you been drinking or something?" It was no secret that Estelle's breath had filled the room with the scent of alcohol.

"No," Estelle said. "I mean, not that much." She slipped on her nightgown and made her way toward the double bed closest to the window. As she did, she bumped the end table with her hip, and a lamp teetered a couple of times like the last bowling pin after a 7-10 split. Estelle lunged for it, but it was already falling to the floor, the light bulb popping with a hollow sound. The room went dark, except for the lights on the motel's walkway that leaked through the thick tapestry curtains.

"Oh jeez, Mom!" Ariel cried. Estelle picked up the lamp and set it gingerly back on the table.

"Don't walk over here, honey," she warned. "Not barefoot, I mean. Glass. A lot of glass. I'll clean it up. In the morning."

Still sitting up in bed, Ariel just frowned as Estelle's silhouette slid into the bed. Estelle pulled a cover tightly to her chin, then said to Ariel, and to herself, too, as if it were going to be that easy for either of them: "Go to sleep. Just go to sleep."

CHAPTER 29

Tony

After a series of restless dreams, Tony woke and sat up in bed. His wind-up alarm clock read three-twenty-one a.m., but he was wide awake. The dumpy place where he had been renting a room—called The Sunset Beach Motel—was a far cry from any beach. It was off Sunset Strip in a seedy commercial area featuring a couple of run-down bars, a hippie head shop, and an adult bookstore with brown butcher paper pasted to its tall front windows. Instead of invigorating sea air, his room was filled with a strong musty scent from the threadbare, stained carpeting.

He rolled out of bed, shuffled to the sink, and drank a glass of water from a plastic cup. He sat down on the edge of the saggy bed. He couldn't remember all of his dreams, exactly, though he was certain that some of them were short, fragmented scenes with Estelle. And her crystal ball, of course.

His mind slipped back to the evening when—after they'd dated a couple of times—Estelle offered to give him a private crystal ball reading in her tent.

"Now, my tall, handsome stranger," she had said with a flair as they sat in the dim light, "I'm about to tell your fortune." She laughed lightly—a musical sound, like wind chimes clinking together.

"Whatever you say, you amazing gypsy you," Tony had replied with a grin as he tipped back on a wood-slat chair. He didn't buy into her crystal ball reading, thought it was just for show, like all the rest of the attractions in the carnival. "Lay it on me, baby."

She untied the top of a velvet bag, lifted the crystal ball with her slender fingers as if it weighed as little as a feather—though it probably weighed ten pounds—and guided it with her palms to the center of the table.

"Alright," she said, "Here goes." She closed her eyes a moment. Then she opened them halfway and gazed languidly into the ball. Her face, illuminated by a small light beneath the table, took on a mystical, almost statuesque expression, and he marveled at the perfect ovals of her eyelids, her small, slightly pointed but dainty nose, the symmetrical hills of her rouged cheekbones. His lips could run across those, and then down her neck, and that's what he thought about as she cupped her hands, letting them float a fraction of an inch above the crystal.

"Does that help?" Tony quizzed, a satirical edge in his voice. "You polishing it? Need some Windex so you can see, or what?" Despite his kidding, he imagined those hands gently brushing the hair on his temples, then sliding around the back of his neck.

"Hmmm," she said. Then she made the sound again, deep in her throat. A pleasant, catlike purring sound, almost.

"So c'mon," Tony said impatiently. His Chevy pickup was parked nearby, a twelve-pack of Schlitz Malt Liquor waiting on ice in a Coleman in the flatbed. He hoped to convince her to drive around with him later that evening, maybe pull up at Lookout Point outside Wanley. "What's the story? Am I getting a new Corvette next year? Signing a contract with Ringling? Am I making a million bucks?"

She didn't reply, just leaned her face closer to the ball. He could see the crystal ball's tiny sphere reflected in her large, almond-shaped eyes. At that moment, she did start to seem wise, and magical.

"Tell me," he goaded.

"Silence," she said with mock authority. "It's not right to interrupt the teller during a reading. Especially if it's a freebie."

"Reading, scmeading," he joked, though a part of him was still fascinated by this whole thing. Plus, though it might have been a little rude, he had the opportunity to gaze up and down at Estelle's shapely form when he was this close to her—her longish auburn hair, the globes of her breasts beneath a lavender-colored T-shirt, her tight faded jeans. He could hardly stand it another second. He could hardly stand it, staring at her without taking her into his arms, without pulling her from the chair, kissing her, and pressing her against the taut side of the stretched canvas. But besides those impulses, he knew that he needed to know her more, to find out what she was about beneath all that exterior beauty. He'd known lovely women before, of course, but he knew she wasn't like any of them. She was more, so much more. Mystery. Complexity. Intelligence. All that.

Speaking in a low tone, she broke into his reverie.

"I see you, Tony Desdiolo. I see you standing by a stream, ready to cross it."

"Oh yeah?"

"Yes. But you hesitate there."

He put his hands behind his head, tipping his chair and rocking backward and forward on the two back legs. "Am I trout fishing, or what?"

"No, you're not. On the other side, there's…there's a woman."

"A woman? Hey, I think I like this."

"It's a woman you're about to connect with. If only you'd cross that stream."

"Hmmm." He smirked a little, still trying to play it cool.

"You are about to look into her eyes, as if for the first time, and be lost there."

"Oh really?" He said skeptically, though inside, he was beginning to feel a little nervous.

"Yes. She's a furtive woman. Still in the shadows. Too shy to say what she feels. You've hardly known she's existed. And…," she hesitated, "and you don't know how much she cares about you."

"So, who's the woman?" he asked, doing his best to avoid the intense, impassioned tone of her voice that suddenly tangled around him. "Bridget Bardot? Sophia Loren, maybe?"

She pulled back from the table, slid out of her chair and took a step toward him in the grainy light. She leaned closer, staring at him with eyes that seemed illuminated by a light from within. He could almost feel those eyes probing into him as if she had some kind of power over him. She lifted her hands to the sides of his face and pressed them there lightly, but still firmly. Her touch felt electric.

"Me," she finally whispered. "Maybe I'm that person on the other side of the stream."

The soft urgency of her words and her closeness gave him an odd, vulnerable sensation. Tony Desdiolo—the macho carny, ladies' man extraordinaire, chugger of six packs, driver of souped-up trucks, and king of the Shooting Gallery—felt himself blush suddenly, spirals of blood circling outward on his cheeks. He hoped she didn't see it or notice that she had that effect on him. Finally, as if he was far down some hallway and hadn't quite heard her, he said "You?"

"Yes," she repeated. "Me."

Tony pulled back from the memory and stood from the bed. He missed Estelle, missed her a lot. He wondered what she was doing right now. Then he thought about the pain she must be feeling about him being gone. Still, he just couldn't get himself to explain where he was, or why. Not yet, not until he knew more, at least. But soon. Right now, it was all too complicated. He hoped it would be a surprise. Maybe it was a completely unrealistic idea, he thought, to think you'd announce that you were adopting your long-lost son as if that would explain everything to Estelle and Ariel. But that's what he intended to do, eventually. That was the idealistic and optimistic part of him. Not like his father. Not like a cynical, indifferent father who slid out a door, walked away to who knows where, without even bothering to say goodbye.

* * *

It frustrated him that Charlotte kept putting him off.

"No more questions," she had said yesterday. "What are you, anyway, the frickin' FBI? We've just gotta wait until the agency—you know—gets back to me. They keep delaying stuff. Can't find the records, they say. Besides that, I'm not even sure if it's even the right agency. I mean, it was years ago…"

"I know, but…"

"Tony," she said, "maybe you should just forget all this shit about the kid. Maybe we'll never figure out where he is. So how about if you just settle up?"

He gave her a questioning look.

"You know—give me that child support you talked about. I mean…" she continued, "I could use it right about now. We could, you know, sort of agree on an amount. Then we'd be good. And you could be on your way…"

"I *will* work that out. But I'm not leaving. At least not until I connect with the kid."

"Never mind finding the kid," she reiterated, her tone turning icy. "You can figure all that out later."

"I can't wait until later."

"Hey," she said, waving her hand in the air, "there's always a tomorrow. Every next day is a tomorrow. They just keep happening, right? You don't have to think about them. They'll always be there."

"Damn it, Charlotte," Tony exclaimed, frustrated. "When *do* you think the agency will get back to you?"

"What do I look like," she uttered sarcastically, "some goddamn fortune teller?"

*   *   *

Now, at three-thirty a.m., Tony wondered if he could go back to sleep. He might have to get some fresh air, maybe pace the avenue like he did some nights. He stood and peered through the motel window's dusty drapes.

The view out there was sad, lonely. Brick storefronts, their windows like blind eyes, were darkened and closed. Beneath a dim streetlight, drops of rain fell as though the dense sky was wringing itself dry. Further down, a neon sign for a liquor store with some of its letters shorted out blinked off and on, advertising EER and WIN. Two working girls—fishnet stockings leading up to their hot pant shorts—strolled the sidewalk, the hoods of their sweatshirts pulled up. A low-slung Pontiac rumbled up next to the girls, idled there a minute, the headlights glaring, then pulled away. Then the wide avenue was empty again. It occurred to Tony that it glistened like the surface of an unmoving river. Or maybe a wide, flattened dream.

CHAPTER 30

Estelle and Ariel

Red lights. Blue lights. Red lights. Their light filtered through the space at the top of the drapes, and when she closed her eyes, she still could see them. Estelle couldn't ignore those neon lights, nor—because they seemed to be shorting out—the rising and falling sound of their slight buzzing, as though there were cicadas perched on the small elm tree right outside the room.

That night in the Royale Motel, it was already four in the morning, and Estelle—her mind still racing after her night at the bar—was restless and awake. All she could do was toss and turn there, listening to Ariel's steady breathing next to her on the double bed. She thought about how Ariel could always sleep and sleep. Some mornings Estelle had to practically pry her limp body from the bed. Ariel was never one to jolt awake with a sudden sound or a touch; she always rose slowly from the dark depths of sleep to the brightness of waking. Estelle understood that she was a dreamer, and her dreams always wanted to pull her deeper toward them.

Ariel stirred briefly, rolling sideways, her left leg extending out of the covers. Estelle saw Ariel's eyes, sliding beneath their lids and noticed her legs twitch. She wondered if maybe Ariel was dreaming of running. No limping. Her evenly matched legs dancing through a field of flowers. *I love this sweet girl*, thought Estelle as she studied Ariel's face. *Let her sleep. Let her dream. That's what childhood's about.*

Yesterday afternoon, when Estelle first unlocked the door with a key attached key holder shaped like a red plastic crown, she noticed that some moths, their dried, dusty beige husks scattered on the wooden windowsill of the picture window. The Royale seemed fairly clean, though the double bed with the once-pleasant chenille bedspread had a couple of cigarette burns and the maple paneled walls were slightly warped and curving in places. On one wall hung a dime store picture of an ocean scene with a blue wave about to crash into a black rock, and on the opposite wall, a mountain scene, which looked like the Rockies, complete with a couple of scruffy mountain goats. The bathroom featured two glasses wrapped in cloudy cellophane, a narrow tin shower stall, and a paper shower mat on the floor with two sea horses facing the drain. Ariel noticed the mat and chuckled, saying the sea horses were cute. On the mat was scripted "Welcome to the Royale Motel—for a Royal Knight's stay." *Witty*, Estelle thought.

Before they checked in, she had stepped into the town's one phone booth on the corner and called her friend Lily back at the carnival.

"Lily," Estelle had said, "We're stalled. Totally stalled."

"What do you mean?"

Staring at the holes in the phone's rotary dial, Estelle told her about the car. "We're in Elmwood Place, Ohio. Wherever that is. Our car's broken down. And we're checking into some dumpy motel for the night. I think we should just turn around. You know—head back to Wanley tomorrow."

"Oh no," Lily said firmly. "Don't think about that."

"Why not?"

"Because. You practically just got started." For a few seconds, Estelle listened to the soft hush of static. "You can't give up, Estelle."

"I feel like I'm going to."

"You can't. I gave up a long time ago. First the divorce. I ended up a single mother, and joining a carnival. You have to keep going. For me, at least. But more so for you." She sniffed, then added. "And then there's that kid to think about. The loveable Ariel."

"Yeah, that kid."

"And if you need more cash for the repair," Lily added, "I'll wire you some money."

"We don't need it yet. But thanks, Lil. We love you. You're a great friend."

"Love you too, Es," Lily echoed.

Just then the long-distance operator cut in, telling Estelle to deposit another seventy-five cents for the next minute.

"Better hang up," Lily said quickly, "Save your quarters. Call me again? But before you go, tell me—are you having a little fun yet?"

"Oh, loads of it," Estelle said in jest, "Tonight we plan to wine and dine at Bud's Café and Truck Stop. They've got waiters in tuxes and linen tablecloths and a lobster special tonight and...." Then she heard a distant click, letting her know that the call was already disconnected.

* * *

Tonight, recalling the sound of Lily's reassuring words and her slow, deep breath, Estelle took a few breaths of her own, thinking they might bring her sleep. But they didn't.

Instead, she worried about the car being fixed. She pictured it, sitting in the greasy darkness of the concrete block repair garage, their trailer unhitched and plunked next to a stack of bald tires. Though she was a little nervous about seeing Cody again, she'd check on the status of the car as soon as the station opened.

She wondered where they'd go next, and the possibility that they'd run out of money. She worried that she was pulling Ariel away from her friends back at the carnival. And what made her think she'd ever find Tony? She knew that he was in a relationship with a woman before he met her. "It was a pretty serious one, even," he confided once, but then declined to say any more about it.

The initial excitement of her decision to search for him was quickly wearing off, thanks to a broken-down car and a broken-down room in a broken-down motel with neon lights that couldn't make up their minds to glow brightly or go dim.

Her mind drifted to the image that appeared a couple of times in her crystal ball. It was Tony's anguished face, surrounded by white dots, like faded stars. Was that vision trying to tell her something? Or did she just imagine it because she wanted so badly to see him?

And, of course, she thought about her time with Cody. What did his sudden, unexpected kiss mean? She shouldn't have let it make her feel like some giddy teenager. She closed her eyes but kept replaying the events at the bar over and over in her mind. Whiskey sours, Merle Haggard's scratchy voice, darts flying through the air, the warning light flaring on the dash, the lights blinking on the dartboard after the bullseye, Cody's face, leaning in to kiss her—all those images whirled around in her mind, coming back to her again and again like they were caught in some endlessly circling cyclone. Moments of doubt, moments of exhilaration, rushes of guilt.

She felt confused, and aimless as those rippling ribbons of dust that blew across the main street of this little town.

Stop, she said to herself, and she squeezed her eyes shut even tighter and rolled onto her side, the sagging springs beneath her creaking.

She got out of bed and turned on the small black and white TV perched on a rickety aluminum stand. She kept the volume off and turned the channel dial. Most of the five channels were snowy screens. The only two stations the TV could pick up were test patterns that looked like the crosshairs of a rifle with a bullseye. The bottom of the screen announced We Are Currently off the Air. Programming Returns at 8 a.m. She clicked the TV off.

She turned her head toward her travel alarm that seemed to be ticking so loudly on the nightstand. The luminous hands on the clock pointed to five fifteen a.m..

She knew she had to continue, as Lily insisted. She had to come up with a plan.

Her first step—after the car was repaired—would be to head east, toward Pennsylvania, where she knew some carnival friends, and then—if necessary—south. Even as far south as Gibsonton, a small town outside Sarasota, Florida, where the carnival crew spent the winter. She and Tony had stayed there one winter, before Ariel was born. Could she make it that far? She knew Tony had quite a few friends in that town, a place nicknamed Carny Town USA by the locals because so many carnival people had settled there.

She'd follow leads if there were any. She'd veer toward hunches. She'd trace the roads on the map that Ariel held in her frail hands: highways that narrowed into thinner county roads that led to—she hoped—some answers. But did she have enough strength to follow them? she wondered. That question echoed through her mind. After all, she reasoned, she was just a woman—with a high school education, and no career to speak of—driving aimlessly in a car with her daughter. She was just a woman, caught in the big, indifferent middle of America.

A headache gnashed its teeth behind her forehead. She eased out of bed in her flannel nightgown and walked to the cramped bathroom for a glass of water and some aspirin. She leaned toward the mirror as if she could see deeply into it. But she knew the truth: mirrors didn't reveal anything about the past, or the future. All they could do was reflect the present. Standing motionless in the filtered glow of the beige seashell night light, she felt like she was tapped in amber, just like those insects she'd once seen in a museum.

She wondered what Tony was doing right now, and how far away he was.

Climbing back into bed and propping two pillows beneath her head, Estelle resigned herself to the fact that she'd stay up all night. She wouldn't sleep. She wouldn't dream. She'd watch her daughter dream, and that would be enough. She'd wait for morning to come, and maybe the first thin shafts of light slanting through the drapes would tell her what she needed to know.

She lay there, letting thoughts blow through her mind like sheets torn from a clothesline in the wind. She listened to the red and blue lights buzz and flicker, flicker and buzz. She slipped from the bed again, stepped again to the window, and peered out at the nocturnal moths, attracted to the light. She watched their frantic wings, fluttering toward the pulsing neon tubes and spiraling around them, then fluttering away into the darkness, then fluttering back and circling the lights again.

*   *   *

Estelle felt awkward as she stood in front of the gas station's cash register at noon, her head still throbbing from her hangover. Cody held out a receipt of the bill for the car repair. "There you go. She's good as new," he said. "I was able to find a couple of recycled parts. So I saved you a little cash."

"Thanks. But if the parts are recycled," Estelle commented, "they're not exactly new."

"Well, good as old, then." Cody laughed.

She glanced at the oily rag on the wall behind him with its question mark-shaped stain. "So, um, thanks," she said. "For getting us on the road again."

"Any time," he said. "And good thing you didn't run totally dry on that oil. The engine might have seized up. And that would have cost a bundle."

"Yes," she agreed. "Good thing." As she slid behind the wheel, Cody leaned into the driver's side window.

"So," he said a little self-consciously, "You're off to somewhere, I suppose. On your mystery trip."

"We are." Estelle clicked the ignition and the car wheezed a little, coughed, then started.

"So where to?"

"Not sure where yet. The road's calling, I guess."

"You know," he said, squinting one eye, "It seems brave to just take off like you're doing."

"Either brave, or stupid."

"Guess most people are one or the other. There's no in-between." A gust of wind ruffled his brown hair, and he leaned in closer. Feeling a little embarrassed, she pretended to adjust the rearview mirror.

"Come on, Mom," Ariel called impatiently from the passenger's seat. "We going or not?"

"In a minute, honey," Estelle said, though she could tell by her tone that Ariel was beginning to wonder exactly what happened last night at the Flat Iron Tavern.

"So, anyway," Cody said, "take care. And if you're ever in the vicinity of Elmwood, Ohio, feel free to stop and say hi."

"Will do."

He stepped back from the window and a wry expression spread over his face. "The earth is flat, you know. That's what we all say around here. So be careful not to drop off the edge."

She nodded pleasantly. "I'll watch for the road signs."

CHAPTER 31

Ariel

Sideshow #66

    Sometimes I have a little fun with my journal entries. Every now and then, I need that. We all do, don't we?

    So here goes. During my spare time, I enjoy walking among or riding or pondering the following thrill rides and amusements. We have some of them at our carnival, and I've seen others at the bigger state fairs. If there is such a thing as carnival poetry (my mom says there is), then saying these names is sort of like poetry on my tongue. So, say them along with me as fast as you can:

    Ring of Fire! Fire Ball! Ducks on the Pond! Down the Clown! Amazing Maze! Mirror Maze! Tunnel of Love! Ferris Wheel! Fun Slide! The Whip! The Waltzer! Wipeout! Sphere of Fear! Sizzler! Spider! Tarantula! Monkey Mayhem! Monkey Wheel! Pleasure Wheel! Wonder Wheel! Wheel of Death! Tumble Bug! Turbo Drop! Bumper Cars! Kiddie Cars! Bumper Boats! Circus Train! Dodge-ems! Kamikaze! Loop-o-Plane! Loop the Loop! Octopus! Mini-Plane! Rock-O-Plane! Roll-o-Plane! Roll a Ball! Roller Coaster! Roller Racer! Round Up! The Pit! The Pendulum! Zipper! Monster! Gravitron! Scrambler! Screamin' Swing! Skydiver! Shoot the Chute! Sky Coaster! Sky Swatter! Sky Diver! Sky Shot! Space Shot! Super Shot! Star Flyer! Super Star! Moon Walk! Swing Around! Swing Boat! Tornado! Hurricane! Fun House! House of Horrors! House of Mirrors! Bounce House! Madhouse!

    There you have it. Feel better? I do already!

Sideshow #91

    Okay. I admit it. I have a love-hate relationship with the World's Smallest Horse. Pinkie Pie (yes, that's her name, but I don't know why) is 27 inches tall. It's a fully grown horse, more than ten years old. They keep her in an exhibit in a plywood stall. She stands there all day long, facing one of the walls. Sometimes it eats the hay from the floor of its pen. It looks like a palomino, with a blondish mane, and big brown eyes with lashes.

It should be a cute and adorable and cuddly little thing, this Pinkie Pie, the World's Smallest Horse. But she's not.

She's kinda angry, and mean. One day when I reached down to pet it, it tipped its muzzle up toward me and bit me on the hand. It really hurt. I guess I understand her anger. What would you do if you just faced a wall all day? And gawkers filed past and laughed and tried to tap you on the back? What would you do if you couldn't take a step forward or backward, or even turn around? I'd feel pretty bad if I always dreamed of galloping but couldn't.

I guess if that were me, I'd bite the hand of anybody who reached down at me.

After hours, Jumpin' Johnny, who runs the Rock-O-Plane, is in charge of Lil' Pinkie. He ties it to a rope that's knotted securely to a metal stake alongside his trailer. I guess Johnny puts up with Pinkie, and she puts up with him. Maybe, after hours, he sits next to her and tells it some jokes to calm its feisty temperament. Jokes like "Okay, little horse. What do you call a bad dream? A nightmare." (Ha ha.) Johnny told me once that she sleeps like a baby, but her legs kind of wiggle and fidget.

Sometimes I wonder why she doesn't just run away. "Because the little critter is lame," Sand once explained. "Even if you set it free," he said, "The thing can barely walk. Couldn't find its way out of a burning barn."

Sad, I know.

Sideshow #63

When it comes to the exciting carnival thrill shows, I enjoy my dad's tightrope show the most, of course.

There are a few other acts, too, that Virgil Sand has rounded up. Such as The Sphere of Fear, where a motorcycle rider does the loop-de-loop. He rides in circles at full speed inside a circular cage. This guy's name is Darwin Ashbury, and he goes by the nickname of The Fast Ass. Others call him The Psycho Cycler. Psycho will tell you his motto is "Always keep a full tank of gas. Especially if you plan on riding upside down." (yuck yuck)

Then there's Ray the Reptile Man. Sand recruits him whenever the show travels through Iowa. Reptile Ray has a skin condition, I guess. Scales, and all that. But for the show, he brushes on a coating of some washable light green paint on his arms and legs and face. Kinda pretty.

I'm also entertained by Boom Boom Bruno, The Human Cannonball. He used to get blown out of a cannon and land in a net about seventy-five feet away. I read about human cannonballs in a book. Here's what I found out: "The first Human Cannonball was launched in 1877 in London. It was a 14-year-old girl named Zazel. The world record for the longest Human Cannonball Flight is 193 feet." To that I say Wow. I'd never climb into a cannon. But I guess somebody has to do it. Boom Boom is from Czechoslovakia or Ukraine or somewhere. But he doesn't want anyone to think he's a foreigner. So he tells people he's from Wisconsin. People ask him "Where you from?" And he answers, with that wacky accent, "Yah, yah, from Mal-vaukee." Then they ask "No, I mean where are you from originally?" And he answers "Yah, yah, Mal-vaukee." Anyway, Boom Boom is not cannon-balling any more. He just unloads the trucks. People say quite a few of his brain cells are missing. They say he probably lost two billion brain cells with each cannon shot. The brain has 171 billion cells in it. (I looked it up.) So, if Boom Boom took off 100 times…well, you see what I mean. I once imagined those neurons inside his head, bouncing around, and not ending up back in the same place. Not a pretty picture.

Boom Boom also has trouble hearing. If you say something to him, he always tips his head toward the side and says "Vhat?" Once I walked right up behind him and said "How are you today, Mr. Boom Boom?" But he didn't hear a word. I guess, after lots of explosions, life has become silent to him. I feel sad for him, and don't want that to ever happen to me. And I want my brain cells to stay right where they are. And—who knows?—maybe even ask a few billion friends to join them.

Sideshow #77

Okay, here's some more stuff about the screamers. I've listened to the riders on many rides. And I've come to one conclusion. The screams coming from The Zipper are the absolute best. They're ear-piercing. They're horrifying. They're blood-curdling. Some of the screams are so high-pitched, you'd swear they were whistles. I mean, if you were a blind person, you could hear that one ride from a mile away. Yet when the ride stops, they line up for another ticket. I guess the screamers are happier than most people. They don't keep it inside. They let it all out. The screamers have the most fun on the entire planet. If you have a spare moment during your busy day, just listen.

CHAPTER 32

Tony

"Sorry," the voice said. No record of a Charlotte Devoe here." Standing inside a stuffy pay phone booth with a stack of quarters on the counter, Tony strained to hear the receptionist above the cars and Harleys roaring past on Sunset Boulevard.

A week had passed. And now another few days. Tony was getting more and more impatient. With no word from Charlotte about the foster care agency, Tony decided to do some investigating on his own. So he called the maternity ward at the hospital Charlotte had mentioned.

"So was she admitted there, or what?" he inquired.

"We have no record of her, sir."

The head nurse in San Francisco gave him the name of a social work agency. He called them, and he got the same response. The mid-morning sun beat on the phone booth, making the air inside it heat up. Tony felt the sweat rolling down his temples.

"Sorry," the word kept slamming a door in his face. "Sorry sorry sorry."

But no one was sorrier than Tony about all the dead ends. He was still determined to locate the boy. He considered driving up to San Francisco soon if he couldn't get any other leads. Maybe he could locate Charlotte's sister. Charlotte said she stayed with her when she took that Greyhound to California years ago. His ideal plan—though he knew it was becoming a less and less realistic one—was to locate the boy, take a blood test if necessary, then claim the boy as his son. If he was still in foster care, Tony would apply for adoption, and eventually bring him back to Wanley.

This past year, Ariel had told Tony repeatedly that she wished she had a brother or sister.

"Really?" Tony had replied.

"Yeah. A friend. A pal. You know—someone I could prank by drawing on their forehead with lipstick while they were asleep."

"What if you really did have a sibling?" Tony had quizzed a couple weeks ago.

"I'd be happy," she had replied. "Not just happy. More like thrilled."

* * *

The next evening, Tony stopped at Charlotte's apartment again. She said she'd be around, and he wanted to pin her down—for once—with some answers to his questions.

He heard loud stereo music playing from inside her apartment as he knocked.

She opened the door. The room smelled of thick incense, and it was easy to see that Charlotte was soaring. Tony wondered what altitude she was in. "C'mon in, stranger," she said, wide-eyed. "Want something to drink? Or perhaps to smoke?"

"No," he said. "I'm not here for that."

"Did you ever meet my snakes?" she asked.

"Don't think so," Tony replied.

"Well come over and see them." She sauntered to the terrarium and pointed to the two pythons inside. "I'll formally introduce you," she said, her voice slurring. "They're named Herald. And Schmerald. Sometimes I call them Adam and Eve. Or Yin and Yang. One's male, and one's female." Then, though nothing was all that funny, she started to laugh.

Both snakes were yellow with pale orange markings on them. Their eyes were an odd orange color that creeped Tony out. "How can you tell them apart?" he asked.

"I can't, usually." With that, she turned, stepped to a cupboard, shook a pill from a bottle, popped it in her mouth, then washed it down with a glass of bourbon.

"What are you doing?" Tony questioned.

"Well, you're here. That means the par-tay's started. So I'm toasting you. I'm celebrating. Anything wrong with that?"

"Yeah, there is," Tony said, chiding her. "And I'm not here to party."

She just gave him a flirty glance, and in a sing-song voice, said "Tony, Tony, dull little Tony, sat upon a wall. Tony Tony, boring Tony, had a great fall." Pleased at her parody of Humpty Dumpty, she burst out with a cackling laugh. "All the king's horses, and…all the king's horses…" She faltered. "What's the rest of it?"

"Damn it, Charlotte," he said, disgusted. "Why do you have to get high all the time?"

"Because I want to," she blurted. Her face went blank, her features drooping like wax melting. "Because sometimes I just frickin' want to."

"Jeez, Char. What's with you, anyway?"

"Nothing's with me." Her back straightened and she seemed to sober up. By now, Tony had noticed that one moment, she was stoned and crazy and outrageous, the next moment, subdued and contemplative. He didn't know which Charlotte he'd be talking to next. "I mean, everything's with me," she smirked. "And, hey, Tony. No fair asking hard questions. I wanna pass my ACT test, you know."

She wandered across the room to the stereo. After scratching the stereo needle across the record once, she plopped the needle on an album, and "Nobody but Me" thrummed through the speakers. She began to sway back and forth, eyes closed. "C'mon," she called. "It's dance time!" When Tony declined, she sashayed over and took a slug from the bottle of bourbon on the dining room table where an array of red pills were scattered across the oak tabletop. She gyrated up to him. "Let's rock out, dammit!" she demanded. Both hands raised in the air, she moved with an awkward motion, like someone trying to get out from under a net.

Tony didn't move.

Holding the bottle by the neck in one hand, she flipped on the strobe lights that she had installed in the corner, and, illuminated by the bursts of bright light, her body moved in a jerky motion. "Don't you love it?" she called, raising her voice over the music. "I mean, when you dance in strobe lights, it sorta looks like you're moving, but not moving at the same time. So cool!"

"Enough, Charlotte," Tony said, grabbing the bottle from her. He felt odd saying it, as though he was disciplining some out-of-control junior high student. "You've out of it. You're drunk and you're stoned already. And it's only nine at night. You need to knock it off."

"No," she said blearily. "No, officer Tony. I am not out of it. I am not out of anything. I just need one more." She scooped up a pill. "Gotta reach my daily quota," she chuckled.

"Listen to me," Tony said. "Just sit down a minute."

Pouting, she plopped onto the couch, and he lowered himself next to her. "I can't stay in town much longer," he explained. "I'm planning to stop at that foster care agency."

"Fos-ter ca-re a-gen-cy?" She elongated the words slowly like she was pronouncing a foreign term.

"Yeah. And what about your sister in San Fran?" Tony lowered himself to the couch.

"Maybe she knows more. Maybe I should talk to her, too. You have her number?"

Charlotte's back straightened and she seemed to rise to the surface of herself and become a little more lucid. "My sister and I, we don't talk anymore. So don't bother. She's some kind of accountant or something. But I lost her number."

"I called the hospital in San Fran," Tony said, hoping to finally pin her down. "Nobody could find a record of you being there. I couldn't locate a birth certificate at the courthouse, either."

"Oh." She exhaled the word like someone just sat on her stomach. "Oh." Charlotte fidgeted with her macrame necklace, strung with beads and shells.

"So, what's up? Did you use a different name, or what?"

"Or what…" she replied. She twisted her lips a moment. "Nobody's who they seem," she finally said. "That's life. Everybody's somebody else. Aren't they?"

"I don't know," he replied, "Are they?"

Her mood quickly shifted again. "Wow, Tone," she exclaimed. "You seem sorta wound up. Maybe you need a beer." She stood. "I'll get you one. And a fancy glass, even." She walked to a kitchen cabinet and opened it. When she reached in, she bumped a container and an array of pills spilled from bottles and onto the floor. "Shit, shit, shit!" she exclaimed, as they skittered across the linoleum and she tried to gather them up.

"What the hell's all that?" Tony asked, walking closer.

"Um it's my little collection," she said, trying to laugh as she pushed Tony away and quickly shut the cabinet door. A baggie of white powder got wedged at the base of one door, and she opened it again and pushed the bag back in. "My happy cabinet."

"You can't possibly be taking this much shit. Are you dealing, or what?" Tony demanded.

She cocked her head to one side. "Well, Tony. You think I make a living off a couple of goddamn snakes on a pier?"

"Char, you've got to find a way to quit all this," he said, confronting her.

She crossed the room and sat down hard on the couch. She nodded, and a distant look came over her face. "I know, I know," she said, closing her eyes. She opened them and focused on a slightly-slanted poster of Malibu Beach surfers taped to the wall. "I'd quit. But guess I'm kinda having too much fun. With Buzz, and the rest, I mean." She looked up at him helplessly. "But there's times I wish somebody could sort of…I don't know, show me a way out. I mean, like you, maybe. You seem so damn stable and all that."

Tony shook his head. "I can't save you, Charlotte. You'll just have to figure out a way to save yourself."

She closed her eyes and tipped her head back, denting the cushion. Then her mood shifted, and she seemed suddenly high again. "Wow, Tony," she blurted. "This is all getting way too serious." She let out a giddy laugh. "It's like a very serious melodrama. Like we're in The Guiding Light or some damn thing."

She jumped up suddenly, made her way over to her aquarium, and bent close to the water. At the bottom of the tank was a toy treasure chest brimming with fake jewels. She picked up a small net, scooped up an orange and beige striped lionfish, and held it above the water. "Hey, Tone," she exclaimed as the fish floundered in the net, its poisonous spines raised. "I've got a little question for you. Does this fish know it's a tropical fish? Or does it think it's a carp or a whale, or maybe a shark or something? I mean, for cripe's sake, how does it *know?*"

CHAPTER 33

The next evening, Tony dialed the number and waited for an answer as he stood in the stale air of a phone booth on Hollywood Boulevard. He had finally located Charlotte's sister, Donna Devoe, in the San Francisco phone directory. Talking to her was a last resort. He'd exhausted all the calls to foster care agencies and only reached dead ends. The phone rang once, twice, three times.

Outside the booth, tourists strolled by on the Walk of Fame, reading the names of the dead Hollywood stars—Marilyn Monroe, Humphrey Bogart, Clark Gable, Vivian Leigh—and gawking at their handprints, frozen in the cement. A few yards away, in front of the Snow White Café and Bar, a street performer—dressed as Elvis—was muddling through a bad version of "Heartbreak Hotel."

"Hullo?" a voice finally answered.

Tony introduced himself and told her he was calling about Charlotte.

"Char in trouble again?" she asked curtly.

"Um, no…"

"You a debt collector, then?"

"Not that, either." Tony proceeded to introduce himself, then said "Charlotte was pregnant thirteen years ago. And I'm…" he paused, then continued. "I'm the father."

"Oh," she said dryly. "So you're the famous Tony."

"I know it's been a lot of years. But Charlotte told me she stayed here with you."

"Right," she said. "Yeah. She showed up here. For a few days, then just took off." A few seconds passed. "You know, we're not in touch anymore."

"I understand that."

"I mean," she continued. "Char's gone off the deep end. Had to bail her out of jail a couple times. But I'm done with all that. So why are you calling?"

"I need to know if you have any details. About where the kid ended up."

"The kid?" she blurted.

"Yeah. Our baby."

There was a long silence, and finally, she said "I think somebody misled you."

"Huh?"

"There was no baby."

"What do you mean?"

"Char...she didn't have the baby. She had a miscarriage."

The words hit Tony hard. It felt like all the air was suddenly pulled out of the phone booth, and Tony heard himself gasp.

Outside, more tourists strolled by. One small kid bent down, laughing, and placed his hands on Mickey Rooney's handprints in the concrete. "Look!" he exclaimed to his amused parents. "His hands are exactly the size of mine."

* * *

Upset, Tony could barely focus as he threw his belongings into his suitcase and hastily checked out of The Sunset Beach Motel. He tossed his suitcase and a Coleman cooler into the flatbed of his pickup.

When Tony opened the door of Charlotte's apartment, his face was slapped by a cloud of smoke and the strong scent of hashish. Loud psychedelic music filled the room. Tony noticed a bottle of pills and some Zig-Zag papers on the dining room table, and he could tell by Charlotte's expression that she was high again.

She jumped from the couch and ran up to him. "You're taking me to Buzz's, right?" she asked, her voice like a gleeful child. "I need a lift." As usual, Charlotte's face was coated with too much makeup. Hot pink lips, smudged black mascara, dark blue eye shadow.

"No," Tony said. "No Buzzy's. No rides."

Charlotte couldn't help but notice the angry expression on Tony's face. "What's up?" she quizzed.

"Why didn't you tell me?" he demanded.

"Tell you? Tell you what?" she asked, her bloodshot eyes widening.

"That you never had that baby. That you had a miscarriage."

A blank look slid across her face like a wave sweeping across sand. She backed away and bumped into the table. Grabbing a bottle of bourbon from it, she tipped it to her lips, took a few gulps, then let out a cough as it burned in her throat. Her hand shaking, she lowered it to the table again. "No baby," she finally managed, her shoulders shuddering with a slight sob. "You're right. You're right right right. It got washed away. So now you know."

Tony just glared at her.

She bowed her head, her hair falling in front of her face. "It was a tough time. You were nowhere around."

"You…you told me you had the baby. All those phony stories about adoption. You were just playing me. You were just…" Tony wanted to say more but could barely find the words.

Charlotte went silent. Her eyes looked sunken and dark, like deep wells without water, her hot pink lips—neither smiling nor frowning—were smeared. As the song on the turntable ended, a hissing sound slid through the big wooden speakers. "I know," she finally said. "I'm a liar. Just a goddamn liar." She tipped her face toward the ceiling, closed her eyes, and her thick fake eyelashes twitched. "Guess it's just, you know, my way." She stared at the floor a few seconds, then stepped over and flipped on the strobe lights. She teetered up to him on high heels as if she'd just stepped off a dizzying elevator ride. "But Tony," she said, intensely, "That's all over. It's in the past. We've got now, don't we?" She tipped her head toward him. "We can always…you know, make everything right again."

"You're crazy." He started to back away.

"Maybe I am," she claimed with a half-smile. Stepping closer, her voice grew softer. "Frickin' crazy." She gave him a half-lidded, sensuous stare. Her eyelids were big, and purple, like bruises. "Still a little crazy. About you, maybe."

Tony flinched.

"I mean, I've had lovers, and all that, she continued. "But never never never anybody like Tony Desdiolo." The flashing lights made her lips look like they were moving and not moving. "It's just you and me now, right? No damn baby. Nothing to pull us apart this time." She tipped her head to one side with a coy, teasing expression, put her hands gently on his shoulders, and leaned close to him.

When he pulled back, she grabbed him by the wrists.

"Tony, please," she pleaded. "You can at least kiss me. You haven't even goddamn kissed me since you got here!" As her fingernails dug into his skin, he felt as though her swirling blue ink tattoos were crawling off her arms and transferring onto him. "It's us two again. I wanna go back.

I wanna start over." She pressed her body against his and puckered her lips, desperately trying to kiss him.

"Get away from me," he said, turning toward the door.

"Come on," she begged. "Come on, Tony." She grabbed his shoulders from behind. "Where you going?"

He whirled around and faced her. "Where the hell are *you* going?" he shouted angrily. "Isn't it time you figured it out, Charlotte?" He strode to the table, and with one quick motion of his arm, swept the papers and pills off it. He slapped the bottle of bourbon. It cartwheeled to the green shag carpeting, the amber liquid glugging out of it in low-pitched gulps.

He stepped out the door, slamming it behind him. The door bumped against the frame and bounced back open. "Damn!" he shouted. He slammed it again. "God damn!" He wasn't just swearing at a door, he was swearing at everything—Charlotte and the lost baby and the Malibu parties and the strobe lights and the dope. But more than anything, he was swearing at himself, for leaving his wife and daughter and coming all the way out here in the first place, all because of a lie.

* * *

In the parking lot, Tony sat in his truck, head tipped back against the head rest, his eyes pinched shut. He felt himself tumbling through the gray air of confusing emotions: anger, frustration, loss, and the humiliation of being used.

Opening his eyes, he saw Charlotte, standing in the back window of her second-floor apartment and gazing down at his truck. Strobe lights fluttered around her for a few seconds until she reached up, pulled the shade, and the window went dark.

Tony clicked the ignition and the dashboard lit up with an orange glow. His truck lurched backward out of the parking stall, loose stones stuttering under the tires, then sped forward.

The next thing he knew, he was following the crumbling cinders of the alley toward a vacant asphalt street. The streetlights looked dim, surrounded by halos of fog. He let that street pull him toward the gray-and-neon buildings of Hollywood Boulevard. He passed a maze of intersecting avenues. Passed nameless taverns squeezed between brick buildings, passed the Roosevelt Hotel where Marilyn Monroe once lived in a penthouse room, passed a stretch of sidewalk littered with early-evening drunks and hookers and bums, all of them like one-dimensional shadows.

Finally, he felt his truck rising onto the slight incline of an entrance ramp.

He was on Route 66 again, heading east this time. The Mother Road. He'd been on this route before, of course; he knew every curve and rise and fall of the pavement. And, the road seemed to know him, too, and though he was different now, it pulled him forward as if it was an old friend, welcoming him back.

CHAPTER 34

Ariel

Questions. They always filled her head.

Was the earth really round, like everyone said? Ariel often imagined it as sort of oblong, and hollow. At least that's the way it felt to her, sometimes as she lay in her bed before sleep.

Tonight was a night like that. Her head buoyed up by her pillow, Ariel pictured herself walking across the carnival lot at night. She missed that place, now that she and Estelle were on the road, stopping at night to park their trailer in seedy KOA campgrounds. Back at the carnival, she knew where each ride and game and food stand was positioned, and who ran them. She knew which games—like the Skee-Ball bowling game—she could slip into through the unlocked back door, and which carny kids lived in which trailer, so to her, the whole place was an odd but familiar playground. When everything was shut down, and her mom thought she was over at one of her friend's trailers for an extra hour, she'd stroll the boarded-up midway at night. It had been her only time to think. She'd stare at the darkened silhouettes of the rides—The Sizzler, with its small cages in which the riders spun themselves dizzy. Fast Eddie had let her ride it a couple times for free. "Hope you come back alive, kid," he joked as he lowered the silver bar to her skinny waist—so she wouldn't fall out when it was upside down. Then he clamped the bar into place with a dull silver cotter pin. It was a strange feeling when the ride picked up full speed, your little cage circling high in the air. Your body was light one minute, then heavy the next. You lost all sense of direction when you were up there. You lost your sense of up and down. Which was okay with her, at least for a few minutes.

She recalled that night she had woken from sleep and noticed Tony, sitting on the step of the trailer, his head in his hands. She sat down next to him and asked, "What are you doing, Daddy?" Earlier, she couldn't help but hear her parents arguing.

"Thinking," he'd replied, putting her off. "Just sort of thinking." Tony was always sort of uncomfortable and awkward when he talked to her alone.

"About what?"

"Dunno. About the moon." He tipped his head back and peered at the clear night sky that was spattered with stars. "It seems to shine. People say that, and write songs about it, and all that. But it's not really shining."

"No?"

"No. It's just a dry landscape. There's no life on it. But the sun reflects off it, so it always looks bright."

"But that's still kind of a good thing, right?" Ariel offered.

"Yeah, I guess," he replied. "If you don't have your own light, you can at least look like you do."

* * *

During their search for Tony, her head began to fill with questions that fluttered frantically. Why do people say "I do" at the altar and then, later break up? What goes through their minds? They make a baby, like her, who grows into a kid. They have a lot between them, don't they? Then what happens? Do they stop feeling it? Or are there other reasons? Maybe, she decided, they just lose their sense of up and down.

She hated it, those first few days after Tony left, when she'd wander out of her bedroom at night to get a glass of milk and discover her mom, still sitting in front of the TV. She noticed tears glimmering on her mom's cheeks.

"You watching a sad show?" Ariel asked her.

Her mom nodded, dabbing her eyes with a Kleenex.

When Ariel walked closer to the TV, she realized it was just a rerun of *Laugh-In*.

"That's sad?" she quizzed, pointing at the screen.

Her mom didn't say anything at first, then finally explained, "Yes. Sometimes funny things can be sad."

A couple of weeks ago, that morning he found out it was missing, Virgil Sand gave the third degree to the newly hired carnies regarding the whereabouts of his famous Bird Child. "Dammit all! "Who the hell broke in there?" Sand shouted as Ariel, standing behind a ticket booth, overheard. She smiled smugly. No one had any answers, of course. Before he stomped off, Sand added "I'm giving a hundred bucks reward to anybody who finds the thing. You hear me? A hundred bucks!" Ariel couldn't help but imagine Sand's hand-lettered poster for it, with a poorly-drawn image of The Bird Child, tacked to dozens of telephone poles:

> Wanted, Dead or Alive!
> THE BIRD CHILD.
> $100 REWARD!

If Sand had cornered her with an interrogation, Ariel would have replied flippantly, saying something like "Mister Sand, maybe the Bird Child was abducted by aliens. Maybe it's being held for ransom." Or "Maybe it decided to roll its jar all the way to Florida and take a vacation," to which Sand would snarl, "Shaddap, ya damn little smart ass."

But Sand didn't even bother to question her. He always hassled her Mom, but he never suspected Ariel, the frail girl with the short left leg. She was the girl who wondered if any boy would ever like her, the way she limped like a klutz. The girl who would be a bad dancer. The little girl who kept waiting for it to happen—to be attractive and tall and nicely rounded on her hips and chest—but who never seemed to grow up.

Still, she knew that eventually—in five years or so, which sounded like a century—she would arrive there, and step onto that lush and fascinating island called adolescence. She dreamed about it: She could get her learner's permit and drive a car. She'd have a new purse with spangles on it, a collection of lacey bras, maybe a handsome boyfriend, some rose-colored eye makeup, and her own record player with a bunch of 45s on the spindle. She'd use her allowance money to buy records by The Lovin' Spoonful and Herman's Hermits and The Beatles and even The Rolling Stones, who her mom said were a little raunchy. She and the boy—who would wear a navy-blue sweater vest and white Levi's and penny loafers—would sway in a slow dance to Percy Sledge's "When A Man Loves a Woman" in the parlor room of his parents' luxurious house, the chandelier lights turned low by a dimmer switch. Just dreams, she knew. Lately, she wondered if they would ever really happen.

As Ariel stared into the darkness of her bedroom, she pictured The Bird Child, lying there beneath the soil. She imagined it, tunneling deeper into the earth, like some strange, secret mole. Down there, it would burrow for answers to the things it kept asking over and over. Like where it really came from, and who created it. Did it have parents—a mother and a father? Was it a fake, or was it once alive and real, with red blood pulsing through its arteries? Maybe it just wanted to know—no matter how small and insignificant it was—its purpose in life. Maybe it just wanted to know love.

When she was tossing and turning like this, she'd ask Estelle to rub her shoulders to help her fall back to sleep. *Switch off your brain and sail into your dreams*, her mom always advised.

But she couldn't sail into those dreams. Not tonight. She couldn't stop thinking about The Bird Child. Couldn't stop thinking that maybe it just wanted to know the real truth—as Ariel did—about all those simple but ever-so-illusive questions.

PART THREE

CHAPTER 35

Tony

As he drove, Tony felt like a small knot in the middle of an endlessly long string.

He couldn't get over the sensation that the landscape was moving past, and he was standing perfectly still, sitting motionless in his truck with four flat tires while his dreams glided slowly, steadily past the windows and away from him.

A couple of hundred miles from LA, the mid-morning sun heated the desert to nearly 100 degrees, and the air inside the cab was sweltering. The road ahead of Tony began to waver, the asphalt transforming into a rectangular pool of water. He drove toward distant water that, the closer he got to it, always kept pulling away. There was no cool water out there, he knew. The highway was indifferent, disguising itself with dust and scraping tumbleweed.

The images from his final days on the coast haunted him, flipping through his brain like a deck of cards being shuffled and reshuffled: Charlotte holding out a handful of reds. Buzzy's chaotic underworld parties where no one was sober. The chrome bow of Buzzy's yacht speeding toward him through the ocean. Charlotte, mouthing apologies like a guppy against the glass of a fish tank. The wasted couple having sex on the beach, the woman whispering "No. Yes. No." The terrarium with the two albino boas coiling as if they were trying to crush the air out of each other. The snakes and the parties and the LOVE tattoo on Charlotte's forearm—he wanted to wipe all of it from his memory the way you'd erase chalk from a blackboard. But though he tried, the images remained, like faint and ghostly marks where you'd pressed too hard on the slate.

He thought about Buzzy and his crew—losers without direction who could spend hours, tripping out, mesmerized by the motions of their own hands.

And Charlotte was a lie. A sad lie. A phony actress sliding in and out of a role. She lied to Tony, to her so-called friends, to herself. She was a woman pretending to be suave and hip on the Santa Monica pier and luring tourists toward her so she could catch some stray dollars and support a habit.

Washed away, she said last night when she finally admitted the truth to Tony. In Tony's mind, those words made the image of the child's face dissolve steadily, like a lozenge. And this morning, as he stood by his truck at a wayside, he felt as though he was standing at the bottom of a deep, dry well, and the rest of the world was up there, a tiny circle of light cut into the darkness.

Now Tony glanced down at the bottle of Jack, its amber liquid sloshing from side to side like some graceful performer swaying her hips. Steadying the steering wheel with one hand, he reached down, picked it up, took a swallow. Anything to pull himself up from the depths, the gloom that seemed to fill him.

A road sign caught his attention. Needles 38. Needles puncturing my brain, too, he thought. To get his mind off everything, he forced himself to focus on the desert.

Out here, away from the steel and concrete of the city, he thought, everything seemed more real. And ancient. No more plastic, no four-lane freeways, no more luring billboards lit by blinking lights. Instead, layers of rock on rock, centuries. Mint-green sage brush tumbling across the lanes. On this side of Needles, the Mojave spread itself in front of the highway like some faded pink and gray watercolor. He passed the wooden frames of Native American stands, where the Navajo locals sold turquoise bracelets and woven blankets and feathered dream catchers dangling from leather strands. He passed Devil Dog Road. Saw signs for Bullhead City and Ash Fork. Towns he couldn't see out there, lost in the hazy heat. This was the low desert, the elevation not much more than five-hundred feet above sea level.

At a station a half-hour from nowhere, he stopped for a soda with caffeine—to ease his headache—and a tank of gas. The concrete block place promised, on the warped tin sign, Ice Cold Coke and Clean Restrooms. Neither one was true. The Coke, clunking out of a stout red vending machine, was lukewarm and the oval bathroom sink was the grimy gray color of a spare tire, like the ones piled high on the side of the building. The station had one pump, and, inside, a rack of faded black and white postcards which pictured none other than the gas station itself, with its big sign that proclaimed, in silver letters, Corky's Gas and Tire.

Corky, the owner, an older man, wore overalls, sported a longish gray beard, and looked like a miner right out of the 1840s gold rush.

"How's it going?" Tony said, greeting the man.

"Puttin' on miles," Corky replied.

Tony lifted the gas pump and began filling his truck. In the small, rectangular eyes of the pump, numbers spun like a slot machine.

"So where you headed?" Corky asked.

"Back where I used to be," Tony replied.

Corky let out a guttural laugh. "Don't we all wanna go back there."

Tony replaced the gas pump, checked the total.

"Well, I sure as hell hope you get there, son," Corky added, wiping the sweat from his forehead with a once-white T-shirt. His saggy eyes slid toward Tony's Chevvy, dully reflecting the sun. "But I'd recommend checking the oil and radiator in that ol' truck of yours first."

"I suppose I should."

"Yessir," Corky continued, chewing on a toothpick so the tip rotated in a circle. "Might need some coolant, if you plan to head across that desert. Things boil over, you know."

"Yeah," echoed Tony. "Things boil over."

Tony checked the antifreeze in the truck, and sure enough, it was low, so he bought a gallon of Prestone, poured half of the green liquid in, and set the bottle on the floor of the passenger side.

On his way to the restroom, Tony spotted something leaning against a shed beside the station. It looked like a large kite made of stretched nylon fabric and wood. "What's that by the shed?"

"That there's a hang glider," Corky replied. "New sport around here, I guess. And over at Big Sur, too I hear. A young fellow passing through one time dropped it off. Said he had to move some furniture in his truck and didn't have no more room. Said he'd come back through to pick it up, but he never did. Was gettin' married, and all, I guess."

"Ever try it?"

"Me? Hell no." He chortled. "I'm not about to jump off no cliff. Unless one of my ex-wives is chasing me, that is."

"Want to sell that outfit?" Tony asked, surprising himself.

"Sell? Why not." Corky's beard twitched, and then he said, "A new hang glider costs a couple hundred, somebody once told me. But if you got fifty bucks, it's yours."

Tony walked to the glider and checked the blue and red nylon material, which looked new. The wood braces were in fine shape, and so was the harness. Probably never been used, Tony surmised. Tucked inside the harness was a booklet of instructions on how to use it. A couple of months ago, Tony had talked to a buddy of his who told him how great it was when he flew one over the cliffs by Monterrey.

"Sold," Tony said. "If you'll take forty."

Corky's forehead wrinkled, dry cracks in an empty watering hole. "I s'pose. That thing don't do me no good just sittin' against a shed."

Tony paid the man and loaded the glider into the back of his truck.

"Plan to do some flying, do you?" Corky inquired.

"I don't know. It's just an impulse buy."

"You some kind of chance-taker, then?"

"I guess."

"Well then, have yourself a blast. But don't try to fly too near the sun." A chuckle rasped out from him.

"Don't worry."

"And," Corky added, "watch out for flyin' saucers when you're up in the sky. One crashed over in Roswell, you know. Strange things happen out here in the desert." He tipped his head back and guffawed.

The man's humor—and the idea of distracting himself by trying out a hang glider—lightened Tony's mood a little, and he felt himself almost smile. "I'll keep an eye out."

But back on the road, the dark cloud of despondency filled the cab of the truck again. He tried to focus on the lines ahead of him on the road and couldn't help but think of snakes cut into short white segments.

He approached a brown sign for the Kaibab National Forest and noticed green pine trees popping up on hills that began to lift their shoulders a little higher with each mile. Deer might step lightly up there, he imagined. Mountain lions might crouch beneath sage, waiting for their prey. Somewhere, unseen, a rattler was shedding its skin. A condor swooped low, then rose again. Everything changing, he thought, or going somewhere. But where was he going?

Miles later, a sign rushed toward him: Flagstaff 15. There, he'd find running water, hardware stores. Stoplights at intersections. Civilization. Nothing ancient there. He'd stopped in that town on his way to California, and now he pictured, along Railroad Avenue, the beer flowing from taps in the small bars with names like The Watering Hole and Bud's Bar and

Trail's End Saloon. Places that would, he hoped, help him feel less lost. The Santa Fe train, its rusty cars coupled, would rumble past every hour or so, rattling the windows of the buildings along Phoenix Avenue. Its blaring horn would drown out the sound of jukebox woofers and tweeters pumping out Hank Williams, or Tammy Wynette whining "Stand by your man."

A half-hour later, Tony lowered himself onto the red vinyl stool of the Elbow Room Pool Hall and Cocktail Lounge. He avoided glancing at his reflection in the wall mirror behind the ornate Victorian wood bar.

"So, whereabouts you from?" the bored, portly bartender asked him, sliding another sweating blue and silver can of Hamm's toward Tony like he was playing shuffleboard.

"Here," Tony replied, so that—with his stained white T-shirt and worn jeans—he didn't seem like such an aimless drifter, "Now."

CHAPTER 36

When they arrived at the town of Defiance, Ohio, the banner above the town proclaimed: WHERE THE PAST MEETS THE FUTURE.

"So," Ariel asked, "Is every little town required to have a corny motto, or what?"

"I guess."

"So, when does the past meet the future, Mom?" Ariel asked as they passed beneath the rippling banner.

Estelle's fingers fidgeted as she held the steering wheel, and she didn't reply.

"Okay, then," Ariel said, pursuing the issue, "When does the present meet the future?"

Estelle tipped back against the headrest. "If I knew the answers, I'd tell you." For the next few seconds, she tried to envision her future. She often hoped it was a straight line—or at least a meandering line that led to happiness. Not just circles and more circles. Sometimes she pictured it as a brilliant place, like a wave of sunlight in a meadow. But lately, when she tried to envision it, all she saw was a vapor, a fog, maybe, with no identifiable shapes in it.

"Mom, I've been wondering," Ariel said, leaning against the headrest. "When I get to be about fifteen, will I be a woman or a girl?"

"Which would you rather be?"

"Don't know. Do I have to decide?"

"No. Not right now."

"Well then, good."

Estelle studied her daughter. Ariel was thin and girlish now, but Estelle knew she'd be growing up soon. Too soon. And that thought scared Estelle—and Ariel, too, she knew. Sometimes Estelle walked in with groceries to see Ariel standing in the cramped pink vinyl-walled bathroom of their trailer after a shower, wearing a white terrycloth robe. She'd be leaning close to the foggy mirror, squinting at herself as if she was trying to discover some clues about what was next for her.

* * *

At the local fairgrounds, Estelle pulled out a picture of Tony on the wire and quizzed the carnival owner.

"Wish we had a feller like that," the owner mused as he filled a bin for caramel apples. "Looks like a pretty good act."

Among the rides, a gaunt carny, wearing a faded blue tank top with oil-stain hieroglyphs exhaled "Nope" with a puff of smoke from his cigarette. He pulled the rusty lever on the Space Cars, a paint-chipped miniature rocket ship ride. The cars jerked to a start, then trundled in a circle as he asked. "So why do ya want to find him, anyways?"

Estelle just turned away. It seemed like the more times she showed Tony's slightly-creased black and white photograph, the heavier and heavier it was beginning to feel in her hand.

Later, at dusk, Estelle and Ariel decided to leave the campground and take a stroll through the neighborhoods of the town. Ariel stopped to look at a girl's rusted minibike, fastened to a lawn by weeds that curled over the handlebars.

In front of one house, they passed a sofa with a ripped cushion sitting next to the curb.

A block further, a mattress—with no sign attached—was propped against a tree.

"Why are people leaving things by the curb?" Ariel asked.

"They're abandoning them, I guess."

"Yeah, but why?"

"Guess they don't want them anymore. So they just drop them off by the curb and hope somebody will pick them up."

"Think someone will?"

Estelle just let a Who knows? expression to slide across her face.

They turned the corner onto a main street that seemed oddly empty, for a town this size. No cars crawling past, no townspeople in sight. A parked car's broken window was replaced by a layer of gray duct tape. Worn trolley tracks embedded themselves in the tarred street that led to a town square with a granite horse trough and a Civil War statue someone had pelted with a bottle of ink. A dark blue stain spread across the soldier's chest. Singling them out as outsiders, a gray 1860s cannon, its mouth open, seemed to aim at them as they walked past.

They finally reached the business district and stopped in front of Ned's Soda. Estelle peered through the tall front window, past the iridescent husks of dried flies clustered on the sill. Inside, just the empty counter with a row of red vinyl stools. Behind the counter, a pyramid of parfait and malt glasses stacked themselves in front of a beveled mirror. One middle-aged soda jerk standing there, holding a glass up to the light. Two teenagers—a scraggy-haired boy and a girl with bleached blonde hair—stood at a pinball machine. As she played, the boy stood behind the girl, his hands propped on her shoulders.

The *ping* and *bleep* and *click* of the machine echoed through the screen door and into the empty street. Feeling a sort of odd welcoming quality of the place, Estelle felt the sudden urge to walk in. As they did, the two teens turned and stared at them.

"Whatdayahave?" the soda jerk asked, collapsing all four words into one as Estelle and Ariel sat down at the counter. He was tall, in his fifties, and above his broad balding head, which was spawning a few wrinkles, was a rectangular white paper cap.

"A strawberry phosphate, please," Estelle said.

His head swiveled to Ariel. "And you?"

"I'll have what my mom has."

"Anything else?" he asked, seeming a little perturbed about their minimal order.

"That's it for now," Estelle said.

"Last of the big spenders, eh?" The man said, then he poured the drinks and slid them onto the Formica counter. Ariel took some big gulps of her phosphate, finishing half of it in seconds like she was dying of thirst.

"So," the man pried, eyeing Estelle's dangling bracelets, peasant blouse, and long red and orange skirt. "You with the carnival in town?"

"Sort of," Ariel answered.

"No, not really," Estelle corrected her. She knew the treatment people sometimes got if they admitted they were carnies. "We're just traveling through."

"Yeah," he scoffed. "Same goes for most people. They all keep going. Davenport. Or Chicago or somewhere. Nobody stays."

"We'll stay here a while, though," Ariel offered pleasantly, pointing at the countertop.

"Well ain't you cute," the man said. "You deserve a free refill." He poured more soda from the spout into her glass, the pink bubbles fizzing on the surface.

"Aw, shit," the teen girl hissed as the silver ball clunked past the flippers. "Gol damn shit!"

"Watch the language there, will ya?" the man called. "We got a kid in here."

As Estelle drank her phosphate, she couldn't help but feel the loneliness of the place close in on her. She couldn't get over it; it felt thick, almost oppressive. The click of flippers and the bing bing bing sound of the pinball machine didn't seem to help. All it did was echo off the high tin ceiling and the bare plaster walls of the place. As the man turned and hunched over a bin, rinsing a couple of parfait glasses, she began to feel like she was caught in that Edward Hopper Nighthawks painting she'd once seen on TV.

So she stood and wandered over to a jukebox in the back corner of the room. Hoping that a little music would fill the emptiness, she dropped in a quarter in and played three songs. She pressed T2, which was Gene Pitney's "Town Without Pity." It was a song she and Tony slow danced to five years ago, back in '63, when they went on an evening date at a small supper club.

As the song played through the frayed cloth speakers, the lyrics poured over her like syrup and she closed her eyes. She began to sway left and right to the music on the bare wood floor. Then she did a slow pirouette. The two teens turned from their game and gawked at her. The girl elbowed the boy and snickered.

"Mom!" Ariel chided with a hoarse whisper. "What are you doing?"

"Oh," Estelle replied, a little startled, opening her eyes.

"Geeze Mom," Ariel exclaimed. "Geeze!"

*   *   *

They walked back toward the campground in silence. Estelle tipped her head toward the sky. The curved dome was opaque, with no visible planets or stars. "Sorry if I embarrassed you back there," Estelle finally said. "I was just remembering...,"

"You were dancing," Ariel said under her breath. "But with yourself."

"Not myself. With Tony. I really miss him."

"Oh."

"Oh is all you can say?" She crouched down in front of Ariel. "Lately I've been telling you how I feel about him. But how do you feel about him? You never really say."

"How do you think I feel?" Ariel responded, her voice suddenly gruff, like it was rubbed with sandpaper. "I want him back. Back at the kitchen table with us. I want him sitting on the couch and watching *Laugh-In* at night. And so do you."

"But what…," Estelle said softly, "what we can't find him?" Though she hated to think of that possibility, she asked: "Or what if he doesn't want to come back?"

Ariel didn't say anything at first. "He does. He definitely does. He just doesn't know it."

Estelle hoped Ariel was right.

Back in the trailer, beneath the lamp, Estelle unfolded the U.S. map like an accordion and lowered it to the rickety coffee table. It was a map she had studied a dozen times since they left. She pointed to a spot. "See this state?"

"Yeah," Ariel replied. "Ohio. You can say it forwards and backward, and it sounds almost the same. O-I-ho."

"See this black dot?" Estelle continued. "That's us."

"My, we're tiny, aren't we?"

Estelle traced her finger along the thin county highway that led to another town. "We could get here by tomorrow. And if we're lucky, there should be a carnival at the fairgrounds. Old Whiskers told me about their schedule."

"And if we're not lucky?" Ariel questioned. "Then what?"

Estelle folded the map in half, in half again, as if it would make their journey shorter. When she slid it into the back pocket of her bell bottoms, it still felt thick and bulky. "Let's just plan on a little luck, okay?"

CHAPTER 37

In the evening, Tony stopped at a small wayside park off Highway 66 and locked both doors. He was fatigued, and the place seemed remote, and a good place to rest for a few hours.

He lay down on the bench seat of the truck and noticed Venus, rising in the sky, shimmering up there like a fleck of fool's gold, floating in a dark pond. It seemed so close, and touchable, almost, and still so far away.

The next thing he knew he was curled in a dark, warm place, and he thought he felt someone's arms, tightly clasped around his chest.

At the far end of the long, narrow tunnel in which they huddled, there was a circular opening. Outside that opening, all Tony could see was the color beige. He could hear the faint sound of frenetic music played by a small band. Trumpets blaring. A snare drum. A high-pitched clarinet, undercut by the low bass of a tuba. The music sped up faster and faster. "If we don't make it," a familiar voice whispered, "Just know I've always cared about you." He knew, then, that it was Estelle.

"What do you mean, if we don't make it?" he wanted to ask, but no words slid out. He couldn't exhale the words because she was embracing him so hard it squeezed his breath away.

Then he was aware of a countdown, of a chorus of voices chanting: Five, four, three, two, one. A brief silence. A drum roll seemed to last forever, and suddenly the word "Fire!" echoed.

With a sharp explosion and a blinding flash, they were jettisoned through the tunnel. Tony felt a tremendous force as they were propelled upward. Estelle held him even tighter until he thought his ribs would crack.

Once they reached the opening, everything moved in slow motion. They slid through a cloud of smoke. On the other side of that cloud, he realized he was flying through the air somewhere beneath a canvas sky, a sky held up by ropes and tall, segmented posts. As they flew, Estelle released her grip and pushed away from him. Next to him, she stretched like a diver in her sequined tights, her legs extended beautifully, heels together, arms pointed skyward, hands clasped as if in prayer. So he did likewise. They rode the air together like two skydivers in freefall. High in the air, Tony felt exhilarated, flying in complete unison with her.

The freefall ended when a knotted rope net lifted itself toward them as if they were two Luna moths about to be captured mid-flight. The net stopped them with a *shushhh* sound. It knocked the wind out of Tony. He felt the harsh rope burns on his elbows and knees, even through his tights.

"Alright," Estelle said to him, and she held out her hand. "Let's take our bow."

He wasn't sure what she meant, but he grasped her hand. He heard the cheering crowd in the bleachers and took a slow bow, following Estelle's lead as the ringmaster proclaimed in a triumphant voice: "Ladies and Gentlemen, the Flying Desdiolos! The breathtaking husband and wife team, shot from a cannon!" Tony squinted into the blinding spotlight, its bright beam hazy from the smoke.

The spotlight was so bright it made Tony blink his eyes. When he opened them again, he realized he was lying on the front seat of his pickup, alone, a scratchy wool blanket pulled over him. It was morning, 6 a.m.. The harsh Arizona sun had already lifted its head to stare at him, and he felt—again—a hollowness in his gut.

He sat up and started the truck.

A half-hour later, hungry for breakfast, Tony pulled into a truck stop alongside a couple of idling semis. The place advertised Good Grub—Open 24 Hrs. He stepped out next to a couple of young hippies. The guy, who looked about twenty, wearing a tie-dyed peace symbol T-shirt, reached toward the radiator cap of his beat-up VW with a gray rag. The girl—about eighteen, braless in a tank top with strings of blue beads around her neck and hemp bracelets circling her wrists—stood back a few feet, watching. Tony could hear the hiss as the boy twisted the radiator cap, then yanked his fingers away, then reached down again, then pulled away again.

"I'd watch it," Tony said as he passed.

The guy flipped his long brown hair and looked through it at Tony. "Huh?"

"That radiator's way too hot. Might overflow. You could get scalded."

"So, like, what do you suggest, man?" the guy inquired, brushing his shoulder-length greasy hair from his face. "I'm not all that mechanical."

The kid seemed a little naïve—schooled, Tony figured, only in psychedelic music, Allen Ginsberg, and dope—so Tony leaned over the engine, then advised, "Let it sit a while. Cool off."

The guy rubbed his scalded fingers on the back of his jeans. "Hey, thanks, dude," he said, lifting his hand and giving Tony a peace sign with a kind of California I-live-near-the-Haight languidness. The girl, lifting her string of beads to her lips and, sucking on one, gave Tony a vacuous smile.

Inside, Tony passed a couple of arcade games, and then a mechanical fortune teller inside a glass booth stopped him. Her face was painted in life-like colors, and she was wearing a peasant's blouse and a black babushka. Your Fortune. Only 25 Cents, the sign said. The scratched glass looked foggy. For a second, he was tempted to reach into his pocket and drop a quarter into the slot, but the mannequin's glass eyes seemed to penetrate him, so he turned away. Plaster and plastic and paint, he thought. Not like Estelle, who was real.

"So, how are we today?" someone inquired. He turned to see a waitress behind the counter.

"Fair to partly cloudy." Surrounded by the oily scent of grilled burgers and French fries submerged in mesh baskets, Tony sat on a red vinyl stool.

"Oh really?" she asked, planting her elbows on the counter and leaning toward him.

"Yeah. But I'm working on eliminating all the gray areas in my life."

After a long look, she smacked her gum and sighed "Well good for you."

He ordered a breakfast of ham and eggs with a glass of root beer. While he ate, he stared at the tiers of chocolate candies behind the counter, and wondered which ones wouldn't melt in the cab of his truck. He turned and perused the postcards on the circular wire rack next to him. Some of them said Greetings from Arizona with a picture of a saguaro cactus, some featured desert Gila monsters on beige sand, or rattlers coiled at the base of rocks. As he rotated the squeaking rack, the gypsy mannequin seemed to watch him. Finding one, he plucked it from the rack. He tossed a dime on the counter, then slid the postcard halfway into the pocket of his T-shirt.

Finishing his breakfast, he gulped the last of the soda from a red plastic tumbler.

"Postcard to home?" the waitress inquired.

"Maybe," he answered.

"How nice. Where you from, then?"

"Hollywood, for the last couple weeks. Now pretty much anywhere else."

"What's wrong with Hollywood?"

"Might as well call it *Hell*wood," he scoffed.

"Funny," she replied. An admiring smile slid through her pale white lipstick. "So, you one of those aspiring actors, then?"

"No," he replied, standing from the counter. Then he added, "But I guess I'm aspiring to something."

Outside, the two hippies still sat there against the wall in front of their VW, its hood open wide. The girl dangled one worn leather sandal from her index finger and stared out at nothing. When the guy noticed Tony, he gave him a languid, knowing nod. They'd wait, Tony figured. Let things cool off. Good advice.

He drove off, and a distant, static-filled radio station played "Turn! Turn! Turn!" by the Byrds. A song about accepting the change of seasons, he thought. But how am I going to do that?

The nine a.m. Arizona sky looked like a worn piece of cardboard. He knew it was blue up there, somewhere. But right now, the sky just looked gray, and beyond that, another layer of gray, and beyond that, more gray. The whole day clouded him over. It smothered him and seemed to be slowing him down when he knew the truck should be going faster. He checked the emergency brake because it seemed like it was still on, and he could almost feel the tires beneath him smoldering with rising heat. He rolled the window halfway down.

He shifted his focus to the postcard on the dash. According to the waitress, the nearest post office with a mailbox was in the next town, twenty-five miles down Highway 66.

The front of the card pictured a happy couple in a red convertible. The silver scripted letters proclaimed *Having a Great Time on the Famous Route 66*. The highway beneath them stretched like a pale string pulled taut between two distant mountains. On the back side, the blank space of the message box waited for a written message.

Dear Estelle and Ariel, he thought about writing. But how could he possibly explain everything he felt in such a small three-by-five-inch space? There was too much to write; the words would bleed off the edge of the cardboard. Besides, he might make it back to Wanley before the postcard even got there. And though he wanted to, he knew he couldn't call her; with the carnival traveling so frequently, they never had a phone installed in the trailer.

He wondered what she was doing right now. Maybe, at seven a.m., she was up and making breakfast, Ariel handing her a half-gallon of milk. Or maybe she was still asleep and dreaming in their soft double bed with the covers flattened on the left side, where Tony usually slept.

As the dry desert air sighed through the half-opened window, the postcard fluttered a little, rising and falling a fraction of an inch off the dashboard as if it were a thin cardboard tongue, not quite saying what it needed to say.

CHAPTER 38

Ariel

Sideshow #79

Sometimes I dream that I live inside a crystal ball. I can't move around much in there, though. It's kinda small. I sort of press my palms to the rounded walls. And I'm still waiting for my future.

Sideshow #80

If I was a fortune teller's ball, I wouldn't be made of flawless crystal. I've decided that I'd be made of glass and not perfect. With lots of bubbles, holding their breaths, suspended inside.

Sideshow # 83

Sometimes I feel kinda like a small puddle with a patch of the sky reflected in it. Like the one I see outside my window right now. Other days, I feel a lot bigger than that. I'm a great blue hole. There's no way anyone can see to the bottom of me. Not even me.

Sideshow # 93

My mom claims that I am a lot like Dorothy in The Wizard of Oz. She says I live in a black-and-white world, like Dorothy, but dream about another.

Okay, a couple questions: are funnel clouds just rainbows that disguise themselves by turning gray and starting to spin? Are rainbows funnel clouds that unravel and then change color? The sky always fills with big questions.

Sideshow #100

Maybe I will sprout wings when I'm older like my mom once told me. She's a wise woman, so I pretty much trust her. But where will the young girl in me go? Will she still be alive in me? Or will she dry up in there and just sort of disappear? Okay—maybe she'll just hibernate and wait for the right time to come back out.

Sideshow #111

Late at night (like tonight, for instance), when I look up at the sky, I wish on a star.

Other times, I wonder: is the moon made of paper? And if it is, then are the stars made of paper, too? And what if they all catch fire? What will the night sky look like then? What will happen to girls' wishes?

CHAPTER 39

Estelle

As they drove down the main street of a small town, Estelle couldn't help but notice the titles of the upcoming movies, surrounded by the yellow bulbs of the overhanging 1930s-style marquee of the theatre.

Romeo and Juliet M-F 7 & 9

Below it, a classic movie was advertised:

Trapeze Sun. Matinee 1 & 3

She'd seen both of those romantic movies in Wanley with Tony.

*   *   *

Her mind jumped back to the day she and Tony were married. It wasn't a usual wedding, but still, it was thrilling, and romantic in its own way. They were on the road in a small town in Iowa and had decided to call a justice of the peace at the local courthouse and hold the wedding at the carnival after hours.

The carnival crew had gathered in the wooden bleachers of Tony's tightrope act tent—a small arena where a wire was suspended thirty feet up between two metal posts. A couple of card tables—stocked with bottles of champagne and Solo cups, paper cups filled with confetti, and a tray of party poppers—were placed in the corners. The whole thing was Tony's idea.

Estelle, clothed in a simple white lace dress she'd bought at a local store, waited at the base of the wire. Her hair was swept up with a lace ribbon and she wore her best jewelry—a string of pearls, a few feathers in her hair which Lily gathered from the ostrich exhibit, a gold and silver charm bracelet given to her by her grandmother. Lily, in a long, flowered blue dress, stood at Estelle's right side, and Fast Eddie, Tony's best man, stiff and awkward in a corduroy sport coat and T-shirt, waited to stand beside Tony. Old Whiskers clicked the button on a cassette boom box that began to play "The Liberty Bell March" by John Phillip Sousa. All the regulars were there watching—including the vendors and the temporary set-up crew. Splat the Clown, looking ordinary without his clown costume and makeup, flipped on the spotlight that illuminated the silver wire.

Tony didn't appear at first.

As everyone waited and the music kept playing, the justice of the peace, an older man with white hair, asked "Where's the groom? Is this going to happen, or what?"

Just then, Tony appeared through a tent flap and entered the arena. He wore a black tux, pink shirt, and black bow tie. He quickly climbed the rungs on the post and began walking the wire. There he was, Estelle had thought: her fiancé, a skilled performer, suspended halfway between earth and sky. A guy with a fireworks smile who claimed, on one of their first dates, "I'll never fall, not ever. Unless it's for you, that is." Because they were spoken by Tony, the words sounded sincere and not the least bit corny. He was a dreamer, a guy who talked about traveling to Paris or Rio or Madrid someday, and at the same time, he was down to earth, able to fix the carburetor of a pickup truck, or a broken fan belt on the chugging Allis-Chalmers motor that ran the Kiddie Roller Coaster. Somehow, she knew, even weeks before she met him, that he was the person destined for her. It seemed that she had sensed him everywhere—he was there, in the sound of a distant stream, in a glimmer of sunlight, in a subtle shift in the wind that she couldn't help but notice.

As Tony continued across the wire at their wedding, Boom Boom Bruno cupped his hands and shouted "Yah, Tony!" from the bleachers, and someone elbowed and shushed him.

Smiling broadly, and with his usual athletic casualness, Tony walked, step by step, one arm extended to his right. His other arm—circling and holding a small glistening object between his fingertips—extended to his left.

Reaching the middle where the wire sagged and swayed back and forth slightly, Tony paused briefly. Estelle gasped a little. Though it was like gravity couldn't weigh him down, he always made her nervous when he was up there. At the far end of the wire, Tony climbed down the rungs, then jumped the last five feet and landed next to Estelle. His legs bent slightly with the impact on the sawdust floor, but he quickly straightened, gazed fondly into Estelle's eyes, and, with a flourish, handed her a gleaming gold ring. The crew in the bleachers cheered.

"You look amazing," he whispered to Estelle.

Then he turned toward the justice of the peace and said "I do."

"We're not at that point yet," the justice said.

"Well I am," Tony replied.

*   *   *

A car horn honking from behind broke Estelle from her reverie.

"Mom," Ariel said. "Are we going to a movie, or what?"

"Oh. Um, no. No." She accelerated beyond the theatre. Gripping the steering wheel, she couldn't stop picturing Tony on that day. She felt like gasping again as she saw him pausing on the trembling wire, halfway between a starting point and a stopping point, a beginning and an end.

CHAPTER 40

Tony

He noticed an elevated rocky formation on the left side of the road. It would be a great place to try a jump, he thought. His back was stiff from driving, so he pulled the truck over.

He slid the hang glider from the back of the flatbed and carried it up to a rocky ledge that jutted about fifty feet over the desert. He climbed into the harness, and counted to three. Then he ran toward the edge and dove, headfirst, into the air.

Tony had been trying out the hang glider at rest stops. He'd studied the instruction manual and tried to follow the directions. The first time, hopping off a small ledge, he flew for just about fifteen seconds, then scraped to the soft sand of the desert, skinning his knees. A measly Wright Brothers' first flight, he told himself, but it was a start, at least. After that, he learned how to adjust the angle of the wings, and how to catch an updraft. Tony recalled his carnival buddy from Monterey, telling Tony about gliding. When they talked once last year, the guy was enthusiastic about the new sport. He told Tony that by catching warm updrafts, he stayed up for three hours, just like those hawks or ospreys that found a thermal and hovered above the landscape all afternoon. "Kind of like a bird, then?" Tony had said to him, to which he replied, "Yep. Just like some damn bird."

Updrafts, Tony told himself. That's what he was about now. No more downers. Just Updrafts. No more mourning the lost kid. Negative thoughts are just flies, caught in spider webs.

This time his flight was a little longer. He glided for about thirty seconds until he landed on the soft sand beyond the rocks. He climbed back onto the rocky point and tried it again. Then a third time. Each time, he glided a bit further. By the third time, he was able to maneuver the hang glider more easily, veering it left, then right, as he leaned into the breeze.

Back in the truck, he felt refreshed, ready to move forward again. He accelerated, the truck clunking over a torn-up stretch of asphalt. A few miles later, he noticed the truck's rearview mirror brightening with red light. He wondered if the sun was setting behind him. Then the rising and falling sound of a siren filled his ears.

"Damn!" he spat as he slowed and pulled over, the cop's big Dodge cruiser nosing up behind him. Tony clicked off the ignition and winced as he watched the heavy-set state patrolman, dressed in a brown uniform with a trooper's hat, saunter up to the truck.

"Going way too fast, mister." the cop chided.

"I hardly realized it," Tony said apologetically as he rolled down the window. "I mean—the empty highway, and all."

"Y'know, we're tryin' to keep these highways safe," the cop said with a rehearsed tone. "Doing ninety doesn't exactly help." He sniffed the air a couple of times like an oversized rodent.

The cop glanced past Tony to the passenger's seat scattered with splayed Texaco road maps, empty Styrofoam coffee cups, crumpled wrappers from burger joints, and a half-finished box of Junior Mints. Tony had thrown a local flier on top of the bottle of Jack Daniels, disguising it. "I notice you got Minnesota plates," the man said. "On some kind of road trip, are you?"

"Yeah," Tony replied, "Sort of."

"Got family somewhere?"

He hesitated. "Wife," he explained, wanting to make himself sound stable. "And daughter."

The cop studied Tony's driver's license, then looked up at the highway, as if pondering the Pass With Care sign, then back at Tony's license. He flipped up the black leather cover of his note pad, scribbled something.

As the man tore out the page, Tony cringed, anticipating the fine he'd have to pay.

"With the cost of a speedin' ticket," the cop related, "you'd pretty much have to sleep in your truck." He nodded ruefully at the burger wrappers. "Go without lunch a few days, even."

Tony grimaced and nodded.

"But," the cop continued, "I'm just givin' you a warnin' this time." He held a pink slip toward Tony.

"Oh. Well, thanks, officer," he said with genuine surprise.

"Just do me a favor, will you?"

"What's that?"

The man wagged his head a little, then slid the ticket pad into its case on his belt, and handed Tony's driver's license back to him. "I see from your license you're thirty-three years old." He said solemnly. "Criminy. You should know better than to be out speedin' like some damn teenager. Your wife and kid need you at home, I bet. And, most likely, they want you to get there in one piece."

CHAPTER 41

Estelle and Ariel

The road transformed. The two-lane state highway lifted them on its concrete shoulders until it became four lanes, then six lanes—three headed west, three east. Even though the traffic thickened, Estelle liked the wideness of the road, liked it that the scraggy pines and hardwoods gave way to a scattering of small houses, and those gave way to larger buildings as a city rose into view. In the front seat, Ariel was napping, having finished a crossword puzzle and a few chapters of *Swiss Family Robinson*. The book slid from her knees to the floor mat as the car drove over a rise in the road.

Estelle navigated through stoplights, following the brown signs that led her through the urban streets. The next thing she knew, she was turning onto Constitution Avenue, where a dozen cabs blurred past.

"Ariel," she said softly, waking her daughter, "You have to see this." Ariel lifted her head groggily and squinted through the windshield.

Ahead, the pale granite monolith rose as if to poke a hole in the azure sky.

"What is it?" Ariel asked, stretching her arms to her sides.

"The Washington Monument."

"Washington?" Ariel gave her a questioning look. "So, um, is there a carnival here, or what?"

"Well, a carnival is based in Salem, Virginia. And that's where I was headed." Estelle flipped up the visor she had lowered to block the glare of the sun. "But I decided we should take a few detours. And detours are good, right?"

"I suppose." Ariel slid the book into a backpack and smiled. "I mean, absolutely."

"Besides, I've always dreamed about visiting Washington since I was a little girl. So our mission has changed. This is now officially a vacation."

Estelle parked the car and paid the attendant dressed in a dark blue suit. "Ready?" Estelle said. "We're going up. On the elevator."

"To the top?"

"I hope you won't get dizzy. It's only five hundred fifty-five feet."

"Mom," Ariel countered, "do I go on the Rock-O-Plane without closing my eyes? Did I ride the Round-up five times in a row with no hands? Without even getting queasy?"

"Point made."

When they reached the entry, the attendant told them that the elevator was malfunctioning. "Closed for repairs," he advised.

"But we can climb the stairs, right?" Estelle asked.

The man nodded. "I guess." He gave Ariel a skeptical look. "I mean, if you want to."

A frown crept down Ariel's face. "Um, Mom," she said in a shaky voice, "I don't know if my leg…"

"We'll take it slow, so you can rest," Estella said. She knew that a lot of walking sometimes caused Ariel to have pain in her left leg. "You'll make it."

"But what if I can't?"

"I'll carry you, then."

"Oh Mom," Ariel countered stubbornly, "You're not going to carry me. I'm way, way too old for that."

A half-hour later, Estelle gazed out the small, barred window at the top of the monument. Below, she saw the national mall she had read about in books: The White House, the Lincoln Memorial, the reflecting pool with clusters of people gathering around it, the Jefferson Memorial. The symmetrical, almost musical patterns of the trees and the copper-topped buildings and contoured lawns. To Estelle, the grand monuments looked so solid, so permanent. Not like her tent and the flimsy wooden stands of the carnival—these buildings were made of white stone and granite and marble. They were meant to last. She marveled at the beauty of the Capital's dome, finished over a hundred years before, and thought about the freedom people fought and died for over the decades. The enormity of it all made her feel choked up.

"Wait 'til you see this." She lifted Ariel, who wasn't tall enough to see the view, and as she did, the window, inhaling the high, cool air, pushed a gust of wind into their faces.

She glanced at Ariel, who looked out at the scene, her thin blonde hair braiding and unbraiding in the breeze. Estelle hoped Ariel was seeing what she was seeing, hoped she was feeling what she was feeling. It was the most a mother could ask of a daughter, wasn't it?

"What's wrong, Mom?" Ariel asked, noticing a tear in the corner of her eye.

"Nothing," she replied, brushing her eye with the sleeve of her blouse. "Nothing's wrong at all. It's just too awesome."

Afterward, they strolled down Independence Avenue toward the huge rectangular reflecting pool. Ariel looked up at the street sign. "Hey, we're walking along Independence Avenue," Ariel said whimsically. "Does this mean we're independent, Mom?"

Estelle just smirked.

Further down the avenue, a sign cautioned Pedestrians Only, and a bright orange roadblock stopped the traffic. Two squad cars idled nearby, their parking lights on, and three policemen stood alongside them. Estelle noticed more police cars crawling toward the intersection and joining them.

A large group of pedestrians—most of them African Americans—filled the crosswalk as the light changed. Estelle wondered why there'd be this many people on the streets. She grabbed Ariel's hand as they fell in step with the crowd.

"You sightseeing, too?" Estelle asked a Black woman next to her as they lingered, waiting for the walk light.

The woman laughed. "Not exactly. So, you joining us?" she asked.

"Sure. We are now, I guess."

The woman, who introduced herself as Pearl, was in her late twenties, with a soft-looking afro hairdo that was large as a basketball. She wore colorful red and blue bell bottoms, sandals, and an African Dashiki-style red and green top with brocade. "We probably won't get very close, mind you," Pearl said.

"Close to what?" Estelle asked.

"The White House, of course."

"Is something going on?"

The woman gave Estelle an inquisitive look. "Yeah. Something goin' on, all right."

As they approached the White House, they heard the sound of voices chanting and clapping. Estelle could see an array of hand-painted signs, but they were too far away to read. "Mom, what are they chanting about?" Ariel asked, but Estelle, unsure, just shook her head.

More people joined them on the sidewalks at the next intersections. The crowd moved like tributaries leading into a main artery. As Estelle looked around, she noticed that except for an occasional White person, most of the crowd was made up of Black people. Soon hundreds of marchers—some of them singing—flooded into the street, and the crush of people gave Estelle the sensation that she was being pushed along by a steadily moving river.

"Step back, step back," a line of policemen and guards, dressed in blue uniforms, shouted through megaphones at the crowd. They pushed the group to either side, clearing a narrow pathway in the center of the street.

"Better do what they say," Pearl advised, and Estelle and Ariel made their way to the curb. "So," the woman said, "you're here for him, too?"

"Who?"

"Martin Luther King, of course. Or his memory, I should say. The reason we're all here." The woman gave her a somber look. "Only five months since the shooting, rest his soul."

"Oh," Estelle said, feeling a little naïve for not realizing what was happening. "Oh, of course." She'd read a brief article in a small-town Indiana newspaper about King's assassination and about civil rights gatherings like this. But—isolated by the carnival and its constant traveling schedule—she didn't think too much about it, nor did she ever imagine she'd be right in the midst of it.

"And I hope you're ready, honey," Pearl said.

"For what?" Estelle inquired.

The woman didn't answer, just nodded toward an open space on the grass where they could stand.

*   *   *

A half-hour later, the three of them were perched alongside the reflecting pool that stretched a third of a mile from the Lincoln Memorial. "Welcome to the anniversary of the nineteen-sixty-three March for Jobs and Freedom," the man at the podium announced, and as he did, a loud cheer rose up from the audience. "That's Ralph Abernathy," Pearl told them.

"Five years ago," Abernathy continued, "Dr. King said 'I have a dream.' Now, less than five months after his death, we vow to carry on that dream! We will not let him die in vain!" With that, the crowd erupted for a full two minutes, waving their arms and their placards in the air as the police, lined on both sides of the gathering, eyed them menacingly. One by one, several Black men rose to the podium; the words *freedom* and *equality* and *justice* boomed through speakers perched solidly in the trees. Estelle felt the words surround her, rising and falling and flowing with a jazz-like revivalist rhythm. She closed her eyes in reverie.

As the men continued their passionate speeches, the words didn't just touch Estelle from the outside. Their voices seemed to enter her and resonate in her core. Words she'd heard only in passing on an occasional nightly news report now touched her deeply. For an instant, she thought that Tony's leaving was a little injustice in the scheme of things, but still, it was wrong, and she felt even more resolved that she had to do something about it. If not for her, then for Ariel.

At the end of the talks, a recording of King's "I Have a Dream" speech played through the speakers, and, as it ended, a tumultuous cheer rose from the crowd. When Ariel pointed at it, Estelle noticed a black and orange monarch flittering over the crowd, looking for a place to land.

* * *

As the march concluded and the demonstrators lingered, a commotion began near the corner of the reflecting pool.

At first, Estella hear one raised voice calling out.

A cop lifted his shield and baton and pushed toward the crowd, telling them to disperse. More cops joined him. Arms shoved at each other. A scuffle broke out. More voices flew into the air like startled or angry birds. A cardboard sign on a wooden stick rose up into the air and came down hard. A cracking sound. A thump. A shout, a scream. A dark object—thrown by an angry-faced young man with a large afro—flew through the air toward the advancing police. They retaliated by throwing a silver canister—a cloud of white gas hissing from it—toward the crowd. One tall man, his eyes pinched shut, picked up the canister and hastily whipped it back toward the squad cars. It bounced off a windshield, cracking it.

In a chain reaction, the screams multiplied into more screams. Like a whirling dust devil that rose and gained strength, shouts rose into the air, bringing with them other shouts. Estelle could feel the tension ripple through the gathering as some people tried to push their way out of the crowd, and others pushed toward the police line.

Suddenly, a group of police in riot gear charged into the group on foot or on horseback. Panic spread suddenly through the crowd like sparks from a wildfire. Estelle grabbed Ariel's hand tightly and held on.

Bodies moved toward Estelle and away from her at the same moment, like protons and neutrons colliding. Some people tripped and fell, some used their signs as shields, some dropped them and tried to run. A mother and her teenage daughter scuttled past them on hands and knees like crabs on a seashore. Estelle saw one policeman lifting his club into the air, almost gracefully, like a maestro lifting a baton at a concert, and then swinging it down hard on top of a gray-haired man's head. There was no music, though: just a dull, sickening thud.

Ariel looked up at Estelle, her face distorted in fear. "Mom!" Ariel cried as their hands were torn from each other. The push and pull of the crowd twisted Estelle sideways, and she struggled to get back to Ariel, who was a few feet behind her.

"Better move, honey!" Estelle heard Pearl's voice shout. "Move now! Don't get caught in this!"

Estelle somehow managed to grasp Ariel's hand again and tried to squeeze forward or backward to get out of the way, but the pressure of the crowd held her motionless. Pungent tear gas assaulted the air. The crowd seemed, somehow, to have become one solid body, huddling to protect itself. Estelle and Ariel cowered there, seeds in the center of a fruit that someone was steadily crushing.

After a few moments, the crowd began to pull apart, like a fabric being torn from all sides, and Estelle was able to break away. She leaned into a run and tugged Ariel behind her. "Mom, I can't run!" Ariel gasped as she stumbled, dragging her left leg behind her. "I can't go that fast!"

Estelle kept pulling her, weaving their way, avoiding the nightsticks that swung like pendulums. She ducked, hearing the snorting of horses, the scrape of hooves on concrete, and the awful thump of wood clubs on skulls. As one mounted policeman reined his horse toward them, his steed snorted and raised its head up and down. Estelle instinctively leaned over Ariel, sheltering her with her arms and body. She felt her daughter tremble beneath her.

Estelle closed her eyes as the horse brushed against her with its flanks and then clomped past them and further into the crowd.

When she opened her eyes, she saw Pearl, sitting cross-legged on the concrete, holding the side of her temple, blood seeping beneath her palm. Estelle grabbed her by the waist and lifted her to her feet. Then, with Ariel in tow, she led the two of them into an empty grassy area beyond the reflecting pool.

She gently eased Pearl—with drops of blood staining her blouse—to the ground.

Estelle wiped the blood from Pearl's forehead with her sleeve. "Stay right here," she told Pearl and Ariel, "Be back in a minute." Pulling a pale scarf from her pocket, Estelle ran to a nearby elegant, Italian-looking fountain. She soaked the cloth in the cold water that sprung from the mouths of white marble cherubs, brought it back, and pressed it to Pearl's temple. "There," she said, comforting Pearl, who was dazed and sobbing.

"Why?" Pearl kept uttering. Sirens rose and fell as squad cars and ambulances rushed toward the scene. "Damn them. Why?"

Estelle watched the crowd disperse as a few Black men and women were shuffled or dragged to police vehicles, their red lights pulsing like arteries. Just then a muscular white policeman—wearing a riot helmet with a visor and a bulletproof vest—marched across the grass and toward them. Holding his nightstick, the cop paused near them, tear gas canisters clinking on his belt.

Pearl—with flowers of blood stains spreading on the scarf—cowered as the cop leaned over the three of them. Then she gave him a defiant look and began to rise to her feet. "I'd stay down if I were you," he advised in a growling voice. "I'd stay right where you're at. Unless you want more trouble."

Then he turned to Estelle and Ariel. "And you two. Better get out of here," he ordered. "This isn't a place for you, ma'am," he added. As if it was on ball bearings, his head rotated to Pearl, then back to Estelle. "Not with these people, if you get my drift."

Estelle instinctively slid her arm around Pearl's shoulders. She could see, in the cop's mirrored sunglasses, the curved reflection of the three of them. "Maybe I *do* want to be here," she said, surprising herself with the words.

CHAPTER 42

Estelle and Ariel

Pearl lay on the couch, with her head propped on the armrest. Estelle, after asking her about concussion symptoms, dabbed an ice pack on Pearl's forehead and applied a bandage Ariel had retrieved from a medicine cabinet.

Estelle stood from the sofa to get a Pepsi from the refrigerator and glanced around at the simple furnishings of Pearl's apartment. On the opposite wall, an overstuffed chair, and above it, music posters of Earth, Wind, and Fire and The Staple Singers, their afros circling their heads like broad black halos. She admired a framed painting of an African woman and man—the woman in a long orange striped dress, the man in a dashiki. Mimeographed fliers were piled next to a stack of books on the coffee table. She noticed *Soul on Ice* by Eldridge Cleaver on top.

"I do really appreciate this, hon," Pearl said as she opened her eyes and Estelle handed her the soda. "You don't know how much."

A few hours later, the swollen lump on Pearl's head subsided, and she felt much better. While Ariel watched TV, Pearl and Estelle sat on the sofa, talking and sipping cups of tea.

"So what do you do in Washington?" Estelle inquired.

"I work at a high school. It's on the other side of town. The bad side, you might say." When Estelle gave her a quizzical look, her voice—resonant with timbre—grew husky. "It's Washington's dirty little secret, that they have a baaaad side of town," she explained. "Everyone thinks this city is nothing but clean white buildings and senators and parties in the White House rose garden, but it's not. Believe me, my school ain't no rose garden." She let out a gruff laugh.

"What do you do there?"

"I'm a guidance counselor. I do what I can for the kids. So what do you do, if I don't mind my asking?"

"I work at...," she hesitated, "I work at a traveling show."

"She tells people's futures," Ariel blurted, turning her head from an episode of *Gunsmoke* on the TV, where Matt Dillon was talking to Miss Kitty. Ariel was always able to tune into two conversations at once.

"I'm, um, with a carnival." Estelle felt a bit embarrassed, explaining this to such an educated woman. "It's not your everyday job," she said, almost apologetically. "But it's a living, though, I guess."

"It's a very important job," Ariel interjected between licks of the cherry Popsicle that Pearl had given her. "She's got a crystal ball. Things appear in it, even."

"Oh?" said Pearl, raising her eyebrows. "Sounds funky."

"Yes," Ariel added, "It's funky. Very, extremely funky." Then she mumbled, "Whatever that means."

"So," Pearl inquired, turning back to Estelle, "can you tell your own future, then?"

"No," Estelle replied. "I guess that doesn't come with the territory."

"Sure you could, Mom," Ariel said. "If you tried, you could."

"Oh, Ariel," Estelle said, fluttering her hand in the air.

"She's still young," Pearl said. "She still believes. And you know, honey," she continued, chuckling, "that isn't such a bad thing. Not a bad thing, at all. Especially when this ol' planet seems so messed up." She took a sip of her tea and set the cup down on the saucer with a clink, a little of the amber liquid spilling over. "Here's the thing. We speak out for a little equality, and we get our heads bashed. Congress dishes out millions to put a man up on the moon. But damned if we can feed our kids on the streets of Chicago. There's hate everywhere. And way too much violence. White against Black, Black against White. Factions, fighting each other. The whole country's gone insane."

Estelle nodded.

"I got sick of it all," Pearl said. "And that's why I'm heading a group in town."

"Group?"

"Well, I'm not a Black Panther or anything, if that's what you're thinking. I'm with CORE."

"I'm not even sure what that is, actually," Estelle admitted.

Pearl laughed a raspy laugh. "Honey, where have y'all been lately? Don't you watch the news, or read the papers?"

"Not often enough," Estelle confessed. "I guess I've spent my life in a tent. I hardly paid attention to what's going on in politics."

"Well, you should have," Pearl offered. "You really should have."

Estelle nodded.

"So, like I was saying, I head a coalition here in Washington. It's for racial equality." She took a slow breath, brushing the back of her hand across the bandage on her forehead.

"So what does your group do, then?"

"We organize rallies. Go into neighborhoods to distribute food and spread the word. Check on textbook selections at schools."

"That's great. I admire that."

Pearl closed her eyes; her dark brown eyelids were big. She opened them, and leaned close to Estelle and spoke in a hushed but passionate tone. "You know, you damn well can't change the world all at once. But you can change society. Maybe one person at a time."

Estelle nodded as the wisps of steam rose from her teacup. Pearl stood and pulled Ralph Ellison's *The Invisible Man* off a shelf and handed the book to Estelle. "This one will light up your mind," she said with a soft laugh. "And I've got plenty more. In case you're interested."

"Well, this will be a change from my romance novels," Estelle admitted, smiling. "But yeah, I'm interested," she said, opening the book.

"So, during all my spare time," Pearl continued, a little irony beneath her words, "I'm taking a night class over at George Washington U."

"What are you taking?"

"A course on the Civil War. What about you? Did you go to college?"

"Me? I flirted with it once, when I was eighteen. But that was a century ago."

"Why didn't you go, girl?"

"I don't know," Estelle replied, a little flustered beneath the intensity of Pearl's brown eyes.

"Well, maybe you should think about getting that degree. You seem like a real smart woman.

"Thanks. But I guess life just got in the way. Then the carnival. I sort of just got stuck there and didn't think about much else."

"And let me guess, hon," Pearl pried. "Might there be a man involved?" She said the word *man* musically, stretching it out into three syllables.

Estelle swallowed hard. "Yeah," she said illusively, not wanting to explain everything at the moment. "I suppose."

"Yep. I had a hunch."

"My dad went away a couple weeks ago," Ariel blurted, turning again from the TV. "But we intend to find him."

"So where are you going to find him, sweetie?" Pearl inquired.

"Somewhere," she replied.

"Where's somewhere, hon?"

"It's where we're going," Ariel said confidently as if it was an actual town they could just drive to. As if they could pull into the city limits and read the sign *Somewhere, U.S.A., Population Tony*. "He won't be that hard to find."

Pearl smiled, the space between her two front teeth showing. "Hey," she said to Estelle, "I dig her straightforwardness."

Estelle glanced at the clock on the wall and stood from her chair. "It's getting late. We should go."

"Where you staying?"

"Out there," she said, gesturing toward the window and their car and trailer parked by the curb. "That's our home on wheels."

"Oh, no honey," Pearl said sharply. "You're not staying on these streets. She nodded at Ariel. "Especially with your baby. That's nonsense."

"Oh, I don't want to impose...."

"You're staying here," Pearl insisted, gesturing to the room. "It's not a palace, I know. But you can have the couch. And your sweetie pie can have the floor."

Ariel jumped up from the oval rug. "Oh, can we stay, Mom? Can we?"

Estelle finally agreed.

"Now let's get you some dinner," Pearl said, turning toward the kitchen. "You like soul food?"

Ariel squinted one eye. "What's soul food?"

Pearl crouched down in front of her. "It's food," she said, patting Ariel over her heart, "For here. Right here."

"Is it every bit as good as carnival food?" Ariel asked, half seriously, and half in jest.

"Oh, it's better than that. I guarantee you'll love it—it'll be the best dang thing you ever tasted."

That evening, with Ariel in a sleeping bag on the floor next to her, Estelle lay on the couch. A phrase Pearl had spoken kept looping through her head. *One person at a time.* The more she thought about the words, the truer they sounded; they were sweet and filling as the soul food they ate for dinner, and she savored them, one word at a time.

CHAPTER 43

Tony

Red and tan and brown. Awesome, he thought as he marveled at the colors of the rock layers in the walls of the deep canyon below. Tony glided left, then right, cradled in the big palm of the wind.

Today, taking a break from driving in the one-hundred-degree desert sun, Tony had toted his Delta glider onto a butte next to a canyon that meandered along the highway. He noticed a trail leading up the side of the canyon, so he knew there'd be a way back after his flight. He hesitated, wondering if he should try it or not, if the adrenalin rush was worth it. As if to answer himself, he ran toward the cliff, kicked off a ledge, shouted "Yeah!" and dove into the air like he was diving into a clear ocean.

As he hovered, the heat from the dry land wasn't even noticeable up there, in the atmosphere. Up there, everything was cooler. He loved that feeling—the wind buffing his face and fluttering his hair with a *hussshh* sound—and he wondered how long he could fly. He was a long way from Malibu now, a long way from Charlotte and her deceits, her snakes coiled around her neck.

As he glided, his mind meandered, and he became almost meditative. Things boil over, he knew, and then they evaporate and disappear. Water becomes clouds. Clouds become water. Then it rains and refreshes the land again. Everything transforms and renews, he thought, doesn't it?

As he straightened the glider, the silhouettes of a couple of birds hovered above him. Their movements were almost imperceptible; they were pieces of black paper pinned to the sky. For the first time in a long time, he felt free, buoyant, unfettered. It was like he was floating on a dream.

For an instant, he fantasized that he could fly all the way to the carnival and see it from high above—a jumble of toothpicks and matchboxes and toy rides. He wished he could glide over Estelle and Ariel, carving concentric circles in the air as they craned their necks toward him. Then he would float down, down, down to surprise them by landing, softly and gracefully, right next to them.

"Hey. It's me," he'd say to their beaming faces, as he spread his arms with a flair.

The next thing he knew, Tony felt the right side of the glider tip suddenly to one side. He sensed a shift in the air, a faster-moving layer, a downdraft. Caught in the cross current, he struggled to right the glider. Lean into it, he thought. That's what his buddy in Monterey had advised. Don't let it take you. But it didn't seem to matter which way he leaned; the current kept pulling the glider down at an angle as if its surface was a small leaf and the wind was pressing its thumb on it.

The downdraft kept its hold on him, an invisible whirlpool pulling him in. Damn, he thought, and then he shouted it aloud: "Damn!" The more he struggled, the further away he got from the updraft that had been buoying him. In seconds, he was in a full dive. It was like he was being pulled down by a net, and there was nothing he could do to stop it. He passed through warmer and warmer layers of air as he nosedived toward a rock outcropping at the edge of the canyon. Desperate, he pulled upward on the nylon wings, but still, the rocks rose toward him. As he approached them, what looked so picturesque and pastel-colored from up there now rushed up to claim him, hard and sharp and unforgiving.

At the last second, he covered his head with his forearms, trying to avoid striking his skull. Pain exploded in his chest like flash powder, then spread through his arms and his hip. He skidded over red rocks that punched and pummeled him with rapid blows like a boxer with sandstone gloves. He felt himself begin to tumble, head over wings over head, down the face of the cliff. The colors blurred: blue and white and red and blue again.

An instant later, as if he was a butterfly captured by some cruel kid and placed inside a sealed, airtight collection box, everything went black.

CHAPTER 44

Ariel

Ariel had it all planned. When they finally found Tony, she'd tell him all about her caper with The Bird Child.

She'd tell him about how she sneaked in there that night, then lugged the glass jar from the display like some huge cloudy egg, and how she finally smashed it on the ground.

Her Dad would understand. It was his kind of stunt, like when he started the empty Ferris Wheel at night sometimes, just to watch it spin at full speed in the moonlight, or like when he wore that orange clown's wig—stolen, temporarily, from Splat the Clown—and popped up outside the trailer's kitchen window on April Fool's day, just to startle Estelle. Ariel pictured herself, telling Tony about The Bird Child's disappearance and imagined him, tipping his head back and laughing hard.

He'd be entertained, and maybe even proud of her for doing it, she thought, for being just a little rebellious against The Almighty Sandstorm, as Tony called Virgil Sand. Proud of her for stepping out of the box and doing something really weird. After all, she was her father's daughter, right?

"Weird is good," he had told her once, "That's why we don't exactly fit with everybody else. And that's why we make a living at it." Tony had said it to her last year, one evening when he was fixing a light switch that had shorted out in the living room. He flipped the power switch on the trailer's fuse box so the whole place was dark, then peered into the wall socket with a flashlight and fiddled with the wires.

"Are we making a living?" she had asked. Sometimes she'd heard her mom and Tony upset as they talked about money.

"Well…," he thought a moment. "Well, sure. At least enough to get by."

"Then why do you always say we're broke?"

He rubbed the back of his neck with his palm. "Well, kiddo," he said, squinting at the red and black wires in the socket, "Maybe we always want what we can't have."

"What's that mean?"

"Well…what I mean is," he said slowly, reaching into the pocket of his navy-blue T-shirt, stabbing a cigarette into his mouth without lighting it. Ariel knew he was always trying to quit. "Well, if you're sort of struggling for money, you always wish you were rich. And rich people, they wish their lives were less complicated. More simple." The unlit cigarette wobbled as he spoke. "But hey, we're neither rich nor poor." He pointed to a tin toolbox. "Hand me that screwdriver, will you Arie?"

"But…" Ariel asked, lowering an amber-handled screwdriver into his palm, "If we're not rich and not poor, then what are we?"

"Something in between," he said with a slight grimace as he leaned toward the wall and attached a thick wire to a bolt. "Kind of like the middle of the tightrope." Ariel began to notice that he used his tightrope comparisons a lot, as if it was the only thing to measure life by. "And maybe that's okay. Because we're rich, you know…rich in experience. Rich in dreams. We're rich because we have each other. And that's a good thing." He finished connecting the wires, eased them back into the socket, and reattached the beige plastic cover.

He dropped the screwdriver back into the toolbox. "Okay, kid. Hold your breath," he said, and Ariel complied, filling her skinny chest with air. He plugged in a lamp, stepped to the fuse box, turned the power back on, then flipped the light switch. The 100-watt bulb sent out a bright glow. "Voila!" he said. "Your dad just created light." Then he corrected himself, saying, "Or I should say *we* created light?"

Exhaling, and blinking from the sudden brightness, all she could do was nod.

So when they found her dad, she'd tell him how her little rebellion with The Bird Child shook up the whole carnival, and how, when the jar shattered on the black asphalt, the glass pieces scattered like shards of ice when a river breaks up in the spring. She'd describe The Bird Child's expression—that kind of sad but relieved look—as she laid it into a shallow grave. She hoped Tony wouldn't ask her something like "So why'd you do it?" because she really wouldn't be able to answer him. She didn't know the answer herself. If he'd insist, she'd have to say "Guess I wanted to let it dream. Maybe I'm just weird, like you." She hoped he'd just laugh and agree.

Then she'd sit down with Tony and tell him all about her new self, about the way she saw life in a different, slightly more grown-up way these past few weeks. She had become weird, clearly weird, but *good weird*, she'd tell him; she'd become very rich in dreams, and he should be proud of her. Maybe he'd even cheer her on, saying "Way to go, kid. Bravissimo."

When they found him, she'd tell him about all that. She'd tell him how she'd try to go to sleep at night, staring at the moon out the window and wishing it was his face. She'd talk on and on about what happened since he was gone—about their wandering road trip and the Washington Monument, where she wanted to drop a nickel from the observatory window but was afraid it might go right through a dog. She'd describe staying in campgrounds where, at night, the lightning bugs glowed on, then off, then on again with a faint buttery light as she limped toward the woods, trying to catch them.

If he was willing to listen, she'd talk to him a lot more than she ever had.

She'd tell him how, next year, she'd be twelve, and she figured she might be on the edge of that cliff known as puberty, and that she was just about to become less of a girl and more of a woman, and that might embarrass him a little. But most importantly, she'd tell him the feelings she'd been holding inside—how he hurt her and Mom by disappearing like that, and how much they both missed him. She pictured him giving her an understanding nod, that unlit cigarette bobbing in his mouth.

She'd have so much to tell him, it would be like a dam of light bursting, all the bright words flooding out without stopping. So much to tell him, she thought. When they found him. Not *if*, but *when*.

PART FOUR

CHAPTER 45

Tony

He flew, spiraling and spiraling in the darkness.

It was an uneasy feeling, this kind of flying, and he wasn't sure if he had wings. But Tony somehow understood he could keep flying, but only if he kept his arms outstretched, the way he did when he was walking the wire. Or the way he stretched them toward the cheering crowd when he did his dismount after his act, leaping to the ground in a black and silver-sequined outfit.

Still, there was no balance here, not for sure. Balance was elusive and velvety. He felt like he could grab onto a nearby cloud to steady himself, but whenever he tried to clutch it, it seemed to evaporate, and he kept falling.

A boy's half-formed face appeared above him. A pale fetus. Then it dissolved steadily, like a small frozen pond, melting in spring.

Tony felt his lungs inflate, then lose their air, then inflate again, like worn tires. He didn't need to try to breathe—it seemed that breath was given to him. It was as if an angel was leaning over and breathing into his lungs. His lungs, expanding, contracting, then expanding again easily, with a hushed sound, like a gust of wind.

Minutes passed. Or hours. Or years.

Then somewhere, deep in the blackness above him, meteors appeared. They streaked across the sky, or the darkness, or the emptiness, or whatever it was. Then two brighter meteors, trailing orange sparks, veered toward him. He looked closely at them: one was Estelle's face. One was Ariel's. Both faces were expressionless. He reached out to catch them in his open palms, but though they seemed to be close by, they were still far, far away.

Each time he lunged for them, he fell into the spiral again, and it took him to an orbit farther away from them. It was like he was caught in a sky dark as a whirlpool of ink, but he wasn't drowning. He was just circling, and circling, and circling. Never landing, just circling.

Then, somehow, he managed to find an opening in the blackness. At first, it was like someone pricked it with the tip of a pin. Then the pinhole widened, and he could see the brightness, steadily expanding. Then he could see a ceiling, then a white wall, then a blinking red mouth. The mouth spoke to him in a language he couldn't understand. *Eeeeep*, it said with a red voice. *Eeeeep. Eeeeep.* He just stared at it, not understanding, as it opened, then closed it, then opened it again.

Then another sound broke through. It was a voice—a human voice. Not the red voice, but a different one.

"Awake," the woman's voice was saying. "So, we're awake. Welcome back."

Tony shifted his eyes and saw a nurse—a plump woman in her forties—sitting in a chair, checking the settings on a machine next to his bed. He felt a pain in the side of his chest as if hot coals glowed inside it. He tried to utter something, but with the oxygen mask covering his mouth, no word slid from his parched throat.

"I'll call the doctor and get him down here," she said brightly as she pressed a button on the wall.

Tony tried to say something again, but the muffled words just disappeared into the plastic mask.

"Don't try to talk just yet," she advised. "Don't go back to sleep. Just stay awake 'til he gets here, okay?" She adjusted the blanket on his chest. "We're glad you're coming out of it. You've been in a coma for a few days." She adjusted a dial and jotted something on a clipboard. "You could have killed yourself, you know." She gave him a pleasant but condescending look, and made a tisk tisk sound, clicking her tongue. "You hit your skull pretty hard during your little jump. Lucky it wasn't a broken neck."

He tried to smile, maybe to say the word lucky, but the plastic mask kept his mouth from moving. The only sound that emerged was "Luhhhay." He tried to move his head a little, but any motion made his skull feel like it was a land mine, about to detonate from the inside.

Behind her, Tony could see a window with slatted blinds, and beyond the blinds, the blackness seemed to be waiting for him. He shifted his eyes quickly away from it.

"Maybe later, after you talk to Dr. Warton, we can get some contact information from you. Alright?"

He nodded slightly, and it hurt.

She stood from the chair., stepped to the doorway, and glanced back at Tony. "That way we can notify your loved ones."

Loved ones. The words echoed in his skull, a place that felt like a huge, empty auditorium. Loved ones. Loved ones. Loved ones.

CHAPTER 46

Estelle and Ariel and Pearl

"So, this road trip of yours. Where've y'all been so far?" Sitting on the grass in a small park, Pearl, smoking a Virginia Slim cigarette, stretched out her legs, clad in bell-bottom jeans with calico patches on the back pockets. Her dark brown skin looked lovely in the morning sunlight that filtered through the leaves of the trees.

"Well," Estelle began, "It's, it's part pleasure trip, and part sort of, well…"

Pearl, her afro billowing from her head, peered at her through her small steel-rim glasses. Estelle could almost see her face reflected in the lenses. "Are you chasing something, hon?"

"Um, well…it's complicated."

Pearl leaned on one elbow. "Honey, I've counseled lots of women at the shelter where I volunteer. They're all got a story. Usually a bad one. And I can tell by the look in your eyes that you've got one, too. So level with me. What happened? This man of yours. So, he took off on you?"

Estelle nodded in agreement.

"Um hum. I see it all the time at the center. A lot of the women are pregnant, and the guy ditches them, and they're left helpless." She snuffed out the cigarette, pushing the lit end into the soil next to her.

"I'm not helpless. I'm making this a kind of vacation, too."

Estelle turned her head toward Ariel, at the playground, and watched her climb a ladder and glide down a slide that was worn to a shine.

"Okay," said Pearl. "Let's hear the story."

She filled Pearl in about the carnival, and Tony, the night he left, the weeks that followed, and her decision to hit the road. She poured out the story quickly, her words cascading like water flowing down a rapids.

"He didn't abuse you or hit you, did he?"

"No, no, just the opposite. He was always great to me."

"Affairs?"

"No. He flirted with women once in a while. But no. Not that."

"Then what happened?"

"I'm not sure what I did wrong."

"Huh huh huh," Pearl laughed a low-pitched laugh. "I like the way you say you did something wrong. C'mon, hon. Why are you at fault?"

Estelle just sat there without replying. There were so many questions she couldn't answer. She knew that since Tony left, she'd lost her confidence. It had drained out of her steadily, like one of those fifty-gallon water barrels outside the food tent with a small hole rusted in the bottom. She wondered how—and if—she could ever get it back.

"Sounds like quite a mess," Pearl continued. "So what's your plan?"

"Well….I want Tony back," Estelle admitted, "but if he doesn't want me….." It felt like a release to let out all these feelings, and at the same time, it was painful to dredge them up again. The hurt was deep, and the more she tried to bring it to the surface, the bigger and heavier it seemed to become. She picked a few blades of grass, then let the breeze blow them away from her fingertips. "Then I… I guess I'm not letting myself think much about that possibility."

"I hear you. You sound a little lost to me," Pearl said, shaking her head, her hoop earrings catching the glint of the sun. "An' that ain't a good thing, you know, to be lost. You've got to be centered. Especially when you've got that little girl. She ain't going to be a pre-teen for long, you know."

Estelle glanced over at Ariel, who had climbed a small tree and was sitting on a low branch, reading a book and swinging her legs.

A few minutes later, Estelle stood at the base of a slide, worn and shiny, and Ariel kept whisking down it, then running back to the ladder, and then sliding down it again. It seemed like she was regressing into a carefree little girl again. Then she climbed on a wooden swing. "Push me, Mom!" she called.

Estelle sent Ariel back and forth a few times, pressing her palms into Ariel's small, bony back as Pearl leaned against one of the galvanized posts of the swing.

Estelle watched her daughter pull away from her hands, and then swing back toward her, then pull away again. For an instant, she imagined Ariel, growing a year older with each push. With one push she was twelve, entering junior high, and getting her period. Then she was thirteen, and taller, her body filling out, then she was sixteen and learning to drive, then eighteen, with a steady boyfriend. Then she was twenty-one and just married and moving out, her dolls left behind in a cardboard box, their plastic eyelids closed like they were planning to sleep for years.

"Higher!" Ariel called. "Underdog! Do an underdog!"

"Oh, Ariel...." Estelle sighed. But she complied, putting both hands on Ariel's back and rushing beneath her so she swung higher. Each time she did, it felt like she was tossing her daughter into the air and letting her go. Then she stepped to the side and watched Ariel, giggling as she swung like a pendulum, arching both legs to keep the momentum going. "Look, Mom!" she exclaimed, "I can touch it. I can touch the sky!"

"You can, you can!" Estelle agreed as Pearl, watching, beamed in approval.

As Estelle watched Ariel swinging far up into the blue, she wished her daughter could always be so happy and carefree. She wished a lot of things for her, and right now, more than anything, she wished that.

A few minutes later, Ariel, beginning to tire, stopped pumping her legs and let herself coast, steadily, to a stop. Then she lowered her feet and scraped her worn tennis shoes in the bowl-shaped indentation carved in the bare soil by the thousands of kids before her.

Suddenly she was back to earth, looking red-faced and a little disappointed. "I almost flew up there, Mom," she exclaimed. "I was almost an angel."

"I know," Estelle replied. "I know."

CHAPTER 47

Tony

Tony turned his head toward the window, its glass divided by wooden panes. The outside was cut into squares by those four panes: a tree in one. A cumulous cloud in another, black power lines sliced the third pane in half, and the corner of a brick wall filled the lower one. Tree, sky, clouds, brick, he thought. The world, cut into segments.

What was out there, beyond them? It seemed that everything had changed since he had this accident. Or maybe it was he who had changed. Or was it both?

Whatever, these past days he could spend hours, lying in the bed, meditating on all the things that were beyond the squares, wishing he was out there again. He never had so much time to think in his life, never had so much yearning to get outside, to find out what was beyond those squares. He'd been in the coma for more than a week, they told him, though it seemed, to him, like a short afternoon nap. He wondered how those few days had passed and eluded him, without him even knowing it. It was like someone took a pencil and erased a sentence from his life and, suddenly, he was a week older.

He wanted the days back. He would have driven all the way back to Wanley by now. He wanted every hour, minute, and second back. But those things just slipped through his fingers like trying to hold a handful of mercury.

"So how long am I stuck in this joint, Doc?" Tony inquired when the doctor, making his rounds, walked in.

"Sorry you consider yourself stuck." The severe man, his half-shell glasses slid down on his nose, frowned. "Without us, you might be dead. You were darn lucky that backpacker saw you take that nosedive."

"Okay, okay, I realize that," he said, more apologetically. "But I just want to know how long."

"A few more days, at least," he said, "until you're stable. We'll do some tests. Head injuries and comas are nothing to mess around with, you know."

"Hey, tell me about it."

Tony, who was off the oxygen machine, was still being fed a painkiller and an antibiotic through an IV. He glanced down at the small tube, a transparent umbilical cord inserted into a vein in his forearm.

The doctor leaned back in his white hospital coat, frayed at the sleeves. "Your stitches look good," he said, peering at the side of Tony's skull.

"I'm glad they're happy," Tony tossed back, but the man remained stone-faced.

"After you're released," the doctor continued, "the concussion might make you dizzy at times. Maybe confused, too. And those ribs are going to be sore. You broke three, you know. They'll take a while to heal. So no heavy lifting."

"Yeah," he agreed. "But can I drive?"

"Anxious to get back somewhere?"

"I am. Yes, sir, I am."

"I wouldn't push it." He scribbled something on Tony's chart on a clipboard, his pen itching across the paper, peeled his glasses off his nose, and stuffed them into a baggy coat pocket. "And," he added dryly, "I'd think twice about that hang gliding. Trying to fly over a canyon is not the best idea," he scolded. "It's a great way to do yourself in at an early age."

"I suppose. But I don't mind taking a risk or two, I guess."

The doctor glanced up from his clipboard. "What are you?" he chided. "Some kind of stuntman?"

Tony just shrugged and, tried to chuckle, which caused a few matches to ignite and burn beneath his rib cage.

The doctor stood from the card table chair. "I have to say, the staff was a little confused, what with a couple of different IDs in your wallet with different addresses. And different names, even." Tony knew what he was talking about—he'd had a guy at a copying shop make up a couple of fake laminated IDs with bogus addresses as a gag. Such as Dashing Desdiolo, from Hollywood, Ca. and Tony D., from Las Vegas. Or Tightwalk Tony from Ringling Brothers, Inc., Baraboo, Wis. "We couldn't really figure out who you were. Or where you were from."

"Join the club," Tony quipped. "Sometimes I can't, either."

"You've been the talk of the nurse's station since you got here," the doctor continued, ignoring his comment. "Even checked with the local police, to make sure you weren't on the run from the law or something."

"Well, I'm not. I'm just running on the airplane fuel you're feeding me in my IV."

"Whatever," the doctor returned with a sting of sarcasm.

As he pulled the door shut behind him, the doctor muttered something about getting some rest. But Tony didn't want to rest. He didn't want to close his eyes. He didn't want to go back to a place that reminded him of the coma, a place where the days were lost easily as water evaporating from a boiling pan. He wanted to stay awake as long as he could, even as the room was darkening. He wanted to listen to the faint beeping sound, and stare at the small light, like a tiny red heart that blinked off, then on, on, then off, as if to whisper to him: Stop. Go. Stop. Go.

CHAPTER 48

Estelle and Ariel

Estelle watched the chaotic but fascinating scene on the grassy area in front of the White House. A group of people—both Blacks and Whites— danced in a circle as skinny, bare-chested men with long hair chanted and played bongos and African drums. Others stood in vigil, holding up hand-painted red and white signs decorated with peace symbols and Black power fist symbols. The signs shouted: End Segregation Now! Stand up Against Racism! and End Police Brutality! Barefoot girls with embroidered peasant blouses and bell bottoms wandered the grounds, pausing by the dancing group or the contingent with signs, handing out daisies from small baskets. All the while, scowling police stood at attention in a line along the curb, eyeing the activities.

Pearl, walking beside Estelle and Ariel, remarked "Peaceful protest. An' that's the best kind. So far, no busted heads."

Ariel glanced down at Estelle's clothes; her long skirt, sandals, and multicolored circles of bracelets were similar to several of the dancing girls. "Mom, are we hippies?"

"What?"

"I heard somebody call carnival people hippies. The cops aren't going to club us, are they?" she asked, her voice nervous.

"No. We're more like gypsies," Estelle replied. "So don't worry."

"Don't be so sure," Pearl said under her breath to Estelle. "It seems like, lately, anybody who looks a little different is an enemy of the establishment."

"So we're targets, too?" Estelle quizzed.

"Just watch your step, that's all," she cautioned. "You saw what happened to me. And, damned if the same thing happened three years ago when I walked the bridge in Selma."

"Selma?" Estelle repeated, and Pearl proceeded to tell her about the famous walk across the Edmund Pettus Bridge in Selma, where police charged and assaulted a group of Black civil rights protestors.

Just then a man in his twenties sauntered up to the three of them. Bearded, he had long brown hair and a washed-out burgundy and white tie-dyed T-shirt. His jeans were held up by a rope belt tied in a knot on one side. "Hey," he said, tipping his chin to Pearl.

"Hey," Pearl tossed back. "This is my new friend Estelle. And her daughter Ariel."

"Far out. Here to do the sit-in with us?" the man asked Estelle.

"Not exactly." Estelle replied.

He lifted his hand in the air. "Hey, that's okay." He shifted on his worn leather sandals. "Maybe you will, eventually. For now, just groove with the movement."

"He's part of our activist group," Pearl explained. "Our resident white male hippie, you might say."

The man laughed. "Hey, nothing wrong with that." He held out his hand to Estelle. "My name's Ezekiel, by the way."

The man pointed to the bruise on the side of Pearl's temple "Jesus, Pearl. What's with that?"

"Had a little run-in with a club."

"At the MLK rally?"

Pearl nodded.

"Damn Fascist bastards," he hissed through gritted teeth. "You okay, Pearl?"

"Much better. Thanks to these two."

Ezekiel bent to one knee next to Ariel. "So, want to join the circle?" He pulled a daisy from his backpack and handed it to Ariel.

"Can I, Mom?" Ariel asked.

Estelle tossed a questioning look at Pearl, who nodded. "Seems pretty tame out there. If there's any trouble, we can pull her back."

"Well, okay," Estelle agreed. "But just for a few minutes. And don't smoke any of their cigarettes, if they offer you any."

"No way," Ariel joked, not quite getting Estelle's implication. "I won't smoke. Not until I'm at least thirteen."

Hearing that, Pearl laughed heartily, and Ezekiel whisked Ariel out to the drum circle. The group chanted "Peace now!" followed by a couple of verses from "We Shall Overcome."

Estelle watched Ariel as she joined hands in the circle and quickly learned the words to the song.

Later, Pearl suggested that they stop at the Civil Rights Coalition at the neighborhood co-op. "It's where I volunteer," she explained.

"So what do you do there?" Estelle inquired.

"Leaflets. You know—for the causes. Racism. Poverty. Fair Housing. And you can bring Ariel along, too," Pearl added. "There are always a few kids hanging out there. Might be fun for her. And, who knows—she might just learn something, too."

*   *   *

In the afternoon, before Pearl picked Estelle and Ariel up to take them to the co-op, Estelle drove the two of them to the Smithsonian Museum of Natural History.

"Why are we stopping here?" Ariel questioned.

"It's a museum." She dropped the keys into her macramé purse and stepped out.

"It's not going to have carnival freaks or anything, is it?" Ariel asked, squinting one eye in jest.

"No, no," Estelle countered, knowing Ariel was thinking of Virgil Sand's tacky exhibit he called Dr. Sand's Museum of Amazing Oddities, the musty tent that housed some of his odd mutants of nature, like the two-headed gopher, a racoon with three eyes that looked like one of Sand's fake taxidermy attempts, a three-legged turtle, and a mouse holding a tiny barbell. Next to those, on a wooden plank, were glass jars of bleached animal skulls, though no one knew what was what. On the back wall was an array of vintage black and white photos of famous carnival freaks such as the Bearded Lady, the Lobster Boy, the Reptile Man, the Four-Legged Girl, the Pig Man, The Living Skeleton, the Camel Girl, and the Human Pin Cushion—a man who pounded nails through his tongue. Sand was overly fascinated by all of that, but the exhibit, which cost two bucks to enter, really grossed Ariel out.

"This place is classy," Estelle assured Ariel, taking her hand. "And, there's something in here I think you should see."

Inside, in the darkened Hall of Gems and Minerals exhibit, they came upon a huge crystal ball in a glass case. Ariel ran up to it and, awed, blinked her eyes at it. As she bent close to read the details written on a plaque, the crystal ball reflected a curved, upside-down image of her face. "Two-hundred forty thousand carats," she said, her breath fogging a small circle on the glass. "Twelve point nine inches in diameter. One hundred six pounds. It's the world's largest. Wow," she exclaimed, "This thing weighs more than I do!" Estelle, pulling out her Instamatic camera, snapped a picture of Ariel, her pug nose pressed to the glass. The flash bounced off the polished crystal and, for an instant, illuminated the room.

"It says that this crystal ball is flawless." Ariel continued. She shifted her eyes to Estelle. "What about your crystal ball, Mom? Is it flawless?"

"What do you think?"

Ariel twisted her lips to one side, and then the other. "I think it's probably a little flawed. And," she added, "flawless at the same time."

"Just like us?" Estelle asked.

"Yeah." Ariel laughed. "Just like us."

* * *

That evening, with Ariel playing cards with a couple of kids in a side room, Estelle sat next to Pearl, sliding leaflets into pre-addressed envelopes. The picture window of the storefront was plastered with posters of blue peace symbols and a sign declaring:

CIVIL RIGHTS COALITION OF WASHINGTON.
FREE LITERATURE. KNOW YOUR RIGHTS!

Inside were more posters, including one with Malcolm X pointing to the sky and the words:

YOU CAN'T SEPARATE PEACE FROM FREEDOM.

On another wall were music posters of Nina Simone, her stare burning through the paper, Marvin Gaye in mid-song, The Impressions, wearing sports jackets and bow ties, Otis Redding wailing into a microphone, and James Brown on his knees, and wearing a cape. The room was decorated with small, mismatched chairs, a couple of Formica-topped lunchroom tables, and a few wooden crates. Ashtrays and soda cans and empty wine bottles with candles in them anchored newspapers and dog-eared copies of *Ebony* and *Newsweek*. Two overhead fluorescent tubes—seemingly too small for the space—bathed the room in filtered light, and a Mahalia Jackson album spun on a turntable in the corner.

Thanks to Pearl's welcoming offer, Estelle had agreed to stay one more night at her apartment before they hit the road again. It was a welcome respite from the highway, she reasoned, and besides, Ariel was enjoying her time here.

Before she began stuffing the envelopes, Estelle read the leaflet's headline, "Civil Rights, Equality, Fair Housing, and an End to Poverty," and opened it to the text. It occurred to her that she hadn't thought that much about the civil rights movement. Besides family activities, she barely had an hour to peruse a newspaper from a local quick mart. For Estelle, civil rights protests and the war on poverty were a million miles away.

But now this room brought it much closer, and into focus. The space was filled with a rag-tag group of White, Hispanic, and African-American students, plus a few faculty members from nearby George Washington University and a couple of older women activists wearing Free Angela Davis buttons.

When Pearl stood up to take a break, the bearded man Estelle had met at the protest plopped down on her left. "So. You're a new recruit after all."

"Not exactly," Estelle said shyly, "but sort of."

"Glad you could volunteer." He extended his hand and gave hers a firm shake. This evening he wore a bright orange and red spiral-patterned shirt and a fringed buckskin vest. The vest was dotted with political buttons. A smile lit up beneath his beard. "Let's see…you're Estelle, right?"

She nodded.

"Cool name," he exclaimed, staring at her with piercing eyes. "It means star in Spanish. Means you're celestial."

"Hmmm," Estelle said. "Never really thought about it."

"Well, you should. Every name has a meaning." He was a couple years younger than Estelle—maybe in his late 20s, and handsome, she noticed. He had a distinct scent of leather and smoke.

"And your name was…." Estelle didn't recall it from that afternoon.

"Zeke. Ever hear of the prophet Ezekiel?"

"Sure. So that's you?"

"Absolutely." He stretched his arms wide, exposing a couple of knotted leather wristbands. "I'm surrounded by a corrupt establishment. It's trying to suppress us all. And I prophesize that we'll bring it down. We're gonna change the ever-lovin' world."

"Hmmm." Estella was a bit surprised by his confidence.

"In the Bible, Ezekiel was a visionary, man," he continued. "He had visions of creatures with four heads that could see all four directions at once. He saw a wheel within a wheel. They were wheels of fire. Wheels of enlightenment. Ezekiel believed that the spiritual is as important as the physical." He nodded. "That's the best way to survive."

"And are you surviving?"

"So far," he said, his voice tight. He knocked his knuckles on the scarred wooden table. "So frickin' far."

Estelle nodded to the stack of leaflets. "So where are all these being sent?"

"To the senators, of course," he affirmed. " And congresswoman." He snorted through his nose. "There's only one, you know."

"Think they'll read them?"

"Doubt it. I mean, they're the ones passing bills that skirt around fair housing. And support funding suburban schools while the inner city ones starve." He raised one eyebrow in a thoughtful pose. "Yeah. It's the same imperialists who allocate all our tax money. You know—so we can kill off the young Black men. A lot of the guys sent to 'Nam are minorities, you know. The war on poverty takes on a whole new meaning over there."

As he continued speaking, he used inflection on certain words, as if he'd often said these things into a microphone in a speech at a rally. He looked at her skeptically, his eyes studying her from her hair to her sandals. "You're not from around here, are you?"

"Oh," she said, flustered, "We're just staying at Pearl's place for a little while."

"That didn't answer my question."

"I'm traveling," she finally replied. "On a kind of road trip."

"Good that you detoured, and took some time to do something meaningful," he said with a nod of approval.

She knew her trip had turned into a series of detours, but, she decided, they were detours she needed to follow. They showed her—and Ariel, too—that there were important issues outside the carnival, that people did more than just set up the Milk Bottle game or pull a duct-taped lever to start the Kiddie Kars in motion. Her few days in Washington made the carnival seem small.

"So how'd you end up here?" she asked.

"I ran away from home when I was seventeen. Dropped out of school. Eventually, I took a few classes at a free university."

"You don't seem like a dropout."

"Hey, I'm self-educated," he said with an undertone of arrogance. "Which is what you have to be if you want to survive. Let's face it—most of what we see and hear on the tube is capitalist propaganda. I mean, the media, and history books have it all wrong. So much of it is bullshit, you know? It's what the establishment wants to you hear. What they want you to believe."

As she listened, Estelle stuffed another envelope, licked the flap, sealed it, then passed it down the row toward the people who were applying stamps. Minor as it was, she felt like she was actually doing something for a cause, and that felt good. She was actually taking a stand, even if it was just sliding fliers into the dry envelopes.

Pearl, a sandwich in one hand, came back from her break and squeezed in next to Estelle again. "So," Pearl said to Ezekiel, "I see you've swooped in on our newcomer."

"Like, you mean Star," he said knowingly, bobbing his head.

"And," Pearl said, directing her comment to Estelle, "I see you've met our resident coalition spokesperson. He delivers the speeches at a lot of rallies."

"So I gathered," Estelle said. "Ezekiel. Like the prophet."

"Oh. Is that what he told you his name was?"

Pearl gave the man a disapproving glance, and he tossed back a smug look. "Watch out for this one," she said, pointing her index finger at him. "Unlike most men, he's smarter than he appears to be."

"Hey, sister, you watch it," he countered.

It was near midnight, and Estelle drank a couple of glasses of wine, which were passed around after the envelopes were finished. She knew it was getting late, and Pearl said she'd drive them back to her place for the night. "Soul Man" by Sam and Dave played on the stereo. Estelle hoped the loud music wasn't waking Ariel, who had been asleep in a side room for the last couple of hours.

In the back room, looking for her coat, Estelle glanced up to see that Ezekiel had followed her there. With a kick of his scuffed suede boot, he closed the door behind him.

"Hey," he said, a half-smile appearing beneath his overgrowth of beard. "Wanna rap?"

"Rap?" she asked, rummaging for her coat, but he didn't reply.

He flopped down on a saggy tapestry couch, reefer in hand, and pulled her to the cushion next to him. "It's cool talking to you, Star. Really cool, you know?" His eyes were bloodshot, and he was clearly stoned.

"Yeah." She thought for a second, then blurted out, "So what is your real name, then?"

"Why do you ask?"

"I'm just wondering." A part of her was interested in hearing this guy's real story.

"Ezekiel's my nickname, sorta," he said almost giddily. "Like, isn't that good enough?"

"No," she said.

"Okay, okay," he said, holding up his hand, a leather and puka shell bracelet circling his wrist. "Okay. It's really Douglas. But if you were me, I mean, you wouldn't keep a handle like Douglas, would you?"

"If it's who you are, you would."

He touched the reefer to his lips and took in a slow breath. The tip glowed reddish orange like a burner on a stove. "Well," he exhaled, the smoke billowing, "it's not who I am, man. It's who my parents thought I was. My old man...he's an admiral in the goddamn Navy," he scoffed. "Named me after Douglas MacArthur."

"Oh?"

"Absolutely. Dad was a gung-ho Annapolis academy grad, even." He made a saluting gesture with his right hand. "And my mom, she's your, you know, quintessential military wife. Schmoozes with all the military bigwigs. They have parties with the goddamn admirals. And both my parents are racists to the core. I had to get out of there. Jesus Christ, I had to."

"So that's why you ran away?"

"That. And a thousand other reasons. But the military crap was the main thing," he said, his eyes narrowing, his forehead furrowing as the words spilled out in a rush, "I mean, my old man wanted to push me into Annapolis, with all the other frickin' recruits. Hail to thee our alma mater. He was practically training me to be an officer when I was twelve, for Christ's sake." He opened and closed one fist and his lower lip quivered a little. "Shit—I even had a goddamn gun in his gun case." He took another hit of the reefer. "Yeah. And now little Dougie's a draft dodger. That's why I can't give out my real name," he explained. "My old man would kill me if he knew. There'd be an execution by a frikin' firing squad right in my own front yard."

"Sounds rough…."

Ezekiel's face smoothed a little, creases erasing themselves. "But now I'm all about justice. Justice and equality and love."

"I wish it was that simple." The thrumming beat from the stereo pulsed through the wall.

"It is that simple," he countered. "It frikin' is. Equality. And love. I mean, what else do we need?" He leaned back on a pillow cushion and inhaled the joint again. "Star," he said, sliding nearer to her. "It's a really cool name." He put his lips close to her ear and whispered her name. It made her nervous, and when she started to stand, he slid his arms around her waist, pulled her back down, and kissed the side of her face.

"Hey," she said, drawing back from him.

He pulled her close again. "Yeah. Hey," he said, "You're awesome, Star." He leaned forward to kiss the side of her face again.

She ducked out from under his grasp and stood. "Stop it!" she shouted.

"Huh?" he blurted, a little surprised. "What's the big hang-up? I thought you were about love, too."

"I don't know what I'm about," she replied. "But it's not this."

"Then what are you here for?" His voice took on a hostile tone.

She rescued her coat from the pile on the floor.

"You're hooked on somebody," he blurted. "Is that it?"

"Right."

"So? Hey, I'm not hung up about that. I'm cool with it." C'mon," he goaded. "You gotta love the one you're with. I mean, that's what life's about, isn't it?"

She didn't reply. Instrumental music thrummed through from the other side of the wall.

Finally, she said "I'm flattered, Ezekiel, or Douglas, or whoever you are. But I'm leaving."

"Okay, Star," he said. "But you're missing out on life, babe," he chided. "You're really, really missing out." With that, he pushed through the oak door to the living room. Like a drumbeat searching for a song, he bobbed his head and shoulders a little as he stepped into the loud, tangled web of the music.

* * *

Estelle stood over her daughter in the back bedroom. Ariel was somehow able to sleep through the loud music. Estelle leaned over and kissed her on the forehead. Ariel stirred slightly but didn't wake.

Her thoughts shifted to Tony, and she pictured him on his tightrope. Was he walking it somewhere? She wondered. Was that silver wire cutting their lives in half? She pictured herself, standing below, waiting for him to make the crossing, hoping he wouldn't fail. So that was her role? she thought. Just a helpless, passive onlooker, never trying the walk herself, just watching him, cheering him on from below, hoping for his success?

Without answering her own questions, she grabbed her coat, woke her daughter, and exited the storefront with Pearl.

CHAPTER 49

Estelle and Ariel

"We'll stay for breakfast." The next morning, Estelle's voice sounded a little weary. "But we should leave right after that."

"So soon?" Pearl stood by the counter, dropping two slices of whole-grain bread into a toaster.

Estelle nodded. "It's been great staying here. But we've got a lot of miles left to drive, and not all that much money left."

Pearl leaned her hip against the counter. "I hear you. Miles to go before you sleep," she added, quoting the Robert Frost poem from Kennedy's inauguration. "I feel that way every day. But just know, hon, that it was real good to have you around." She lowered her eyes to the linoleum floor. "I'll always owe you for patching me up after that cop took a swing at me."

"You owe me nothing. I think I owe you some things. I owe you a lot, actually."

Pearl reached to the cupboard, pulled down some Shredded Wheat, crumbled a biscuit into a bowl. The toast popped up from the silver toaster. "So," she said, "you off to track down that man of yours?"

"I guess that's the plan."

Pearl set the two pieces of toast on kitchen plates, buttered them, and handed one to Estelle. "Listen—if you come back through here, the door's always open for you. There's a lot of unfinished business around here, you know."

Estelle took a bite of the toast and nodded. "I admire you, Pearl. You know—for your activism."

"I don't have a choice, hon," Pearl said, pouring milk on a bowl of cereal for Estelle, one for Ariel, and then one for herself. "It's just what I do. I just hope it makes some changes for the good. Who knows what America will look like in ten, or even fifty years? A lot better, I hope."

Minutes later, after Ariel rolled up her sleeping bag and Estelle gathered her belongings, the three of them stood by Estelle's car, the leaves from the low-hanging branches of an elm casting fluttering shadows on the hood. "So, Miz Estelle the fortune tellah," Pearl said, "Before you leave on your next leg, tell me—what's around the corner for me?"

Estelle lowered her gaze to the keys in her palm. "Hmmm…" In her mind, she pictured the battles that might lie ahead for Pearl: the protest marches, the tireless hours handing out leaflets and writing to legislators, the dull wooden clubs, trying to beat the dreams from her head. "I can't say exactly. But what I can say is that it's good. It might be a hard road, but it's a good one. And the right one."

Pearl smiled broadly. "I'll take that, hon. Sure sounds real fine to me. In fact, I think it's already happening."

Pearl bent to one knee and gave Ariel a warm hug. Ariel muttered a sad "Bye," sniffed, and straightened the daisy that she'd started wearing in her hair. Then Pearl stood and embraced Estelle.

"And how about my fortune?" Estelle asked, turning the tables. "Tell me what you think."

"Your future? Don't know for sure. But what I do know is that you've got to be yourself, honey. You dig my meaning?"

"I'm trying."

"I learned that a long time ago," Pearl continued. "It's the way I survived. Whatever you decide to be, just go after it a hundred percent. You don't have to be great at it, just be strong." She leaned against the rough bark of the elm and laughed. "End of lecture. I know you didn't ask for it," she exclaimed with a hearty laugh, "but damn, sometimes I just can't help it."

"And you, baby girl," Pearl said, nodding at Ariel, "You've got a great life ahead of you. Just follow this fine lady's footsteps." She nodded at Estelle. "You can't go wrong."

As they drove through the streets of Washington, Estelle glanced into the rearview mirror and noticed the Capitol building and the pale spire of the Washington Monument becoming smaller. After a few blocks, as if the earth itself was slowly absorbing them, they disappeared from view.

CHAPTER 50

Tony

Finally released from the hospital, he stood outside the glass doors, stretched his arms wide, and took a gulp of air, feeling like he was waking from a long sleep. He was in a way, after those days in the coma when he was caught in a dark nothingness. This morning, the midday sun cupped his face gently in the palm of its hand. Standing there in the bright parking lot, Tony knew exactly what he had to do today.

He glanced at his hang glider in the flatbed, which the rescue crew had brought with them after his accident; the nylon had only a few small tears. It was obvious that he had taken the brunt of the damage.

He exited the hospital and drove east for a couple of hours; beneath the floorboards, the pavement crooned its steady, one-note melodic song. The range of mountains—the western edge of the Rockies—began to lift their broad shoulders. The first time he drove through them, the mountains seemed so massive. But this time, as he aimed his truck in their direction, the mountains looked almost small to him. Rather than growing larger and more intimidating as he drove toward them, they seemed manageable. They seemed like someplace he could be.

For a second, he remembered Ariel's question when she woke and emerged from her bedroom that night he left. "Where you going, Daddy?" he heard her call. He felt guilty, but he didn't turn to answer her.

This morning, he approached a smaller road that intersected the highway. Like a compass dial pointing north, the chrome hood ornament of the truck seemed to be pulled in that direction. And almost without even realizing it, Tony cranked the wheel and followed it.

He didn't question why. He was detouring; that's all he knew. Maybe the sound of his own wheels was making him a little crazy. All he knew was that he was that the steering wheel was speaking to his fingers, and he was turning it toward those mountains.

There was something he needed to do. Not just needed, but compelled to do.

Steadily, the asphalt road began to rise, and to narrow, squeezing in on him with sagebrush and sand and weathered boulders.

A half-hour later, the asphalt crumbled to gravel, then to dirt, and then, eventually, it became a rocky trail with two ruts in it. He drove slowly on that small, steep, remote path, the tires bumping over rocks, the engine heating up, and finally, he felt the truck chug a few times. The truck lurched to a stop.

He heard himself laugh.

He stepped out, leaving the driver's side wide open. He knew it didn't matter if he left the truck just like that—door open, the keys still in the ignition, its beeping sound crying out.

He noticed a small trail—vague, but discernable—leading upward along the steep hillside. He surmised that it was used by gold miners seeking their fortunes long ago, and, before them, by the Native Americans, who were hunting, or maybe on a vision quest. And even before them, it was traversed by deer and bighorn sheep and mountain lions and whatever else lives up in those hills and has a compulsion—no, an instinct—to climb.

He felt that same instinct now.

So he reached into the flatbed, grabbed his hang glider, and slid it out. He lifted the glider to his shoulders and began to carry it up that rugged trail, the low scrub pines scratching at his legs and ankles, the sharp, loose rocks rolling out from under his scuffed tennies. The hang glider's tip scraped over pale-green sage and he had to angle it between the narrow rock outcroppings. It was bulky and cumbersome, but, Tony decided, not too heavy to lug up this path. His bandaged ribs ached as he climbed, and sweat dampened his t-shirt, but it didn't matter. He'd keep going, finish this climb; he'd follow this trail as far as he could.

He knew there was something he needed to do with the glider, once he got there. Something important. That's what mattered.

As he climbed, he dislodged a couple of rocks. He watched them, tumbling below him, bounding against the other rocks embedded in the trail, then eventually wedging against a tree trunk or an outcropping. It was the way of rocks, he decided: to be at rest, and then to be uprooted, to roll, to click against other rocks, and then to come to rest again. As one tumbled below him, Tony admired the way of rocks.

On one section of the trail, he stumbled on a bulging tree root and fell forward. Extending his arm to break his fall, he cut the palm of his right hand on a sharp shard of granite. "Ahh!" he exclaimed. Dark red blood seeped from the burning gouge in the center of his palm.

Then he noticed his leather wallet—which had jostled out of his jeans pocket—splayed open on the path, the bills sliding out of it. The wind lifted the top bill—a ten—from the stack and blew it away. Then another bill—a one. Then another. They fluttered off a ledge, then dropped twenty feet down. Instead of scuttling down the rocks to try to retrieve them, he let them go, watched them scrape and skitter down the steep terrain. They didn't matter right now.

As the bills peeled away, he felt as if layers of himself were peeling off, too. They peeled away like the layers of an onion or the rings of a tree until he was down to his center. His very core.

He was no longer Ping Pong Tony or The Dashing Desdiolo. Instead, he was just plain Tony Desdiolo. Tony Desdiolo, idiot, and runaway father. Tony Desdiolo, who didn't have a lost child, like he'd always pictured. Tony Desdiolo, whose unrealistic dream of adoption had tumbled away.

He rose from his knees to his feet and continued up the trail.

He knew what he had to do.

After another half hour of climbing, he reached a precipice. Panting in the thin air, and wiping the sweat from his eyes, he stepped onto a large, flat, limestone slab, an altar smoothed by wind and sand for thousands of years. He set the hang glider down and gazed out over the hazy bruise-blue mountains. From this pinnacle, they seemed to stretch all the way to the end of the earth, though he knew they didn't.

He sat down and pulled the wrinkled photo of Estelle and Ariel from his pocket. It was a black and white Polaroid shot, a favorite of his, though he'd kept it folded and stashed in the truck's glove compartment and hadn't looked at it for a long time. In it, the two of them stood in front of the fortune-telling tent, Estelle with her head tipped slightly sideways, giving the camera an insecure but inquisitive look, and five-year-old Ariel, a melting sno-cone dripping from her fingers, her eyes squinted as if the sunlight, angling between the concession stands, was too much for her. The picture was worn from being carried around so long, and the pale crease marks looked like grey wires in front of the two.

Tony studied the picture, and as he did, Estelle and Ariel's faces seemed to become brighter and brighter until they stung his eyes, causing him to close them.

In the next few seconds, his faults and weaknesses rushed through his mind: his vanity and ego, his constant quest for fame, to be a star in the carnival, his restlessness, and—most of all—his leaving his wife and child behind on this aimless quest. He felt guilty for it all.

Still, just facing those realizations was freeing to him. It made him feel light, unburdened. His head was finally clear. He wasn't who he used to be, and it felt liberating, like nothing he'd ever experienced. He felt like a crystal in a dark cave, glowing from the inside. Or like the fire in an ember before it burns.

Then he opened his eyes and looked away from the photo, tipping his head toward the sky: the setting sun was caught, held still by the sharp edge of one silhouetted mountain slope.

It would be dark soon, he knew. He reminded himself of the purpose of this climb. And he had to fulfill it.

He set the photo next to him on the flat rock and placed pebbles on the four corners so it wouldn't blow away. As he did, he suddenly felt like crying. He felt like crying, because of the mountains. Because of how far away from Estelle and Ariel he felt. Because of the blood on his palm—the same blood that ran through his veins ran through little Ariel's veins. And through the veins of the baby Charlotte lost. He lowered his head and sobbed a few seconds.

As his sobs subsided, he tried to compose himself. He crossed his legs, slid his arms onto his knees, palms up, and straightened his back like he'd seen some meditating people do on the cliffs overlooking the California beaches.

He took a few long, slow breaths and began to meditate, to think about the meaning of his life. Things he hadn't focused on for a long time. He thought about love, or what he believed was love. There were many sides to the emotion, he realized. Sometimes love simply disappears and evaporates into the high, thin regions of the hazy atmosphere. Sometimes it's a power that can pull things together. Sometimes love is what people leave behind.

Whatever form it took, he decided, it was love—just love—that mattered most of all. Maybe it was that infinitely simple, he thought, and that infinitely complex.

He inhaled deeply, held it, then released his breath steadily, expelling the stale air from his lungs. It made a sighing sound, like the first gust of wind on the day the earth was born.

His thoughts tunneled deeper, deeper than they'd ever gone before, surprising him. He pondered his smallness—he was nothing more than a tiny, tiny speck, not even a freckle on the massive face of the earth. Thought about how his measly life span was no more than a single molecule on a road that stretched for hundreds of miles. And how many years did he have left?

He stood up, and lifted the gossamer hang glider, which felt suddenly light, almost weightless. *Where you going, Daddy?* a voice asked from somewhere far away, but he didn't answer. He walked to the edge of the rock, held the glider above his head by its handles, and looked down at the steep drop-off below him, the teeth of the jagged granite and slate ledges.

It was a sheer drop-off. A thousand feet, at least, to the basin of the canyon. A stream at its base, thin as a blue thread. He felt the pull as a gust of wind slid its palms under the glider, beckoning him.

With both arms, he raised the glider as high as he could, and held it there, the wings wobbling.

Then, with one quick motion, he reared back and tossed the glider into the air, watched it pirouette on a current, spinning once, twice, three times. With a sharp sound, the glider struck an outcrop, the wood cracking, the frame bending, the nylon fabric tearing to shreds. The glider scraped and cartwheeled down the mountainside until, far below, it reached the dark seam of a rock crevice, dropped into it, and disappeared.

His face lifted into a smile. He was happy to see it break into pieces. Hang gliders didn't matter. The bills in his wallet didn't matter. His ego didn't matter. There were so many things that didn't matter anymore.

Tony lowered himself onto the rock platform again. He felt relieved because he knew where he was going, finally, and what he had to do. He looked down at his upturned palms—one of them pale, covered with a layer of fine dust, the creases crisscrossing it like a map to somewhere. The other was caked with blood that surrounded the deep cut—a wound, that, though it was still bleeding a little, was already beginning to heal.

CHAPTER 51

Estelle and Ariel

Ariel laughed and pointed as Estelle drove past a cage in someone's front yard. Inside it, a chimpanzee gripped its fingers in the wires and hooted at them. Behind another house, what looked like a large gray shed seemed to shift slightly as they passed. When the shed moved again, Ariel realized it was actually a ten-foot elephant, chained to a metal stake.

A few blocks before, they had passed a wooden billboard, featuring a little person in a clown's suit, announcing:

Welcome to Gibsonton, Florida
Carney Town, USA

Gibsonton was a town that carnies—both current and past—gravitated toward, since they were accepted there. For years, famous carnival people wintered in the town, and eventually settled there, sometimes even keeping tamed bears or rusted rides in their yards as if they were lawn ornaments. For Estelle, the town was full of pleasant memories. It was a place where she and Tony had once escaped the cold winter of Minnesota. That year, the winds blew snow into high drifts along the sides of their trailer as if trying to prop it up. Once in Gibtown—as people referred to it—they developed friendships with the enclave of carnival workers who also wintered or retired or just hung out there.

"Cooool," crooned Ariel as they drove the back streets and passed a house with a brightly-colored Candy Korn trailer parked in front. "I'm really beginning to like this place."

Estelle maneuvered down a half-paved back street that crumbled at the edges. She noticed an empty lot with the Dodge-em Cars and the rusted remains of a rusted Wipeout ride, its lights missing, its metal beams and arms folded inward like a dead spider's legs. At the end of the street, she recognized Joanie's place—a trailer home that seemed to have three sections. It had an addition, painted a faded green, then another addition with blue siding. A low palm sprouted on one side of the small yard, and a cypress tree, pale moss hanging from the branches, leaned on the other side. A three-foot cactus grew from the rotted boards of the overhanging eave next to the front door.

Joanie was famous on the carnival circuit as the "Half-Girl," a sideshow sensation. Born with no legs, she was just two and a half feet tall, and her husband Del was, ironically, the World's Tallest Man who was eight feet five inches tall. Estelle knew that it was definitely a strange town. Where else was the elected mayor a little person, and the fire chief a towering eight-foot man?

Estelle hoped that Joanie, a busybody who knew almost every carny in the area, might have some information about Tony.

The house—stuffy with too-warm air—smelled like cat litter and beer and stale smoke, and when Ariel walked inside, she plugged her nose. Several cats scattered across the living room carpet in front of them. The room was decorated with large orange and white striped curtains that looked like they'd come from a cheap circus stage show or an elephant's parade costume. The walls were cracked, and uneven at the corners, as if the place was settling and couldn't decide which way to lean. A small end table lit up with plastic and glass figurines: elves, ballerinas, dancing bears, and a ringmaster. Beer cans, some upright, some tipped, decorated the coffee table between them, along with a few balls of frayed yarn. In one corner, a faded purple lamp with green bead fringes. Joanie, who was about 50 years old, sat on a worn purple pillow that propped her up on the velour couch. Her shoulders barely reached the center of the back cushion.

"Nope," Joanie was saying, "Can't say as I've seen 'im." She sipped on some chocolate-flavored Yoo-hoo, the bottle pinned between her deformed, fingerless hands. In the den, the TV was tuned to an episode of *The Price is Right*, its giddy theme song blaring.

"Handsome fella, though, as I recall, your Tony. A real good catch." Joanie's voice was surprisingly loud and husky, especially for a person with such a small body.

"Well, I guess you could say he's uncaught right now," Estelle related.

"Shit and piss. Sorry to hear dat," Joanie said through her speech impediment caused by a harelip.

Estelle, at the edge of the couch, bumped her elbow against an ashtray, its base a small red bean bag, and it fell on the floor, spewing out a couple of unlit but half-finished cigarettes. When Estelle picked it up, Joanie remarked, "Them are just for the taste. I don't inhale."

Just then, one of her six or seven or dozen cats—Estelle wasn't sure how many—sprung to the couch, scratched a cushion with its claws, and then leaped off again. The cat turned and glared jealously at Estelle. It had one gray eye and one blue one.

"Damn cats," barked Joanie, giving it a scowl. "Noodles always wants attention, damn her." Then back to Estelle: "So, jeepers creepers," she said, glancing down at Ariel, who, kneeling on the floor, played with a calico cat that climbed on her shoulders, "Tony just up and leave? How come?"

"That's what I'm trying to figure out."

"Hey, Misty!" she shouted to a cat that had climbed halfway up the drape, "Cut that crap out! So," she said, rolling her buggy eyes back to Estelle, "You try Dottie?"

Big Dottie was the famous 500-pound fat lady who also settled in the town. "Yeah, I did, and she hasn't heard anything."

"That's a dollar and forty-nine!" Joanie called out, answering Bob Barker's question about the jar of tomato sauce on *The Price is Right*. She turned back to Estelle, "You still with Sand and his bunch up there in Minnesota?"

"I guess."

"Good ol' Sandman. That sonofa bitch. I hear he swindled a couple dozen show people. But—shit and piss—nobody could prove nothing."

On the dung-stained carpet in front of them, two cats, paws outstretched, leaped over and over each other, as if they were in a trained show. And Estelle figured they might be.

"Yeah, Sand can be slippery all right," Estelle agreed. "He still owes me for part of my last month."

"You claim that money, gal," Joanie said, tipping forward.

"I'll see," Estelle replied.

"Don't just *see*, dammit. Shoot, cash in while you can. Or else bust his goddamn head." She let out a laugh, finished her bottle of Yoo-hoo, set it on the coffee table next to a few empties, then called out: "That's ninety-eight cents!" when Bob Barker asked for the correct amount for a package of spaghetti. "Ninety-eight, I'm telling ya!" Then back to Estelle: "I should be on that damn show. They never get it right. They're nincompoops, y' know? They don't have half a brain." She pursed her lips at the empty bottle and exclaimed: "Hey! More Yoo-hoo!" She gestured toward Estelle with a half arm. "Yoo-hoo for you too?" she cooed.

"Um, no thanks," Estelle said, trying not to laugh at Joanie's odd, rhyming question.

"How 'bout sweet-cheeks there?" she asked, nodding her chinless face toward Ariel. The cat Ariel was petting meowed demurely, then, for no reason, hissed and clawed at her. "Damn cat! Knock it off, Road Kill," Joanie spat. "Or I'll lock ya in the cage out back!"

"Nope," Estelle interjected. "Ariel's okay. She had a soda at the Carnival Café before we stopped." Estelle stood, anxious to leave the weirdness of Joanie's dim living room. Still, she felt sorry for her, stuck in this dingy house, sorry that the woman's only success in life was due to a birth defect.

"Gimmie a minute," Joanie trundled on a square board with wheels to the kitchen and brought back two bottles of Yoo-hoo, both of them sweaty with condensation.

"Oh," said Estelle, "We couldn't."

"Oh, you bet you could." Joanie closed her eyes briefly, calling back a memory. "You know what Big Del used to say when he brought me one of these?"

"What?"

"'Here you are, m'lady,' he'd say. Use to practically bump his damn head on the top of the kitchen doorway as he brought one to me. He was eight feet, five and a half inches, y'know. People always forget to mention that last half inch." She motioned her arm toward their publicity photo, framed on the wall, where Del wore a cowboy hat while holding little Joanie, the Half-Woman, in his arms. The caption read The World's Strangest Couple. "He used to say, real suave-like, 'You're the queen, y'know.'" She sniffed, a faraway look in her eyes. "Yeah," she continued, her voice softer, "Del's been gone a whole six years already. When we decided to get married, we eloped. We were the big love story of the carnival, y'know."

"I'm sure you were."

"I've all but stopped touring since he's gone," Joanie mused. "I done it for years, y'know, and now it's only once or twice a year. But I might just stop altogether. Maybe sort of rest on my laurels."

"So what shows are you doing these days?"

"Guest appearances. That kind of stuff. Conventions or circus days celebrations over in Tampa. I can still do my acrobatics. Y'know—cartwheels and handstands and such." She beamed a crooked smile and did a handstand. "Did you know I could climb up a ladder backward, using just my arms?" Estelle smiled, aware that Joanie was able to do some amazing tricks, despite being born without her legs and with two deformed hands. "People pay to see a person like me, you know." Joanie pointed the stub of her hand into her concave chest. "We're different, y'know. But we're still people. We have feelings, like everybody else. We can fall in love, and be loved. Like every other goddamn person. So it ain't exploitation, like some say. It's money. And you don't have to do a damn thing except pretty much sit there. So how can you turn that down?"

"I see your point."

The cat tiptoed across the end table, knocking down a ballerina statue. "Noodles!" Joanie called. "Get the hey off that!"

"Well, thanks, Joanie. We've got to get going." Estelle steered Ariel from the seedy carpet and toward the door. She didn't want to stay in this sad place much longer, with Joanie, making her way through life after the carnival by scraping close to the ground.

"Sure ya don't wanna stay longer?" Joanie tipped toward them from her creeper. "I could whip up a real good lunch. After all, I still have half an appetite!" As she said her joke, she chortled a strange, guttural-sounding laugh that sounded like bubbles popping through mud.

Estelle laughed along with her. She couldn't help but picture Joanie reaching to the bottom shelf of the refrigerator, making stale sandwiches to be washed down by the weak chocolate flavor of Yoo-hoo. "Thanks for the offer," she lied, "but we just ate."

"Welp, okay. Hey, it was real good to see ya again, ya damn mystical psychic you."

"Same to you."

Joanie, with both arms, held out the bottle of Yoo-hoo for Ariel. "You forgot this. A Yoo-hoo for the girl. One for the road. Somethin' to grow on, you might say," she quipped.

Ariel looked at Estelle, who nodded, and then took the bottle from Joanie and thanked her politely.

Joanie rolled into the front entryway with them. "Hey, sorry I couldn't help ya more about Tony boy. Shit and piss." Then she added, "Yep, my man stuck with me for a whole lotta years. It was big of him, right? Heh heh." She gurgled a laugh. "And I made a small contribution to him too, eh? Yeah…" A nostalgic smile smeared her face. "I mighta been the Half Woman, but he was twice the man. And then some."

Estelle said farewell, backed out the door and, with her foot, blocked the bolting Misty from making a quick escape.

As she towed Ariel back to the car, she could hear, through the screen door, Joanie calling to the TV: "That's two-fifty for Chef Boyardee! Two-fifty, you nincompoops!"

On their way out of town, Estelle pulled into the Showtown Restaurant and Bar off Highway 41. It was a colorfully painted place where she and Ariel ordered a lunch of sloppy Joes served on paper plates. The air hung heavy with grease as Estelle asked around about Tony—to no avail. Ariel, who ate only part of her sloppy Joe, saying it tasted like dog food, wandered around, staring at the odd, hand-painted murals on the walls—one with a four-eyed ringmaster wearing a top hat. Another one, entitled The Ringmaster in the Sky, depicted a kind of God-like bright light bursting through a hole in the clouds and shining on a miniature traveling show.

Estelle left a tip, walked past the hand-lettered sign that advertised Karaoke and Conch Fritter Night, and the two hopped back into the car, which she'd parked in the restaurant's side lot. As she tried to back the car up, she heard a low-pitched grinding sound. She hit the brake, then backed up again. Something scraped beneath the car. She put the car in neutral and jumped out to see that a concrete parking block was caught under her front bumper, the Falcon dragging it. She stood there, frustrated, trying helplessly to lift the front bumper of the car. "Great," she spat, walking back to Ariel's open window. "Apparently, we've been captured by the Showtown Bar."

"Don't make me go back in there, Mom," Ariel pleaded. "Please. Isn't there a Macdonald's anywhere around here? Or is this whole town just plain creepy?"

Just then a middle-aged man stepped out of the low-slung, rusty sedan that was parked next to them. The big man was bald, his face round, his body even rounder. "Need help, Ma'am?" he asked politely.

She nodded, and he leaned over and slid both hands under the front bumper. "Hop back in and put 'er in reverse," he said, and as she did, he hefted the bumper above the concrete block. The carriage scraped a little, then the car lurched a few feet backward and was free.

Estelle rolled down the window and thanked the man. She pulled a few dollar bills from her purse and tried to hand it to him.

"Nope," he said, blushing a little and waving the tip away. "It's nothin'. I used to be a strong man in a show. Some things still come in handy once in a while, right?"

CHAPTER 52

Estelle and Ariel

Estelle leaned back on the sand and let her eyelids close as the sound soothed her, mesmerized her. The waves rolled in, and broke close to shore with a whoosh that softened to a sigh. Then, like blue tongues tipped by white foam, each wave pulled back into the mouth of the ocean again. Far off, in the bay, the masts of boats swung gently back and forth like metronomes, keeping time. Above her, the palm fronds rustled as they lifted, then bowed their heads.

The remote powdery white sand beach extended for at least a mile. On this Florida shore, she could breathe the warm sea air, which tasted sweet and fragrant. It was so much different than the confines of their trailer, its narrow walls made of brown mahogany paneling that seemed to absorb light but still echo sounds. It was so much different than the confines of the carnival with its cluttered, clanking rides, their steel support beams like prison bars, closing her in each day.

It had been a long jaunt, this trip, and after two-thousand miles, it had nearly reached its end on this shoreline. Where had the journey taken her?

Here. Here, she could stroll with her daughter. Here, Estelle slipped off her sandals and Ariel, barefoot but limping, walked along this in-between place where the ocean meets the land. Estelle felt the fine, wet sand massaging the soles of her feet. On this shore, she could look up, and instead of seeing the caged riders in the rust-red Rock-O-Plane, she looked at the curved shapes of seagulls, grey and white and buoyant as they banked like kites on the warm exhaling winds. Here, Estelle could glance behind her and see her footprints, quickly washed away by the rushing waves.

It was as though there was no past here, she thought; whatever was behind you was quickly erased. There was just the present, the place where you took the next step on the smooth, untouched sand.

"Mom, can I go in the water?" Ariel asked as she walked in her silk swimsuit—with hamburgers and French fries printed on it—and sipped on the bottle of Yoo-hoo that Joanie gave her.

"Of course you can."

With Estelle sitting on a beach towel, Ariel tiptoed a few feet into the surf, then dashed back to shore as, one by one, the waves chased her. Estelle called out: "Not too far out there, honey. Watch out for those bigger waves. Looks like the tide's coming in."

Ariel just gave her a neutral, almost indifferent stare, as if to say *Maybe I will. But maybe I won't.* She kept wading a little deeper toward the waves that slapped against her waist. Ariel was like that: seemingly compliant, but, lately, her attitude was sprinkled with a hint of independence and rebellion. Estelle worried about Ariel, not just because of the depth of the water and the power of the waves. She worried about her sweet little girl growing up in the next couple of years. She worried that kids in junior high would make fun of her one short leg, that some heartless smart-ass boys would mock her by limping behind her in the hallway. Estelle knew that when Ariel crossed the bridge to adolescence, she wouldn't be the same. There'd be boys she'd have crushes on, there'd be hormones and broken hearts and mood swings and arguments, there'd be temptations like dozens of apples hanging from nearby branches, and Estelle wanted to prepare her daughter—and herself—for those moments.

Estelle realized that—traveling with the carnival each summer, and sometimes missing school a few weeks in early fall—her daughter had a little less experience than other kids. Still, it was an equally important kind of experience: at the carnival, she learned not only about bets and chance but about delight and wishes and dreams. It was an escapist place, a place where people came in nightly, trying to forget their worries for a while, not caring if they wasted some hard-earned money on games or sugary candy. They bought their young sons or daughters some giggles on the Mini-Space Ship ride, some screams on the Swinging Chairs. They'd stay for a while, maybe win a small teddy bear, then go back to their lives, somehow a little more able to face the doldrums of their jobs or their humdrum existence. Maybe their drab lives seemed a little brighter because of the carnival. Or, she wondered, did their lives just seem more faded and sad, once they exited the galvanized steel gate with the colorful banner? Estelle hoped that, when Ariel was older and looked back, she'd see her carnival years as a joyful time, coated with bright colors.

"Mom!" Estelle's thoughts were interrupted by Ariel's panicked voice. "Mom!" she cried.

Estelle looked up to see Ariel, being pulled farther out into the ocean, one hand trying to paddle, the other hand waving frantically in the air. *A rip tide?* She wondered with a sudden panic, jumping up from the beach towel. Estelle had read the rip tide warning in the park's small pavilion, but she never imagined that one could occur in such shallow water, since Ariel had only waded up to her waist.

Estelle rushed into the water, and as she did, she felt the strong pull on her ankles and knees, a suction-like power, as if the ocean itself was inhaling. It seemed as though the powerful current could carry her, and her daughter, all the way to the deep middle of the ocean.

"Don't swim against it!" she cried, remembering the warning sign's advice. "Swim sideways!"

"I can't, Mom," Ariel sputtered. "Can't!" She was already about fifty yards away from shore. "It's too strong!"

"You can. You can!" Estelle called, and as she did, she dove into the water and swam toward her daughter. She'd save Ariel, she told herself, or else she'd drown trying.

The rip tide pulled Estelle quickly away from the shore, so she was swimming twice as fast as she normally could. The confluence of incoming waves and the outgoing current made the water choppy; eddies and swirls of salty brine rose and fell, splashing her in the face. Still, she somehow kept focused on Ariel, who looked blurry as she waved one arm in the air.

That waving arm. That one frail arm. She had to reach it, she thought. Had to. She finally caught up to Ariel, who, exhausted, had just gone limp, her head sinking a few inches beneath the surface. Estelle lifted her and saw her pale face, her flaxen hair flattened to her skull. Dazed, Ariel coughed out a mouthful of water.

Estelle rotated onto her back and pulled Ariel close to her chest. "I'm not letting you go," she gasped, and she paddled with one arm and fluttered her legs as hard as she could.

The rip tide still tugged her away from the shore. She quickly felt exhausted; fatigue began to overtake her, as if her muscles, her whole body was filling with heavy sand. It seemed inevitable that, at any second, she and her daughter would sink to the bottom of this scenic, palm-lined bay with the crescent shoreline—a place that looked so peaceful when they arrived. The thought crossed her mind that, hours later, some fisherman would discover their lifeless bodies rising and falling in the waves.

Then a defiant voice in her brain shouted: No. Don't let that happen. Don't let it end like that.

Somehow, she gathered all the strength she had left, her muscles woke, and she pulled at the water again with her free arm and kicked both legs even harder, swimming parallel to shore to escape the current's grip. Suddenly she felt an extra push and looked down to see Ariel's legs, fluttering along with hers.

Seconds later, Estelle felt the rip tide's pull weaken, and then, like a fist unclenching, it finally released them of its grasp. She paddled toward the shore and finally felt the soles of her feet touch the solid sand. The two of them collapsed onto the beach, gasping, holding each other tightly.

"You saved me, Mom," Ariel exhaled after they'd both caught their breath.

"No, you saved me," Estelle replied.

"Maybe we saved each other."

* * *

An hour later they lay on their beach towels, the mid-morning sun coating them with a yellow warmth. Estelle rolled to her side to check on Ariel. "How are you feeling now?"

"A little dumb. I mean, for getting caught in that. But good, now that it turned out okay," Ariel said. "How about you?"

"The same. Good. Thankful, too, that we made it." Estelle closed her eyes for a few minutes, and her thoughts returned to her visit with Joanie.

She realized now that she wasn't like Joanie. Not at all. She didn't feel like half a woman. She felt powerful enough to pull her daughter from the huge mouth of the sea. For the first time in a long time, she felt ready to move forward, no matter what images might reveal themselves inside the crystal ball. The sun and the waves and the moon-shaped crescent of the beach and the cries of the seagulls and the menacing riptide that couldn't claim them—they all made her feel suddenly stronger than she thought she could be.

It was as if she had been drowning these past weeks, helplessly controlled by tides and currents, and finally, she was able to save herself. Her lungs aching, she was able to burst through the surface and gasp in a welcome breath of air. She was complete now, this moment.

She wished Tony was here to share her feelings.

Just then Ariel—who had strolled down the beach—came running up to her.

"Mom, look what I found!" she exclaimed. She held up a large crème spiral shell she'd plucked from the sand at the edge of the water. Estelle studied her: her daughter, with dark blonde hair drying in the sun. The rosy color returned to her face, her eyes wide, greenish-blue irises glistening in the angled sun.

"Wow. That's pretty." Estelle took it from her, held it to her ear, and closed her eyes.

"What are you doing, Mom?"

"If you hold a shell up to your ear, you're supposed to hear something."

"So what do you hear?" Ariel asked, tipping her head alongside Estelle's, as if she wanted to listen, too.

"The world," Estelle replied. "I hear the whole world." She focused her eyes on Ariel and her lips quivered. "Today I almost lost you."

"But you didn't, Mom. I'm here. I'm right here." She noticed something glistening on Estelle's cheek.

"You're crying, Mom."

"I know."

"So are they sad tears, or happy tears?"

"Both, I think." She stood and dabbed her tears with their light blue beach towel. "Let's get back to the car. Okay?"

"So, we're on to next town?"

"No, not the next town, Ariel. We're going home."

CHAPTER 53

Tony

  Tony cruised into the small Iowa town just before sunset. He tried to contain the swirl of emotions he felt inside himself: a mix of anticipation and excitement, and something else, too. It was fear. A fear that Estelle wouldn't take him back. Tony felt that fear tightening steadily in his chest, making it hard to breathe. Once he found her, he wondered, would she even talk to him, or would she just angrily turn away from him?

  Algona, Iowa. He'd seen this town almost a dozen times. It was a stop on their carnival's annual summer tour, and he had all the late summer stops memorized. Algona in mid-August, then Red Wing, Minnesota, then back to their home base in Wanley at the end of the season. He'd always thought of Algona as a dull, ugly place as he drove through it. But today the town looked quaint to him, almost charming, with its two-story brick facades and its parking meters, painted alternately red and blue. A kitschy banner was strung over its wide Main Street. The banner featured two dancing cartoon potatoes—one wearing overalls, the other a dress—advertising the town's locally-famous Potato Daze.

  Pulling up at the one stoplight, Tony spotted it: a Sand's Magical Shows and Amusements poster, taped inside the front window of the town café. He read the sign, which featured an out-of-proportion cartoon of a Merry-go-Round. The dates on the poster assured him that the carnival was still in town today—Sunday—its final day, from noon to six. He glanced at his watch. It was already 5:45. He knew he'd have to hurry; they'd be packing up in fifteen minutes.

  His muffler—punctured with a few holes from the long drive—growled, but he was careful not to push the truck over the limit. He couldn't get pulled over. He'd paid his share of fines in small towns before, roaring down the streets at 45 in a 25-mile-per-hour zone. But today, things were different; when his speedometer needle angled toward 29, he eased off the accelerator. He glanced in his rearview mirror and noticed the town cop's squad car, following him for a couple of blocks.

At the next stop sign, Tony gave the squinting cop a quick wave. Satisfied that Tony was no bank robber on the run, the cop wheeled around the corner and toward the city park.

Approaching the fairgrounds, Tony felt elation, a sudden lightness, as if the truck's retread tires were lifting a couple inches off the cracked pavement. He was ready to explain everything to Estelle. About where he'd been and what he had planned to do. He'd open his arms to her, show her who he really was. Then he'd bend to one knee and give Ariel a loving embrace.

He hoped Estelle and Ariel would see the change in him.

He'd read once that a family is like a wheel. The heart's like a wheel, too, he thought. Sometimes it goes where it needs to, and other times it wobbles right off its ol'axle. Love, he thought—it's a little like a wheel, too, isn't it?

At the fairground's gate, an overweight middle-aged woman—wearing a red and white striped apron and a paper hat with Potato Daze on it—motioned him to stop. "We pretty much close up in a couple minutes," she cautioned, "But if you still wanna pay for parking…" He hastily paid the dollar admission charge and squeezed his truck into a space between a beat-up Buick and a blue Mustang.

Jumping out, he headed toward the midway, which looked nearly empty. Just a few customers lingering near the food wagons. With a rush of adrenaline, he leaned into a run, the familiar rows of games blurring on both sides: Skee Ball, Tip the Cat, Fire Alley, Money Wheel, Gone Fishin', Down the Clown. He thought he heard someone call his name—maybe Dickie's nasal voice, calling from the Tater Toss, a corny game adapted for this town's festival. But Tony didn't have time to stop and talk. All he could think about was finding Estelle and Ariel.

But when he finally reached the spot where her fortune-telling tent should be, he came to a sudden halt. In its place was the sno-cone stand. He gasped, wondering if Estelle had moved her tent from its usual place. He broke into a run again, veering toward the back lot, where the crew parked their mobile homes. There, he recognized the rounded hulls of several trailers, but their Rollohome, with its distinct pastel side panels, was nowhere to be seen.

"Well, I'll be damned," a voice barked from behind. "Fancy seeing you here."

He spun around to see Virgil Sand, his stubby arms crossed in front of his chest.

"Greetings, Virgil," Tony said, extending his hand. Virgil didn't do likewise, just stood stiffly, arms locked like they were soldered together.

"What the hell you doing here?" Virgil scoffed. Dressed in a maroon blazer with gold trim, he looked like an usher at a cheap theater.

"Estelle," Tony exhaled, still feeling short of breath. "I'm looking for her. She around?"

"Fraid not," Virgil said, his right eye twitching. He planted his elbow on a stack of bent cardboard boxes—a new shipment of stuffed toys for the games. "She and Ariel ditched out. Been gone a while. Decided to take a furlough, I guess."

The realization made Tony go numb. He swallowed, and it felt like dry splinters were caught in his throat.

"You know," Sand announced, straightening, his spine arched as if he was standing at military attention, "you got a lotta gall, showing up here." He spat on the packed dirt. "I mean, shit. After you took off without telling a soul. Four weeks, even. The first nights, I had to scramble. Just to find something to fill in for your goddamn act."

"You're right. I'm sorry about that. But I…"

"Well sorry doesn't cut it." Sand wiggled his pug nose as though he smelled something foul. "At least the clowns threw together a little skit for a couple days after you left. A juggling act. Some sorta comedy mixed in."

"I guess sorry doesn't cut it," Tony admitted. He adjusted the rolled-up sleeve of his denim shirt. "But I thought I'd…" Tony stammered. "You know, maybe team up with the show again." His supplicant tone surprised even him.

"Team up?"

"Yeah. Fast Eddie and I could set up the act, have it ready in a day."

"That's not possible," Sand scoffed. "There's no slot for you anymore. And, let's face it. You were screwing up that tightrope gig more and more often."

Tony flinched a little. "I know," Tony admitted. "But I'll work on it."

"I don't think you heard me right. The show went on without you, Tony. In fact, I hired a fellow from over in Portage. Young guy, about 20. Real muscular. Does a real good strong-man weightlifting schtick. Lifts Cotton Candy Mandy straight over his head with one arm, even. The crowd loves it." His face filled with a patronizing smile. "So you see, Tony, you're done. You're replaced. You're pretty much dead and forgotten."

The words stung, but he let them roll off him and shifted the conversation to the most important thing on his mind. "Do you have any idea where Estelle and Ariel went?"

"Where they went?" Sand flailed his arms. "Who the hell knows? Estelle's been gone more than a couple weeks. Somebody said she was headed all the way to Gibtown. Disloyal, she is. Went AWOL. A goddamn deserter. Just like you." Sand pivoted and marched away.

Tony leaned his shoulders against the cool wires of a cyclone fence. He felt stalled, unable to move forward or backward. He wasn't used to being so directionless, so out of control, and he hated that feeling. A creased map of the United States stretched out in his brain. He had no idea where his wife and daughter were on that map.

Then a realization struck him: For weeks, he'd been pursuing a phantom child. He'd been chasing an illusion, something that wasn't there in the first place, and in the meantime, he might have lost what he already had. His solid home, his real family. He slid down, his back against the fence, and sat. He covered his face with his hands.

Minutes later, he looked up and noticed, a few yards away, the closed Mirror Maze. He had set up the front panels of this attraction numerous times, though he'd never been inside it.

Thinking it would distract him, he walked to it and hopped over the turnstile. Inside, he followed a narrow dark hallway where he couldn't even see his hand in front of his face. The plywood floor was slanted, and he held his arms out from his sides to keep from stumbling. At the end of the hall, a strobe light flashed, assaulting his eyes.

He entered the hall of mirrors. One mirror turned him into a squat, two-foot-tall person, another one stretched him until he was rangy and giraffe-like. The next one inflated his head and body like a balloon, and another one stretched his face two feet long like some strange creature made of elastic. The images should have been amusing, but they weren't.

In the next room, two floor-to-ceiling mirrors were anchored on opposite walls. He stood in front of one of them—a mirror that didn't distort but simply reflected. There he was, a man in rumpled clothes with a vacant expression on his face. Behind his reflection was another reflection, and behind that, another. He stepped on a raised plywood panel and it clicked, tripping a recording. As shrill, mocking laughter from the ceiling speakers surrounded him, he glared at his reflection—a reflection that repeated itself, each one smaller and smaller, until the image became too small to see.

CHAPTER 54

Ariel

At night, when Ariel was halfway between waking and dreaming, a conversation played through her head:

"What are you?" Ariel heard herself ask.

"I'm a bird child. You know that, don't you?"

"So you can talk, after all."

"Does it sound like I'm talking?"

"Okay then, tell me this—who made you?"

"How should I know?"

"Are you actually part human and part bird?"

"So they tell me. It's up to you to decide."

"Come on, be honest with me. Who made you?"

"Maybe God did."

"But why?"

"Because he wanted to create a joke of some kind."

"A joke?"

"Sure. He set up a very orderly planet, and wanted to create a little amusement."

"God's a joker, then? Somebody who's supposed to be serious, but he's just some kind of clown?"

"If he actually did make me, then I guess the answer is yes."

"Well, I don't think it's funny."

"Okay, not funny, then. But curious. And weird, of course."

"Are you blind?"

"Maybe."

"Like Helen Keller? I read all about her."

"I guess so."

"Okay—if you're blind, how do you know so much?"

"I learn from within. Or at least that's what I try to do."

"And how do you do that?"

"Don't ask me. I just do."

"So, will we ever find my Dad?"

"What do you think I am, a genius?"

"I thought you were smart."

"Well, I'm not. Remember, my whole life is inside this murky five-gallon jar. It's not exactly a penthouse."

"But does my Dad still love me?"

"Does anybody really love anybody?"

"Yes, they do. I hope so, at least."

"Good for you, then. A little hope never hurt anyone."

"When will I grow up?"

"Whenever you want to. Whenever you decide it's time."

"You mean I can change myself?"

"Yes. If you think you can, you can."

"So, what do you think about the kids who come to gawk at you at the carnival?"

"You mean those normal children? Sometimes I laugh at them. And sometimes I feel sorry for them."

"Why?"

"Because most of them have no wings."

"What do you mean, *most* of them? You mean some do?"

"I want to stop talking. I'm tired, and I need to sleep."

"But I'm asking you something."

"Put me back in my jar and close the cover tightly, will you? Last time you left the cover loose. And that annoying calliope music kept me awake."

"Wait. Before you sleep, just tell me—what do you mean, most of them have no wings?"

"Did anyone ever tell you that you ask too many questions?"

"Did anyone ever tell you that you cause too many questions?"

After Ariel asked that, there was no reply.

PART FIVE

CHAPTER 55

Estelle and Ariel

At dusk, Estelle coaxed the chugging Falcon up the hillside, where it hesitated, shuddered, then rolled to a stop at the top of the five-hundred-foot bluff. Estelle and Ariel stepped out next to the Scenic View sign. Sand's Magical Shows and Amusements had just set up in the Red Wing, Minnesota fairgrounds in the valley below. Standing in front of the engine that ticked as it cooled, Estelle and Ariel gazed down at the scene.

"Well, here we are," Ariel said.

The view of the carnival below looked so familiar to Estelle, and so foreign at the same moment. There it was: a place she loved and hated. It was a world of its own, all right, a wonder.

After years of being surrounded by it, Estelle came to understand that a carnival had the power to transform any empty, ordinary field. And even if she'd become a little tired of it, she could still see it through her daughter's eyes when they arrived at each new destination. Ariel, transfixed and sitting on the front steps of their trailer, would watch it all happen.

First, a caravan of semi-trucks, their dented side panels closed and padlocked, pulled onto a vacant lot. The field was usually lumpy, and uneven, with some scraped bare spots and a few oval bowls of mud. Sometimes the field was adjacent to a salvage yard, and bordered by a row of rusty cars, their blind headlight eyes staring endlessly. After the trucks and semi-trailers and campers wheezed to a halt in a cluster, the vehicles might be mistaken for being part of the junkyard.

But they weren't. Metal rectangles rose quickly rose from the flatbeds and one by one they fused together to form platforms for games, ramps to the Mardi Gras or the Haunted Mansion. Plexiglass-windowed ticket booths—held down by ratcheted orange straps—unleashed themselves and anchored at the entry gates and at strategic points across the field.

Aluminum chairs—with cotter-pinned metal bars acting as safety belts—unstacked themselves and clamped onto sturdy chains to become the Jitterbug Swings. Booms slid off the flatbeds of semis. The vertical track of the Ring of Fire rose up, and guy wires steadied it so it wouldn't roll toward the horizon. Cages that looked like places to house small animals or wild dogs fastened themselves to steel beams and became the cars of the Kamikaze, which drained the blood from the rider's foreheads and spun them so fast that the whole countryside blurred. As if jealous, the Octopus threw its steel arms toward the sky.

Bolts attached themselves to steel beams, and beams gathered strings of yellow and red lightbulbs as the next ride lifted itself from the earth. All the while, the air filled with the scents of cigarette smoke and sweaty tank tops and chewed tobacco. The sounds of power drills and clanking wrenches and shouts and strings of swear words mixed with the buzz of blaring boomboxes as workers hunched over and hefted and cranked, swinging their elbows and grunting as if they were lifting the whole planet.

One by one, vertical two-by-fours seemed to grow from the barren field like a small, forest of saplings without leaves or branches. Then that forest grew horizontal appendages, creating rectangles for the array of game booths. Taut canvas walls stretched across the beams and were littered, from top to bottom with stuffed teddy bears and long-armed monkeys and giraffes, mass-produced in Japan and filled with sawdust, maybe, but still very much alive.

One by one, squat tin sheds tossed off their cotter pins and reversed their sliding windows, exposing small deep fryers for the mini donuts and corn dogs, tubs for cotton candy, deep wells of sticky brown or cherry caramel, and rows of red apples. Large plastic globes filled with lemonade that, once the switch was on, flowed from the top of the globe in a perpetual yellow waterfall. Red and orange pennants jumped from their rooftops and flapped madly at the wind.

The flattened Bounce Castle inhaled air and inflated like an orange and red vinyl cloud.

Next, beige tents billowed from the ground like canvas mushrooms. Estelle's tent always rose like a mystical azure and white striped bubble from deep within the earth. Or so she liked to think.

Finally, wires and more wires. Wires—like arteries and veins—slithered everywhere across the midway. Motors hooked up their lifelines to the High Voltage truck with its monstrous generator that would soon—like a life support system connected to a comatose patient—begin to pump its resuscitating electric lifeblood.

The entire entourage was always on wheels. Twenty-one trailers—each stenciled with the red, white, and blue words Sand's Magical Shows and Amusements—were always ready to move, to roll forward, to stay in motion. But for five days—from Wednesday through Sunday—the caravan anchored in one place at a fairground, transforming that barren plot of land.

And then, at last, eight hours later, on opening night at dusk, it happened: The generators sputtered and spun, kicking out carbon smoke, and roared to life. Frayed speakers released calliope music, creating the mood. Backfiring engines that powered the rides roared and popped. Strings of lights opened their eyes across the expanse of the ramshackle town. The lights flickered at first before they glowed, as if they were hoping they wouldn't burn out before the first customer stepped through the entry gate.

Like its name, this traveling show really was something to behold, Estelle thought, as long as you didn't look too closely. Dull wood and tin and steel somehow transformed into what was a living work of art—a bright, enticing canvas of sights and smells and sounds. From high above, if you saw the place at night from an airplane, it might look like a small but complex city, bursting to life where no city existed the day before.

And that's how it looked right now from this bluff. Though she hated to admit it, Estelle caught herself thinking that it might even look magical.

"Yes," she finally replied to Ariel. "Here we are."

CHAPTER 56

Estelle and Ariel

Now that Estelle was back, it seemed like nothing had changed. She strolled among the off-kilter booths of the games and the plastic ducks circling in the water murky of the Ducks-on-the-Pond. Dust and exhaust entwined with the scents of sugary cotton candy and sickie-sweet cherry popsicles. Splat the Clown, his face smudged with red and blue grease paint, was hunched in his usual spot near the corn dog stand. A few kids clustered around him as he twisted long, thin balloons into poodles and heart shapes that sometimes popped before he handed them to the kids. Further down, fairgoers lined up to enter the creepy Haunted House, with its amateur-looking painted 1940s front panels featuring grotesque images of ghosts and Jack-in-the-boxes and witches. Its colors seemed to fade a little more each year.

Ariel squeezed Estelle's hand excitedly, letting Estelle know she was happy to be back. After all—it was her home, in a way.

One of the carnival's posters on the wooden fence caused Estelle to stop. The poster announced, to her surprise: *Here Today! Estelle the Crystal Ball Reader!*

Before she could think more about it, she heard a squeal of delight and looked up to see Lily running toward them with open arms. Lily embraced both of them in a joyful hug.

"You're back!" Lily exclaimed. "You don't know how much I've missed you two!"

"Same here," Estelle replied, returning a warm hug.

"This place is brain-numbing without you." She bent down to Ariel and said, "And you, you sweet and smart girl. You light up this whole place."

"I feel the same about you, Lily," Ariel said.

Lily hesitated, then quizzed, "So, I hate to ask, but... no Tony?"

"No Tony."

"Oh. I'm really sorry to hear that, dear. I really hoped you'd find him."

"That makes three of us," Ariel said.

"So," Lily inquired, "You're back for good, then?"

"I don't know," Estelle replied. "I mean, we've only been here fifteen minutes."

"Well, well. Lookie who's here!" The boisterous voice of Virgil Sand interrupted them. "The prodigal daughter returns." Resting one hand on the Cobra car, Sand always seemed to appear when you least wanted him to.

"Hello, Virgil," Estelle said flatly.

"Greetings and salutations," Sand said with a snide undertone. He bent toward Ariel and, in a condescending voice people use on a toddler, uttered "Hello again, little girl."

Ariel replied with an exaggerated baby voice. "Mister Sand, you ever find that Bird Child you were looking for?"

"Why no, I didn't," he said, his face turning crimson with the mention of this sore subject. He crouched in front of her and removed his straw hat with the rakishly tipped brim. "Why?" he asked anxiously, his receding hairline visible on his broad forehead. "You know something about it?"

"Nope. What would I know?" she said, a twisting irony in her voice. "After all, I'm just a little girl."

"Heh heh. Yes. Of course." Sand stood, and turned to Estelle. "You know, now that you're back, you and I better have a talk. A business meeting."

"Yes, we better," Estelle said, still upset about seeing the poster with her name on it.

"Okay then. In my office."

"Your office?" Estelle questioned.

"Well, certainly," he said with a chuckle. "I don't do business on the midway. Besides, I've got all my records in there."

"Let's catch up later, Lily," Estelle said to Lily, and Lily grabbed Ariel's hand and led her away, saying "Tell me all about your adventures. And Maria Luz can't wait to see you again."

In his office, Sand plopped down on the wooden captain's chair and propped his elbows on the desk blotter.

Estelle could smell the scent of his Brut cologne mixed with a faint scent of garlic and booze.

"So," he began, "Back from your great big vacation, are you?"

"I guess."

"Yeah, I pretty much figured you'd show up again." He tipped his head to one side. "Because you love this place so much, right?"

"I saw you still have my posters up," Estelle said with a cool tone. "Can you explain that?"

"Aw, those are just some extra ones, I guess. We had so many printed, we just had to use 'em," Sand explained. "We're all about the environment around here, you know."

Estelle could see right through the flimsy excuse. Sand was, as usual, luring in fairgoers with his famous false advertising. She could just picture him saying to potential customers, Oops, sorry—guess she's not working the tent tonight. But hey—we got lots of other attractions. And a ton of rides you can go on.

"So," Sand inquired, "So, I s'pose you're wanting to do your fortune teller thing again?"

"I'll think about it," Estelle said. She knew she drew in lots of customers, and that, once the word spread in a town, she garnered plenty of cash for Sand, and cash was what he was all about. Tony once claimed that, if he could amass enough of it, Sand would sleep on a bed of gold bullion.

"But your gig, your place in the show, well…I didn't promise nothing, you know. Not after you left that way. A defector." His oversized head tipped back. "And, there's this new girl. She's done a couple of gigs. I've been negotiating with her."

"Negotiating?"

"Yeah. Her name's Maude. But I'm calling her Mesmerizing Miranda. Catchy, eh?" He stood from his chair and paced the floor in front of his desk. "She's just a temp for now, mind you. Can't be here some weekends. She's on work release, actually." He let out a puffy laugh. "I recruited her from an outfit over in South Dakota. Guess she got in a little trouble over there." He sniffed at the air with his pug nose. "Anyway, she's a self-proclaimed psychic of some kind."

"Oh really?"

"Yep. But your gig was a winner. So it's a deal, then? You'll start up again?"

"I didn't make any deal. I might come back. But," she added, "only if you give me that back pay you owe me. And I'd also like a raise."

"Raise? Back pay?" He made a soft puhhh sound, like a worn tennis ball being struck by a racket. "Well, shit—pardon my French, as they say—but we can't just dip back in the kitty and sorta pull out extra money. "Then again…" He turned to the small window, and seemed to study the warped side of the mini donut stand, as if that was extremely important. He placed his hand on his chin as if he was deliberating issues of national security. "I s'pose I could ponder it." He straightened the lapel of his too-large sport coat and walked toward her with his bow legs. "And maybe we can work something out." His head seemed to wobble like it was on a pedestal. "I mean, if we can come to an agreement."

"Agreement?"

"Yeah. I bet it gets real lonely in that trailer. Without that runaway husband of yours. If you know what I mean." He winked. "So maybe I'll do you a real nice favor, out of the kindness of my heart," he said. He reached out, ran his hands along her bare arms, and lowered his voice. "If you can do likewise."

Estelle pushed his hands away and took a step back.

He advanced on her again, slid his hands around her waist, pressed his crotch against her hip, and lunged to kiss her on the neck.

She slapped him in the face.

Surprised, he pulled back, then lifted his palms into the air in a gesture of mock innocence. "Cripes. No need for that. What's with you, anyway? I'm just trying to make a business agreement here. I'm just talking about business."

"And that's all I'm talking about."

"Okay. Okay. Let's not get all worked up."

Estelle turned toward the door to leave.

Sand called: "Oh, by the way...your ol' hubby was looking for you."

The words made her spin around. "Tony?"

"Yeah. I saw him. A week or so ago. Down in Algona. He was askin' 'bout you."

"What...what did he say?"

"Not much. He was just stopping through. Then he just up and left again. Kind of a drifter, he is. It's his way. The same way he picked up in the night and left you."

Estelle gave him a heated glare.

"That's your kinda guy, I guess," he added with a sarcastic smirk.

"Sand, you're such a jerk."

"Heh heh heh," he released a stifled laugh as if the conversation had just taken a humorous turn. "Aw, Estelle, c'mon." He tipped his head to one side and tossed her a paternal look. "I know you don't mean that. After all, I'm your Uncle Sand," he said with a lilting voice. "The Sandman." He spread his arms out like a ringmaster. "The Great Sanderino. We run a safe, clean show around here," he said, spewing out his usual clichés. "You know that. We're one big family. We treat each other right. And you know you love me."

Estelle just shook her head at him in disgust, pushed through his office door, and let it slam behind her.

* * *

"What are we doing, Mom?" Ariel quizzed a couple of hours later as they walked toward the far end of the midway. The carnival had closed at 10 p.m., and everything was shut down.

"Something we've never done. I arranged it with Fast Eddie. We're getting a private ride. On the Round Up."

"But mom, you hate scary rides. And besides, you're afraid of heights."

"Exactly."

Ariel just gave her a puzzled look as Estelle took her hand and pulled her toward the ramp.

Fast Eddie waited there. "You two sign the wrongful death waiver?" he asked, and then he burst out with his usual cackling laugh. Not only was he Tony's best friend, he was the carnival's best jokester, too. He arranged practical jokes for just about everyone on the crew. Fake vomit on a table. Rubber dog poop on a chair. Woopie cushions. A fly in an ice cube. You name it, and he had every corny prank covered. One time he took a couple of scary cadaver mannequins from the Haunted House and placed them as riders on the Tilt-a-Whirl. "Sure you want to ride this?" he had asked the little kids waiting in line, who suddenly looked up, terrified. "That ride'll scare the life out of ya," he said, pointing to the cadavers.

"I don't take nothing too seriously," he once told Estelle. "That's how you survive around here."

Estelle had talked to Eddie earlier that day about letting them ride the Round Up after hours, and he agreed. "Long as Sand don't catch me," he replied. "He'd throw a fit and bill me for the gas. And probably the electricity, too."

Lifting the entrance chain, Eddie held out his open palm. "That'll be a thousand bucks," he said. Ariel wrinkled her nose at him and he just smirked and said, "Just kidding, cutie. For you, it'll only be a hundred."

"Oh Eddie," Ariel quipped, "Don't be stupid."

"I am what I am. Don't knock it until you've tried it," he laughed. "Now git in there, you two." He swung his arm toward the ride. "I don't have all night. Unless you're planning on riding that long."

"No way," Estelle said, feeling anxious as they walked up the ramp to the platform. She and Ariel took their places next to each other, leaned against the cage-like wall, and hooked the rubber-coated safety chains in front of their waists.

"Hold your horses!" Eddie called. "Whadaya think you're doing?"

"Getting ready to round up on the Round Up," Ariel said. "What else?"

Eddy gave them an admonishing look. "Shoot, you can't stand next to each other. Gotta stand on opposite sides of the wheel. You want this dang thing to break loose and roll across the field, or what? The platform's gotta be balanced."

"We are balanced," Ariel quipped as she walked to the other side of the ride, "Except for the days we're unbalanced. Then watch out."

"Shut up and ride, kid," Eddie teased, and after she and Estelle chose two slots opposite of each other, he pulled the steel lever and started the ride.

The huge cylinder spun faster and faster, and then it began to rise slowly, lifted by a hydraulic arm. Estelle could feel a thousand tiny wings fluttering in her stomach, but she pushed the sensation away. And even though she wanted to shut her eyes tightly, she promised herself that she'd keep them open. Whatever it took, she'd face the fear. As the ride rose, it felt like the earth was beginning to slant.

"Here we go!" Ariel yelled from the other side as the huge wheel spun faster and rose higher until it was finally vertical.

Estelle felt the force pressing her back to the metal mesh behind her, and she could hardly lift her arms. "Try letting go!" Ariel yelled from the other side, lifting her hands over her head to demonstrate.

Estelle hesitated, and then Ariel yelled again. "Come on, Mom! Try it! Let go!"

Estelle released her tight grip on the hand railings and realized that, due to the centripetal force, she wouldn't fall when the cylinder was straight up. Though they felt leaden, she forced her arms up and reached above her head. At that moment, the rushing of the wind that tousled her hair, the force pressing against her body, and the crazy spinning streaks of the stars in the night sky, caused her to let go a spontaneous scream.

When she did, Ariel screamed back at her.

Estelle returned the scream, and Ariel echoed it again. With each dizzying rotation, Estelle screamed louder and louder, letting out all her pent-up, swirling emotions. She screamed for herself, for Ariel, for Tony. Especially for Tony. And though she knew it was impossible, she hoped he could somehow hear her.

CHAPTER 57

Tony

He craned his neck and squinted. There it was, just fifty yards away. His trailer. *Their* trailer: his and Estelle's, and Ariel's.

The moonlight seemed to shimmer in a layer on its roof, and the small oval living room window cast a buttery yellow spotlight to the ground below. To Tony, that yellow light looked lovely, as if it were the last light on Earth. He leaned into a run, his heart beating hard in his heels.

The carnival had returned to its home base in Wanley, and earlier that evening, Dickie Higgins had stopped at the park outside town where Tony had been camping. He'd been staying there, waiting for any word about his wife and daughter. Higgie alerted him that Estelle had returned. "Just in case y' wanted t' know," Dickie had said in his usual phony Irish brogue.

"Just in case?" Tony had replied, trying to contain his excitement. Of course he wanted to know.

Now, as he approached the trailer, he could smell the faint ozone in the air. Distant flashes of lightning flickered and lit up its pastel pink and blue siding. He pictured the array of bumper stickers pasted to the trailer's back panel: souvenirs from Wall Drug, Devil's Lake State Park in Wisconsin, The Badlands, and various towns on the carnival's summer tour. Then there was the *I Heart Carnivals* sticker with a red heart, which he and five-year-old Ariel pasted next to the license plate. That one, and the image of the daughter he'd taken for granted—not just taken for granted but sometimes even neglected—made Tony feel choked up.

Closer, he saw the flowerbox of impatiens, and imagined their small petals closed for the night. He spotted the Welcome sign on the slightly dented front door. He remembered the evenings when the smooth voices of Johnny Mathis or Sinatra crooned through their small Sears stereo in the bedroom, a bedroom where he had felt Estelle pull him close, her eyes locking with his in an intense, loving gaze. A deep, understanding look that, whenever he felt empty, could fill him, buoy him up, make him feel whole. More than anything, he needed that gaze right now.

When he reached the front door, he hesitated. He didn't climb the three steps and knock. Instead, on an impulse, he thought about making a grand entry. It was the showman in him; he never wanted anything about his life to seem ordinary. An unexpected entrance would be more fitting, he reasoned, and it would, hopefully, be a memorable surprise for Estelle and Ariel.

So, he climbed the small metal ladder attached to the back of the trailer, then pulled himself onto the flat roof. As he walked, he tried to step lightly, though the aluminum roof panels still popped softly under his feet. He pictured Estelle, looking up, wondering what that sound was. Would she recognize his footsteps?

On the far side of the roof, he lay down on his stomach, hooked his black tennis shoes on the chrome luggage rack, then lowered himself until he was even with the living room window. There, through the barrier of glass and a gauze drape, he saw, upside-down, the life he'd missed for the last weeks: Estelle, reclined on the green couch with an afghan pulled up to her chin, and Ariel, in a new pair of plaid pajamas, legs crossed on the floor, tossing the letters from Alpha-Bits cereal into the air and catching them in her mouth. The bluish light from the late show on the black-and-white TV radiated to the corners of the room, giving both of their faces an angelic glow. When something funny appeared on the screen, they both burst into laughter at the same time. Tony watched the scene for a minute, surprised that neither of them noticed him. They seemed so comfortable there, just the two of them. Did they even need him back here? a doubting voice inside him asked. Would they welcome him back, or were they better off without him?

As he hung there, Tony felt a throbbing in his temples, the pressure of the blood rushing to his face. He couldn't help but think of the stories of Harry Houdini, suspended upside-down inside his famous 250-gallon Chinese Water Torture Cell, with chains wrapped around his chest, and his ankles clamped into wooden stocks. During one almost-failed performance, The Great Houdini, running out of air, struggled, unable to get out of his straitjacket, and desperately tried to signal the axe-wielding attendant to break the thick glass.

Tony took a slow, long breath and held it, hoping he was about to pull off the greatest comeback stunt in the universe. Or would he fail, and die trying?

Break the glass, he thought. Break the glass. Break the damn glass.

A minute later, when he exhaled, it occurred to him that maybe this was a ridiculous idea. Why, he asked himself, did he decide to return to his family this way?

With that thought, he pulled himself back onto the roof and stepped softly back to the ladder.

He knew it was about time to finally climb down. About time to knock on the door and face Estelle. Face Ariel. Face himself.

CHAPTER 58

Estelle and Tony

Estelle unlocked the door. Seeing Tony standing there, she opened the door just a few inches, then held it there. Knowing this might be complicated, Estelle instructed Ariel to go to Lily's.

"But Mom…!" Ariel protested. "It's Dad!"

"I know," Estelle replied. "But just go. I'll come and get you in a little while." Ariel reluctantly left through the back door. But before she headed to Lily's, she impulsively ran to Tony, who, seeing her, bent to one knee.

"Dad," she said with a sob, throwing her arms around his neck.

"Ariel," he whispered, returning her hug.

Tony rose to his feet and turned to Estelle. The moment Tony looked at her again, his life—which felt like it was reeling and off-kilter—seemed to right itself. Standing in her pink nightgown, Estelle appeared lovelier than he remembered her. A strand of her auburn hair—more red-tipped than he recalled—fell across one eye like a spiraling streak of fire.

The past few days, Tony had rehearsed this scene a hundred times as he sat by his campfire in the park, scribbling versions of what he would say. One night he woke at three a.m. and, using a flashlight, composed even more apologetic sentences.

But now, standing in front of her, all those words seemed useless and small. Feeling self-conscious but trying to look casual, he hooked his thumbs in his belt loops and stood there in his tight charcoal gray t-shirt as a drizzle was beginning to fall. He leaned toward her, his jaw tense, as if hesitant words were held captive inside his throat.

Caught in the gaze of Tony's blue eyes, Estelle felt as though her skin was almost transparent, made of glass. As if it would protect her, she folded her arms.

In the past, Estella had, at times, pushed the door shut on Tony when he took off during their short-lived arguments. But she couldn't do that now. She felt conflicted and fragile, like a thin fabric torn down the middle. Part of her wanted to lean forward and embrace him, another part of her wanted to clench her fists, pummel his chest and shout at him. She had a thousand things to say to him, words she'd kept inside for weeks, words waiting to rush out from her.

Instead, she was silent. She'd hold back, she told herself. She'd wait for what he had to say. The passing seconds seemed to stretch out, and the two of them were like awkwardly rocking boats—tethered side-by-side to a dock, bumping together, then pulling apart, then bumping together again as the tide moved in.

Finally, Tony managed to say something. "Um," he said. Then "Um, well, I'm back." The words tasted stupid on his tongue, like he was some Neanderthal, trying to grunt out a few first words.

"So I see."

"Okay if I come in?" he asked humbly. "It's kind of starting to rain out here."

She took a step backward. "Oh? Well, it's been raining in here since you left."

Her words had an angry edge to them, which was exactly what he had worried about.

Reluctantly, she opened the door wider. As Tony stepped into the unlit kitchen, he appeared to be half man, half boy. Estelle flipped the light switch, and the fluorescent glow caused the lines to dig into his face, making him suddenly years older.

Feeling self-conscious in her sheer nightgown, she grabbed a long-sleeved shirt from a hook behind the door. Sliding it over her bare shoulders, she realized, ironically, that it was Tony's frayed blue denim shirt, left behind these past weeks.

His eyes shifted to the wall beyond her, where a couple of months ago, he had pulled out a nail and never got around to spackling the chipped wall. There were a lot of things he'd left undone. He peered through the archway to the living room and said, "The place looks good. Real good." When she didn't reply, he focused back on Estelle and, hoping to warm her cool expression, he managed a tight grin. "And so do you."

Estelle didn't respond. "You know," she finally said. "You've got a lot of nerve, just walking in here like nothing's happened." Her words scraped from her throat. "Like you haven't been gone for almost four weeks."

"Yeah, okay. I realize that…"

"So where were you?" Her pale cheeks suddenly glowed scarlet.

"I was....well...," he stammered, tugging at the neck of his T-shirt as if it were too tight.

He forced a stifled laugh. "Hey, not even I knew where I was." As soon as he said the words, he realized they sounded flippant, elusive.

"That's no answer, Tony, and you know it."

"Well, it's sort of complicated." He swallowed. "I was sort of off the rails that night. And I guess I got impulsive."

"You guess?"

"I was trying…um, just trying to figure out some things."

She waited for more. In her mind, these vague excuses couldn't make up for his disappearing act, the slice of their lives that he'd taken and could never give back. During the awkward pause, the TV in the living room sent out little flickers of light, and a newscaster announced the oncoming severe weather.

"I'll try to explain," he continued, glancing down at one of his tennis shoes, the lace untied, then back at her. "I mean, it's a long story. I don't know where to begin."

Estelle leaned against the Formica countertop. "Damn it, Tony—I had no idea if you were alive or dead. I didn't know what to say to Ariel. I mean, how do you think she felt when her father just walks out the door one night and doesn't come back? She needs more stability than that."

Tony flinched. "You're right," he said, his lips pinched, "Not just some guy on a wobbling wire. Some guy who keeps falling off." He took a long, uneven breath. "But that's not who I am anymore." He stepped closer and placed his hands gently on her shoulders.

These past weeks, Estelle had yearned for Tony's touch; her longing had swept over her daily like a wave, and right now she wanted to lean into him and press her lips to his. Instead, it took all her strength to pull back from him and say, "No, Tony. You haven't even begun to explain."

Outside, a storm was moving in. Far off, lightning jabbed at the earth, and thunder shook its fists.

"This is hard," he began. He studied the back of his hands. On his left wrist, darkly tanned from the California sun, a pale oval where he had worn his watch, a watch he lost somewhere during his hang glider accident. "But I have to level with you. It's about a kid. A child…"

"What do you mean, a child?"

He grabbed the brim of his ball cap, lifted it, then placed it back on his head. He lowered his voice to a hushed tone. "There was this woman. Someone I knew before I met you, and...."

"A woman?" she gasped. "What are you trying to say, Tony?"

"I'm saying, I'm just...." He stammered, his quick and jumbled explanation not coming out at all like he intended. "I, I went out west. To California. To try to locate her."

"So you went out there to find an old girlfriend?"

"She located me somehow, I guess. She sent me a letter, and..."

"About getting back together?"

"No, no. I had no intention of that."

"Then what, Tony? What was it about?" In her mind, she couldn't help but picture him, staying with that woman. The very thought of it stung her deeply.

"It was about, um...a baby."

"A baby?"

"Yeah," he admitted. "She had gotten pregnant, and I..."

"Pregnant?" Estelle gasped. "With your baby?"

He nodded.

Shocked, her entire body jolted, and she took a quick step back from him. "I can't believe you hid all this from me!"

Tony went silent. For the next few seconds, he felt like the air pressure in the trailer had suddenly changed as if someone had quickly opened and closed the front and back doors. "I know, I know," he finally admitted. "I should have told you."

"You had a child with someone?" Her voice rose in disbelief. "And I'm just finding out about it now?"

"No. There's no child," he continued, fumbling with his explanation.

"What? You're not making any sense."

As the storm moved closer, the overhead light fixture flickered, then hesitated, then flickered again. "Listen, Stelle...," He reached out and slid his hands around her waist, hoping to pull her close. "I had a plan. I couldn't do what my dad did to me. So I had to..."

"Stop," she exclaimed. "Just stop!" Numbed by hurt and disbelief, she couldn't muster anything else to say to him. Tears burned her cheeks like acid. Pushing him away, she rushed to the door and stepped out into the rain.

* * *

As the cold downpour soaked her, Estelle ran a few yards from the trailer. She could hear Tony, calling her from behind. Reaching the tin awning of the Fun House, she ducked under it, then pulled on a back door, which was unlocked. She stepped in and closed it behind her.

She walked down a zig-zagging hallway, then stopped, leaned her shoulders against a wall, and took a few quick breaths to try to calm herself. The hallway was almost pitch black, and she wondered if she'd be able to find her way back out. Either way—with what Tony just told her, she felt more lost than she'd ever felt in her life.

Noticing a faint light, she began to walk toward it, feeling her way along the crooked angles by pressing her hands to the slick walls. At the end of a hallway, she reached a large picture window, open so fairgoers could watch the people inside.

Standing outside of that window was Tony. Lightning flickered, and she was certain, with each burst of light, that he could see her, too.

It was beginning to hail.

White pellets fell around him. They struck Tony on the top of his head and his shoulders. But he didn't move, or even flinch; he just stood motionless, an anguished expression on his face.

Seeing that expression and the white hailstones, Estelle instantly recognized the puzzling, fleeting image of Tony that had appeared twice in her crystal ball. Tony's face. The black background. The white pellets surrounding him.

She realized that her vision must have been a prediction of this very moment. And she also knew that—no matter if the outcome was positive, or tragic, or something in between—that she'd have to let this scene play itself out. She had to accept whatever was next.

Tony stepped close to the window and mouthed her name. He said it again. A third time. Then he lifted his hands and pressed them to the window.

She lifted her hands and did the same.

For the next few seconds, they stared intently at one another, their hands, with fingers outstretched, pressed on opposite sides of the window. Though she knew it wasn't possible, she thought she could feel the heat from his palms radiating through the thick glass.

And she knew, at that moment, that they both had to return to the trailer and talk.

CHAPTER 59

Tony and Estella

Back inside the trailer, Tony and Estelle sat opposite each other at the kitchen table. As Estelle listened, Tony explained what had transpired in the past weeks. He told her about Charlotte, about the child he had hoped to connect with, about his futile search at adoption agencies, and, finally, about the unexpected, sad end of the story.

After a long silence, Estella said, "I don't know what to think of all this. I'm still hurt. I'm angry. And there are lots of things I need to say to you."

Tony, his elbows on the table, leaned toward her. "Okay," he said. "Go ahead."

"While Ariel and I were on our road trip, I had a lot of time to think," she began. "And I faced some challenges."

He nodded.

"And one day it dawned on me. I've spent years telling other people's futures, and all that. But I never figured out my own." She tipped her head toward the ceiling. "It's a big world, and I have to know how I fit in it. Things have changed, Tony. I've changed. I'm feeling more confident," she continued. "I did some things I never thought I could do. I even rescued Ariel from the ocean." She focused on him again, her brown eyes intense. "The point is, Tony, we both need to change."

"Oh?" He didn't mean it to come out as a defensive or flippant response, but that's what it sounded like.

"For one thing, I need you to be more honest with me. At times I don't know what you're thinking. Or what you're feeling. I hate it that you sometimes bury things."

"Yeah, I guess that's a bad habit of mine."

"I wish you'd just told me about everything. Charlotte. The letter. All that. It would have saved us both a lot of anguish." Her words seemed to linger, filling the small kitchen. "I wish I knew what was going on in your head."

"Sometimes I don't even know what I think. Or what I feel. Guess I just act on impulses."

"I hope you realize how much Ariel missed you when you were gone. She loves you dearly, in case you haven't noticed."

A guilty expression spread over Tony's face, and he bowed his head.

"There's one other thing," she said. "A big thing."

"What's that?"

"I'm starting to think we need a break. From Sand and his rules. His underhanded dealings. Sometimes I feel like this place is suffocating me."

She stood from the table and stepped to the window. The rain had ended, and the still, humid night seemed to be pressing itself against the windowpane. "I have dreams that go beyond this carnival," she said softly. Estella turned and faced him. "That's all I have to say."

The silence between the two of them stretched for a few long seconds. Though he knew it probably wasn't the right response or the one she had hoped for, Tony felt himself shrug.

Not getting the reaction she hoped for, Estelle felt tears emerging on her eyelids. "I hope you have someplace to stay," she finally told him. "It hurts me to say this, but I can't just let you walk back into my life like this. Into our lives. Not right now."

*   *   *

Later, back at his campsite, Tony sat for hours near the campfire beside his tent. He fixed his eyes on the coals in the firepit that were soggy from the recent thunderstorm. He imagined them bursting into flame, though he knew that, tonight at least, they couldn't.

He looked up toward the sky, where the thick bank of clouds was steadily opening into a wide hole. Within that opening, a broad glistening veil of stars from the Milky Way appeared. Some were faint, some brighter.

So many stars up there, he thought. Hundreds. Thousands. Millions. He read once, as a kid, that some stars had burned out and died millions of years ago, exploding into supernovas. But now their light was just reaching the earth.

He thought about how many years he had left before he would be gone, nothing left of him but a faint memory in someone's mind.

But more than anything, he thought of Estelle. And Ariel. The hurt he caused them. The light they gave to him. The light he needed to survive.

He pictured himself these past weeks, driving all night across the country and never really reaching his destination. He tipped his face back, letting the light from the stars enter his eyes. Then he closed them and imagined that light brightening—at least briefly—the darkness inside himself.

CHAPTER 60

After a night of restless sleep, Estelle woke to a clunking sound. Groggy, she slid out of bed. She checked Ariel's bedroom and saw she was still sound asleep, wrapped in layers of her blue quilt. She strolled to the kitchen, opened the cupboard, and pulled out the tin of Folders to make a pot of coffee.

As she did, she heard the odd sound again. Then it stopped, and she heard a soft hushing, like water running through pipes, and wondered if the spigot on the side of the trailer had been left on.

She rose to her tiptoes and peered out the window. She was surprised to see Tony, a tin watering can in his hand. As he watered the impatiens, he bumped the aluminum can against the wood frame of the flower box. Watering wasn't something he ever did in the past; it was always up to her or Ariel to be the caretakers of the fragile plants.

She tapped on the window, and he lifted his head toward her and nodded.

When she opened the back door of the trailer, he was standing there, an apologetic look on his face, the watering can at his side. "They looked a little wilted," he explained. "Needed some reviving." He tipped the watering can and let the last drops of water splash on his t-shirt. "Me, too, I guess."

Estelle laughed lightly.

"And the answer is *yes*," he said.

"Yes what?"

"Yes to all the things you talked about last night." His words, choked with emotion, were sincere, honest, bare. "Yes to working on it. Or at least trying to."

"You know, Tony," she cautioned. "What I said about changing… It isn't just for me and Ariel. It's for all three of us. We'll all work on it."

"I know, I know," he agreed, his face opening into a wide smile.

"Well don't just stand there," she said. "Better come in. We've got a lot of catching up to do. And there's someone who's still sleeping and would love to wake up to you."

"You?" he asked, stepping through the doorway.

"I meant Ariel." A smile rose to her lips. "And yes, maybe me, too."

CHAPTER 61

Tony and Estella

With the blinds closed and the shades drawn, Estelle and Tony stood in their bedroom. The narrow walls of their room were silent, and waiting.

There were no more highways, state lines, caution signs, or lost crumbling roads pulling the two of them away from each other. No parched deserts or oceans or endless plains, no thousands of miles separating them.

No angry or doubting words pushing each other away.

It was just the two of them now, staring at each other in the near darkness on opposite sides of their double bed. For a few moments, it was enough, just to gaze like that, as if seeing each other for the first time.

The two of them whispered each other's names and their names were like music on their lips.

They slid onto the bed at the same time, the static electricity sparking in the sheets.

Estella reached toward him. Even in the dim light, Tony could see the fine lines branching across her delicate palm. He wished he was a palm reader, and that he could trace each line, and each line would bring him closer to her.

He reached toward her, and their fingertips, just inches apart, finally touched. It was an effortless gesture, but still infinitely complex, and infinitely beautiful.

Tony knew that her touch was the only touch that mattered, her face was the only face, her kiss the only kiss. As their lips met, he felt a sudden rush of exhilaration, a sensation like he was racing down a highway at a high speed: he rushed past the blurring rows of carnival games, past his petty, flawed egotistical self, past the ghost of his father and the sad, unmarked grave of the lost child to a place where the road ended. There, he reached a bright, ethereal place where everything was azure blue and shimmering and new.

When he opened his eyes again, he was back in the present, staring at Estelle.

Tony realized that it might be a long journey, but Estelle would help him make his life whole again. Not an imitation of who he thought he was, but the real him. He might be just flesh and bone, he might be obsession and broken dreams and failure, but still, it was the real him, opening himself to her, all his layers peeled back, his inner self revealed. He'd tell her that, and hope she would understand, hope she would forgive. Right now, he began the conversation with just three words. "I love you," he whispered.

And when Estelle whispered the words back to him, Tony felt them enter him and seem to bloom inside him. They were three small, simple words, and at the same time, they were the biggest and clearest and most important words in the world.

Outside the thin walls of their trailer, the whole planet might have been falling apart. There might have been earthquakes, fires, tornadoes, wars, tragedies. A kaleidoscope of chaos. But inside this small room, everything was perfect.

With a soft sigh, they met in the middle and made love tenderly, passionately, their bodies finally closing all that distance that had been between them.

CHAPTER 62

Tony and Ariel

Early the next morning, Tony leaned over Ariel's pink bicycle. They always kept the small girl-sized bike strapped to the back of the trailer whenever the show traveled, and Ariel could use it to ride around the local fairgrounds.

"How long's this chain been off?" Tony asked.

"A while," Ariel answered. "I hit a bump, and then off it went. Guess I was going too fast."

"Huh," he said, twisting his lips to one side, "I know what you mean." He leaned over and studied the black and silver chain that dangled from the pedals to the ground. "You're not going anywhere without this. So let's take care of it." He flipped the bike over onto its handlebars, then lifted the chain and placed it around the small gear on the rear axle. Next, he eased the chain onto the larger gear by the pedals. Keeping one hand on the chain to guide it, he slowly started pedaling the bike, securing the chain back onto the gears. "Hand me that wrench over there, will you?"

Ariel complied, pulling a wrench from the gray toolbox next to them.

"This could use some tightening."

Ariel watched as he worked the wrench on the rear axle, his elbow swinging side to side like a pendulum.

"There," he said. "It won't come off again, I hope."

He turned to her. "You know, we should get you a new bike. Not these kiddie-sized ones, but a full-sized one. You've almost outgrown this one."

She patted the fender. "Yeah, but I still like it."

"I know. But I bet you'd like a new one. Let's think about it, for next year." He eyed the front tire, which was sagging slightly. "Tire looks a little low." He reached for a hand pump and pumped up the tire. "Okay," he said, "ready for takeoff."

"Thanks, Dad. You're good at fixing things."

"Yeah," he said, wincing a little. "Sometimes."

"Yeah," she echoed, "sometimes."

"I'm guessing you didn't put any miles on this bike lately. I mean, with you and your mom on the road."

"You're right," she said, sighing. "And our little trip didn't end up all that well. I mean," Ariel continued, "A lot happened. And it was interesting to see new places, and all that. The Turtle broke down. Then we survived a riot. I learned about civil rights. And women's rights. And I became a hippie, sort of, for an hour, at least. Then I met a half-woman who gave me Yoo-hoo. We drove fifteen hundred miles through nine states. And ended up at the ocean. But…" Her lips dove into a frown, and her hazel eyes pierced him. He waited for the rest of her sentence. "But we didn't find you."

Tony shifted his weight uncomfortably. When he was nervous, or unable to find the right words, he'd usually reach for a drag of his cigarette. But he'd quit smoking. So instead he just fiddled with the faded brim of his blue Dodgers cap as if it needed adjusting. He looked down at the tops of his bare feet, the blue veins in them branching out, then back at Ariel. "But I'm here," he finally said. "Consider me found."

Neither one said anything for a few seconds. Finally, Tony bent down on one knee next to her. "Before you give the bike a spin… Um," he began, struggling for what to say, "I need to, you know… Tell you what's been on my mind." Ariel sensed, by the way his words seemed to skitter, that he was about to say something that meant a lot to him, something hard to express.

"Sure," she said, encouraging him.

"I know that sometimes I sort of ignore you. I get preoccupied. I get…" He noticed her sad expression. "But from now on, I mean, it's not all that easy for me, but we can talk. Talk about anything."

"Anything?" she said, her voice lifting.

"Yeah. If you want to, that is."

"Oh," she said enthusiastically, "I want to."

A pained expression slid across his face. "I feel really bad about leaving you like that." He took her hand. "I know I probably caused you and your mom all kinds of worry."

"You did," she admitted, her voice choking up. "Our lives turned upside down, kind of."

"I'm sorry. Really sorry. But you should know that I thought about you all the time I was away. And I missed you. You know I love you, right…?"

"Right. Of course. You're my dad." Ariel thought she noticed a tear glistening in the corner of Tony's eye, a rare tear. She felt her eyes welling up, too. Tony took off his ball cap and seemed to peer into it. Inside, the concentric salt stains circled each other. He slid the cap back on, brushed his eye with the sleeve of his shirt, then lowered himself next to Ariel again. He wiped her tears away with his fingertip, then studied her for a few long seconds.

"You know, when you grow up… When you leave the nest someday, you're going to be smart and strong and beautiful, like your mom."

She tilted her face toward him. "Is that a prediction?"

"Hey," he chuckled, "That's your mom's department. But, anyway… um. What I'm trying to say is… You're beautiful right now."

"But not smart?" she teased.

"Okay, okay. Smart, too. Ah, heck," he exclaimed, flustered, "you know what I mean, right?"

"I get it, Dad. I get it."

"But hey, let's focus on today." Tony lifted the bike and flipped it over onto its tires again. "There," he exclaimed. "Everything's right side up again."

"I hope so," she replied. Then she asked, "So, things are good with you and Mom again?"

"Not good," he nodded. "Great."

Ariel beamed as she slid onto the bike again and placed her feet on the pedals. Looking up, she waved at Estelle, who had been watching them from the kitchen window.

"Try it out," Tony said. "Let's see how fast you can go." He nodded toward the empty midway. "In fact, I'll race you."

She glanced down at his feet. "But you're barefoot."

"Doesn't matter. Let's go."

She pedaled slowly at first, with Tony jogging alongside her as they passed the kiddie Teacup and Little Swan rides.

Leaning into a sprint, Tony pulled a few yards ahead of her. "Hey!" he shouted. "Come on! Catch up!" She pedaled harder, and the bike sped up. She gained on Tony, and by the time they reached the thrill rides at the far end, she was side by side with him, both of them laughing. "How's it work?" he asked between breaths.

"Good" she called. "Not good, great!" As the wind fluttered her hair, she kept pedaling on the path that extended beyond the carnival grounds and into a pine tree-lined field.

A few yards later, she noticed he wasn't paralleling her anymore. She stopped pedaling, coasted, and turned to look for him.

He was already far behind her. As if he was winded and out of breath, he slowed, came to a stop, leaned over, and put his hands on his knees. Then he straightened again, raised one hand, and waved at her. And though he knew she couldn't hear him from that far away, he grinned and called, softly, "Yeah. Keep going, Ariel. Keep going."

CHAPTER 63

Tony, Estelle, Ariel, and Virgil Sand

He stood on the plywood platform, the sawdust floor thirty feet below him. Even though he hadn't taken a step yet, he felt his legs trembling, as if the air in the tent was cold.

He knew he would get back to this walking eventually. He had to. After all, it wasn't just a hobby or a pastime, was a part of him, a deep part.

He also knew that after not walking it for a while, the braided steel wire would burn beneath the soles of his feet. This kind of journey was never an easy one. A distant announcer's voice scratched through the speakers. "Ladies and gentlemen—introducing the Dashing Desdiolo!"

Long seconds passed, but Tony didn't move. The fifty-foot wire to the other platform seemed to stretch to fifty miles, and he felt paralyzed there. He wondered: If he fell, could he try to stop the fall by grabbing a fistful of air? Though he knew that a tightrope walker should never look down, Tony couldn't help but glance briefly at the crowd, fidgeting on the bowed wooden bleachers. Their faces seemed small, and far away, like spilled confetti. He thought he heard one kid with a half-eaten mop of cotton candy whine, "Is he just gonna stand there forever?"

Stand there forever. The words jabbed at him like boxing gloves, trying to knock him off the platform. Was he just going to stay in one place and not move again? Drops of sweat slid down his forehead, stung his eyes, then rolled down his cheek like tears of sorrow or tears of joy. For an absurd moment, he imagined himself standing here for hours, days, years, and growing old—his hair gradually graying, his shoulders hunching.

Why did he keep trying to prove himself? he thought.

The announcer's voice echoed again. The crowd looked up in expectation. The spotlight waited as it glared at him, an unblinking, searing white-hot eye. The taut wire waited. The whole damn planet seemed to be waiting.

It was then that he spotted them, standing in the open doorway of the tent. Estelle and Ariel. Their hopeful faces tipped toward him, calmed him. After all, he was doing this walk not for himself, or to amuse some peanut-crunching crowd, but for them. For Ariel, with her endless enthusiasm. For Estelle, who amazed him with her beauty and her strength—not just on the outside, but on the inside, too. She wasn't false, or strobe-light illuminated, she was just herself—true, and real.

As he nodded to the two of them, realizations rippled through his mind. From today on, he decided, he wouldn't let the wire possess him. He'd still live his life spontaneously and passionately, but now, whenever he walked forward, he would pause to see the landscape on both sides. He'd feel the wind rush up to him and swirl around him. He'd take the time to notice a hovering hawk in the sky, almost motionless, balancing gently on the updrafts. But most of all, he'd pause to appreciate the faces that love him. Yes, he decided, from now on, his life would encompass all those things.

So, he extended his arms gracefully to his sides and closed his eyes. Then, lifting his right foot from the platform, he opened them and took that first, tentative step onto the quivering wire.

* * *

Tony opened his eyes and Estelle was there, next to him in the bed, her head resting on a pastel blue pillowcase. Her eyelids fluttered. She seemed to be waking at exactly the same moment that he was. She rolled her head slowly toward him, and then her eyes opened fully.

"Morning," she said, her voice still velvety with sleep.

And it was. But not just any morning, but a gorgeous morning, he thought. Here, close to her. The first bright beams of sun slid through their narrow window, waking the room.

"Morning," he echoed back to her.

Love, he thought. That was what was at the other side of the wire he kept trying to walk across. It was always there, waiting for him to recognize it.

Love was his destination. Estelle was his destination.

And before she could say another word, he parted his lips to tell her so.

* * *

An hour later, after the three of them finished breakfast, Tony stood from the table. "How about the three of us go for a walk?" he offered.

"Sure," Ariel responded. "Where to?"

"Oh, I don't know—around the midway. Or," he laughed, "Who knows—around the planet, maybe."

They strolled among the rides, which were still motionless and slumbering, waiting for the first riders to climb onto them when the gates opened at noon.

Suddenly, Virgil Sand appeared, bustling toward them from between the Bumper Cars and the Tarantula.

"Well, well," he uttered, his voice brimming with sarcasm. He tipped his wide-brimmed straw hat back. "If it isn't the three runaways. All in one place, even."

"Yeah, we are," Tony replied curtly.

Sand turned to Estelle. "By the way, Estelle, I was just looking for you. We need to have a little meeting."

"What about?" she asked.

"Let's step into my office. We need to talk in private."

"No way," Estelle said, giving Tony a knowing side glance. Tony had heard all about Sand's touchy-feely episodes with Estelle, and that he also mauled some of the young mess tent girls against their will, even causing one girl to quit.

"Oh, oh, well, okay. Whatever. Then over here." He motioned her around the corner of a semi to a flatbed and sat on the edge of it. "A little privacy. Just you and me." He patted the wooden platform. "Cozy up by Papa Sand."

"I prefer to stand," she countered.

"Alright, then." He eased himself off the flatbed and stood next to her. "So as it turns out, I made a decision. An executive decision, actually," he said with a pompous flair. "Here's the thing. This new girl, Mesmerizing Miranda, is joining the show. She's just part-time, though. She's agreed to work at base pay, even." He clapped his hands together enthusiastically. "She's got crystals, Tarot cards, the whole schtick. For a price, she even holds seances sometimes, with some fake ghost images projected on the wall of her tent. She's got a little smoke machine hidden under her table. Works pretty good."

"Is that so?" Estelle said incredulously.

"Sure. The customers are real convinced. You know—that they've contacted their lost loved ones." He raised one eyebrow in a mock-thoughtful expression. "You know—kind of like your phony fortune-telling biz."

"It's not phony," Estelle said angrily. "And neither am I."

"So," he continued, ignoring her comment, "I assume you still have your gypsy gimmicks? Your magic ball and all?"

"It's a crystal ball. And it's not a gimmick."

"Semantics, my dear," he chuckled, using one of the few big words he prized. "Just semantics."

"Anyway, the bottom line is, I can still make room for you here. Miranda's not sure about coming back next season. You can set up your teller thing again. So we have a deal, then?"

"What about my back pay?"

"Oh yes, that little matter. I had a feeling you might bring that up." He pulled a checkbook and pen from his jacket pocket, scribbled a check, and handed it to her.

"Thanks."

"So we're all good, now, right?"

"Not exactly."

"Why not?"

"Because I quit."

"Uh, what?" Sand's whole face seemed to squint. "I don't think I heard you right."

"You did. I'm quitting the show," Estelle said firmly. "I'm done with this place."

"Well, well," he said, "Aren't you little miss uppity." He stuffed his checkbook back into his pocket. "But I guess that does solve things, then, doesn't it?" he said, his voice laced with passive-aggressive hostility. "You know, I'm actually glad you're quitting. I was only letting you back in on a trial basis, out of kindness. In fact, I was planning to fire you eventually anyway. If Miranda goes full time, that is." He forced a chuckle. "Yep. Makes it all a lot easier on me."

"Are we done here?" She glanced back toward Tony and Ariel.

"Just so you know," Sand added, "Miranda's doing real good." He nodded. "Nice gal, too. Slinkier than you, kind of. Plus," he added, "she's more—how should I say this—cooperative than you are. So, if you ever come back to the show, and find it in your heart to feel cooperative, just let me know." He puffed out a heh heh heh sound, winked one puffy eye, then put his hand on her bare arm, his fingers crawling upward from her wrist to her elbow.

She pushed his hand off her arm. "Get away from me. You're such a creep. And you don't know how much I despise you!"

Tony, who had been overhearing the conversation from the corner of the semi, stepped in. "Is there a problem, Estelle?"

"Yes. Sand's the problem."

"Sand, why don't you just back off," Tony demanded.

"You keep out of this, Desdiolo," Sand barked. "We're negotiating. You have no say in anything around here."

"I have a say in whatever I want," Tony fired back. "And so does Estelle. So why don't you just negotiate your way into your office and crawl back in your hole."

"Pfffft," Sand scoffed. "As I recall, you're no longer part of this show, Tony." He rubbed his chin with his thumb and index finger, pretending to be thoughtful. "And, what's more, your trailer's parked on my property. That means you're trespassing. You're here illegally. You're breaking the law." His face filled with a hostile squint. "So I want you out of here."

"We'll leave whenever we want," Tony countered. "On our terms."

"Oh really? In that case, I'll just call the boys in security. They'll throw you out."

Tony laughed. "Fast Eddie runs security around here. And he happens to be my best friend."

Sand's lips wrestled like two pink worms. "Well, then, better yet, I'm calling the damn cops on you."

"Go ahead and call them," Tony said. "Maybe I'll tell them about the little pickpocket scheme that you set up."

"Scheme? What scheme?" Sand said with feigned innocence.

"It's no secret. You send a couple of local guys to work the crowd at the entrance gates. And you split the take with them. And besides that..." he continued, "Everyone knows you fake the ride revenue. So you could pay a lower percentage to the towns on our circuit."

"How dare you try to accuse me of that..."

"Lily discovered it. When she was balancing your record books," Tony added.

"Lily? Ha. What does Lily know, anyway?" Sand snarled. "I mean, she's from Puerto Rico..."

"It's true. She found one real record book and one fake one in a file drawer." Tony pointed at him. "So that makes you the criminal, Sand. Maybe we should be calling the cops on you."

"That's ridiculous," Sand countered. "Those things never happened."

Estelle cut in and said "And what about molesting the new temps on the crew?"

"Huh?" Sand puffed.

"Everyone knows what happens if a girl is called into the office by Handy Sand."

"That's a lie," Sand said. "I'm just a cordial person, is all. Very gregarious. You're both making up things about me. You're both just worthless, phony liars."

"There's nothing phony about us, Sand," Estelle replied defiantly. "We're real. It's you that's the phony."

"I took The Bird Child!" Ariel blurted, the words bursting from her lips.

"What?" Sand gasped, stepping closer to her. "What did you say?"

"I'm the one who took it. Your famous Bird Child."

"Ariel, what on earth..." Estelle exclaimed, but Tony gave her a knowing nod.

"It had enough people laughing at it," Ariel added.

A mottled red color began to fill Sand's face as if hot magma was rising beneath his skin. He bent toward Ariel. "Where is it!" he hissed through gritted teeth.

"How should I know?" Ariel replied flippantly. "Maybe it went to heaven. Or limbo. Or wherever Bird Children go."

"Tell me!" he demanded, his voice rising shrilly. "Tell me, goddamn little freak!" Enraged, Sand grabbed Ariel by the T-shirt and lifted her off the ground.

"Get your hands off her!" Tony shouted, pulling Ariel out of Sand's grasp.

"Go to hell, Desdiolo!" Sand roared. He took a swing at Tony and missed, then shoved him in the chest with both hands, knocking him backward.

Regaining his balance, Tony charged, swung his fist, and hit Sand hard in the jaw. With his hat flying in the air, Sand fell backward on the muddy ground, a stunned look on his face. Tony pinned Sand down and raised his arm to strike him again. He held his fist there a moment, realizing he could knock this buffoon senseless if he wanted to. Seeing Sand cowering beneath him, Tony lowered his fist and stood up again. "*You're* the freak," Tony said, his voice calm, but intense. "You are. And don't you ever touch my daughter or my wife again."

Sand sat up, rubbing his jaw. He pulled his straw hat out from under him, then stood slowly, dusted off his slacks, and straightened his sports jacket. He popped the dents out of his crushed hat, then placed it carefully back on his head. Then he tipped his chin toward the three of them and tossed them an indignant look. He turned and marched a few steps toward his office, then spun around and faced them. Lifting his arm, he pointed at them menacingly, as if he was about to deliver some final insult or decree. "You three… You… you're…" he stammered. His mouth opened and closed, but nothing more came out. For once in his life, Virgil Sand was lost for words.

CHAPTER 64

Ariel and Tony and Estelle

Later that morning, Ariel and Estelle sat on the front step of their trailer, sipping glasses of lemonade.

As the carnival opened its doors and came to life, Ariel listened to the clunk and clank of the rides, the rise and fall of the rider's shrieks. She was always amazed by the way people wailed in terror on thrill rides like the Fireball, the rollercoaster that propelled riders upside down fifty feet in the air on a 360-degree circular track. You could hear them all the way to the entrance gate. Clutching the lap bars that were worn to a shine, riders screamed like they were dying, and yet they always seemed willing to line up for another ride.

They survive, Ariel thought. They always do.

"I've got a little story for you." Estelle said, interrupting Ariel's thoughts.

"What's it about?"

"Well, it's kind of a parable, I guess. About a famous showman."

"Tony?"

"No, not Tony. Harry Houdini. I've been reading about him lately."

"Yay," she exclaimed. "Another Houdini story. Let's hear it."

"You know he did lots of escape tricks," Estelle began. "He freed himself from handcuffs, from padlocks, from city jails. Even from maximum security prison cells."

"Um hum."

"Everybody was baffled. The police searched him before every escape. To make sure he had no hidden tools with him." She tipped her head toward Ariel. "Know how he did it?"

"How?"

"He swallowed keys and picks. Then, when he needed them, he coughed them back up."

"Hmmm. Sounds kinda gross."

"Yeah, maybe it is," Estelle laughed, "But let me finish. The point is, he could always get himself free." She paused. "So, you see, the keys were inside him. His favorite sentence was 'My brain is the key that sets me free.'"

"Cool." Ariel squinted one eye. "So what's the point, Mom?"

"Well, maybe it's a little like us. Me, you, your dad. The keys are inside us. Maybe everybody has the keys," Estelle continued. "You know—to their own destiny. We just need to find them."

"You mean to cough them up?" Ariel said, chuckling a little.

"You're making fun of my story," she said. "But, anyway. It's just something I've been thinking about lately. Sort of a crazy idea, eh?"

"Not crazy. It makes sense," Ariel said. "Thanks, Mom."

She looked up at Estelle fondly. "So, does this qualify as one of those memorable mother-daughter moments?"

"I guess," Estelle agreed. She laughed lightly. "Or maybe a mother-daughter-Houdini moment, is more like it."

"Either way," Ariel replied, "it works for me."

"So, listen," Estelle said, changing the subject, "Tony and I have been talking. How do you feel about taking a trip? A vacation, I mean."

"A vacation? All of us, this time?"

"Yeah. All of us. Out east, maybe?"

"Sounds awesome."

"So, anyway, we were thinking…. Tony always wanted to see the beaches on the east coast. Like in Hilton Head. Cape Hatteras. St. Augustine. All that. And you always wanted to go to that island in Virginia, right? The one with those wild ponies?"

Ariel nodded eagerly.

"When you were eight or nine," Estelle recalled, leaning against the trailer door, "you used to blab on and on about those ponies. You're not too old for that already, are you?"

"Of course not."

Estelle stood from the step. "That settles it. We're going, then. "And," Estelle added, "I want to stop in Washington, too. To see Pearl again. We'll work it all in. That's the plan." Estelle took Ariel's small hand in hers and patted it. "At least one of your dreams might come true."

"More than one. But," Ariel hesitated, drawing a circle in the soil with her bare toe, "You and Tony shouldn't make promises, unless…"

"We intend to keep them," Estelle added, quickly finishing the sentence.

"I better get back inside," she said, standing. "We've got a lot of planning to do."

"So," Ariel inquired, "when we get back, are we joining a carnival again?"

"Not this one, anyway." Estelle walked over to the flower box and plucked one of the red and white impatiens. She returned to Ariel. "But who knows? We might find another one to join. Or maybe we'll do something entirely different. We'll find out what's best for us."

"And what's best for us?"

"What feeds our souls, maybe," she said, her voice softening. "Like everything else, we'll figure it out as we go." Rotating the stem between her fingertips, she spun the flower clockwise, then counterclockwise, making it blur into pink. She gave Ariel a knowing look. "Guess that makes us true gypsies."

"True gypsies," Ariel echoed. "I like the sound of that."

Estelle slipped back into the trailer and Ariel stayed on the step for a few more minutes. She focused on the remodeled Fun House. The day she and her mom returned to the carnival, they walked through it, and they both noticed that the building had been remodeled. Its warped and splintered plywood floor was replaced. These past weeks, when they were looking for Tony, Ariel was filled with doubts. She was beginning to think that families are what other people have. But now she felt like there was still a chance for them. Solid floorboards, she hoped.

* * *

In the living room, Estelle folded a T-shirt and placed it into a cardboard box. She had labeled four boxes: One with *Donate*, one with *Save*, one with *Sell*, and a fourth, containing items she wasn't sure about, with a question mark. She and Tony had decided to downsize a little before they took off on their vacation. "Less weight to tow behind us," Tony had said.

"There's a thrift shop in Wanley," Estelle told Ariel, who was helping with the sorting. "We might sell a couple of things tomorrow, on our way out of town. We'll donate the rest to Salvation Army. Including these." She lifted two of Ariel's small T-shirts with strawberries and balloon designs on them. "Right?"

"Right," Ariel agreed. "I've kinda outgrown them. Maybe some kid could use them."

Ariel had also grown out of her usually squeaky Minnie-Mouse voice. Estelle noticed, for the first time, that Ariel's voice—lower in pitch and more melodious—sounded surprisingly like her own.

When Estelle sat down to plan their itinerary, Ariel slipped into the bathroom and dabbed on some makeup from Estelle's old Revlon bottles she'd found at the back of the medicine cabinet. It made her cheekbones look more pronounced in the mirror. She also noticed that she'd actually gained a little weight; her skinny body looked like it might even begin to have a faintly curved shape. Not an actual teenage girl's shape, she knew, but still, it was a start. And her brain would grow, too, she hoped, giving a lot more room for all the thoughts that would find a home inside it.

When Ariel walked back to the living room, Estelle stood from the table.

"Rouge?" Estelle asked, noticing Ariel's cheeks.

"Yeah," Ariel answered. "But I can wash it off, though," she added quickly.

"No. Leave it on. Looks nice."

"That's what Lily said. She let me try some of hers."

"Lily?"

"Yeah. I stopped at her trailer a while ago. She said she'll come over to say goodbye before we leave. She told me she was going to miss us madly. And so is Maria Luz. Said they love us to the moon."

"I hope you told her we feel the same about them."

"Of course."

Ariel walked to her bedroom, reached under her pillow, and pulled out her secret journal. Back in the living room, she held it out to Estelle. "Voila! Here it is. My Blue Sky Notebook."

Estelle gave her a surprised look.

"You can read it," Ariel said meekly. "I mean, if you want to. Or else put it in that Save box, and read it later."

"There's no way I'm waiting until later." Estelle opened the cover and peered eagerly at the first entry. "I'm reading it right now."

"Just don't read it out loud," Ariel requested. "Might embarrass me."

"Got it," Estelle replied. "I'll just embarrass you silently." She kissed Ariel on the forehead. "Thank you, honey. I'll cherish this."

"Don't cherish it too much, though. I want it back. I'll probably write something in it tonight. If I had the time, I think I could probably write a whole book."

* * *

A half-hour later, Estelle lifted the wooden box containing the crystal ball.

"We're not selling that, are we?" Ariel asked. She had overheard Estelle talking to Tony, saying they might need extra money to finance their trip. Estelle had once speculated how much the ball might be worth—most likely a couple of hundred dollars.

"Bet it's worth a lot," Ariel offered, leaning closer to it. "Right?"

"Right. The first day we came back, Virgil Sand offered to buy it. Said some new girl might be able to use it. Then he offered me a measly twenty bucks for it. When I declined, he said 'Then how about twenty-five?'"

Ariel snickered and scrunched up her face. "So, you told him to take a hike, right?"

"Of course. I'd never sell it to him. Not for a million bucks."

With that, Estelle lifted the ball. As she did, it suddenly rolled from the heels of her palms onto her upturned wrists, then balanced there awkwardly.

"Oh, don't drop it," Ariel said, reaching over and easing the ball securely into Estelle's palms. Ariel imagined its weight: heavy in her mother's hands, but, maybe, at the same time, light as a soap bubble. Or a dream.

Estelle contemplated it for a few seconds. "This ball has powers, you know," she said, raising it in front of her face. "It always has. It always will. And I'm pretty sure that it gives you powers, if you believe."

"So it *is* real, then?" Ariel's eyelashes fluttered a little as if a bright light had just shined into her face. "What you do is real, after all?"

Estelle didn't answer at first. Finally, she said, "It's as real as you want it to be. This ball…" Her voice took on a nostalgic tone. "This ball was your great-grandmother's. And your grandmother's. And then it was mine. And someday, I planned for it to be yours." She closed her eyes, then opened them. "And maybe today's that day." She lowered the ball toward Ariel. "Hold out your hands."

Ariel complied, and Estelle placed the ball into her palms.

"But mom…," Ariel protested. "What if I'm not ready? I mean, what if I…"

"Shhhh," Estelle said, touching Ariel's lips with her index finger. "Don't ask any questions. Just take it. Just accept it."

Though it made her nervous, Ariel couldn't help but feel like she was cradling something precious, or even magical. For years, she had heard about a crystal ball's powers. If light through a window shined on it, it could, like a prism, project a rainbow of colors onto a wall. But if direct sunlight struck it just right, it could send out an intense, focused beam, start a fire, and burn down an entire house.

As Ariel held the ball, the tiny, branching lines in her palm appeared much clearer than she'd ever seen them. And suddenly her small, thin hands looked magnified, and larger, and a lot like her mother's.

CHAPTER 65

Ariel

She knew what she had to do. The night before they left the carnival, Ariel tiptoed into the living room.

* * *

She pictured her mom and dad in this room, just last night. Near midnight, still awake, Ariel had opened her bedroom door a couple of inches and peered out. Estelle and Tony were sitting close to each other on the couch, watching the last few minutes of a show before the network went off the air. When the screen turned to snow, Tony had clicked the TV off. The living room went silent, and dark, except for the creamy moonlight, filtering through the window blinds and lighting the floor like a row of ivory piano keys.

Tony stood and took Estelle's hand. "So," he said, "You want to dance?"

"Dance?" Estelle gave him a flirtatious smile and laughed. "There's no music, is there?" To Ariel, it sounded like her mom was just playing along with him.

"There's music," Tony replied, "There's always music." And the two of them began a graceful waltz, swaying back and forth in the moonlight.

Watching them, Ariel felt a warm rush of emotions. It was a deep-down thrill. Way better than any ride on the Fireball. Better than anything. She knew she'd write about it in her journal, and that the words would just about glow on the page.

* * *

Tonight, Ariel crept into the kitchen, slipped quietly out the door, and grabbed a garden shovel from the flowerbox. She began to walk toward the far end of the boarded-up midway.

Everything seemed strangely silent tonight. The only sounds were unseen nighthawks making their lonely *eeer eeer* sound before they circled and glided away. As she walked, she could almost feel the light from the full moon coating her skin, and she liked that sensation.

Ariel glanced one last time at the Octopus ride, its silhouetted limbs frozen. When she reached the exhibit Virgil Sand had set up during the time that she and Estelle had been gone, she stopped. She scowled at the words on the orange sign nailed over the door:

THE AMAZING CATFISH WITH LEGS!
EIGHTH WONDER OF THE WORLD!
IT COULD SWIM IN A RIVER, OR WALK ON DRY LAND!
See it now for only One Dollar!

She recognized the sloppily painted sign as Virgil Sand's handiwork. She also recognized the exhibit's wooden ramp and display trailer. It was the same one that was used for The Bird Child. The whole idea upset her. She hurried up the ramp and wedged the garden shovel behind the sign. Loosening a nail in one corner, Ariel pried at the sign with her fingernails and finally tore it off, revealing the original, slightly faded sign:

THE AMAZING BIRD CHILD
An Oddity of Nature!
An Eighth Wonder of the World!
See it now for only Fifty Cents!

Ariel carried the Catfish sign behind the exhibit and, with a quick motion, flung it into the long weeds. As she did, one of the nails—its sharp silver point poking through the wood—scratched the palm of her hand. A drop of blood appeared, and she wiped it away. It beaded up again. She studied the blood—the red, rich blood, and felt glad. After all, she reasoned, it wasn't just her blood. It was her mother's blood, and Tony's. And her grandmother's. It would make her grow up. Blood is strong, she thought, and sometimes bleeding makes you stronger.

Reaching the end of the carnival grounds, Ariel noticed that the six-foot side gate was padlocked shut, a chain coiled around the galvanized posts. She yanked at the chain a few times, but it wouldn't budge. She'd have to climb it. She knew it would be easier if she could push her bare toes through the wires. She took off her shoes. Her left shoe clunked to the ground, and the thick cork lift bounced out of it. She tossed the shovel over, then grasped the cyclone fence with her fingers, and pushed her toes into the diamond-shaped openings. Her skinny arms—chicken wings, Estelle once called them—pulled her upward steadily. Her legs—bare below her shorts—shivered a little from the strain, and finally, she reached the top of the fence. She swung her right leg over. Her left leg dangled on the other side. She squinted at her klutzy leg.

She swung her leg over quickly and balanced there, the aluminum bar cold beneath her thighs. For a moment she felt like her dad must feel when he walks the tightrope, and she wondered if she inherited some of his craziness, and hopefully, his skill.

Then, without another thought, she leaped. Her mother taught her that. Sometimes you have to leap into the future, Estelle had told her yesterday. You just have to leap without thinking, because it's what you're feeling that's most important.

Ariel felt herself flying the amazing distance from the fence to the earth. It almost felt like she was falling in slow motion. She landed hard on both legs, the soles of her feet striking the packed dirt with a thump.

She expected her left leg to buckle with the impact. She expected a burning jolt from a sprained ankle or knee, expected her body to tumble forward in a somersault and then sprawl there as she clutched her weak leg and writhed in agony.

Instead, the leg held.

It was stronger than she thought.

Ariel picked up the shovel, and the next thing she knew, she had leaned into a jog, and that jog turned into a gallop, almost, as she ran across the asphalt parking lot. It surprised her that when she ran at full speed, she wasn't at all clumsy like she expected. She didn't trip or stumble or veer off course. The doctors had cautioned her about running, but they were wrong. For a long time, she felt like the world was off-kilter, and she was walking uphill. But now it seemed level again. It felt great to run like that. Not just great, but amazing.

At the far edge of the asphalt, she stopped.

She knew exactly where to dig, of course. Bending over the spot, she began to scrape the soil away, layer by layer, careful not to push the shovel tip too hard.

First, a small, curled foot appeared at the edge of the bubble wrap she'd used to cushion The Bird Child when she'd buried it weeks ago. Then the rest of the odd-shaped limb. Then the round shape of the torso. As she unwrapped it, Ariel could see The Bird Child's bowed head, its tiny, pitiful, half-formed arms clutched close to its chest as if it was keeping some secret—or some coiled pain—inside. She slid her fingers beneath it and began to pull it from the soil. It resisted slightly, as if, like a seedling, it had grown tiny roots and was holding onto the earth. She tugged at it again. She pulled harder, and on the third try, it pulled loose.

She brushed a few pieces of dirt off its body and the two small wings on its back. It still felt rubbery, but more real than she remembered, and the translucent skin seemed to give off a glow from the inside. Whether it was real, or plastic didn't matter to her, though. It was whatever it wanted to be. It was what it was—The Bird Child, the one and only Eighth Wonder of the Entire World.

Through its bulbous, half-closed eyes, The Bird Child seemed to stare at her as if recognizing her. It seemed to ask: What will you do next?

Would she take The Bird Child with her? Would she carry it back to the trailer and secretly slide it into a box, the one labeled with a question mark? Would she hide it, then maybe—a year or two from now—pull it out again? Or would she drop it off on the doorstep of Virgil Sand's office with a hand-written note that would befuddle and anger him? A note proclaiming, in bold letters: **Don't ever take advantage of me again.** Then she'd sign it: **Your Little Pal, The Bird Child.**

But maybe, she thought, she could just wrap it up, cover it with soil, and bury it again, letting it rest there. Give it back to the earth, and let it remain what it was in the first place: a mystery. A pure and simple yet deep mystery, an oddity that was part one thing and part something else. A creature that was—like a lot of regular humans—caught between two worlds.

Ariel knelt over The Bird Child for a few minutes, deciding what would be best. Whatever she'd decide, it would be her secret. No one would know but her, and sometimes that's what made you stronger, she thought: keeping something precious inside, something no one else can touch or spoil.

At that moment, she knew what she needed to do.

Without hesitating, she cradled The Bird Child in her palms, rose from her knees, and stood. She gradually brought The Bird Child up to her waist, to her shoulders, though it almost felt like it was rising on its own. She hoped it could see—or at least sense—the sky above it, the kiss of milky moonlight, and the spray of stars that looked like silver bubbles caught in a dome of darkened crystal. She hoped it would finally be free.

She lifted it high, high, higher, as if she believed it could fly.

THE END

About the Author

Writer and teacher Bill Meissner is the author of twelve books, including four books of short stories and five books of poems. His novels are *Summer of Rain, Summer of Fire*, and *Spirits in the Grass*, which won the Midwest Book Award.

He taught creative writing at St. Cloud State University, and now acts as an occasional writing coach and presents readings and creative writing workshops at area colleges, high schools, elementary schools, and book clubs. He has won numerous awards for his writing, including a National Endowment for the Arts Creative Writing Fellowship, a Loft McKnight Award, a Loft-McKnight Award of Distinction in Fiction, a Minnesota State Arts Board Fellowship, and several PEN/NEA Syndicated Fiction Awards for his short stories (one of which was selected by Kurt Vonnegut, Jr.).

Meissner grew up in Baraboo, Wisconsin, also known as "The Circus City"—the birthplace of the Ringling brothers and their first circus. As a teenager, he worked at the Circus World Museum, vending peanuts, cotton candy, and snow-cones to museum visitors. His boyhood home was located a block from the county fairgrounds, and once, as a ten-year-old, he rode the Rock-O-Plane nineteen times in one day.

Bill's interests include rock music, photography, baseball, vintage typewriters, and travel—especially to tropical/beach locations such as Mexico, Costa Rica, Puerto Rico, and the U.S. Virgin Islands. He lives in Minnesota with his wife, Chris.

Printed in the USA
CPSIA information can be obtained
at www.ICGtesting.com
JSHW080000110324
58906JS00002B/8